CONFESSION
TO A
DEAF GOD

CONFESSION TO A DEAF GOD

Memoir of a Mekong River Rat

Gary R. Blinn
Lt., U.S. Navy

To order additional copies of this book, contact:
Xlibris Corporation
1-888-795-4274
www.Xlibris.com
Orders@Xlibris.com
16471

CONTENTS

INTRODUCTION

INNOCENT

SEA DRAGON

BACK TO THE LAND OF THE ROUND EYES

CAT LO

L.S.T.
Hot Rivers

CAM RANH

SHORT TIMER

THE REAL WORLD

EPILOGUE

DEDICATION

There were not many of us who served on Swift Boats. About 80 Patrol Craft Fast were in-country. Each boat had a crew of six plus a Viet interpreter. Crews served for one year.

Two-thirds of those who went to Vietnam were volunteers. They accounted for 77 percent of the combat deaths.

This book is dedicated to my shipmates who are "Still on Patrol." The World War I poet, Wilfred Owens, said: "These men are worth your tears. You are not worth their merriment."

SN David L. Boyle	2/14/66	Woodland, CA
BM2 Thomas E. Hill	2/14/66	Knoxville, TN
EN2 Jack C. Rodriguez	2/14/66	Jackson Heights, NY
GMG2 Dayton Rudisill	2/14/66	Greensburg, KS
BM2 Raleigh L. Godley	5/22/66	Lawson, MO
EN2 Gale J. Hays	10/18/66	Falling Rock, WV
QM3 Eugene L. Self	10/18/66	Carteret, NJ
BM2 Hubert Tuck	10/18/66	Lenoir City, TN
GMGSN Alvin L. Levan	10/25/66	Catawissa, PA
BM1 Kemper S. Billings	10/29/66	Burlington, NC
MRC Willy S. Baker	11/15/66	Buffalo, TN
BM3 Harry G. Brock	11/15/66	Odessa, TX
RM3 Bruce A. Timmons	11/15/66	Ft. Lauderdale, FL
SN Daniel E. Moore	2/22/67	Omaha, NE
BM3 Terry L. Davis	2/24/67	Parma, OH
SN Gary W. Friedmann	3/11/67	Lebanon, PA

SN Dennis R. Puckett	3/29/67	Lees Summit, MO
LTJG William Murphy	11/19/67	Madison, WI
BM1 Bobby D. Carver	12/6/67	Richmond, CA
EN2 Carl R. Goodfellow	12/23/67	Waterproof, LA
GMG2 Billy Armstrong	6/16/68	West Helena, AR
OM2 Frank Bowman	6/16/68	Walterboro, SC
BM2 Anthony G. Chandler	6/16/68	Warner Robins, GA
EN2 Edward Cruz	6/16/68	Inarajan Guam
RD3 Gerald D. Pochel	9/4/68	Otis, OR
BM2 John McDermott	9/7/68	Pittsburg, KS
BM3 Richard C. Simon	11/3/68	Ellsworth, WI
EN2 David L. Merrill	11/6/68	South Bend, IN
BM3 Peter P. Blasko	11/8/68	Southern Pines, NC
BM3 Stephan T. Volz	11/8/68	Lakewood, CA
Ltjg Richard C. Wallace	11/8/68	Norfolk, VA
BM2 Steven R. Luke	12/6/68	Provo, UT
EN2 John R. Hartkeemeyer	12/17/68	Hamilton, OH
BM3 Gerald R. Horrell	1/5/69	North Hollywood, CA
Ltjg Donald G. Droz	4/12/69	Rich Hill, MO
QM3 Thomas E. Holloway	4/12/69	New Castle, IN
BM 3 Richard L. Baumberger, Jr.	5/5/69	Mansfield, OH
EN3 Dewey R. Decker	5/15/69	Ionia, MI
GMG3 Richard W. Stindl	5/15/69	Beloit, WI
BM3 Robert A. Thompson	5/19/69	Downey, CA
RD2 Kenneth P. West	6/22/69	Butte, MT
EN3 Albert M. Fransen	7/2/69	Las Vegas, NV
GMG3 Glen C. Keene	7/2/69	Fairhope, AL
GMG3 Stephen J. Penta	8/12/69	Revere, MA
LTJG Robert L. Crosby	9/26/69	South Hamilton
QM2 Richard L. Wissler	10/2/69	Willow Street, PA
LTJG Kenneth D. Norton	10/7/69	Lady Lake, FL
RD3 Craig W. Haines	2/17/70	Keyser, WV
RD3 Frederick D. Snyder	5/17/70	Moab, UT
QM2 Lanny H. Buroff	7/6/70	Chicago, IL
QM1 Joseph P. Jurgella	10/25/70	Stevens Point, WI

If you go to The Wall in Washington, D.C., please leave two flowers. One for the life they lived; one for they life they didn't. They were not "wasted."

INTRODUCTION

*All the wrong people remember Vietnam. I think all the people
who remember it should forget it, and all the people who forgot it
should remember it.*

Michael Heer

A NOVEL

Please let me call this book fiction.

If the stories I tell sound true . . .

well . . .

I wish they were not.

*   *   *

Some names are real, some are not.

*   *   *

Some chapters are in the present tense. Some are in the past. I'm sorry if that makes it difficult for the reader, but that's the way the incidents are in my head. It bothers me too.

ACKNOWLEDGEMENTS

In 1974, I attempted to write a non-fiction book about Vietnam. I put a blank sheet of paper in an IBM Selectric and started "page 1," thinking I would write from 7 p.m. to 11 p.m. every Wednesday. I was focused on accuracy of detail and as a result, I was not writing about the raw *feeling* of the war. I was missing the big question, "What was it like to be there?"

That book is now appropriately buried in a manila folder at the bottom of a drawer.

Twenty-five years later, details, facts, even reality were just mist, so I tried again, this time as a novel:

1.) I had spoken to a psychologist and explained that at age 55, I was remembering more about the war. When I was in my thirties and forties, I thought that I had swept most of my experiences under the rug. By my fifties, these experiences had come alive and bugs were crawling out of my head. He said, "It's normal."

2.) In a brief course at Esalen in Big Sur, I gained confidence in my writing and found my writer's voice. Elaine Hughes was a wonderful first teacher.

3.) Back in Nebraska, I discovered the "bracelet" format. I could write short choppy stories and link them together. This allowed me to write in spurts. When I felt happy, I wrote an upbeat chapter. When I felt somber, I wrote about death.

4.) Barbara Schmitz introduced me to Natalie Goldberg. I understood the reason for my first book's failure: Vietnam had not had time to "compost" in my mind.

5.) Barbara also stressed the importance of not editing my work before it was complete. Earlier I had tried to write only what was appropriate. Later, I realized that war is mankind's most "inappropriate" activity; to confine a war novel to appropriate events is to strangle it in its crib.

6.) I've learned to write about the "feeling" of being in combat. I no longer need to worry about details as I had in the past. The Defense Department has warehouses full of documents with details, but very few of those works focus on how it *feels* to get shot at.

7.) One night I awoke at 2 a.m. with characters literally screaming to get out of my head and onto paper. At that moment, I knew I was becoming a writer.

8.) My wife, Diane, made the very helpful suggestion that the *structure* of the writing parallel the *content* and that both fit with the *voice*. My book is fragmented: parts are missing, there is overlap, and parts simply do not fit together. War is like that.

9.) Karen Spray and Gina Baker deserve very special thanks for typing and editing all of this.

10.) Why write, given that most writing will not get published? The key for me was to write for *myself*. Esalen taught me that such an exercise was vital. i.e. I could take the "bugs" from my mind and push them onto paper. By closing the three-ring binder, I contain the bugs. I could view them when they need viewing, but I could also keep them safely between the book covers.

11.) *Alice in Wonderland* was written for just one person. Like Lewis Carroll, I wrote this book for one individual, my son.

12.) Finally, an apology. No memoir is accurate, especially 30 years later. I tell the truth, knowing that much of it is fiction. This is how I remember; if a reader disagrees with certain parts . . . all I can says is that I hope he writes his book. Writing is good for the soul.

Norfolk, Nebraska
October 2002

THE SHRAPNEL'S EDGE

When a Russian B-40 rocket explodes, the warhead ignites and sends a shockwave that travels at 1,800 feet per second. The metal shell casing breaks into small pieces that are propelled at twice the speed of sound. Before impact, the warhead is perfectly smooth. An even, geometric green cone. Then it is no more. It is just pieces propelled mindlessly in every direction. The pieces of shrapnel are jagged at the edges. Rough. Hard. Dull. Shiny. Bent. Sharp. They go into the aluminum hull of the boat. They go through metal, plastic, glass, or mattresses. Through radios and bone. Through fuel tanks and through flesh. You can pick the big ones out of boat hulls or out of people. The tiny pieces stay imbedded forever.

No two pieces fit back together. One minute the warhead is whole. Then one ten thousandth of a second later it no longer exists. The jagged pieces cannot fit together again. Some disappear. Some go to the bottom of the muddy river.

One day I pulled a piece out of the side of my boat, Inky Bite 97. It was about an inch long. Narrow, curved, and jagged. Like a thin strip of an orange peel. It had missed me by an inch or two. Later, I had it cased in plexiglas. The two-inch cube set quietly on my desk. A paperweight. After a year I put it away.

I had kept it partially as a reminder that I didn't get hit. It missed my head. There it was, still hot. By my right ear. Then I tried to keep it in plastic permanence. Then I gave it away.

It didn't really miss me.

INNOCENT

*There are times when somehow we slowly divest ourselves of shame
and begin to speak openly about all the things we do not
understand.*

Czeslaw Milosz

ARMORED

"You can be anything you want to be, Gary, just promise me you, you won't go armored." My dad was pleased when I responded that I wanted to be a surgeon, to fix shattered bones like the Army doctor who repaired my elbow when I was four. To be a doctor was a noble goal, better than driving tanks.

When I was in grade school, I spent long hours in the warm house of my grandmother's sister, Aunt Jo. Both her sons were casualties of World War II. Eighth Air Force. She had photos and mementos in a shoebox of Clayton and Kenney and their bombers. As a grade school boy I was equally interested in a special treasure in that box: the belt buckle of her great-uncle, Cap Wilson. He had been shot at Shiloh. Shot in the belt buckle. Wow. And as a kid I wondered what the scar on his belly had looked like. I held the twisted oval with "U.S." on it and stared at it for hours at a time. Living campaigns of a civil war 90 years before. Curious about every detail.

My dad didn't talk very much about his role in Patton's armored division in World War II. I remember him saying only a few things:

- ˘ His best friend was Sergeant Saltzgiver. He called him "Mother" Saltzgiver. He saved Dad's life more than once, but I never learned the details.
- ˘ On the landing craft, minutes from Normandy Beach, Dad was eating cookies. He turned to the guy beside him and said, "Wanna cookie?"
- ˘ At St. Lo, where Patton's tanks ran into very heavy resistance, Dad's tank was stranded. They expected a German to put a Panzerschreck round into them at any time. They were alone and blocked. It must have been for a very long time because

the tank crew had to piss in their canteen cups and throw the urine out the top tank hatch. They were trapped inside. Surrounded by Germans.

Sometimes he would talk for a few minutes about Hitler's mountain hideaway at Berchtesgarden. He was also at a concentration camp (perhaps Dora), but he didn't talk about that. Not ever.

He had a friend named "Renner." He said the name exactly like a little boy would speak of a big brother that he admired.

Earlier, at Fort Knox, General Patton had promised that the Allied Forces would go through the Germans "like crap through a goose." At St. Lo, Dad said the Germans went through the Americans "like shit through a tin horn." I thought it was funny even if I didn't understand it.

His tank was called "Lonely."

He volunteered simply because he was curious and didn't want to miss anything.

His N.C.O. was Sergeant Zollner. It struck me that Dad's buddies—Renner, Saltzgiver, and Zollner—all had German names.

His was the first allied tank to cross the Siegfried line, the German defensive line of fortification.

That's all he ever told me. I was curious to hear more, but Dad didn't go any further. Sometimes his lip quivered though.

When I was in my last year of high school in 1962, Dad asked what med program I had chosen. Without thinking I replied, "I'm not going to be a doctor after all; I'm going to West Point and go armored."

I didn't get tanks. I didn't get selected to go to the U.S. Military Academy at West Point. I did get my second choice, the U.S. Naval Academy at Annapolis, Maryland. I graduated in 1966 and volunteered for two tours in Vietnam. I was curious and didn't want to miss anything.

It has been 30 years since I was in-country. This story of what I saw from 1967 to 1969 is more complete than my Dad's, but not by much. Many memories are lost. Others are confused, and still others are hidden, too sacred or too profane to be disturbed. I said it's been 30 years since I was in-country; that isn't true. I go back every night.

MADDOX

President Kennedy got us into Vietnam; he sent the advisors. He almost got us into a full nuclear war over Cuba too. Most Americans like to forget that. Most do not know that the polls taken shortly before he was shot indicated that he would not be reelected in 1964. He was losing his popularity rapidly. He liked James Bond novels. At the time, I wondered if reading Ian Fleming's fantasy of 007 made our President too adventuresome.

In the summer of '65 I was in Pensacola, Florida, in summer flight school. The news of the North Vietnamese torpedo boats attacking the U.S.S. Maddox and the C. Turner Joy, two of our destroyers, was on the T.V. in our bachelor officer's quarters. All of us were frozen to the screen. A day or two later when our Navy jets destroyed most of the North Vietnamese Navy, we cheered. We were proud.

Some of us worried aloud that the war might be over before we could get there. We talked of petitioning the Superintendent of the Academy to allow us to be commissioned early. In World War II, the classes graduated in three years instead of four. Many of us did not care about the Bachelor's Degree. We just wanted our "butter bar" insignia of an ensign and orders to combat. (Others among the Brigade of Midshipmen were more thoughtful.) At the time, we didn't know that there would be all the combat anyone would want. Eleven more years.

The most popular author among us was Ian Fleming; like Kennedy, we too enjoyed reading Bond novels.

*   *   *

A few months later the Captain of the Maddox admitted that he wasn't so sure he was attacked by North Vietnamese torpedo boats after all. He said it was probably just false echoes on the radar from the choppy seas.

Fact or fiction? Hell, it didn't matter. By then, like James Bond, we had been issued our license to kill.

A MOOSE AND
SAN FRANCISCO

When I told my dad that I was going to Vietnam, he asked if
I wanted to go moose hunting. It wasn't something that I would
have expected as a parting vacation. We drove to northern British
Columbia where we met a guide named Ken Kylo. Ken was just
what I expected of a Canadian moose guide. Competent and quiet.
We rode in his pickup even further north into the woods. It was
late spring but the snow was still deep. We needed snowshoes to
walk around. The cabin was small and warm. The cook was an
alcoholic who was trying to dry out. He was a good cook. Spicy.
Wild game. He smoked a lot.

We hunted for three days in the deep snow. The pine woods
were beautiful. I became worried that we would not get a moose,
but Dad said that was part of the game. The guides take you to
places without much to shoot at for the first couple of days. Then
after you've had a hunt, they take to a place where you were sure to
make a kill. As usual, he was right.

On the fourth day, Ken took me on a snowmobile far up a
logging trail. A narrow band of light snow was on the road. Deep
green woods on each side. I stood vigilant in the road; motionless
for half an hour. Then without warning, an enormous moose
appeared beside me. Silent snow, then a big black moose. Close. I
shot. Then all was silent again. No moose.

I stood there wondering what to do. I thought I had seen the
moose flinch when I shot. Within a minute or two, an Indian
guide who worked with Ken arrived. He looked at the snow and
said, "You got him." We walked off the road about a hundred

yards and found the moose wounded and lying in the snow looking at us with uncomprehending eyes. Big brown eyes.

I had to shoot him in the head to end it. His eyes were astonishingly big; they looked right into me. Questioning.

Dad was delighted. The Indian said, "Damned good shot" about three times. That's a lot of talking for an Indian. Dad took the hindquarters of the moose back to Nebraska in a little trailer. When we said good-bye, he looked like he would cry.

I flew to San Francisco. I knew a nurse in Oakland who said I could stay with her for the two days before I left for Vietnam. I had known her for three years. She had a nice apartment on a steep hill. She shared it with a French roommate. It took a while for me to realize that her roommate was a lesbian; it took a while longer for me to realize that she was too. It didn't matter. I had a couple of days to see the town and have fun.

Instead I slept. A lot. I did absolutely nothing. Oddly, nothing seemed important anymore. I lounged around the apartment and read newspapers. I didn't even look to see what was happening in the Bay Area. I just read and watched T.V. Then I took a bus to Travis Air Force Base.

If you do not understand this chapter, that's okay, neither do I. Perhaps I should have compressed it. Maybe a moose and a lesbian shouldn't be in the same chapter.

I should have said: "One would think that for his last 48 hours before going to war, a man would do something interesting, not just lie in bed and read newspapers. It was 1967, I had believed that I was a good hunter, but a very big moose surprised me. Embarrassed me. The moose had big eyes and it didn't comprehend what I was doing to it. I was depressed about leaving Dad, and killing the moose, and learning that my friend was a lesbian."

Jesus! Even compressed, those thoughts are still hard to understand. Maybe somehow they fit together. Probably not.

I'm sure that at the time I was confused too . . . afraid as well . . . but officers are not allowed to show such emotions—even to themselves.

SEA DRAGON

THE TONKIN GULF YACHT CLUB,
the most exclusive yacht club in the world.

J. JARVITS (DDG66)

I was in flight training in Pensacola, Florida. I had just finished aerobatics and was in carrier qualifications. I was doing catapulted takeoffs, and arrested landings, "bouncing off the bird farm" when April 26th arrived. Time for my annual physical. I suspected that my eyes were no longer the required 20/20. I attempted to memorize the eye chart.

The flight surgeon asked me to read the letters on the eye chart. "A D Q R V," I responded.

"Next line."

"M O P S V T," I reported.

He looked me straight in the eye and said "Son, you can't see worth a damn!"

I responded, "I know, sir. But I stand number one in my class. I can fly!"

He didn't miss a beat in retorting "Not after today."

Shit. In those five minutes my career as a naval aviator ended. The aviation command wanted to put me in the "back seat." They wanted me to become a bombardier, navigator, or radar intercept officer. I explained that I stood first in my class and had often scared the hell out of myself. I couldn't imagine going for a ride with the worst pilot in the class. My roommate hit a tree with his wheel a week before, and we had a tree branch hanging from the light fixture in our apartment above our breakfast table. Gallows humor of another close call.

I asked for orders to "anything in Vietnam or the South China Sea war zone."

In the meantime, to stay busy, I volunteered to be a guinea pig for the space program. They were working on obtaining a database of how well people could compute and simultaneously endure discomfort. I was spun around in a machine that applied one or two G's to my body. After my blood had literally gravitated from my brain to my butt, I was asked to compute problems like "determine the square root of three" in my head.

Four weeks later, my orders arrived; I was to report to the U.S.S. J. Jarvits, a Hawaii-based destroyer that was on her way to the South China Sea. I took a quick moose-hunting vacation with my dad, and then met my new destroyer in the Philippines. Upon coming aboard the ship, I was given two jobs by the captain. I became the gunnery officer and also the missile officer. Unofficially, the most junior officer acquired an additional job: S.L.J.O. "Shitty Little Job Officer." As the S.L.J.O., I was responsible for about ten time-consuming tasks, like the monthly audit of all of the controlled drugs aboard the ship. Counting doses of morphine one by one.

Another necessary but irritating job was that of ship's librarian. I was to open the glass-enclosed bookshelves from 2 p.m. until 4 p.m. every Sunday. Checking each book out and receiving returns. The problem was that about 40 percent of the crew was on duty at that time. I was warned the most popular book, *Chilton's Auto Repair Manual,* was often missing. I asked what would happen if I lost a book. The answer: "Nothing." I asked how to get a replacement. The answer: "The Pearl Harbor librarian would replace them free." I couldn't believe my ears. The ship's policy limited readership and wasted the time of everyone in order to tightly control an asset that could be replaced free! I called the Pearl Harbor library and ordered 30 copies of *Chilton's Auto Repair Manual.* I removed the locks on the bookshelves as soon as the ship put to sea. My logic was simple; the books could not be stolen. They had to stay within 300 feet of the library! The policy became simple: Take any book you wish, but before the crew could get liberty upon arrival in port, the bookshelves must be full. I was proud of my managerial prowess; the best way to do a shitty little job is to eliminate it.

I had no idea of the shitty jobs that lay ahead.

SEA TRIALS:
A GUIDED MISSILE SHOT

Among its weapons, the Jarvits carried guided missiles. Tartar rockets were intended for surface-to-air use. That is, to shoot down enemy aircraft. One day, we were ordered to conduct a live firing test. One junior officer was to remain topside to watch and to record his observation. Our test was a failure.

After the aborted shot, we gathered in the wardroom. Solemnly, the captain placed the tape recorder on the green felt table. A young voice began, "This is Ensign John Schuler, the official topside observer aboard the U.S.S. J. Jarvits. Thirty seconds, twenty seconds . . . the missile is out of the hatch, it is on the rail. Ignition. Airborne. Oh! Jesus Christ! It's going bananas!"

The captain looked at us with disappointment. It would be hours before the electronic telemetry would be processed. Perhaps it would give a clue why our missile failed. It was sobering to realize that the primary firepower on our ship did not work. When called upon, it went bananas.

SEA DRAGON

"Operation Sea Dragon" was a remarkably stupid idea. The admirals believed that because the Navy was losing so many aircraft in North Vietnam, we could reduce the losses by giving the coastal targets to conventional ships. Destroyers could shoot about eight miles, so if they closed within two miles of the enemy's shore, they could hit any target within six miles of the coast. And because 80 percent of the Viets lived on the coast . . . we could "disrupt" (that was a word they liked a lot, "disrupt") . . . we could disrupt their war effort.

So on a typical mission, we would close in against the coast of North Vietnam and shoot. The targets were supplied by intelligence reports. Shoots were day and night, usually lasting about half an hour. Then the ship would retreat to a safe point ten miles offshore. We would take off battle gear and go to the wardroom to eat ice cream. Antiseptic and clean. An odd way to fight a war. Eating cookies.

The operation was a qualified success. Imagine: a Navy ship sits off shore shooting at targets inland. Things it cannot see. A Viet battery of large guns is positioned near the coast. Dug into cement bunkers. It gets to shoot at a big target—a Navy ship—that it *can* see. Would you rather be in a hidden bunker or sitting out in the middle of water like a duck?

When they shot at the Jarvits, it was amazing. It looked like a giant had thrown a handful of rocks. First muzzle flashes in the distance, then a 40 second wait, and then splashes all around us. Seven or eight guns shooting at us all at once. Just like the movies. Actually, that's what I said to myself the first time that we got shot at: "Just like the movies." It gives pause.

At first you look at it all in disbelief. Like Pierre in *War and Peace* who, in his first battle, says to himself, "Why do they want to kill me? I've always been a good person." Later you slowly begin to comprehend that you could actually get hurt, no matter what kind of person you are. Later still you come to the conclusion that you *will* get hurt if you do it long enough.

CAPTAIN TARR

Commander Donald Tarr, U.S. Navy, U.S. Naval Academy class of 1951, was the commanding officer of the guided missile destroyer U.S.S. J. Jarvits. He was also the most influential mentor that I had ever had. Because I too had graduated from Annapolis, he welcomed me aboard by assigning me not one job but two: Gunnery Officer and also Missile Officer. Both were full time assignments in the peacetime Navy. On Sea Dragon, both jobs were even more important.

Captain Tarr was a scholar. An exciting person with an inquisitive mind who liked to do experiments. One week he would be experimenting with a new schedule for rotation of the watch and general quarters assignments. The next week he would be attempting a controlled test of sleep deprivation on himself.

Evening meals were fascinating learning experiences. Captain Tarr would pose a question and then ask the 12 officers at the table for their advice and input. He would give us a crisis situation, such as a fire in the gun mount or a direct hit to the Combat Information Center. We would respond with what we would do, how we would coordinate with one another. In the process, we quickly got to know our fellow officers much better. We learned who could be counted upon to act quickly, who could think imaginatively. Most importantly, we learned who we could trust.

Captain Tarr did not invent the use of scenario planning for Naval warfare. As I said, he was a serious student; he had learned well. From the master: Admiral Lord Nelson. As Napoleon ravaged Europe, Admiral Nelson was given the task of breaking the back of the French Navy. Without a Navy, Napoleon could not invade the British Isles. Lord Nelson chased his adversary, Admiral Villeneuve, across the Atlantic. He sailed for over a year without ever touching shore. Finally the British fleet caught the French Armada. Nelson gave but one order to the ships and men in his command:

ENGLAND EXPECTS EVERY MAN
TO DO HIS DUTY.

The Battle of Trafalgar commenced, and soon the French fleet was sunk. Annihilated. Napoleon was denied the sea; Britain ruled the waves. England could now go on the offense on land.

Sadly, at Trafalgar, England lost the greatest admiral in history. Lord Nelson died of a gunshot wound. As the battle was ending, he was quietly standing on the deck of H.M.S. Victory. The bullet entered the top of his shoulder and exited below the opposite ribs. He had given no orders during the battle; none since the simple "England expects every man to do his duty." His strategy had been embedded in each of his trusted captains long before. After the battle, he gave but two: he ordered his fleet to anchor. Then as he lay bleeding to death, he turned to his most trusted officer and asked Captain Hardy to kiss him as he died.

During the previous year while Admiral Nelson chased the French, he had a daily meeting of the captains of each of his ships. Each day he posed a new problem. "If the French come with the wind from port, what shall we do?" "If the French outnumber us two to one, how will we modify the attack?" "If we have four ships that are hit and sinking, do we save the men or let them die as we focus on sinking the French?" By the time they reached Trafalgar and caught the French, everyone knew what to do in every eventuality. From the most seasoned captain, to the roughest gunner, to the 12-year-old boys who were "powder monkeys." By God, the British sailors knew how to sink the French. They knew courage. They knew initiative and coordination. They knew each other. As brothers. And as Professor Russell had stressed in the classroom back at the Naval Academy, they knew audacity.

But why did they spend so much time on how to set up the fleet of 24 ships? Positioning them with care before the battle? The answer was simple; it was the age of black gunpowder. Once the first broadside was fired and 400 cannons belched black smoke into the air, it was impossible to see. During a battle none of the other warships could see the flag hoists from Nelson's flagship. Once the battle began, every captain had to maneuver his ship on the *wishes* of Lord Nelson, not upon the *orders* of Nelson.

Within every crew the preparation was evident. The British gunners could fire four times as fast as their French counterparts. More accurately too.

Captain Tarr *was* my Nelson. He treated me as a respected fellow naval officer. He gave me responsibility far beyond my comfort zone. I was officer of the deck, in charge of a warship with nuclear weapons capability. I was only 23. Three hundred men depended on me to do the right thing. Three hundred "souls" as the Navy calls them.

The captain appreciated being kept well informed. At night as he would leave the bridge and go to his quarters to sleep, he would say, "Wake me often so I can sleep well." After a gunshoot he would even ask his officers, "What should I have done differently?" Only a skipper with immense confidence can be so open to those under his command. Once during a major gunshoot, I had a five-inch round stuck in one of my guns. Two hundred pounds of shell being heated by the cherry-hot barrel. Soon it would detonate of its own accord. A "cook off." At the time, the gun was pointed in the direction of friendly forces. Captain Tarr ordered us to break off the engagement with the enemy rather than risk killing friendlies. Later he called me into his quarters and grilled me for 30 minutes, exploring every alternative available at the time. Double checking again and again that we had done the right thing. That no alternative was better. That every measure would be taken to prevent a recurrence.

We were fighting the North Vietnamese with our steel ships. No longer "wooden ships and iron men." America's Navy sang "Anchors Aweigh," not "Heart of Oak." But truly, being a member of Captain Tarr's officer mess was like dining on the H.M.S. Victory 150 years before. Lord Nelson's ghost was the thirteenth diner at every meal.

It was an honor to serve such a skipper.

It was an honor to be part of the rich naval tradition.

A year later in the Mekong River, Captain Tarr, Professor Russell, and Admiral Lord Nelson would stand beside me on my boat and keep me safe.

INCOMING 155 MM SHELLS

On our first mission, we came under heavy attack. The first round landed a few meters off the starboard bow. The waterspout from the explosion went straight up. Like a geyser.

The executive officer, who was standing about three feet in front of me, ducked. He crouched behind the radar. Without thinking, I too genuflected.

Then I stood up and realized what I had done. I looked around to see if anyone had noticed. For no more than one second, I had gone into a crouch. I was embarrassed at my foolishness. A bad example. Hell, stand up and *look*. Either the round hits you or it misses. By the time you see it hit the surface it is too late anyway, so you might as well face it standing up. Look out the bridge and watch to see the muzzle flashes on the beach that give away the enemy's gun locations. Pay attention so you can shoot back. You can't do that hiding behind steel.

The next rounds came in a cluster. All missed us. I grinned at the executive officer. He was a Lieutenant Commander. Fifteen years my senior. His next move was less pronounced. By the time the firefight was into its third or fourth minute he was no longer ducking. He only flinched with each near miss. I continued grinning at him, at the enemy beach, and at the shells landing around us.

Cowardice is contagious. I caught it in less time than I could think. A fraction of a second. Bravery is also contagious, but it takes slightly longer to move from one person to another. We are all brave. We are all cowards. It all depends on circumstances. Obviously, it's easier to be brave if you are with others who display it. But on any given day . . .

*   *   *

Buddhists say "Wake up, be here now!" Meaning stay alive in every sense of the word. Notice things. Be in the day. That was remarkably easy to do in combat. Like it or not, one must stay in the moment.

This was the period when I was richer than I had ever been or would be again. I had nothing I wished to purchase except an occasional pack of cigarettes. We were paid every two weeks. My paychecks piled up uncashed.

At the time there was a popular country western song entitled "I Dreamed I Was There in Hillbilly Heaven." The song tells of a person who, in a dream, goes to heaven and meets and hears all of the great country singers who have passed away. It concludes: "And then I woke up, and I'm sorry I did."

For weeks after we greeted one another upon taking the early morning watch with, "And then I woke up and I'm sorry I did."

OLONGAPO POLICE DEPARTMENT

After a month on the gun line of Sea Dragon, the ship stopped for its first rest and relaxation, R & R, in Subic Bay, Philippines. We would be there five days. The Subic Naval Facility is adjacent to the city of Olongapo. Olongapo is a port town: old-fashioned, dirty, and raw. Many other R & R spots in the Pacific were better, but for repairs to the ship, nothing could compare to Subic. The enlisted men were eager to visit the bars with girls who had mastered enough English to say, "Buy me a drink."

Each evening one junior officer was selected to go to the Olongapo Police Department. "O.P.D." The job was simple. Just remain at the station the entire night in case a sailor was arrested by the police. If the Philippine police arrested an American, the naval officer on duty was to take him into custody and return him to his ship where he would face military justice. The purpose was to keep Americans out of the Philippine judicial system. It worked well.

After a quick sandwich, I walked a mile through muddy streets to the old brick police station. I found an uncomfortable wooden bench by the door and quietly began to read a Joseph Conrad novel. By 10 p.m. business began to pick up at O.P.D. Various quarreling people were pulled into the station by the Filipino law enforcement officials. By 11 p.m., drunks of all sorts were reeling in. I watched the brooding desk sergeant with amazement.

Some of the locals were released with a soft warning, but others received real and violent threats. Still others were carried through a door, which I presumed led to a subterranean jail. It certainly was interesting watching justice being dispatched. Moths circled around the naked light bulbs. At about 2 a.m. three pre-teenage boys were brought to the station. The desk sergeant beat them with a two-foot red rubber garden hose and threw them back into the muddy street. I asked the janitor what their crime had been; he said that he thought they were pickpockets but was not certain.

The little boys had hardly scattered when an officer dragged in three girls. They were dressed in tacky, yet slightly formal, dresses. Mid to late teens. They, too, were the unfortunate recipients of rubber hose whacks thrown indiscriminately upon ears, hands, backs, faces, and legs. They clustered in a tight, frightened group. I would guess each got more or less a half dozen bruises before they too were thrown out the front door. (I never did understand their crime. Their beating seemed harsh to me, but as best I could understand it, both they and the sergeant thought they had gotten off easily.)

Things were quiet again, and soon the roosters in the street were crowing. As the sun came up, I said good-bye to the gloomy desk sergeant and put my book under my arm. I had witnessed an entire spectrum of punishment, all met out to about 30 local Filipinos by a desk sergeant and a couple of clerks.

No Americans had fallen into the island's wheels of justice that night. Presumably the U.S. Navy's shore patrol had picked up any marginal sailors before they offended the local police.

As I walked back to the ship, I enjoyed the beautiful sunrise, the smell of the street, and the feeling of having experienced a night that was truly unique. Every T.V. sitcom, police drama, and soap opera had played out before me. In three dimensions and in living color.

Justice, if that was the word for it, was swift. Perhaps capricious, definitely memorable. I somehow felt much older after spending just ten hours at O.P.D. I was part of this wild environment, yet also filled with bemused detachment.

During the night, I had read Joseph Conrad's *Lord Jim*. As the morning sun rose over the muddy backstreet, I felt that I somehow understood it all. Like I belonged in the Orient.

NASTY BOATS

It was 0200, something big was happening. Earlier radio traffic had informed us that two very high-speed boats would transit our operating area. The J. Jarvits was to remain at a distance. That was all that I knew; the rest was secret. Whatever this special operation was, it was important enough to force our destroyer to cancel a major scheduled gunshoot.

We were up north on Yankee Station. Way up north. Almost off Hai Phong Harbor. In a very dangerous place.

Perfectly on schedule, we saw a tiny yellow blip on the radar screen. Then another close behind. Both of the boats were coming straight north, paralleling the coast. Two of us bachelors had come up to see what was happening. Each of us was huddled around the green screen, watching the two yellow dots move. "How fast do they go?" someone asked. "Let's plot 'em." With each sweep, the position was plotted and timed. Then came a gasp. "Jesus, those boats fly!"

Warrant Officer Bearton stepped up. He had been deeply involved in intelligence work and was doing special secret work on electronic countermeasures. A project that was beyond belief. I can't tell you more; I wish I could. I still can't even tell you the name of the project. At the time even its *name* was classified, perhaps it still is. Seeing my enthusiasm, the warrant told me a few facts about what I was witnessing on the radar screen. Here is what he said:

> "The two boats that you see are called P.T.F.'s, but they are affectionately known as "Nastys." The U.S. has only a precious few. They are elite. Eighty feet long. Paper-thin mahogany and fiberglass hulls imported from Norway. Sixty-nine tons displacement. The engines produce over

6,000 horsepower. They have mortars, guns, and a lot of secret weaponry. They do missions that scare the pee out of the rest of us. Speed is over 45 knots."

We looked with awe at the plots on the radar screen. "Over 45 knots" was a whopping understatement. Six thousand horsepower made those boats unbelievably fast. Napier Deltic Engines, a cousin of Rolls Royce, caused those mahogany hulls to fly.

The show was just beginning. As the two Nastys came between the J. Jarvits and the shore, they abruptly turned left and within seconds had merged with the coast. The lazy sweeps of our radar screen now showed only the North Vietnamese landline. Those crazy bastards had driven straight into a river. Deep into enemy territory. Without slowing down. Pitch black. Holy shit.

The warrant had already told me more than he should have. The captain and the executive officer were by my side looking at the now blank radar screen. Minutes passed. I wondered about the fate of those men. Had they been discovered? Had the North Vietnamese sunk them?

Five minutes. Ten. Total silence on the bridge. Fifteen. We shifted from one foot to another, glued to a 16-inch screen. Then it happened: both boats popped out of the river mouth like hounds from hell. An involuntary cheer emerged from all of us. We grinned at each other in awe and amazement. Both boats quickly turned south and were on their way to safety. Their mission appeared to be accomplished.

Clearly "Nasty" boats were *the* most dangerous job in the Navy. Presumably the tiny force needed volunteers to man those beautiful boats. In a Catch-22 way, because of their secrecy, it was impossible for most junior officers to even know of the existence of such craft, let alone volunteer.

Now I was one of the few who knew about Nastys and had seen what they could do. Warrant Officer Bearton had told me things about them that I had no right to know; I didn't have the security clearance. I looked into the captain's face. He smiled at me.

The pieces fit together. Earlier the captain must have authorized Bearton to tell me. He could see a fit.

After that brief glimpse, I wanted duty on Nastys more than anything in the world. Far more than anything in life.

A NAVAL OFFICER AND
A CHINA SAILOR

There were two officers who became close friends of mine. Lieutenant Becker was a good-looking, crisp officer who was eager to get back stateside to his 24-year-old loving wife. From her photo she looked like a studious coed with the body of a dancer. Becker was to be discharged upon completion of the cruise; he wanted to take an ocean liner back from Honolulu to San Francisco so he and his wife could just enjoy a shipboard romance. Becker grinned as he planned his cruise; he was the ship's engineer so he also hoped that he could convince the cruise ship's captain that he should get a VIP tour of the ocean liner's engineering spaces. Becker would soon be working for Ford Motor Company. In just a few months, he and his lovely wife would have a nice ranch house.

My other friend was Lieutenant O'Boyle. He was the weapon's officer. My boss. Because the Navy does not allow alcohol on board, he was sober most of the time. Ashore, he was often bleary-eyed and staggering. O'Boyle was in love with a bar girl in Yokosuka, Japan, named Tomiko. She was stunningly beautiful with long black hair. She wore white dresses too. She lived in a little house on an unpaved street. A street with chickens walking outside and women carrying pots on long sticks. It looked like a house in a Japanese woodcut. O'Boyle had sailed on two previous cruises to the Orient. He had even flown back to Japan to see Tomiko once. When the J. Jarvits steamed out of port at the end of R & R, O'Boyle stood on the fantail. Alone. Watching the city disappear. He was a true China sailor; he fit in Asia and nowhere else.

Both Becker and O'Boyle outranked me, so at supper they could choose seats away from the talkative chaplain. I had to sit next to him and hear story after story about the lepers on Molokai. Jesus, just what I wanted to think about as I ate my tuna fish sandwich and french-fries. I knew I would never meet a leper anyway.

Becker and O'Boyle. An apple pie homecoming king and an alcoholic Irish China sailor. The Navy needed both. If God existed, She probably preferred Becker. As for me, I liked the Irishman better; he was far more interesting.

THE PADRE

The chaplain on board was an odd duck. He had served for several years on a leper colony. Ugly, with a raspy voice and limited intellect. He wasn't Catholic, but we called him "Padre" anyway. "Reverend" sounded too respectful. Halfway through Operation Sea Dragon, the Navy sent him stateside and replaced him with a straight-out-of-med school M.D. The entire crew was delighted.

I had heard "There are no atheists in fox holes." I didn't notice anyone becoming more religious as we got shot at more often. On the contrary, as things got more dangerous, we simply grew more tired and more preoccupied with day-to-day worries.

Secretly, I was delighted to see that everyone else in the 300-man crew shared my feeling of finding far more comfort in having an M.D. nearby than a strange chaplain.

That's not to say I was an atheist. I marveled as a kid at all of those little bumps on my dog's nose. That perfect pattern proved to me God does exist. My imperfect life and this insane war proved just as well that while God exists, there is no evidence that he is *benevolent*. Twenty years later, near base camp Everest, my tentmate, a brilliant Episcopalian priest, confirmed that mine was a very old question that had bothered thoughtful spiritual people throughout history.

The Braille bumps on my dog's nose were my sacred scripture. I was in a weary, mellow frame of mind when I climbed up the ladder for the next gunshoot. Three hours of sleep just wasn't enough.

ROUTINE GUNSHOOT

The J. Jarvits had been on the gunline for 20 days. Straight. Shoot up the North Vietnam countryside in the morning, afternoon, and again two or three times at night. We received fire on most of the missions. Everyone was in a state of being half asleep and half awake.

Someone had a copy of *In Cold Blood* by Truman Capote. It was a very violent book by the standards of the day. Two ex-cons kill a family in Kansas. One killer even says, "I liked Mr. Clutter right up to the moment I cut his throat." Incomprehensible. They even killed the Clutter's teenage kids.

The book was so fascinating, so exciting, that we all wanted to read it. The solution was simple: we tore the paperback into sections of 20 pages each and sent them round-robin. Each guy anxiously awaiting the next installment. It seems odd today to think of men in war anxious to read a book about murder and being shocked by it.

*   *   *

One death is a tragedy.
A million is a statistic.

Lenin.

JUST ANOTHER VILLAGE

In this blur of gunshoots, one night we were assigned a target that was a staging facility. Some town in North Vietnam where the N.V.A. troops were massing to go down south. Ammunition, men, equipment. The target village had a nondescript name, An Hoi, followed by the coordinates CP 006 135.

The Combat Information Center is the nerve center of a ship. It is dark inside with just the glow of radar screens and small focused lights. On the starboard side is a table where the gunfire is supervised. Three of us huddled around the table: I was the gunnery officer; Ensign Wagner was an engineer who worked as my helper unless the ship was damaged, then he would take charge of the damage control party; and Warrant Officer Bearton, a sarcastic, bright little guy.

I took the message, skimmed it with sleepy eyes, and laid out the big chart to find our target. The small town's name came into sight after a brief search. I circled it, took another swig of coffee to wake up, locked the chart onto the table and began to layout the gunshoot plan.

For naval bombardment, one really needs to know only two things: where your ship is and where the target is. Armed with these two positions, you simply compute a range and bearing (distance and direction) and you shoot.

Destroying a target thoroughly requires a little more skill. Over time, I became skilled. Here is how to destroy a village:

1.) Start with about 15 rounds of high explosive shells timed to go off in the air above the village. This is a surprise. "Daisy Cutter" shots that kill anyone outdoors. Animals, people, whatever.

2.) Assuming the people run for cover, you next go to ground shots. Let the high explosive shells hit the ground and explode. Thirty rounds. Walk them left to right and up and down. Cover the target with shots like a checkerboard.

3.) Now it is time to catch it on fire. Most houses are bamboo, so you lay in 15 airbursts of "Willy Peter." White phosphorus. Walk the rounds. White-hot phosphorus raining down on everything.

That will do the trick.

After the gunshoot, we took off our headphones, stood up to stretch and refilled our coffee cups. We were almost asleep on our feet. Small talk. Still slightly nervous. "Tell Saigon mission accomplished."

Wagner, who normally had a cherubic smile, looked frightened. In the dim light he touched my sleeve, while still looking at the gun chart. "Look at this," he whispered. His finger was on a village that had not received our fire. "An Hoi (1)."

"What the . . ." I started.

"Look," he said. An Hoi (2) had been my target. *Two* villages. Three klicks apart with the same stupid name! An Hoi (1) was at coordinates CP 006 135. We, in our haste, had just seen "An Hoi" and wiped it off the earth. But it was An Hoi (2) at CP 007 133 that we had devastated. The proper target was 1.8 miles away from the village that we had destroyed.

Oddly, it took a full minute for it all to sink in. Wagner and I sat down at the gun table and stared in disbelief. "What do we do now?" I asked myself. We had just eliminated an entire village. Men, women, kids, dogs, ducks. All gone. It was the wrong fucking vil. The "target," the village that was the troop staging area, was three klicks away. Obviously, not a target anymore. Whoever had been in An Hoi (1) had run for cover when the shells started landing 3,000 meters away.

We stared at each other for another ten seconds in silence. We were alone at the table. I shook my head. "It was my fault. Totally. But maybe it's best to forget it. Too late now."

"Yeah," he said. Then sadly, "Let's go." We walked out into the pilot house and went to sleep.

The trouble is, it couldn't be forgotten. I had destroyed a village that wasn't a target. Totally. In cold blood.

Lt. Calley

Later, I read of an Army officer who lost control. His men murdered innocent people in a village called My Lai. People wondered how it could happen. How Americans could look innocent people in the eye and kill them. I know how you can wipe out a village full of people. But I didn't look them in the eye.

Capt. Barger (newsitem)

The Air Force fined the navigator of a U.S. B-52 bomber that accidentally bombed the Cambodian town of _____ August 6. Capt. Thomas Barger was fined $700 and given a letter of reprimand. Three other officers also were disciplined after an investigation of the incident in which 137 persons were killed and 268 wounded.

That's $5.11 per person for each one he killed. Eventually Captain Barger paid a higher price, I'm sure. Maybe he was tired, perhaps in a hurry, maybe he misread the chart.

Maybe I'll go to hell. Maybe it will be crowded.

HONG KONG HILTON

At age 23, I thought I was mature. A combat-hardened man. That might be true in part, but basically I was also just a naive kid from Nebraska.

When the J. Jarvits docked in Hong Kong for R & R, I was simply in awe. I had never seen such a beautiful city. You do not visit Hong Kong; you are overwhelmed by it. Gigantic buildings next to rickshaws. The wildest nightlife on the planet juxtaposed beside proper British men and women wearing white and lawn bowling on the common green.

The bachelors were the first to "hit the beach." Married guys would trade duty with junior officers so the bachelors could maximize their time ashore in the wild ports. In return, the married officers would get off the first days upon return to Pearl to be with wives and family.

In Olongapo we had been given a long list of things we could not do, a list of places we could not visit. As the ship docked in Hong Kong, the X.O. read the orders for Hong Kong: "You may not carry a loaded speargun in downtown Hong Kong. Dismissed."

That was it. Only one restriction in Fragrant Harbor. That is why it had been a pirate haven for over a century. Visitor-friendly in every sense of the word.

The enlisted crew rushed off to Wanchai, a section of Hong Kong that had been "entertaining" sailors since the days of wooden ships and iron men. The best tattoo artists in the world. The best strippers, the best bar girls. Wanchai was a city within a city. Marshall Field had said in his Chicago department store, "Give the lady what she wants!" Wanchai mirrored that motto. "Give the sailor what he wants." Truly world class.

We junior officers took a tour of Wanchai, hosted by a few of the more senior officers. After an hour or two of looking at beautiful first-rate strippers and drinking third-rate scotch, we retreated to the Hong Kong Hilton. Modern, western, comfortable Hong Kong Hilton. A mile from Wanchi. Very good food, a fine massage (yes, just a massage), and then down to the bar. Johnny Walker Black Label. Big, soft leather chairs. Dim lights, a great place to talk, interrupted discreetly by a stunningly beautiful pencil-thin Cantonese waitress in a classic silk dress. Heaven, with no closing time. Heaven, with no irksome Ten Commandments.

At about 1:30 a.m. the operations boss, Lt. Neeley, quietly walked up to the bar and then climbed on top of it. He proceeded to dance a fantastic soft shoe routine on the ebony polished bar. People at the bar held their drinks in their hands politely, as Neeley danced along the long semi-circle of glistening wood. When the performance was over, the bartenders, the waitresses, the entire audience gave a mild applause and resumed where they had left off. As if such things happened every night. Neeley climbed down and resumed drinking with us.

It was all so very . . . civilized. So appropriate.

Hong Kong was exotic and foreign, yet truly the most comfortable city I had ever seen. Comfortable even in the middle of the night. I knew that I could live there. More accurately, I could live there *forever*, without wanting to return to the U.S.A. That was exactly what had happened in the earlier days of the Royal Navy and later the U.S. Navy. "China Sailors" were men, like my friend Lt. O'Boyle, so attracted to the Orient that they refused to return. When asked why they chose the East, they would only smirk.

1967. Had I been born a hundred years before, a subject of Queen Victoria, I would have been a China Sailor. Perhaps in another life I was.

You may not understand why an American would renounce the West . . . you would if you had taken the Star Ferry across the harbor or if you had seen Neeley's soft shoe routine on the onyx bar of the Hong Kong Hilton.

WIBLICS

In addition to shooting up the North Vietnam coast, the Sea Dragon ships were also charged with the responsibility of sinking any Viet ship running down the coast delivering weapons and supplies from North Vietnam to the Viet Cong in the south. Such gunrunners were called "waterborne logistic craft," or "WIBLICS" for short. In America's Civil War, there had been some magnificent stories of blockade runners that brought contraband from Europe and moved vital supplies from port to port in the South.

Our job on the destroyer was to identify such craft and sink them. Curiously, there was no limit on size, so in theory and in fact, if a fisherman took his boat from north to south along the coast, he could be identified as a gunrunner and sunk.

Now think for a moment. How many great fishing areas are likely to be exactly straight offshore from the fisherman's homeport? Fish go up and down the coast. Boats with nets move accordingly. As a result, every boat goes out to a given depth of water and then moves more or less up and down the coast. Obviously the wind is also a factor. It blows boats around, causing them to move parallel to the coast or randomly. In either case, it is seldom straight out and straight back.

So what does a Viet fisherman do? Well, with a wife and several kids, the answer is simple: he goes fishing. It is all he knows how to do. With a per capita income of $200 per year, he can't afford not to work. So he goes fishing. He and the eldest two kids climb into a sampan the size of a log and lay out nets.

Meanwhile, there is a big destroyer two miles away tracking his boat, along with up to 30 other fishing boats. Day and night. Especially at night. Most Viet fishermen prefer to fish at night. They lay out the nets and then hang a small lantern above the water. The fish are attracted to the light. Kids climb into a "basket boat" and make a big circle paddling from the sampan around the fish and back to the sampan. Then daddy pulls up the net and, hopefully, a fish or two appear in the net.

Add to that, the imprecision of radar. From the destroyer, a small sampan looks like a big wave or a bamboo pole with a flag, which were often used to mark fishing areas. One sweep of the radar would show 20 blips, the next 15, and the next 22. Which are waves? Which are boats? Which are marker fish sticks? Absolutely no way to tell.

Basically, the radar on the J. Jarvits was designed to find an enemy aircraft or a ship of steel, not a wooden boat the size of a log that sits only 12 inches above the water. You can try to plot movement. You can try to be careful, but the combination of odd targets, poor radar returns, and just ignorant men and kids trying to catch some damned fish to eat made the job impossible. A sailor who came down from Mount Olympus could not figure it out. Poseidon himself would tell you to give up.

Sadly we didn't. We blasted the shit out of WIBLICS. We called them enemy targets. I wondered if I should do a thoughtful analysis; using probability and statistics and real case examples, I could prove we were shooting at inappropriate targets. I could prove it with analysis of the radar returns. I had "stars" at the academy. I stood in the top 5 percent of my class. My major was systems analysis engineering.

So I continued to think about doing an analysis, fantasizing that I would be flown to Pearl Harbor to present my findings to the Commander in Chief of the Pacific. CINCPAC. Fantasizing that my McNamara-like quantitative study would change the war.

Four months later I was still fantasizing. Just a butter-bar ensign looking up at the brass. Still assuming that if the Navy is doing it, it must be right.

In those four months, we blew up a hell of a lot of Viet fishermen.

Saint Peter was a fisherman. He also holds the keys to heaven. Uh oh.

BEACH

Chief Petty Officer Beach was in charge of the ship's guns. As the gunnery officer, in theory, I was his boss. Given that I had been aboard only a few months and that he had been a gunner's mate for 25 years, it was clear that in truth, there was little that I knew and less still that he didn't.

There was only one problem. Beach was truly the laziest person on the ship. He spent most of his time grooming his perfect handlebar mustache. He could always be found in the chief's lounge, which was affectionately known as "the goat locker." He drank coffee, ate, grew fat, and slept. If a problem arose with a gun, the young enlisted men would politely knock on the goat locker, whisper the problem to Beach, and Beach would give his advice without getting up from the table. He refused to go to the scene of the problem. By remaining still, he avoided burning any calories at all. In general, fat people are masters at efficiently avoiding movement. This allows them to burn fewer calories than normal people. By arranging their lives to minimize movement, overweight people gain even more weight from the food they eat. Beach was fat. His laziness contributed to his caloric gain.

Yet he was extremely competent. He had limited needs. The single thing he seemed to enjoy the most (beyond food) was watching the ship's movies. Especially "Beach Blanket Bingo," an incredibly simple movie starring Annette Funicello, in which young women in bikinis did basically nothing. The crew enjoyed that movie as well, and as a result, we did not trade it with other ships. It stayed aboard and played almost every other night.

The five-inch guns in the fleet were experiencing a major problem. Without warning, the big guns would explode while firing. They would literally blow themselves apart. It was as if the Navy ship had hit itself. The shell would explode inside the gun turret. No one in the Navy knew why it was happening. Each week we would receive another bulletin speculating on the cause, suggesting an adjustment to make that might cure the problem. Later we would receive yet another notice of a sister ship that had a gun blow up. Basically nothing remained of the gunner's mates in those turrets that exploded.

It was hard for me to climb into the turret of our ship knowing that the cause of the explosions had not been found. As an engineer, I assumed that the answer was relatively simple. Perhaps each shell was being rammed into position too hard. Perhaps the shells were creating friction causing a spark, perhaps . . . but try as we might, we simply could not find the cause.

Later I read about a reporter who was invited by the U.S. Air Force to visit the secret facility at Cheyenne Mountain, Colorado. Upon his arrival, the reporter noticed several men attempting to repair a broken escalator. The Air Force brass deluged the reporter with details of how, if called upon, America's exotic missiles would leap from their silos and fly with pinpoint accuracy to the center of the selected targets half way around the world. At the conclusion of his three-day briefing, the reporter noted that the men were *still* trying to fix the escalator!

Our gun problem seemed to be much the same. Ours was a very sophisticated ship with very sophisticated weapons. The crew was bright and well trained. We were capable. Sadly, solving the problem took more than we had. We worked at it. We tried various solutions. They all failed. So in the end, we approached each gunshoot with a combination of excitement and anticipation and also a sense of dread. Taking our chances against the enemy was part of the big game. Taking our chances against our own weapons was insane.

Later, while conducting a routine review of pay records, I was shocked to see that Beach gave most of his pay away. Almost 80 percent of his pay was earmarked for the United Fund. I would never have imagined a person could be so generous. He lived on the ship, he ate well, and consequently he didn't need much money. Yet most people would have saved some money, or purchased a few things for themselves. Not Beach. He gave it all away. Beach was even more complex than the ship's weapons system.

IRON HAND

The U.S. Navy had two aircraft carriers on station every day. One was off North Vietnam; that location was called "Yankee Station." The carrier that steamed off the coast of South Vietnam and supported our troops there was in "Dixie Station." Older destroyers worked in the south and escorted the carriers. Only once did we get orders to escort a carrier. That tour was remarkable, only because of its boredom.

The likelihood of a U.S. carrier being attacked at sea was basically nonexistent. Nonetheless, the Navy insisted that carriers be protected by a screen of two or three smaller ships. There was little to do except watch the aircraft launch against targets in the north, and then later count the aircraft returning. The Phantom II's made an eerie whistling as they landed. Aviators joked that their job was to convert jet fuel into noise. Phantom II pilots converted fuel into a howl.

For us on ships, the feeling was of envy. The pilots of the Navy strike aircraft were flying over enemy territory inflicting damage. Accomplishing something. They were going into harm's way. On the other hand, when we were escorting carriers, we were simply boring holes in the ocean. All of us were eager to get back to Sea Dragon.

The most hairy-chested job among the pilots (who called themselves "drivers" as often as pilots) was one called "Iron Hand." Those were the men whose job was to attack the enemy's air defense missile sites. In other words, the "Iron Hand" pilots had the specific job of going against the enemy locations designed to shoot down aircraft. It was a truly dangerous task. We found it difficult to pull ourselves away from the radio while air strikes were in progress. To hear the flow of war moving, men giving one another support in the face of enemy fire. I felt like a little kid again, reading G.I. Joe comic books. But this was all in real time. Just a few miles away.

We on the destroyers screening the carriers were doing nothing. No danger, no excitement, just tagging along. Listening to the huge P.A. system on the carrier play the song "Spirit in the Sky." The refrain was "That's where I'm gonna go when I die. Take me up to the spirit in the sky . . . ." After two weeks, the J. Jarvits was ordered back to the more dangerous mission; it was good to get off Yankee Station screen duty and back to Sea Dragon.

The carrier was 20 miles off the shore of North Vietnam. On Sea Dragon we would be within a mile or two. Close enough to shoot at them and close enough to get shot at. On occasion, we were called upon to pick up pilots whose aircraft had been damaged but were fortunate enough to get "feet wet." They had managed to get back over water before going down.

On Sea Dragon, our 5-inch guns shot a shell that was exactly 5 inches in diameter and about 20 inches long. It weighed several hundred pounds and could be shot as far as eight miles. The North Vietnamese shot ordnance back at us that was basically the same. It was a fair fight. It was what honorable combat was all about.

Sea Dragon wasn't as dangerous as flying Iron Hand. That was okay with me. There is a limit to how much danger a sane person should seek.

At about this time, our ship's commanding officer, Commander Donald Tarr, was given orders to Washington, D.C. His successor, Captain Bill Carpenter, was a capable, good person, but Captain Tarr had been my first mentor in combat. That person is, and will always remain, a very special individual in the heart and mind of a young officer. I missed him. I felt more vulnerable without him in command.

A GREEK DRAMA

For a week we were assigned to a special task force: Oresteia. It seemed to be an odd name.

Later I looked into the meaning of it. At the time of the Battle of Troy, a young prince named Orestes was obligated to kill his father's killer. The Greeks also had an equal obligation not to kill one's mother. Young Orestes was caught. Unable to reconcile his dilemma because it was his mother who had murdered his father.

I was just an engineer. Unfamiliar with most of the classics. Yet I couldn't help wondering if the operation had been deliberately named by a rebelliant liberal arts student who delighted in teasing that our task was also one in which there could be no "good" answer. Like a classic Greek play, all of the alternatives led to a disastrous consequence.

INSIDE HAIPHONG HARBOR

Late one night we were suddenly ordered into Haiphong Harbor. We were steaming past the huge minefields into the enemy's biggest harbor. We were alone. It was dark. Pitch black. We were putting our ass on the line and there was absolutely no one who could help us if we got in trouble.

We stared at each other with wide eyes. Excited. Disbelief at what was happening. Helpless with where our orders were carrying us.

An odd but obvious thing about the Navy is that there are no deserters. It is impossible to leave; all of the men are literally "in the same boat." The only way to escape is to not get on the ship in the first place. For that reason, missing a ship's movement is a very serious court-martial offense.

So anyway, there were 300 of us in one steel hull going into the center of the enemy's principle harbor. Hopefully our captain knew why we were on this crazy mission. If so, he was not giving us an explanation.

We steamed around inside the lion's mouth for what seemed like half an hour. Then without warning we were ordered out. It appeared to be a senseless mission. Clearly it was dangerous. As far as I could see, it had accomplished absolutely nothing.

No explanation was ever given.

Imagine a German ship in World War II being ordered to sail up the Thames River to London. By itself. Naked. If someone were to tell such a story it would be held in disbelief. Yet that is the equivalent of what we did on a dark night in the summer of 1967.

I'm glad we did it. It was like mooning Uncle Ho.

GLOBE, ARIZONA

We had a young quartermaster named Troy from Globe, Arizona. He enjoyed teasing the cowardly chief who was his boss. One night before a major gunshoot, Troy hooked the chief's headphone to the fire extinguisher hanging on the wall. You heard me right. He connected the end of the chief's phone line to the little black hose coming out of the fire extinguisher.

When the chief arrived on the bridge shortly before the 3 a.m. gunshoot, he put on his headphones and attempted a phone check. Puzzled, he bent down and followed the cord to the wall. He stared at the fire extinguisher in disbelief. The darkness, the preposterousness of it all. Talking into the hose of a red fire extinguisher. He shook. He muttered, "Oh damn it, oh damn it, oh damn it," and shook more.

Covertly, the rest of us looked at him. Eyes teasing cruelly. He was much too frail to be here. He couldn't contribute . . . except as the butt of our humor.

We were amused by his fear. It was transparent. Perhaps having one coward in combat was good. It made the rest of us feel braver. Whether we were, in fact, more brave than he was another issue. Like having a class dummy back in third grade; he was good for the rest of us.

One night when I was the officer of the deck, I found that Troy was also on watch. I asked about his home in Globe, Arizona. He explained that it was dry and desolate. Apparently Globe is a somewhat lonely place. I told Troy that I too was from a place far from the sea.

Troy said something else that night. He said that his dad was a prison warden. The task of executing prisoners weighed heavily on his father. He liked the job, all except for killing

people. I said that I could understand. On further reflection,
the warden's dilemma became elusive. Agony over killing one
person at a time. One person who in all likelihood was actually
guilty of something.

OM

Om is the Buddhist chant. "Om" is a primal sound of man and nature.

Put your hands over your ears. Right now. Listen. You will hear it. Om, om, om, om . . .

The engines of a warship make the same sound. Like a mother's heartbeat comforting the unborn baby. I could hear the sound all night in my bunk in the junior officers quarters. Four of us, the youngest officers. All in one cabin affectionately known as "Boy's Town."

True sounds.

Om. Om. Om. Om.

Some say "Om" should be chanted in three sounds. "Aum" as the Hindus sing:

"A" for Brahma, the Creator God.
"U" for Vishnu, the Preserver, and
"M" for Shiva, the God of Destruction.

PLAINSMEN

It was a warm gray evening. Light rain made the sky and ocean merge into one. A nice time to be on the bridge. The commodore came up with a smile. A crisp brown uniform. A special cup with a shield on it held his coffee. I greeted him and he stood beside me watching the ship's bow cut through the South China Sea. After almost a quarter of an hour of silence, he spoke: "Where are you from, Son?"

"Nebraska, Sir."

"Good state. I'm from there too. Did you know that Nebraska has the highest per capita of naval officers of any state?"

"No, I didn't, Sir, but I can understand. My dad used to say, 'A jackrabbit must pack his lunch to get across the state.'" A slight grin crept upon me. The commodore turned and looked at the sea with a fatherly smile. That smile was for me.

We had both run away from one of the most boring places in America. There was a 25 year difference in our ages. We had joined the Navy to seek adventure, and here we were, two plainsmen looking out upon the flat featureless sea. A hydraulic Great Plain. Soft rain. Comfort in our protective steel home. Gentle rolling hills. Moving like waves of grass.

We stood together on the bridge for an hour of silence. Communicating.

The great Lakota chief Black Elk would have understood.

AROUND THE WORLD

One day, we were to relieve some other ships on Sea Dragon. Apparently the confidential message traffic became so intense that the commodore reverted to a practice that had been common in the days of wooden ships: he called a face-to-face meeting. Six Navy ships convened in one spot in the South China Sea and five launched small boats. Five Navy skippers, or their executive officers, motored over to the host ship.

It was odd to see six warships parked in a big circle. Odder still to see small boats scurrying from ship to ship. White wakes reflected the bright sun of the South China Sea.

I walked on deck. Enjoying the show. Sitting on a bollard near the fantail was an old Navy chief. Beach. His right index finger permanently curled into the white coffee cup. He mumbled something. At first I didn't believe he was talking to me. He spoke again, and I turned around to see who else was with us. We were the only ones. I looked at the side of his head and asked, "Are you talking to me, Chief?"

"Yes Sir," he replied. "Did you ever see anything like it?"

"Like what?"

"Did you ever see anything like *this*?" he asked again. His hand swept the horizon and all of the ships with boats scurrying about.

I grinned. It did look odd. "No, Chief, I never did."

He turned to me and his eyes twinkled. "I been around the world seven times, I seen two world's fairs and a goat-fucking contest, but I ain't never seen a zoo like this before!"

I grinned and winked. What a great line. He needed me to meet him on the fantail. Otherwise that Navy phrase, constructed as he sat in solitude, would be lost. He knew how to use English. So memorably that, for weeks after, I would say to myself "I been

around the world . . . ." Then I would grin. The Navy is a
brotherhood of care and humor and sarcasm. Of suffering and of
love. Mostly it is a brotherhood of *experiences*.

ANZIO

*Life does not cease to be funny when people die anymore
than it ceases to be serious when people laugh.*

George Bernard Shaw

We went into a hot mission off Vinh. The coastal guns opened up on us all at once. The entire coast came alive. Bright pops of light. Like popcorn. Blinking. Each was a round being shot at us. The muzzle flashes looked tiny. Innocuous. Even friendly.

It takes about 40 seconds for the shell to fly through the air. It takes so long that big guns even compensate for the amount the earth turns under the shell as it is flying. In 40 seconds, the earth revolves several feet.

Anyway, 40 seconds later all hell breaks loose. Shells begin landing around the ship like a giant had thrown a handful of rocks. Splashes left, right, in front of the ship. Splashes every goddamned place. The good thing is that it is all the same. There is no place to hide. Left or right it makes no difference so you might as well grin and enjoy the show. It's exhilarating. It is truly *the* big show.

We shot back as fast as our guns could fire. The target was an ammo dump. Finally after we had shot 40 or 50 rounds and had seen incoming shells several times that number, there was an enormous explosion. The target seemed to go into convulsions of successive blasts. One on top of the other. We stopped shooting. We just watched. The North Vietnamese ammunition was literally blowing itself apart. Each secondary explosion set off another and another and another. The people there were truly experiencing hell on earth.

Winston Churchill said, "There is nothing more invigorating than being shot at." We grinned, slapped one another on the back and laughed. We were happy, proud, and unharmed. As the ship steamed away from shore and we secured from general quarters, two of us walked through the main mess deck. Standing by the "goat locker" was an old Navy chief who had been in the Mediterranean in World War II. He looked at us with an air of superiority. "That was good shooting, sir," he said. "But in '44, the big war, on a cruiser, off Anzio, Italy, I saw our gunners shoot an Eye-Talian off his motorcycle with the eight-inch guns at four miles."

We stood in shock. The old goat had just said that he had seen a projectile the weight of a small car hit a person four miles away. Out of respect, we could not say it was a lie. Yet to call it the truth would be a huge stretch. Let's just call it lore.

But that's not the point: the point is that no matter how good you are, there is some warrior who has done better. No matter how brave you are, it still isn't enough. Even the bravest are eclipsed by the murky boundary of fact and fiction. If Hector was brave, Achilles was braver. Leonidis, Spartans, Admiral Lord Nelson, and Mars. You cannot match them. It is beyond reality. Beyond life.

To meet them, you must go beyond your own humanity . . . and you can't do that.

*   *   *

Late that night we received an important bulletin from the Navy's ordnance department. They had found the cause of the gun mount explosions. Some of the ammunition had been improperly produced. The primer was not driven fully into the base of the shell. When the rounds were jammed into the gun, the primer moved forward a tiny fraction of an inch. Not much, but it was enough to create friction which caused a spark which caused an explosion before the round was fully inside the gun. We surveyed the ammunition. All rounds with suspect production numbers were thrown overboard.

The North Vietnamese might kill us, but after that night we could sleep knowing that at least we would not be killing ourselves.

We had confidence again. Hell, we were so good that we too could shoot an Eye-Talian off his motorcycle at four miles . . . maybe five.

ORDERS

Eventually, the J. Jarvits was dinged up a little. The ship was worn out from fighting. It was time to limp back to Pearl Harbor. After six months, our tour of duty was over.

In transit eastward while crossing the Pacific, I wrote a letter:

From: Ensign Gary Robert BLINN, USN, 701383/1100
To: Chief of Naval Personnel
Via: Commanding Officer, U.S.S. J. JARVITS (DDG66)

Subj: Duty in Vietnam, Request for

1. It is respectfully requested that I be assigned duty in Vietnam. On 29 September 1967 I returned from deployment in WestPac during which the J. JARVITS was primarily involved in Operation SEA DRAGON. As both Gunnery and Missile Officer I have had experience as G.L.O. firing the ship's 5-inch/54 battery against various targets in North Vietnam. I received my qualification as OOD(I) on 28 September 1967.

2. The J. JARVITS is presently scheduled for a regular yard overhaul period and consequently I will have little opportunity to gain more at-sea experience during the next year.

3. I will eagerly accept any duty in Vietnam. However, as a 23-year-old bachelor I feel the duty in P.T.F. (Nasty) or P.C.F (Swift) or L.C.M. (Monitor) in that order

would offer the most challenging and rewarding opportunity for me. I would also accept any MAAG/ mission or other shore duty in-country.

Gary R. BLINN
ENS, USN

Dear reader, please read that letter again. It is more significant than it first appears. A young man, age 23, is saying that what he wants most in life is to go into the most dangerous combat available to him in the Navy. I wanted Nastys or Swift boats. Both were successors to the P.T. boats of World War II, whose motto was "They Were Expendable." What causes us as humans to wish for such? Childhood games or family? A dad who had served with Patton or a grandfather with Pershing? Brainwashing by an institution with 110 years of experience or testosterone? Stray electrons in the brain or God? Perhaps just a dented Civil War belt buckle.

At that very time, there was a caring, thoughtful young woman in Maryland. Wise, soft, and pretty. Her wishes were quite different. But that had been in June of 1966. Fifteen months before. A very, very long time ago.

PINEAPPLE FLEET

The U.S.S. J. Jarvits, the 66th guided missile destroyer commissioned into the U.S. Navy, finally returned to her home port. Pearl Harbor. The wives and families waved and cried as they saw their loved ones along the rail.

Months earlier the junior officers had all traded leave in Asian ports with the married men. As a result the married guys rushed ashore as soon as the ship tied up. We bachelors remained aboard on duty for the next few days. Married men happy to have the first moments free with their loved ones. Single men pleased with the extra night or two they had spent in Hong Kong and Japan.

The ship was tired. She had literally worn out her guns from shooting. Days and nights off North Vietnam had left little time to repair boilers or radars or anything important. We had been dinged up a little by North Vietnamese shrapnel. Nothing meaningful, but the ship now needed as much tender love and kindness as the men.

I watched the hugs and kisses on the pier and then went to the forward gun turret, closed the hatch, and sat inside in dark silence and thought of Diane back in Maryland.

The following day a fellow bachelor officer, Tom Farmer, asked if I wanted to share an apartment with him. A week later we rented a lovely apartment in Honolulu near the beach. I bought a motorcycle and commuted to Pearl. Every third day, I had duty and had to spend the nights aboard ship. Days went fast. There was a lot of work to do. No matter what happened, Tom would say in a mock Hawaiian voice, "Ain't no big thing brudda."

I invited my dad and sister to come out to Hawaii and see me for Christmas. I met a nice tall blonde girl who was going to the University of Hawaii and who also lived in our apartment complex.

I enjoyed driving the motorcycle on small back roads in Oahu, but most of my free time was spent in solitude. Work on the ship was proceeding very fast.

After only about six dates with the blonde, my orders came from The Bureau of Naval Personnel. I got my Swift boat! Not my first choice, which had been the Nastys that ran the rivers and coasts of the North, but at least I had a river/coastal boat, even if it was the smaller slower craft in the South. I had requested in-country duty in mid-October. It was not yet Christmas. I had no idea the turnaround would be so fast. Apparently not many people were volunteering for small boats. At the time, that seemed odd to me.

I told my new girlfriend to find a college boy. She was 21 and I was 24, but I felt 10 years older. Maybe 20. I sold my new motorcycle, and I went to the base library and checked out a laundry bag full of books on guerilla warfare.

Then I called my dad and told him what I had done. His voice was soft. He cleared his throat once or twice. Then he said, "Well, if that's what you want . . . ." I told him to cancel his plane ticket to Hawaii and to tell my 16-year-old sister that the vacation she had been planning was not to be. Perhaps I could see them later, after Swift training.

Finally I went to the bedroom, stripped off my clothes and opened the top drawer. I pushed aside the white T-shirts and found one that was faded. Frayed olive drab. I tossed two new Hawaiian swimming suits in the garbage. One still had a price tag. They were both brightly colored and had blue and red flowers on them. At the bottom of the drawer was a six-year-old navy blue swimsuit. Solid, almost black in color. I put it on and started to put on my Adidas too. Then I thought better of it; my feet needed to be toughened up, they were soft.

I walked barefoot out the apartment door and across the street to the hot sunny beach at Waikiki. I went for a very, very long run.

RACCOONS

Vietnam was a war that asked everything of a few and
nothing of most in America.

Myra MacPherson

A few days after the ship limped into Pearl, I went to the hospital in Hawaii to visit a friend from the U.S. Naval Academy.

It was a nice clean facility, but shockingly *big*. The ward was long, with beds on each side. Just like in the movies. A few smiles came my way. Most of the men didn't care one way or the other if a visitor came in. Some just stared at the ceiling.

Many had black eyes. Like they had been in a fight. Both eyes. Gray. Blue. Black. Purple. Vacant. As if they did not comprehend. The concussion of an incoming round landing nearby breaks blood vessels with ease. Especially the delicate ones around the eye sockets.

People who have not been shot at cannot understand. People who have been shot at cannot comprehend either.

Joe started waving to me when I was still five beds away. It wasn't easy to talk to him. The explosion of a Vietnamese shell had blown one small piece of white hot metal into him. Right into the center of his nose. The shrapnel proceeded through his nose and straight into his sinus. His nose was four times bigger than it had been, but still, it was a lucky wound. I asked how he felt and his response was the curt Midwestern phrase, "Can't complain; they operate tomorrow."

We had ten minutes of fast "catch up" banter on what had happened during his absence. Then the conversation abruptly stopped. Nothing left to say. Just quiet discomfort. We said a hurried self-conscious goodbye. I almost ran out of the hospital.

It is very difficult to be around the wounded.

It is very difficult to be around yourself sometimes.

LITTLE HOUSE ON THE PRAIRIE

So why did I volunteer? Let me try to explain, even if it seems to ramble. My grandmother lived in the sandhills of Nebraska. Crookston. Named for General George Crook who was one of the few cavalry generals who understood the real issues of the Indian war. As a small child, I spent the summers at the home of my grandmother; my dad's mother. Her house had lots of mice. Grandma was as Irish as Fagan's Goat. When my cousin Linda and I would promise, "We will not do that again, Gram, we will be good!" Her curt response was: "I've heard sparrows fart before." How can you not love an old imp like that? One of my earliest memories is awakening at dawn to go with her to check the almost 20 mousetraps in the house. With luck we would catch six or eight per night. She had an old black stove with a roaring fire. My job was to hold each of the dead mice by the tail and throw them into the hot fire one by one. It was like an old German fairy tale. Gruesome and bizarre. Mouse hunting was the highlight of each morning. Experiencing the true feelings of Hansel, or playing the part of a child of the Pied Piper's Hamelin. Experiencing life's myths at age three. Living it. Learning to hunt. A mousetrap is surprisingly violent: when the spring slams down, it often hits the mouse head with such force that the eyeballs emerge from the socket. Tongues swell. A body shot to a small mouse can eject viscera through the anus. Believe me, a child notices such things.

My mom's family lived ten miles away on a ranch near Valentine, Nebraska. Cherry County was named after Lt. Samuel A. Cherry. A cavalry officer who was shot in May of 1881 by one of his own men. I knew I would have liked him. Good looking and brave. He went out to retrieve a hard-drinking thief and deserter named Thomas Locke; his mission failed. Lt. Cherry's ghost was everywhere. My grandfather's ranch was only two miles from the old calvary fort adjacent to a place called "Deer Hollow." In the 1880's, the cowboys and the soldiers who came to town eventually became too rowdy for the local sheriff. So the Valentine sheriff ordered that the houses of prostitution be closed. The whores simply reopened shop nearer to the fort. They called it "Deer Hollow." I liked that innocent sounding name. I liked living on the site of a whorehouse for the Indian-fighting cavalry. In fact, by the time Deer Hollow was established most of the Indian skirmishes were long over.

My grandfather was truly the last of the real American cowboys. He had to quit school in the third grade to earn money to support his polio-stricken brother. He had skin like the leather of an old saddle. Even the whites of his eyes were weather-beaten. His name was Lawnie Beed and he could think like an animal. He would say things like, "Sit on this rock. A deer will come by soon." Without fail, everything he told me was true. As a kid, I assumed that all old men knew how to do such things. Only when I grew older did I realize that it was magic. He was my Merlin. I loved him so much that I attached myself to him like a happy tick. People in town called me "Beed's shadow." He never went to church; perhaps that is why he was so perfectly holy. Once he and I and my friend Bobby Mac had been fishing for half an hour without a bite, I asked, "When will they bite?"

He said, "Just wait a few more minutes." Within a half an hour we had 50 crappies. It was magic. I was his Wart, Merlin's young King Arthur.

On the ranch we had two absolutely worthless buck Indians. (Today we use the words "male native Americans," but in the early 50's they were simply "Indians.") Levi and Adam Highhawk would often go on drinking binges that could last for several weeks. My grandfather would quietly inform me that the Highhawk kids had nothing to eat. That was good news for me; it meant that he would take me out to shoot a deer. It didn't matter that I was much too young to have a deer license, or that the season hadn't opened. Ranchers like my grandfather fed the deer in winter along with their cattle, so they naturally felt entitled to shoot a few. Gramps would always pick out an old doe, a "dry" doe that was beyond bearing a fawn. I would shoot and clean her. That evening, he and I would take the carcasses to the two Indian women. Six or eight kids shouting with glee, as I helped deliver the meat. I was not a killer. I was a hunter, a provider, one who fed the children. I was 12. How many grown men living in cities in America have ever truly "put meat on the table"? Most never will.

As a child I just assumed everyone lived out the life of hunter, fisher, cowboy. I was experiencing that mysterious passage into manhood. Girl's bodies tell them when they have become a woman. For a boy, there must be a right of passage, a first paycheck, a first kill. The very lucky ones will have a wise old man to guide them.

I remember only once when Gramps did not do as he said. It was early morning and we were having a huge breakfast of bacon and eggs and homemade bread and chokecherry jelly. There was a knock on the door and my grandfather answered it. It was Levi Highhawk. He was swaying from foot to foot, so drunk he could hardly stand. He slobbered out, "Lawnie, I can't work today."

Gramps stared at him in fury. "Damn it, we've got hay to put up! Goddamn you Indian, you stand right here on the porch while I go get my gun so I can shoot you!"

"Finally," I thought to myself. "He's finally going to shoot Levi." I stared in amazement as Levi simply stood still. I expected the man to run. He just stood in drunken haze awaiting his fate. But Lawnie Beed didn't shoot the Indian after all. At the time, I thought Gramps would shoot Levi. He always kept his word.

In addition to supporting two marginal Indians and their families, we also had the help of the town drunk. "Shots" Morgan was a good worker when he was away from the bars in town. Two Indians, an alcoholic, and a 12-year-old. We put up a lot of hay that summer.

City people might think that not much happens in the prairie. That's really not true. When I was young, a rattlesnake bit me on the shin. When I was 12, the coyotes ate my dog. When I was 13, two families of Lakota froze to death near our ranch; Gramps made me stay in the pickup, so I didn't get to see the bodies. Later that summer, a young Lakota shot a patrolman and hid in a complex of canyons. The sheriff organized a posse to go in to get him. I wanted to go with the cowboys and carry my rifle on my little horse. I didn't get to go. The Indian, whose name was Grandsinger, wisely climbed onto the highway and surrendered to a passing motorist.

I saved a man when I was only nine. Gramps and I had been fishing on Big Alkali Lake. Nearby were two men from Omaha standing in their boat, shouting and drinking. One fell overboard. His friend was too drunk to help him. Reluctantly my grandfather rowed our boat to the drowning man. Gramps held him by both arms from the stern of the boat, unwilling to pull him aboard. It was my job to row. It took a long time, but eventually I got the boat ashore. The drunk stood up on the beach, coughed up water, destroyed his own camp stove and cursed. He didn't bother to thank us. Mrs. Highhawk was always careful to show her appreciation. I didn't want to be associated with city people; they were not civil. They were poor fishermen as well.

I was the only kid in my grade. Our one-room schoolhouse had only six students. Twins in one grade and no one in another. The other four of us had no peers. The bookshelves were well stocked with one copy of each subject. K-8. Our teacher was Flo Conners, the wife of the manager of the U.S. Wildlife Game Refuge on the Niobrara River. She was a wonderful kindly person, skilled in the things far more important than teaching. We simply went to the bookshelf and took whatever looked appealing. I read history, science, and math. I could, and did, go for months without reading spelling or grammar texts. Predictably, my education was irregular, but it was *my* very own education. Books formed the banquet; I took what my appetite wished. If I wanted to read *The Charge of the Light Brigade*, I did exactly that. If such reading made me curious about that failure and the role of the commanding officer, Lord Cardigan, I moved on to study him. Then I would study the entire Crimean War. No one objected. Flo was a resource to help us find our own answers. It was a very good way to learn about the things that I believed that I needed to know. I needed to know about war, heroes, and how to make gunpowder. I needed to know about weapons and honor and the surge of history. I had to try to keep up with my friend Bobby Mac.

Superimposed over all of this was life as a ranch-hand on the prairie, and life in a cowboy community with its own unique sense of values. Let me give you just one example: one morning my grandfather Lawnie Beed and I were having breakfast at the Home Café. The cowboys were talking about a curious event from the night before. A middle-aged Lakota woman ran out of a bar chasing a Lakota cowboy while shooting at him. Her weapon was a .22 revolver. This .22 revolver had a magazine of nine rounds, not six. She fired all nine shots while running at a fleeing man. She never missed! That's right; she put all nine rounds into the poor fellow. She shot him in the heel, in the elbow, in the ear, every damned place. Now the cowboys at the Home Café didn't mention whether or not the unfortunate recipient of nine bullets lived or died. To them, that wasn't particularly important. What mattered was that the Lakota woman was one hell of a shot. No one in the café was foolish enough to believe he could match her skill. That woman could *shoot.*

As a kid, I could tell from looking at a blood trail where the animal had been shot: frothy pink blood is from the lungs, red spots are a muscle shot, dark lumps indicate a gut shot.

*   *   *

Looking back on my childhood it is now apparent that my going into the armed forces was inevitable. To volunteer for Sea Dragon and to later go on to something more dangerous was a foregone conclusion.

Sea Dragon

The ship's 5-inch/54 fires on North Vietnam

A destroyer under fire off Haiphong
(note splash of incoming round landing astern)

BACK TO
THE LAND
OF THE
ROUND EYES

TOO GOOD FOR HER

After Sea Dragon, I briefly returned to Nebraska. My mother lived in Valentine. Immediately upon greeting Mom, she began to talk about Cheri, a 20-year-old cowgirl, and how wonderful she was. Within an hour of my arrival, Cheri had come to the apartment. My mom's matchmaking instinct was so strong that Cheri and I were literally pushed out the door.

Given that I had no option, I invited Cheri to go to the Home Café where we had coffee and shared a piece of chocolate cake. I discovered that she was somewhat in love with a local guy named Ted who inspected cattle brands. That's right. A brand inspector. A law officer who insured that cattle were not stolen. She wore a red high school letter jacket with a big "V." She talked about having four kids and living on the prairie with a quarter horse and going to rodeos.

An hour later, I returned to my mom's tiny bare apartment alone. She began to grill me. "How did you like Cheri?"

"Fine," I said, staring at the white kitchen table.

"She's a wonderful girl," Mom stressed.

"Uh, huh."

"You came back early."

"Mm," I mumbled as I stretched a foot.

"Are you going out with her tonight?"

"No," I glanced away at the white gas stove.

"Why?"

"I dunno."

"Why!" she shouted, surprisingly loudly for such a small woman.

"I just want to sleep," I said truthfully.

"You think you are too good for her!" my mother shouted.

I stared in disbelief. She thought that I was being a snob because I had a college degree in engineering and Cheri had only worked in a Rexall drugstore in a tiny cow town. How could I explain that I didn't fit anymore? This girl had chosen a boyfriend who would insure that she *never* left the prairie. His occupation tied him to this land.

On the other hand, I had worked hard to lose all connection with my past. I had lost touch with America. I had done things in the war zone that I regretted. I no longer fit. Not with my own mother, not with a cowgirl named Cheri, and not with Valentine. All I wanted was to get back to Vietnam. I wasn't better than Cheri, but I was sure as hell different. Bright cherubic face in a varsity jacket. Jesus, I'd feel more at home drinking cheap scotch with a whore in a bar in Olongapo.

My mother was going ballistic. I didn't want a girlfriend. Hell, I didn't want any friends. I didn't want to be in the land of the round eyes. Like a China sailor, I didn't fit in. Certainly not here. I had been with my mother less than two hours and I couldn't wait to leave.

The Tonkin Gulf was familiar; the East was both right and true.

America, cow towns, and my mother were insane. Truly. Insane.

SEARCH AND DESTROY

*Find and destroy the enemy; to destroy or seize his
equipment, foodstuffs, medical supplies and base areas;
and wherever possible, destroy his political and military
infrastructure.*

COMUSMACV

That was what the Pentagon expected us to do. The TET offensive began 31 January 1968, at a time when 50 percent of the South Vietnamese army was on furlough. The V.C. captured 36 provincial capitals and occupied the grounds of our embassy in Saigon.

Ho Chi Minh had put into practice what our General Westmoreland was only talking about. Ho Chi means "He who enlightens." The old man was certainly enlightening America's generals.

In the days of wooden sailing ships and corporal punishment, men were punished with a whip that had nine braids. The "cat-o-nine-tails." By tradition, it was stored in a black bag. As the prisoner was tied hand and foot with his back exposed, the flogger would "take the cat out of the bag."

I had just arrived at Coronado, California, for Swift training when Uncle Ho let the cat out of the bag.

SMALL BOAT TRAINING

Our preparation for Swift boats was reasonably straightforward. Ten weeks in Coronado, California. Five crews at a time. The time was split between classroom and practice. After a morning of lectures on subjects like diesel mechanics, we would then practice for the afternoon on an actual GM diesel that propelled the Swifts. Obviously the engineman on each crew was the most knowledgeable, but the intent was to cross-train us so that the other five people could fill in if the engineman were to become a casualty.

Over time, we rotated through every inch of the boat. Radios, guns, radar, hull, and much more. The drills began early in the morning and ran without stopping into late evening. The instructors would order us to take a training boat out to sea off Coronado and then begin to give us a series of tests. For example, we would have an exercise involving an eight-inch hole in the hull caused by a Russian-made B-40 rocket. Next an exercise that required repairing the steering mechanism. Then we'd have an exercise that involved both: a big rocket hit which would cause the boat to begin sinking and simultaneously cause damage that made steering impossible. If we passed, we would do the test again with only half of the crew; the other three people would sit on the cabin roof, simulating being dead or wounded.

The seas off San Diego were stunningly beautiful. The weather was perfect, warm and mild. It was hard not to enjoy each day. As we moved to night exercises, it was still fun. Finding elusive targets in the dark, boarding them, and searching for weapons. The instructors dressed and acted like Vietnamese. We would try to interrogate them using our newly-acquired Vietnamese language skills.

The U.S. Navy taught us elementary Vietnamese in a truly unique way. In an intensive two-week course, we were placed in a room with a young and pretty Vietnamese girl. We were in groups of only eight sailors per instructor. It was a very pleasant experience. We enjoyed it and the young Viet instructors seemed to enjoy it too. They wore the traditional dress, discussed culture, and taught us rote phrases of questionable use; such as, "Which way did the enemy go?" Some said the girls were daughters of Viet aristocrats and that was how they got such a plum job. That was fine with us; the girls were bright and charming.

The Vietnamese language is quite unique. Like Lakota, which was translated by Catholic priests, Vietnamese was translated more than a century earlier by French nuns who used our alphabet and added notation on how to pronounce/sing the vowels. Thus a westerner can learn the Viet language reasonably quickly compared to mastering the ideograms of the Chinese. With symbols inserted above each vowel, you could pronounce a word like "ca" any of almost a dozen ways; the same word could mean anything from "mother-in-law" to "rice." Cå, cá, cà—each had a different meaning. We could find the word in our dictionary and come surprisingly close.

The best part of training was the gunshoots. We enjoyed cruising to a nearby island and shelling it. Although the Navy tried to make all our training realistic, in fact it was hard to truly believe that what we were doing in sunny California would be the same as our life in-country.

Our instructors had each spent a year in Swifts in Vietnam. All were veterans. They didn't socialize with us. They seemed somewhat remote in a soft, philosophical way. They looked at us with sad, vacant eyes. As if they simply couldn't express to us what we would soon encounter. The things that *really* mattered. Perhaps the Navy told them not to give us the details that would make us reevaluate our willingness to do a voluntary tour. Perhaps the real knowledge of how to survive a tour was simply not translatable.

Like little kids, we thrived on stories of war. One that made the rounds was a young officer who was being interviewed for a combat job. To test his ability to think quickly, he was asked, "What would be the implication if Ho Chi Minh were to suddenly die now?" The candidate's response was immediate, "One less Commie to kill sir!" Allegedly, he got the job.

Weekends were free. One skipper and I spent almost every Sunday skydiving. We had a good chance of getting hurt during the next year anyway, so we decided that we might as well jump out of airplanes over the desert at Elsinore, California. It was exhilarating.

The amphibious base at Coronado had a small lounge for us. Just a few chairs, a coffeepot and a Coke machine. It was a nice comfortable place to relax and talk. The only time it became uncomfortable was when the wounded Navy SEAL was there. The SEAL had been shot in the head six months before. His speech was difficult and slurred. His left side was partially paralyzed and he walked with a difficult shuffle. Six months earlier he had been in truly perfect physical shape. Now he was crippled badly. The real difficulty was that he wanted to talk. He wanted to spend time with others between his long daily sessions in physical and speech therapy. As new Swifties psyched up for our next assignment, being around the wounded SEAL was uncomfortable. We tried to be friendly, but long conversations were draining. We were honing our skills for war, moving away from being caring humans. He was alone, reminding us of our human frailty.

The SEAL's head wound reminded me of a cartoon I had on my wall when I was a boy. The right half of the cartoon was covered with dozens of tiny dots. In the center of the left half was one tiny dot. Alone. The caption of the cartoon was, "Germs avoiding a fellow germ who caught penicillin."

RACEHORSES

Dad joked that I was a racehorse. I had been bred in Kentucky. In 1943, Mom lived in Elizabethtown while Dad was in tank training at Fort Knox. I was born in April of 1944, seven weeks before he landed in Normandy. The boat that carried his tank onto the French beach was a slow little landing craft made by the Higgins Boat Company of New Orleans. Higgins also manufactured P.T. boats. General Eisenhower thought so highly of the landing craft on D-Day that he said of Mr. Higgins, "He's the man who won the war for us."

On D-Day, Mr. Higgins called all of his boat builders together. Most were women. He said, "As you know, today the boats we built are carrying our troops to France. Please join me in a prayer." Then he said, "Let us pray that we made every piece of every boat *perfect.*"

In 1958, when the Higgins Boat Company went out of business, some of its naval engineers and boat builders went to work for another New Orleans manufacturer: Stuart Seacraft. Stuart built our Swift boats.

Twenty-five years after my dad's boat ride, I was now skipper of a Swift boat. A legacy. Kentucky. Higgins.

950 horses.

S.E.R.E.

Survival

The "S" in S.E.R.E. is for "survival." The Navy didn't tell us how long we would be on survival. They just loaded us into busses and took us to the area 30 miles away. California wilderness—not exactly Vietnam. It was bounded by a river; we were not to cross it or go beyond the power lines, which were three miles into the distance. Six crews, 30 men. All of us in an area about 15 square miles. They dumped us off the bus with nothing. Just the fatigue uniforms on our backs.

"Survive," they said. Nothing more. Then they drove away. We had no idea when we would return. It could be one day or many days in which we would have to live off the land. Eating a few plants and berries and drinking from a stream. We were told to stay separated. For the first day it was fun. Getting away from the Navy. Outdoors. Just looking for a snake or a mouse to eat. By the second day, I was becoming sunburned. Slowly I realized that after years of the Navy using this piece of land as a survival range, it had been stripped of all edible plants. There simply were no small animals to eat. Just an occasional little gray lizard, and they were remarkably hard to catch. By nighttime I was exhausted. It was easy to sleep; insects were not as bad as I had expected.

Slowly I became weaker. Lack of food creates a splitting headache. I was sorry that I had not cheated and slipped a few aspirins in my pocket. All of life is a tradeoff, but in survival it becomes quite clear. Is it worth looking for food, or do you save strength and just hunker down? It was taking more calories to search for food than I was getting from the few handfuls of roots and leaves that I found. I ate a few ants, but stopped short of caterpillars. Some are poisonous. I wished I knew more about flora; I vowed to read a book on edible plants in Southeast Asia.

Two years before, in flight training, I had been on a three-day survival course in Pensacola, Florida. I teamed up with Harvey Esty, my flight school roommate. We gave up looking for food on the second day. Finally we took off our clothes and sat in a big mud hole to get cool. We began singing TV fast-food commercials. Our favorite was: "Whatta Burger, treats your palate right, Whatta Burger, it's a true gourmet's delight."

We laughed and planned our trip to the Whatta Burger Drive-In upon our return. Clearly it was improper. If I had to survive, I wouldn't sit in a mud hole and sing about food. But to survive the survival course . . . well, then it was okay.

But this training was different. I would be in Vietnam in three weeks. I couldn't afford to make a joke of it. Yet it was all so futile. I was growing weaker and there just wasn't much to eat. Most frightening was the fact that as we grew weak, we also became progressively more stupid. Without food, a person simply cannot think clearly. Soon I'd be in Indian country, I would need to think.

Evasion

An aerial bomb exploded. That was the sign that the bad guys were entering the area. The instructors were dressed as V.C. or North Vietnamese Army. They knew every inch of the training range. We had gone a few days without food. Now our job was to evade capture.

The next day I was discovered. The little cave that I had dug with a stick was pathetically small. My feet stuck out slightly. That was all it took; the instructor found me so easily that it was embarrassing. I had heard noises the day before, so I knew that I was not among the first to be found. Still, I thought that I should have done a better job of evading capture.

Resistance

We were taken to a P.O.W. camp. It was designed to look like the real ones. The guards were dressed like North Vietnamese soldiers. The camp had been designed by men who knew. A few had actually escaped from the real camps in Vietnam, but most of the staff and techniques were modeled after P.O.W. camps in Korea. Earlier we had been told that some of the instructors had formerly been prisoners in Korea. They knew both sides, prisoner and guard.

We had signed confidentiality agreements before the course began, promising that we would not give details of the curriculum. As an ongoing program, it would ruin it if future classes knew what to expect. Nonetheless, I can tell you a little about it because on occasion a trainee would get seriously injured. More than once, the Navy had to justify the program to the U.S. Senate Armed Services Committee. Earlier classes had had a death or two and many injuries over time. So some of the curriculum became public knowledge.

Each of us had a secret. Mine was "Mary had a little lamb." My interrogators' job was to get it out of me. You can guess how they went about it. Hanging me by my arms until they became numb. Then stuffing me into a tiny black box in the fetal position. Then out in the sun, face down and left alone for hours. Then . . . on and on.

Slowly I began to realize that with enough time, almost anyone will break. Everyone is afraid of something. Afraid of heights? They had that. Afraid of drowning? They strapped you on your back with a washcloth over your face. The more water they poured on the cloth, the harder it was to breathe. Afraid of being alone in a box in the dark? On and on, the interrogators kept trying new tricks. The old movie phrase, "We have ways of making you talk," is true. Beyond belief.

I did not tell them "Mary had a little lamb." With enough time, they would have gotten it out of me. No question. Obviously they stopped short of true torture, but they told us what *might* happen. One torture "scheduled" for me for later was to have my eyelids cut off. I knew that, if real, that would be one thing I could not resist. Imagine having your eyeballs dry out. No lids to blink. You would pray for blood to moisten them, but blood would eventually coagulate.

The camp was Spartan. No food. Bugs in the stinking rags they called beds. Awakened at all hours. They tried to make it real.

One amazing part of the program was that at night in the P.O.W. camp, they had us sit on our haunches and listen to a political lecture. Communist indoctrination. They told us propaganda. How badly the U.S.A. behaved. How well the Soviet system worked. Actually, the lectures were surprisingly interesting; they made some legitimate arguments. My favorite part was "News from home." Baseball scores, business, politics. Mostly true. Some falsehoods mixed in. They told us that George Burns had died; we believed that. The comedian was about 70. They also said Robert Kennedy had been shot and killed. Preposterous. Not two brothers in a row. They told us that at Tet the whole country had risen up as one against America. The U.S. effort in Southeast Asia was doomed. Probably true. It was amazing that if you get "news" containing both facts and lies, the lies often seem more likely to be true than the actual news events.

After getting mixed news for a few days, a person has a hard time later sorting out reality. We soon learned that the news on Robert Kennedy was in fact all too true. As for George Burns, he lived another 25 years or so. The Tet offensive wasn't a victory in the military sense of the word, but it broke America's support for the war. That news was true and false at the same time. America couldn't stand the loss of 2,000 men in one and a half weeks. Although the Communists lost 50,000, our press and TV made it vividly clear that, in spite of the Pentagon's claim that we were winning, the enemy had control.

I can't tell you how long each session of S.E.R.E. lasted. The mystery is a vital part of the program. Not knowing how long you would survive or evade or be in the P.O.W. camp resisting.

Escape

The last "E" in S.E.R.E. is escape. Our job was to escape from the camp. One day I was taken to the Viet prison commander's hooch for punishment. I was told to stand in the sand in front of the little shack. My guard went to the door and entered. A few moments later, he emerged. I had been asleep. Standing up. I had stood there stupidly. Sleeping on my feet. For a full 20 seconds.

Shit! The moment he grabbed me to bring me inside, I realized that I had failed. Twenty seconds! Unsupervised. I should have bolted. That was my only chance to run. I missed it. I was sleeping. Standing up.

At about 4 a.m. one morning we heard sirens and rifle shots. Our P.O.W. camp was "liberated" by friendlies. We plodded outside to face bright lights. We sat in a circle and a nurse looked at each of us. We were given a tin canteen cup containing two large spoonfuls of hot oatmeal. Each of us cursed and asked for more. The cook simply said, "You can have seconds later if you want."

Our stomachs were so shrunken that after a few teaspoons of oatmeal we were stuffed. Not a single person could eat seconds.

We climbed onto the bus and each of us was given a container of orange juice. Within minutes we were all fast asleep. The bus proceeded back to our Coronado base in the warm California dawn.

I have never had a meal as good as that oatmeal. I have always regretted that I didn't seize the moment to escape. I truly learned more in my few days of S.E.R.E. than I learned in any other brief period of my life.

In general, our group was a good one. No one gave up his secret. (Anyone who told the secret was disqualified from going to Vietnam with an elite group.) Two of the 30 made good on their escapes. Only two.

The class before us had suffered three broken bones at the hands of the interrogators. None of us had any damage beyond sunburn, bug bites, and slight malnutrition. We had all passed the course. We were ready to go to our new assignments in-country.

I was confident in myself. Proud that I had finished the course. Yet I was humble in my knowledge that a good interrogator could break me in a matter of days. No question. A razor to my eyelids would work. I probably had a hundred other weak spots as well. All psychological Achilles heels that, if touched, would make me confess that Mary had a little lamb.

*   *   *

The Roman stoics were not afraid of pain or death. Marcus Aurelius said, "Nothing can happen to any man that nature has not fitted him to endure." Yet they *were* afraid. They were fearful of losing control, of being overcome by emotions, and of not doing their duty. Every person is afraid of something; the question is, can we prepare ourselves for likely events that will impact our lives? Can we somehow control our reaction to the unknown?

*   *   *

To me, the most touching part of Homer's *Iliad*, is when the Trojan Hector attempts to say good-bye to his infant son. Hector is going out to fight; it is certain that he will be killed by the Greeks. Probably by Achilles, the greatest of the Greek warriors. As he bends over the child's bed, his son looks in terror and screams. Slowly Hector realizes that it is his battle helmet with its magnificent plume that frightened the boy. Hector removes his helmet and the child smiles as it recognizes its loving father.

It is one of the most touching scenes in all of literature. Hector loves his wife and son so very deeply. Yet he is a warrior. He has no choice but to meet Achilles and die. The familiar loving face of a father and the helmeted fierce soldier are one and the same. Hector's child does not understand. His wife knows that it is beyond them all. The Orientals would call it karma, the Greeks fate.

*   *   *

Beyond comprehension. Far beyond human understanding. So what do you do if captured when you are told that you will have your eyelids cut off? I'll tell you what I'd do. I'd sit in a mud puddle naked and sing. I'd sing, "Whatta Burger, treats your palate right!"

THE BOAT

Ships are safe in the harbor.
Ships were not built to stay in the harbor.

By the end of our training we knew every inch of a Swift boat. We were cross-trained so thoroughly that each of us could fill in for any other man should he be wounded. We would make repairs over and over until we could do it accurately and fast. Then we would practice again in the dark. I began to feel confident in my ability to handle almost anything. To anticipate. To outfox the adversary.

Then one night, the California Highway Patrol taught me a lesson. Another Swift skipper had purchased a beater car from someone on the base who was shipping out. A few such low value cars exist on every military base, changing hands every few months. Registration and license are done annually, but in between, the paperwork often just lies in the glove compartment skipping the formal registration of one or two interim owners. Badger had purchased such a car. A gray Hudson Hornet. It looked like a dirty jellybean.

Badger had a girlfriend in San Bernardino. By coincidence, Victoria, a girl that I had known back in Nebraska, now lived there too. On certain weekends, we would leave the San Diego base after boat exercises on Friday. We did not need to be back until 0700 Monday morning. San Bernardino was only 110 miles away.

One night, we were returning to San Diego. It was 0400. Out of nowhere a California Highway Patrol car crossed in front of us. The officer pulled a gun and aimed it straight at Badger. Before the Hornet was fully stopped, two more highway cruisers were beside us. One on each side. The guy on the right had a .44 Magnum pointed straight at my head. They announced that we were to get out slowly, showing our hands. Then they forced us to lie on our stomachs on the road, arms out. They took our wallets. My head was only three feet from Badger's and I whispered, "What in the hell did you do?" A patrolman told me to be quiet and gave me a soft kick on the knee. They frisked us and they searched the car. All the while they had guns trained on us. We could hear their radios, busy trying to identify us.

Then it was over. After about 15 minutes, one patrolman told us that we could get up. He apologized and called me "Lieutenant." The other shook Badger's hand. They explained that two extremely dangerous men were on the loose and that Badger's strange car fit the description perfectly. They didn't suspect that we were bad guys, they were *certain*. They apologized again and drove away. We got back in the Hornet and slumped in our seats. It took a few minutes before we could laugh.

But it wasn't over. That incident haunted me. I was truly helpless during the entire 15-minute shakedown. Badger and I were surprised. Ambushed. Unable to think quickly. Like S.E.R.E. this incident took away any hubris. I had been ambushed by a patrolman. A year earlier, a moose had snuck up beside me.

In small boat training, we were psyching ourselves up. Telling ourselves that we were trained for any eventuality. Trained to think quickly and stay mentally one step ahead. If those men had been V.C. and not California Highway Patrol, I would be a prisoner. No question.

It was all so damned humbling. It was as if I had psyched myself up to win the Indy 500 and then backed my passenger car over my mailbox.

We weren't late for Monday morning formation. We made it just in time. I don't know about Badger, but I concentrated more than usual. The day's lecture was on pilothouse instruments and controls. Radars, radios, and the depth gauges. The instructor said to always leave the depth gauge on the "shallow" setting, never "deep." We wouldn't need it except in shallow and shallow was where we were going to find ourselves most of the time.

That night I went to the officers club and ordered a big steak. Just as the waitress set the sizzling steak before me, an earthquake struck. The building began to rock, and the diners slowly and quietly walked outdoors. Huge power lines swayed above the building. Then another tremor followed. After about five minutes, the other people began trailing back into the dining room. I followed; this was the first earthquake I had experienced.

At my table lay the steak, cold and white. It was covered with dust. The ceiling of the restaurant was made of suspended acoustic tiles. The shaking had made the papery sawdust fall like snow. So I washed the cold steak off with half a glass of wine and ate it.

I know the reader will say that my earthquake story isn't very exciting. Sometimes things that should be exciting just aren't profound. As for the Hudson Hornet story, it too may sound routine. But it was different. It bothered the hell out of me. I had failed again.

VICTORIA

If any question why we died, tell them, because
our fathers lied.

Rudyard Kipling

San Bernardino, California. I spent several weekends with Victoria. Not that far from San Diego where I was in the ten-week training program to become a Swift boat skipper.

Victoria was tall and thin and had long raven hair. She looked like Liz Taylor in the movie "Cleopatra." Perhaps because of that she wore long plain white dresses. Several months prior, Victoria had left a convent only weeks before taking her vows. I was just moving from the Western to the Eastern Hemisphere. She had decided to leave the heavenly and spiritual to go back to the earthly. Her decision to move was bigger than mine.

31 March 1968 we were drinking Scotch and making love and sleeping. And then it was time to turn on the T.V. President Johnson looked us in the eye. He said that he had an important message for America. I held hands with Victoria as he spoke directly to me. The President told me that the war would take all of his energy. He didn't say he could or would end it. The message was that he would not run for another term. I thought he said that he would halt the bombing, and, he would *try* to end the war. It wasn't really clear what he was promising. Something about "peace through negotiations."

No lights were on in the hotel room. When I turned the T.V. off, we found ourselves alone in the dark. Within a few days I would be back in Vietnam for my second tour. Victoria would go on with her life. Maybe she would write to me. Probably not.

It was surreal. For an instant I thought, "We could just drive up Highway 101 to Vancouver and start a life." That thought, whether it was a brilliant thought, a logical thought, a cowardly thought, or just fantasy, took only a second.

In Vietnam I had longed to get back to "the real world." Now I was in the real world and my predicament was insane. In hours, I'd be in a wet jungle, not this hotel room which smelled of sex and lovemaking.

Victoria squeezed my hand. She winked.

The Boat

Swift boat in South China Sea

CAT LO

War is an ugly thing but not the ugliest of things.
The ugliest is that man who thinks nothing is worth fighting
and dying for and lets men better than himself protect him.

John Stuart Mill

Between 1964 and 1973, 16 million draft-aged men
dodged America's military service.

INBOUND FLIGHT

The World Airways flight to Saigon was scheduled to leave Travis Air Force Base at 1500. A comfortable time to depart San Francisco for the all night flight. We arrived three hours before departure; each of the crews formed a small cluster in the cavernous waiting room. Quiet. No wives or girlfriends. An occasional poker game. A few people just reading alone. Some actually sleeping on the linoleum, recuperating from a hard last night of parties. The five Swift crews that had finished training in Coronado would all be flying to Vietnam on the same aircraft.

At 1430 a sergeant shouted, "Flight 1473 Zulu Delta to Saigon, line six!" Obediently we formed a line and walked across the tarmac to the 707. As we were about to ascend the stairs, a petty officer ahead of me turned to a boyish-looking enlisted guy and asked, "Got your ticket?" The young man instinctively slapped his hands against empty pockets. For a moment he had a frightened look in his eyes. Then the petty officer let out a loud roar of laughter at the panic-stricken 19-year-old getting shipped to Vietnam, worried that he had lost his ticket.

The flight was smooth. To pass the time, I read a horror story: *Rosemary's Baby*. We arrived over Vietnam early the next morning. Everyone was eager to see the country from above. As we crossed the coast, it looked green and peaceful.

Twenty minutes later, we were on approach over Saigon. Suddenly the left side of the aircraft came alive with men speaking. Nervous. High-pitched. Pointing down. An occasional curse word. Faces pressed against the windows.

I got out of my seat and pushed my way to the left side too. A pair of helicopters were circling a neighborhood of Saigon. Every now and then, one aircraft would dip and fire a rocket at a target.

Involuntarily, I too shouted a curse. American helos were rocketing a portion of the capital. This was Saigon. Supposedly the safest place in Vietnam. Our choppers were shooting down at our own city. Each time a rocket was launched the passengers of our aircraft emitted a shout. About two seconds later a louder sound erupted from the men as the rockets hit a building below.

Actually the scene was not unfamiliar. We had all seen such air attacks many, many times on the T.V. news. We had to tell ourselves that this was different. The small windows of our passenger jet were not T.V. screens. This was real, not the Walter Cronkite CBS news.

Real war. Not a movie. Not T.V. Each of us had a birds-eye seat.

We didn't even need a ticket.

TON SAN NHUT AIRPORT

When our jet arrived in Saigon, our crew deplaned on the tarmac and walked toward the terminal. Midway, we passed "Graves Registration." Body bags were lying like cordwood waiting for the final trip on the Freedom Bird. The aircraft that brought us would take the dead back. It was a greeting from hell. The ditty, "If I die in the combat zone, box me up and ship me home" changed from fiction to non-fiction.

I was upset and angry. *How* could the Army be so goddamned stupid? My virgin crew was frightened and demoralized after only five minutes in-country. Of all the places to pile bodies, why was the Army so unprofessional as to put them in the sun and under the feet of these completely unseasoned kids?

It was going to be a very long year.

CARIBOU

Of the five crews that landed in Saigon, two crews were to proceed to Cat Lo, the Swift base at the mouth of the Mekong. Badger and I began walking to the smaller tactical airport, which was one half mile from the big airport. Someone told us that we must go there to get a hop to Cat Lo.

Badger and I each led our crews of five men past the body bags and down the rows of quonsets and aircraft. Finally the 12 of us arrived at a non-descript quonset with a few small cargo aircraft beside it. I went up to the empty desk. Inside, it looked like an airport counter in a small town in Nebraska. Six or eight chairs and a small blackboard with four flights written in chalk. All destinations of places unknown to me. New Viet words. I shouted once or twice. Finally an overweight Air Force sergeant came out of a room behind the desk.

"Yes," he said.

I looked him in the eye. "Yes, Sir," I corrected.

"Yes, Sir," he responded in a surly voice.

"Our two crews, there are 12 of us, have urgent orders to Cat Lo." The fat sergeant took the orders and disappeared.

Five minutes later he returned and said, "Check in again sometime tomorrow."

I was furious. "Look," I said. "Our orders are urgent. I don't know if you have passengers with higher priority than that, but my job is to get our crews to a river base that is short-handed. Check again!"

The Air Force enlisted man waddled back through the closed door; I heard a voice from behind say, "I'm not flying today. Not there. It's too hot. Forget it."

Back again came the sergeant. "Tomorrow . . . Sir."

"Ok," I responded. "If the Air Force is afraid to fly us in, I understand. We will be back at 0800 tomorrow."

The sergeant looked relieved that he had won. I surprised him with what I had to say next, "So here is what we will do. We will leave our crews here in your waiting room today and tonight. In the meantime, we two Naval officers will find the highest-ranking Air Force officer in Saigon and we will report to him that his operation is afraid to fly us out. That someone, and I do not know who . . . yet . . . is a coward."

Badger looked at me with surprise, but he followed me as I turned to the door. "Men, stay here; we will be back shortly," I ordered our crews.

Before I got to the door, the Air Force sergeant shouted that he would try again. An hour later we were on a caribou passenger plane and on our way.

*   *   *

It was late when we arrived. No one met us. We just stood in the dark for an hour. Hot, wet, scared. Finally a big gray bus drove up to take us the last ten miles to Cat Lo. It looked like a cheap school bus except that the windows were covered with wire. Like the buses they use to transport prisoners. The wire was to prevent V.C. from throwing a grenade through the window into the bus.

It was dark when the bus drove through the biggest cemetery that I had ever seen. Miles of crypts. Above ground. A great place for an ambush. If the bus were to take a rocket, we would all be trapped inside. I wished the windows did not have wire over them.

The bus had a few bullet holes. The driver explained that the cemetery was controlled by V.C. The A.R.V.I.N., or army of South Vietnam, was afraid to sweep it. They were also superstitious of graveyards. The generals in Saigon refused to give permission to bulldoze down the crypts, so the bus just drove through it all. As fast as an abused and poorly maintained school bus could go. The bus driver called the huge cemetery "Death Valley." I made a note to myself to never go anyplace without a weapon.

It was almost midnight when we arrived in Cat Lo. We were welcomed by a black metal sign with a smirking cat. "COSDIV 13." Someone gave each of us a sandwich. I found the officer's hooch and entered. It had a row of ten cots on each side. Most had gear on them. A few bunks held a sleeping person covered with a mosquito net tent. Only two were vacant. I took the vacant one on the left. I sat in darkness and ate my sandwich.

I rolled some clothes into a pillow and laid down. Exhausted. Within a few seconds, I was covered with mosquitoes. It didn't bother me if they bit me, but the noise of them around and in my ears was bothersome. I put a sock over each hand and a shirt over my head. Within minutes I was sleeping like a baby.

ROCKY

The Quonset hut came alive as the sun rose. Noise of weapons being cleaned, boots knocking off mud, even the crowing of roosters. A couple of guys walked past my bunk and said, "Welcome aboard."

As the new kid, I decided I should roll out of the pad and explore my new home. The shower was cold river water. As I was putting on khaki trousers and an olive drab shirt, one of the Swift officers told me there would be a formation in 15 minutes. It seemed odd, a formal formation on a muddy riverbank.

The officers and men were standing around. I introduced myself to a few. Then a disheveled Navy lieutenant appeared. A stocky, dull-looking guy. He nodded at me, then frowned and called our group to attention.

"Some of you obey orders. Some of you seem to have a hard time even listening to orders. Some of you are smart and others aren't so smart. On occasion, you not so smart ones go where you shouldn't and you get shot at. Sometimes you get hit too. I told you I don't like to do the paperwork when you get shot. Stay out of the Bassac river! Fox, come up and get this!"

A good-looking guy came front and center. The C.O. pushed a Purple Heart at him and turned around to grab another. "Barry!"

Another young officer came forward and received the same treatment. Then the stocky C.O. shouted, "Dismissed!"

I stood aghast. I had just witnessed the awarding of the Purple Heart to two naval officers who had been wounded in action. The C.O. had made the presentation ceremony look like a reprimand. It was clear that he disliked both young men. It was clear he disliked all of us.

"What was that all about?" I asked later.

A tall thoughtful officer introduced himself. "I'm Pat Lang, Ops Boss. Welcome to the Black Cat Division. Costal Division Thirteen. You just met our C.O., Rocky. He was a former football player, so he may seem abrupt."

Later I would learn the facts: Pat Lang was the person who ran Costal Division Thirteen. He was diplomatic, smart, caring, and had been a Swift skipper for his first six months in-country. He also knew what life on the boats was like. The C.O. gave me the impression of a washed-up athlete who was of very limited intellect. Fortunately for all of us, he was not on base much of the time. Instead he spent much of his time in town, in a room above the Red Horse. The Red Horse was a bar and "massage parlor." Lang, the number two person, ran the Black Cat Division. It appeared to me that whenever Rocky made the four-mile trip from Vung Tau back to Cat Lo he caused trouble.

The two men who received medals were both excellent skippers. Barry was funny and smart and an electrical engineer.

Fox had a wry sense of humor. Heir to a small manufacturing company. Rocky hated him. Only a few weeks before my arrival, Rocky had threatened Fox by saying, "I will ruin your career with my next fitness report on you!"

Fox responded, "The only way you can hurt me with a fitness report is if you roll it into a little tiny ball and stick it in my eye."

So in the first hour of my first day in-country, I learned that my pig-eyed C.O. was odd. I wondered if he was both incompetent and dangerous. Lang, the second in command, had taken control. Apparently, he ran the place properly. Hopefully Lang minimized danger to us all. The critical factor seemed to be whether or not we could keep Rocky busy with nightlife in town. Believe it or not, my life depended on it.

As Rocky's jeep disappeared, I realized this was very, very far from what I had expected.

Dangerously insane or humorously insane, in the end what mattered was how much control I had over my own boat's operations. For the first few weeks, I would just keep my head down.

CAT LO

After the awards ceremony, I returned to my bunk. A solidly built officer named Anderson stopped me. "That's the sniper bunk," he said, pointing to where I had slept the night before. "Look out the window. See the ten-foot cement wall around the base? See the tall tree just outside the base? Well, on occasion, a V.C. sniper climbs the tree, sits on the limb and shoots over the wall through the quonset window into this bed. A Swifty got shot last year sleeping in that damned bunk. Nobody *ever* uses it."

"Thanks," I responded meekly. I stripped the bunk and moved my gear to the other vacant bunk on the opposite side of the quonset. I wondered why someone didn't just go outside the base perimeter and chop down the damned tree. Or, they could put a locker in front of the window to block the view. Both solutions seemed logical, but I was just a new kid. Surely someone had previously thought of cutting down the tree.

So a guy had been shot while in bed. No one bothered to say if he died. The incident was over a year ago, perhaps no one here remembered him personally. As a midshipman, I had been on an old submarine off Key West a few years before, and I heard a World War II story of a guy who was sleeping in the top bunk. The boat hit a mine and the explosion caused him to fly up to the ceiling and hit his head. He fell back onto the bunk unconscious and with a cut on his forehead. The submariner had won the Purple Heart without waking up!

The water supply had been poisoned by the V.C. several months before. No one in Cat Lo trusted it. Not even to wash off their toothbrush. There was an old open can of warm beer in the head for that. People showered with their mouths held tightly shut.

On the brighter side, there was lots of beer available. Nothing stronger; never drugs. For serious work, we simply couldn't afford to have a drug-head around. It would have endangered all of us. Fifteen great officers. Impressive individuals as far as I could tell. Men who knew what they were doing. Good strong guys whose judgment could be trusted.

I looked at a footlocker riddled with bullet holes. I asked how that had happened. How could the V.C. have blasted the inside of our quonset? Marlow cheerfully told me that Anderson, the guy I had met earlier, had shot it. He had emptied an entire magazine of a Thompson sub-machine gun on his own locker! The gun accidentally went to full automatic. Anderson couldn't stop the firing, so he trained the muzzle on the place where it would do the least harm. The gun proceeded to shoot automatically. Without anyone touching the trigger, it riddled all of Anderson's gear. Clothes, books, boots, everything.

In the 1920's, the Thompson was a gun used by Chicago gangsters like John Dillinger. It was a temperamental and worthless weapon. It fired .45 slugs in a notoriously inaccurate fashion. Why anyone would use it in Vietnam was beyond me.

So I was a new kid. A virgin. In-country only a night and a day. My new friends had names like "Jack Daniels" and "Inexperienced Romeo." They shot up their own lockers. They didn't bother to take the time to chop down a tree from which snipers shot at them. The C.O., Rocky, lived above a whorehouse in town. The Grand Hotel served good lobster. The guys tolerated a V.C. barmaid in the camp because she was young and pretty. It was foolish for me to ask about the "rules of engagement" which were the official conditions in which U.S. forces could use deadly force. No one cared.

I walked over to the mess hall for a cup of coffee. Tomorrow my crew and I would get a check ride to determine if we where qualified for patrol. Over coffee, Anderson told me an odd piece of lore: each day, whichever boat had the southern most area, had the duty to give the weather report. A week before, Fox had been on station. At 0600 he transmitted his weather report on the radio: "This is Inky Bite 37 off the mouth of the Bo Di River. Temperature is 70 degrees, visibility unlimited, wind from the south at . . ." (A strong 'rat-tat-tat' could be heard on the receiver) . . . Fox went on, "We are taking automatic weapons fire now. Anyway, wind is from the south at ten knots. We are returning fire, and the sea state is two with small waves of three feet . . ." The crazy guy was getting shot at and he casually continued to give a routine weather report! Some of these men, perhaps all, just didn't give a damn.

They just didn't give a rat's ass, even if their life depended on it. Furthermore, it was perfectly clear that they didn't give a damn if *my* life depended on it.

The mission of the Swifts was changing. Earlier in the war, they were responsible for keeping the coasts clear. They performed that job so well that now practically no smuggling of arms or supplies came from the north by sea. Everything came inland through Laos and Cambodia on the Ho Chi Minh Trail. As a result, Swifts were being used more and more to patrol the rivers. Much of the coastal work was transferred to the cutters of the U.S. Coast Guard. Swifts worked with the small boats called PBR's (Patrol Boat River) and with larger armored boats called Monitors. The techniques of combat were totally different from what we had learned in Coronado.

Obviously, I had a lot to learn, but it wasn't clear exactly who was going to teach me.

HANK

The real training for life in-country doesn't begin until you are in the bush. Instructors back in California would preface remarks with, "Listen up! If you do not, or you forget what I say, it will kill you." We would pay attention all right, but once in-country, everything was a "Listen up!"

There were roughly three crews for every two boats. Two crews shared a boat until a senior crew shipped home. Then one of the duos got his own boat and the more junior of the pair was assigned a new kid. As a result, new kids were trained by crews that had been in-country only two or three months. I was lucky. I was assigned to Hank. Naval Academy. Class of '65. Hank was an excellent skipper. Each member of his crew took time to help the corresponding person on my crew. Engineman to engineman, bosun to bosun, and so on.

Some antiwar people say that the military mind is a case of arrested development. Perhaps there is something to that. Like Peter Pan, we were on the Island of Lost Boys. Normal rules of civil conduct didn't apply to us. And we had our own toy, a quarter of a million dollar boat that could kick ass. Perhaps it wasn't "Peter Pan" as much as "Lord of the Flies."

Hank told me not to allow our crew to use AK-47's. The Chicom rifle of Russian design worked far better than our own U.S. made M-16. But the AK-47 emitted a loud "clack" each time it fired, a sound far different from our U.S. weapons. That was normally no big deal, but if you were off the boat doing an exercise on land, and using an AK, you'd get greased by friendlies. In the prairie we shot only when the game could be identified clearly. Here people shot at sounds. Hell, they'd empty a clip on a slight movement of a bush. You didn't need visual confirmation that it was a target. Shoot first. Think later. It was actually faster than that. There wasn't even time for the nerve signal to go to the brain and back down the arm to the finger. It was as if you hand squeezed off the round with its own primordial cells doing the thinking.

Hank explained how to tell where a fishing boat was based just by looking at the shape of its eyes. Each junk had eyes painted on the bow so that is could find its way across the South China Sea. The shape changed from circular at one end of the coast to narrow slits at the other.

For a new kid it was difficult to tell which situations called for serious consideration and which did not. One moment we would be in the "What can they do to us, send us to Vietnam?" frame of mind. Later we would be focused and professional, then back to not giving a damn. The old timers knew when each was appropriate. The new kids got it all wrong.

Hank also taught me the subtle difference between "toi doi" and "xin loi." The former means, "What the fuck?"; the latter simply, "Sorry about that." We used both phrases often.

Early one morning Hank and some other skippers were laughing conspiratorially. I asked what had happened. They explained that Hank had given three entire boxes of Ex Lax to his Viet interpreter the afternoon before. He told the Viet it was chocolate candy. The Viet ate all three boxes. Ate 'em down with a wolfish grin.

They thought it was extremely funny. So cruel it was hysterical. The Viet had spent the entire night on the pot and was now so weak and dehydrated that he was unable to go on patrol.

As I watched Hank and his crew depart without their Viet interpreter, Anderson leaned over to me and said softly, "Did you know Hank suspects his Viet of being a V.C. agent?" I had had no idea; I had thought Hank would have told me of anything so serious. Anderson went on, "He and Barry are going up the Bo Di today, Hank didn't want the Viet, Tan, to be aboard."

It was beyond belief. Insanely funny and deadly serious all at the same time. That incident distinguished itself—even by Swift boat standards.

Four thousand square miles of Mekong Delta. Mangrove swamp. Toi doi; clearly I had a lot to learn.

TEX THE BOSUN

Tex was the youngest of my crew. A freckle-faced kid from Texas. The bosun is the person responsible for the boat in general. Hull, paint, everything that did not require specialized training. Tex was a good kid, but, at age 19, he was too young to be on the boat. Perhaps we all were.

He liked to listen to the radio. Armed Forces Radio. The news was usually watered down, so most of the information we received was simply baseball scores and the like. If you wanted to know casualties for the week or get details of the latest protest on the mall in D.C., you had to read *TIME*.

One morning we were listening to A.F.R.N. Just after they opened with "Good morning Vietnam," they gave the news. At the end, they always had an in-country story. One of the more memorable involved a couple of guys on long-range recon patrol. L.R.R.P., pronounced "LURPS." The radio reported that two men out in the bush built a small fire and poured beef stew C-rations into a pan and began to cook. Suddenly an adolescent tiger burst through the elephant grass. He walked straight to the pan, knocked it over, and ate the beef stew. The cat then gave a sideways look at the frightened LURPS and sprang back into the bush.

That was the kind of news A.F.R.N. carried. Tex liked the radio show more than the rest of us.

One day Tex was eating spaghetti and meatballs out of the can. I was looking at a chart nearby. With childish glee Tex held up a fork with a white, yellow lump at the end and declared, "Uhmm look, a potata!" As he popped it into his mouth I gave him a distracted look. Ever so slowly I tried to understand this latest dose of verbal information. It didn't compute. There are no potatoes in spaghetti . . . at least not normally . . . but still . . . he just said . . . my muddled thinking was interrupted when Tex spit out a golf ball-sized lump of pure cold yellowish-white grease.

We laughed as Tex cursed his container of cold spaghetti and threw it overboard.

I reflected on the process, how it took several seconds for me to realize there are no potatoes in spaghetti. When presented with the absurd, we often have to give absurdity the benefit of the doubt and assume it is ourselves in the wrong, not the facts. Absurd things occur, especially around here.

A year before something similar had happened on Sea Dragon. We were close off Hanoi with another destroyer. Shortly after midnight, the other ship abruptly turned toward the North Vietnam mainland. I was in charge on the bridge, my first thought was that perhaps I had missed a radio message; perhaps I was supposed to do the same. To go where our fellow destroyer was headed seemed incorrect, but perhaps there was a change. As I was trying to figure out why I was wrong, my Assistant Office of the Deck shouted, "He's going into the minefield!"

Oh, of course, but why didn't I see that first? We jumped to the radio and transmitted, "You are standing into danger!"

A young voice on the destroyer responded with a curt "Roger." Their ship came to an immediate stop in the minefield. We stood at the radar screen and stared. Our captain promptly appeared on deck in his T-shirt. Slowly the other ship turned and proceeded very, very slowly toward safety. I watched the radar screen, an involved spectator. If the other ship hit a mine and sank, would our ship go into the dark minefield too? To save their crew, would we risk all, or would we take a half measure like anchoring off the minefield and sending in a lifeboat to save 10 or 20 men at a time? Ever so slowly the other ship emerged from the minefield unscathed. A different voice came on the radio to thank us. Their captain had taken over from the junior officer, probably a fellow just like me. I suspected that captain would not go back to sleep that night.

What bothered me was why it took me so long to process the information. Why can we humans react in a fraction of a second in one situation and yet take several seconds or even minutes in another?

In five or ten seconds a lot can happen. A ship with 300 souls can hit a mine and sink. Or a kid can eat a spaghetti potato.

KELLEY, THE ENGINEMAN

Kelley maintained the General Motors diesels in perfect condition. He said they ran "like a striped assed ape". I pretended to know what the simile meant. At general quarters, Kelley manned the 81-mm motor on the fantail. Because he was so far away from the pilothouse at G.Q., he wore a set of phones. Navy men who wear communication phones on their ears must also wear an oversized helmet. That gray helmet looks odd because it is so wide, wide enough to write on the back. Kelley wrote in white paint:

"When I die, bury me face down so the world can kiss my ass."

He was as proud of that phrase as he was of his photo of his son. I thought it was curious that he wrote "when" and not "if." The remainder of the phrase sounded just fine with me.

Kelley grew up in West Virginia. His family was very, very poor. As a kid, he stole coal at night from the local mine. That supplemented the family income. Little kids stealing coal worth, say $10 per ton. A seven-year-old could steal 50 pounds of coal in a night. 25 cents. Jesus!

We had a guy who's old man was a millionaire in the squadron and we had guys from families as poor as those in a Dickens novel. All in the same boat, so to speak.

Kelley was always on an emotional high. He called people "Ace" or "Slick" or "Girls." He said one musician on Armed Forces radio sang "as beautiful as wind whistling up an aardvark's asshole." From his poetic vocabulary, I'm sure you have already guessed that Kelley was a career enlisted man. A "lifer." He told Tex, "If brains were gas, you wouldn't have enough to run a pissant's motorcycle." Tex just laughed and tried to think of a rejoiner. Kelley's favorite phrase was one he used daily, "We're Hacksaw Indians. We can hack anything."

At times Kelley could become a slight irritant, but he was a very, very good mechanic. Our boat's engines screamed like banshees. In World War II, P.T. boat sailors had a ditty:

"Some P.T. boats go forty knots
Some go thirty-nine
If we can get our boat to run at all
We think we're doing fine!"

With Kelley, we did just fine. Two General Motors 12 cylinder diesels producing 475 horsepower each. He was a giant of a man; as a child he had lost both front teeth. He seldom wore his dentures, so his grin was huge. Terrifying.

One day Kelley returned to the boat with a blood pressure machine. I have absolutely no idea where he found it, but the 97 now had a blood pressure machine as part of its standard equipment. As luck would have it, the following day we picked up two suspected V.C. Kelley told me that he thought he could get the V.C. to confess. We called for the interpreter to grill the little guys and both had stress in their voice. After five minutes of fruitless interrogation, Kelley got the B.P. machine. He put the cuff on the upper arm of one suspect and began pumping the rubber bulb while showing his demonic, toothless grin. The armband grew tighter. Then Kelley told our Viet interpreter, Nguyen, to tell the suspect that the machine would blow his arm off.

The V.C.'s eyes grew huge. Kelley weighed 250 pounds, so he was three times as big as his adversary. Kelley put his nose in front of the suspect and told Nguyen to tell the little guy to confess and tell where the V.C. were hiding. The V.C. stressed that he was innocent. Kelley tightened the blood pressure machine armband further. The suspect was wide-eyed, wet with sweat, and trembling. He looked like he would pee his pants. There was no question that he expected the toothless devil to use the tightening armband to blow off his limb.

In the end, Kelley did not get a confession. If we had had a stethoscope at the time, we could have gotten the V.C.'s actual blood pressure. It was a shame that we didn't; I'm sure little Victor Charlie set a record. From the look on Chuck's face, I'd guess 300 over 250, maybe higher.

THOMPSEN,
THE QUARTERMASTER

Thompsen was from Belzoni, Mississippi. He liked watermelon almost as much as he liked cars. He wanted an Oldsmobile 442. He also got a packet of seeds from his aunt. He had found a spot of sandy soil that was perfect for growing watermelons. I asked for details, but he explained that it had to remain secret or his melons would be stolen. He talked about how good the melons would be and how much he would enjoy his new car. He planned to return to college after this tour. The G.I. Bill would help a lot.

One guy read the *Congressional Record*. But Thompsen read *Playboy*. One day while he was looking at the centerfold, he took a toothpick out of his mouth and said, "That's a clean-looking snake." I didn't know what a "clean-looking snake" was, but that was okay. Some things Thompsen said were beyond me.

Anyway, I never got to taste Thompsen's watermelons. Maybe he ate them all, or maybe they didn't grow. I never knew. When I was a kid, I had a book about Johnny Appleseed. He planted apple seeds all over the U.S. Maybe someday Thompsen's watermelons will grow all over the Delta.

The quartermaster is responsible for navigation of the boat. Radars, depth gages, charts, and avoiding running aground on sandbars. Thompsen was my second in command. He made Second Class Petty Officer in record time. He was smart; he would do well in college when he went back.

One day, he and I took a tiny fishing boat out and visited several villages on the Mekong. Just two guys plus an interpreter in a dinky little boat. If the V.C. wanted to kill us we were just sitting ducks. Two vulnerable guys looking things over while paddling around with a grin. Nothing happened. It was a good day. Although I didn't get to taste the watermelon, I did save a photo of us in the sampan looking happy, embarked on another hare-brained adventure.

Armed Forces Radio was playing and some damned hippie girl had been singing about "man's inhumanity to man." I didn't pay any attention to the lyrics, but Thompsen did. He stressed that it was impossible for a person to be inhumane. Humans behave abominably. They may not be angelic, but even if they are obscene, they are still behaving like humans . . . humanly. Thompsen would do very well in college. Maybe he would enjoy philosophy. He'd scare the shit out of the 18-year-old freshmen when the class discussed ethics. Vietnam was a fucking graduate school of ethics.

KID, THE RADIOMAN

Kid was good at his job. The radios worked. All four of them. Unlike the boat hull or guns or engine, the radios were always a little mysterious. Temperamental. Subject to "atmospherics." But when we needed to communicate, Kid insured that we could do so.

He was a good sailor. Nice smile. A mop of reddish hair. But his eyes always looked slightly sad. Kid didn't talk much. That's funny; you would expect that a guy who specialized in radios would like to talk. Sometimes Kid drank too much, like a typical 19-year-old. He was quiet after a hard night. We all were. Bouncing around in a little boat is painful for your head. Stomach too.

Kid called all Viets "gooks." I ordered him not to use the word. We had Asian allies: Viets, Koreans, and many Americans of Oriental descent. Kid would cease using the word for a while and then revert. I tried to explain that we couldn't "win the hearts and minds" if we had a prejudicial vocabulary. My lectures made me sound like a windbag. I'm sure of it. Eventually I let him call them "gooks" because, on occasion, I slipped and did the same.

The Romans had a god. Baccus. He was the god of wine. The god said, "I bring you wine. It makes you slightly crazy so that you can withstand the gigantic insanity of life."

Sad-eyed Kid. A freckle-faced kid with a tattoo on his shoulder. SÁT CÔNG. "Kill V.C."

JAKE, THE GUNNER

Jake was our gunner's mate. He maintained our weapons in excellent shape. In combat, everyone fired weapons except the quartermaster, Thompsen. He drove the boat. Under fire, his job was to get us out of trouble without running into a sandbar or shore or putting our boat in the line of fire of another Swift. Getting out of a hot spot was more important than shooting back at the enemy.

In a firefight, the rest of the crew would be very busy. As the skipper, I stood in the pilothouse door with an M-16 rifle or an M-79 grenade launcher. The radioman fired an M-16 or a .30 caliber. The Viet shot an M-16. The engineman was on the fantail with the single .50 and the 81-mm mortar. Jake, the gunner was in the gun tub above the pilothouse manning the twin .50's. The bosun was shooting and also loading the mortar. Hopefully it stayed noisy. When a gun jams, the silence is terrifying. With Jake, the 97 boat didn't have guns that jammed. Ever. .45's, .38's, .50's, .30's. Each of our more than 20 weapons was perfectly clean. Each glistened with a light coat of oil.

I said it was noisy. A .50-caliber machine gun emits 170 decibels; anything over 140 causes humans permanent hearing loss. The .50 caliber was originally designed to shoot down aircraft. We had three .50's aboard. We used them on people.

As skipper of the boat, I usually stood in a hatchway half in and half out of the pilothouse. I could touch or shout at Thompsen at the helm. In the gun tub, Jake stood on a plate half above the pilothouse, so his feet were near my waist. While firing, the hot spent brass shell casings rained down onto the floor. Each making a tinkling sound as it bounced on the aluminum deck. It was odd; the loud and fast "Bang, Bang, Bang" of the big weapon and the soft "tinkle" sound of the empty discarded shells. It sounded like a child playing a delicate little triangle in the midst of insane chaos.

Jake was as quiet as Kid. Shy and thoughtful, he intended to make the Navy a career. He was married, but seldom spoke of his wife. Icy blue eyes and a nice smile. He was also a crack shot. Like all of the crew, Jake was professional. He had volunteered for Swifts. I was lucky to have him on Inky Bite 97.

One night we were playing with the math of converting U.S. weapons which use "caliber" (100 caliber is an inch) into the world standard "millimeter" (25.4 millimeter per inch). "What is a service .45 pistol in millimeters?" Questions like that.

Thompsen teased Jake with "There are three kinds of gunners . . . those that are good with math and those that are not."

Jake didn't laugh. He just smiled politely. We were all going deaf; perhaps he did not hear the joke.

THE VIET,
A CASUAL OBSERVER

Each boat had a Viet interpreter aboard. Most were good people. They had no choice; every young Viet man served—one side or the other. Riding a Swift was often safer than the alternative of the Vietnamese Army, and on Swifts the food was very good. So the little guys worked hard. Most of them smiled; all had excellent English skills. Only a few were lazy.

We were only partially confident that they translated the wild stories of the locals accurately back to us, but that was to be understood. They often avoided conflict.

That last phrase—they avoided conflict—sounds truly goofy. Actually the Viets were shooting the hell out of the Americans, the French, the Koreans, and themselves. Still, one-on-one they tried very hard to keep harmony. That wasn't easy. In their tight "tiger suits" of camouflage, they watched us vandalize cemeteries, frighten people, and behave badly. Mostly out of frustration. They shared stories and gave us friendship bracelets of brass.

It was rumored that the V.C. prisoners we handed over to the Vietnamese Army authorities were often beaten, and on occasion, killed. "Field interrogation," it was called. Brutal. Murderous. We Americans didn't want to know. We just turned V.C. over to the South Vietnamese; what happened next was out of our control. We told ourselves that it was their war after all. For our prisoners, we had to respect the Geneva Convention, but once we turned them over to the South Viets . . . well . . . yet the Viet on our boat never seemed to be upset or to take it personally. He would watch his countrymen being handed over and show no concern. None at all.

Most interpreters were named Nguyen or Tan. Most had a photo of a girlfriend. Most got seasick easily. Their payment was about $300 per *year*.

One night while we were on patrol, I smelled the horrible stench of an electrical fire. I pulled the throttles to neutral and sprang from the pilothouse into the main cabin. There the stench was stronger, and I rushed toward the engines. Suddenly, I stopped in disbelief. Earlier in the day we had traded eggs for lobsters with a local fisherman. Nguyen had taken one of those lobsters and decided to cook it. He placed the lobster directly on the glowing hotplate stove in the galley! The poor crustacean was trying to walk across the pink hotplate; its legs were black and smoke was coming from its little cinder-like feet. My Viet looked at me with pride. The lobster was making a noble attempt to walk, but his legs were disappearing from under him. Finally the poor creature stopped. I watched the show in horror. I was pleased that Inky Bite 97 was not on fire, but somewhat amazed at the torture I was witnessing. Finally, the lobster stopped moving. The Viet then pinched the tail and flipped the lobster over to burn its back. The bottom of the one pound "bug" was black, the sides green, and now the top of the shell was turning pink. After another minute or two, Nguyen removed the lobster and began shelling it. Burned bottom, pink top, and the rest raw. He ate the lobster with his fingers, a nod, and a smile.

I climbed back into the pilothouse and gunned the boat ahead. We needed a breeze to blow the sickening smoke out of the main cabin.

The next morning I showed the Viet how we Americans cook lobster. I superheated the big Navy coffee pot and boiled the five remaining creatures to a lovely pink. Then we Americans ate our breakfast feast. I was surprised to note that our lobsters had acquired a slight taste of coffee. Worse, for the next few days our coffee had a hint of lobster.

Two weeks later, Nguyen disappeared. Our next interpreter was named Van. He didn't trade his allotted egg for lobster. Apparently he liked eggs better.

THOMPSEN AND KID

Thompsen had a dream. An Oldsmobile Cutlass Supreme. With a toothpick hanging from his mouth, he would explain why he wanted that particular car. He would discuss not just the wonderful features of that machine, but he would also tell you why he picked each option. Limited slip differential, red with white interior, special radio—the list went on. Best of all, he would go on to discuss how he would drive it. Even where he would park it in the parking lot of the community college. He had been in school for a semester with no car. Now he would return. GI Bill paying tuition. A year of Navy pay for the car. He could *see* himself in that Oldsmobile coup talking to pretty young women. We could see it too.

Kid had a round face and expressionless eyes. Young and old at the same time. He was very, very quiet. Kid might say ten words all day. On occasion he had a bad hangover, so it was inappropriate to talk to him anyway. He was a good radioman, a good person, but at age 19, Kid did not seem to think beyond this tour of duty. Melancholy isn't the word for someone who doesn't want to think of the future. Maybe he didn't have one. Maybe none of us did.

*   *   *

But, I didn't think such big thoughts at the time. I didn't talk to Kid about his life. Instead, I told him not to put so much Tabasco sauce on his C-rations or he would get an ulcer.

NIGHTWATCH

We were lying off a river mouth. Midnight. Hoping to catch a gunrunner sampan. "So why did you volunteer for Swifts?" I asked my crew one by one.

Kelley thought for a while, and then responded softly, "Well, my wife sure as hell didn't understand."

Kid made eye contact and muttered, "I dunno."

Tex just grinned.

Only Thompsen could explain, "Well, I wanted a car. And I wanted to continue school without the pressure of tuition. Last time I had enough money to eat or pay tuition, but not enough for both. So I thought the G.I. Bill would help. Maybe I'll finish this time. Yea, I will. So, Skipper, why did you volunteer?"

"I guess I wanted to see the country. Curiosity. Just curious. My dad said the reason he volunteered for tanks with Patton was because 'He didn't want to miss anything.' Sounds pretty feeble now. But oddly true. I think I was in a hurry to get in-country to see the people and the villages. I did a tour on Operation Sea Dragon before. A destroyer doing gunshoots off North Vietnam. We just shot up stuff. Reported targets. Concentrations of soldiers, trucks, factories, villages, whatever they said was a target. I wanted to see face-to-face what I'd been shooting at."

I began thinking about the night that I destroyed the wrong village. But that was a year ago. Eleven hundred klicks north. My crew wouldn't have thought that it was such a big deal.

C. RATS

The master box of C-rations contains nine smaller boxes, each an individual meal. Two of the nine were breakfast. Scrambled eggs. Cold scrambled eggs eaten out of a can are okay, but usually not anyone's first choice. So the two breakfasts get eaten last. The other seven have a main course, a dessert, and a third can which usually has vegetables. Only the main course is listed on the outside of the box. My favorite was ham and lima beans. But that box always contains pound cake for dessert. The spaghetti and meatballs came with a can of peaches. The peaches are good. If you are fast, you can get the ham and beans from one box and steal the peaches from the other. That leaves the goddamned pound cake for someone else.

Don't get me wrong. Pound cake is good even after five or ten years in a can. The problem is, it's impossible to get it out of the can.

On the chain around our necks we all carried a "P-38" can opener with our dog tags. The tags were wrapped in tape so they wouldn't make noise when we moved, but the P-38 was always ready.

Anyway, you take this tiny little can opener and make about 15 cuts and the top comes off the canned pound cake. But the cake doesn't come out. So you do the same to the bottom. Then you push it through. But even then it is difficult to extrude. On one end the jagged edges hamper the extrusion. At the other, the edges all point inward toward your finger. Most of the time you get cut.

Kelley was a giant of a man. His fingers were like sausages. He liked pound cake even if he cut his fingers, even if his pound cake emerged with blood.

Kelley was missing both front teeth. Jesus, what a sight! A guy with no front teeth eating a Twinkie-sized piece of pound cake with blood on it. It's enough to make you not want to eat your peaches.

KILLER BOB

In a free-fire zone, the 76 boat flushed out a V.C. The little guy was only ten yards away from Bob. Instead of shooting, Charlie just jumped up and ran carrying his AK-47. Black pajamas, no hat, no shoes. The V.C. was up and running for his life. Truly.

Instinctively, Bob raised his M-16. He emptied it on full automatic on the little guy who was running straight away. He emptied his entire clip. All 19 rounds. Missed. Every one. From point blank range.

After that, he was nicknamed "Killer Bob."

Oh well, I imagine he did succeed in getting Chuck's heartbeat up to 200 beats per minute.

No harm done.

AS DIFFERENT
AS NIGHT AND DAY

Early Evening at the Pier

Boats bob by the pier. I'm with my brothers. Laughing, teasing. Full stomach and almost normal. Thoughts bouncing around the work being done: refueling my boat with diesel, bringing food aboard. A few papers under my nav charts, operator's traffic and the like. A dog-eared book, a new K-Bar knife. Kelley checking the engines and Jake rearming. Two boxes of .50 caliber, six crates of mortar rounds. A dog barks. A few white seabirds flying over the pier, indifferent to the war. A normal day at the office. Almost like the real world.

Midnight Ambush

Night and day difference. No sound except water splashing against the hull. A rhythmic, metallic "thunk" as periodic as a heartbeat. Comforting. A few bugs. Sticky, sweet, dirty, sweat-mud smell of the Mekong. Few stars. Listen! Smell! Look! Every animal sense alive. I look at my watch. 0212. It's dangerous to daydream. Touch the M-79 grenade launcher in my hand; it is as comforting as a child touching its mother. This little metallic bastard can save my life. I trust it. I need it. Listen. Smell. Look. Glance at the watch again. It must be 30 minutes later; shit, only seven. Nothing moving but eyeballs. Thompsen's eyes make contact for just an instant. In 12 hours we'll be back at the pier. We can handle anything at O Dark Thirty.

A night ambush drains your guts out. Dog-tired.

Daylight/Back at Base

It was over. Nothing profound, but what is noteworthy is that if you didn't get hurt or killed, you go do it again the next day and night. And if you were still healthy, you did it again and again.

A Joke

Years later I heard a joke about a tough boss who said: "We are going to have a sales contest. The winners get to keep their jobs."

SUNRISE

I thought to myself, "Dad will be going home to supper with my sister right now." She was applying for colleges and eager to get away from Nebraska too. Dad would be tired and worried. I thought of them as I ate a piece of pound cake. Sitting by the shining clean gun tub, leaning against the twin .50's, and looking at the sunrise. Bright red. I wondered if my dad was looking at the same sun right now, for him, in the west. Our radio was playing so loudly that I could hear "Good morning, Vietnam!" from the top of the pilothouse. Thompsen was looking at a chart that had gotten wet so often that it was hard to read. Kelley was joking around and looking for food. He was getting fat.

Jake climbed into the pilothouse. He stood looking out the window. Silent for five minutes, then he retreated back to his bunk. Later, up on the gun tub, someone said something to Kelley and he responded with a silly, "Don't hit me, Masa, don' hit me! I do it, I do it!"

I had some odd skin rash on my ear. Probably from sleeping on the rubber-covered bunk. I made a note to get some alcohol and to wash the damned pads down with disinfectant. They were covered in new and old sweat. Lang had given us our third totally quiet day in a row; it was good to have Rocky away from the base. It was good to look at the beautiful blue South China Sea. The morning temperature was a nice 70 degrees. I picked the pound cake out of my teeth with a little Swiss army knife.

The Supremes were singing a bouncy song, "Baby Love," as my fingernail picked at the rash on my ear.

All in all, life was good. I had never felt so *alive*.

SWIMMER

All Swift boats had removed the toilet from the head; it was too hard to clean. With three guys sleeping in the main cabin, it was too disruptive to have someone come down the stairs, turn on the lights, and relieve themselves a few feet from men trying to sleep. The aluminum metal amplified the noise.

As a result, Swifties simply pissed over the stern.

One night, in particularly heavy seas, a sailor on another boat fell overboard. At the time, the boat was about a mile off a section of jungle that was a designated free-fire zone. In other words, it was 2 a.m. and he was in the water off a coast controlled by the bad guys. His crew didn't discover his absence until sunrise. By that time the boat had covered a huge amount of coastline. The Swift radioed that it had lost a man overboard. Other boats joined the search. Late in the day, they found the sailor—still swimming.

He said he decided to float and swim until he was exhausted. He would not risk going ashore unarmed and being taken prisoner until he absolutely had no choice. He remained hopeful throughout the night and through most of the next day. It was lucky that we found him.

I can't remember the guy's real name; everyone just called him "Swimmer."

BEACH BOY

Kid was walking toward me. Barefoot in the sand. His red-brown hair was bleached by the sun. Big freckles. A grin. Perfect white teeth. He had recently purchased a new watch, a Seiko. He looked like any happy teenager in California. Like a movie scene. But his eyes betrayed him. His eyes looked so very, very tired with the sad squint of weariness. Crow's-feet flanked each baby blue eye. As he walked, his dog tags swung across his sun-burned chest. Dog tags wrapped in olive green tape to keep them silent.

Not California after all.

DINNER CONVERSATION

Back in Cat Lo, an hour before patrol, I slid my tray onto a table with four other Swifties. Elliott was talking about Mesopotamia. He said:

"Damascus was the home of the finest early sword-makers. They discovered that if swords were heated white-hot and then plunged through the bowels of a Nubian slave, the blade emerged both stronger and more flexible. Slaves were cheap, weapons were valuable.

What they didn't know at the time was that they had discovered tempering. Quenched in liquid, the metal's molecules rearrange themselves to produce steel that holds an edge and yet will not break.

Cooling the hot blade quickly could have been accomplished just as well by dousing it in water. But the sword makers of Damascus hadn't learned that yet. They knew only that the desired results were obtained by thrusting the hot blade through the guts of a slave."

From there the conversation bounced around in a random fashion. Fox was complaining about a misfire in his motorcycle. He was unsure if it was safe to drive it to town; it was not good to be stranded between Cat Lo and Vung Tau at 0200. No one knew anything about motorcycle mechanics, so the conversation shifted to sea snakes. Several of us had seen the migration—thousands of snakes swimming underwater in a formation that looked like a giant snake itself. Like a river under water. Yellow-brown, neurotoxic, and lethal. Impressive. Like the river Styx that borders hell.

One skipper had a fungus growing on his face. Big white spots. There was some discussion about how to treat it, but the damned things were hard to kill. He looked like he had albino birthmarks on his neck and cheeks. I wondered if he would be able to kill the fungus before he went home to round-eye girls.

Someone said something about "God missed the boat." Others laughed, but I didn't get the joke. Phrases were jumbled. "No adult supervision" and "pucker factor" were used to describe a run up a hot river. I retreated into my head and thought of a photo that Jim Mann had taken of a dead lizard. Jim had worked on some shoots for *National Geographic* before coming to Swifts. He had a 35mm Nikon. He was the only person with a good camera. The salt air of the sea was so corrosive that most cameras became inoperative within three months. For an amateur, it was better to buy a $6 camera and dispose of it.

Elliott asked a question, a Japanese Koan: "Who would you take with you to a most dangerous place?" Several people responded with their answer. Most elected to bring someone strong and brave. Elliott gave a mysterious smile and then said, "I would bring a *child.*" The answer was profound; caring for a child would *force* you to be your very best. The table was quiet for a minute as we thought of the implications.

I said that in reading Greek myths, I was surprised that some mortals declined to become a god. The reason was that because gods are immortal, they cannot die. Because they cannot fear death, they cannot be brave.

Then someone said he had read of a sailor on a wooden ship who had been shot in the head. With a bullet in his brain, as he lay dying, the sailor asked for an orange. Apparently it was a true story. The poor guy had asked for an orange. The incident happened in the War of 1812.

One person said that he saw a movie in which a wolf was shot. The wolf tried to lick the wound to make it better. The bullet in deep flesh. The dog just licking the bloody surface. It was a horrid image. I was saddened by the story of innocence. Wounded innocence of animals.

That image was enough to trigger a memory of another skipper. He said that at his dad's funeral, his aunt told him a story about his father, a father who had been in reconnaissance in World War II and hardly ever spoke about the war. One day when the skipper was a boy playing by the dinner table, one of the guests complemented his father on what a good person his son was. "I killed German boys as good or better" the father whispered. The guests at the dinner table were silent for a full minute. The WWII vet had blurted out a sad, true, shocking expression of guilt. By the end of the war, Hitler was sending boys of only 10 or 12 into combat against the American troops. For those who had to kill them, there could be only gut-wrenching sorrow. German boys as good as—or perhaps better than—America's own sons.

I looked at my plate. My macaroni and cheese was gone. Apparently I had eaten the damned orange goo because my stomach began to hurt. I looked around the table and then at my watch. Thirty minutes and my crew would go out on patrol.

As I stepped out of the quonset, I suddenly thought about how many stars had floated above our tiny ranch in Valentine. I tipped my head back; the sky was overcast. Only a few stars tonight.

Suddenly, I had a compelling urge to learn to play the banjo.

STARLIGHT

I went from the mess hall to the Operations office to pick up the new codebook, intelligence reports, and the highly classified starlight scope. The starlight scope was a heavy telescope that magnified the faint light of stars by a factor of a thousand or so. This device made it possible to see things at night almost as clearly as in the day.

On the boat, Kid and Jake were talking about certain Chinese weapons that were in use by the V.C., "Chicom" 107mm and 122mm rockets. Kelley had the engines purring like tigers, Thompsen was at the controls. I ordered "Lines in, underway," and went down to the galley for a cup of coffee. I thought of going to graduate school, perhaps business school. But how do you take the G.M.A.T. exam while in-country?

As Inky Bite 97 turned her bow to the South China Sea, I thought of Bob Hope. The week before he had a big show in Saigon with *Playboy* girls and a band. That would have been fun. Once, a Filipino girl did come to Cat Lo to sing American songs. I missed seeing her. The guys said she had a husky voice and knew all the words. The guitar guy who accompanied her was awkward, skinny, and played so loudly that it was hard to hear the girl. They said she wore a micro, red, see-through dress. That made it better. I could understand that Bob Hope would not have time to come to a stinking mud shore like Cat Lo, but I didn't feel it was right for the Navy to schedule the Filipino girl for just one show. Half of us were on patrol, so half missed seeing her body through that red dress.

By now the Swift was scooting down the coast at 30 knots. Sea spray, warm sun set. Kelley was up in the gun tub. Thompsen came over to my side with his impish grin.

"Skipper," he said, "now I know why we are here. It's called the domino effect. I read about it in *TIME*. See, the State Department believes that if just one country goes Communist, the neighbor will go Red too. Then the next, and then the next. Like, say, if Nevada were to have gambling and prostitutes and wild parties, then of course the Mormons in Utah would too."

I winked at him and saluted with my coffee cup. "You got it, but keep it quiet or they'll station us in Utah. No, wait, maybe they'll station us in Nevada to keep the showgirls from all converting to Mormons. That would be worse."

Thompsen grinned. It was fun to have him aboard.

*   *   *

The next day, about noon, we beached on a tiny island to have a picnic. The guys fanned out with their plates. Eggs and ham. We ate meals more or less at random on 24 hour patrols, some of the crew sleeping, others awake. Consequently, it doesn't matter if you have breakfast at noon or midnight. Anyway, as the guys fanned out, Tex shouted that he had found a cave. We stood around the perimeter of it, and then searched the island for a second entrance. Finding none, we returned to the two foot hole and threw a couple of concussion grenades down it. Kid grabbed the M-79 and shot once, then strapped on a .38 and a flashlight and went into the black hole.

I felt uncomfortable. Kid was the smallest of my crew, he seemed to want to go, but I didn't know the proper technique for cave reconnaissance. Kid made some noise as he searched in the dark; we shouted a word or two, but he didn't hear us. After a few minutes he emerged. "Just some papers and old cans, nothing else. Guys have been there, but all I could see were tracks. Maybe bad guys, maybe kids."

So we ate our eggs and looked at the sea and at the Viet coastline a mile away from our island. I must have worried about Kid's safety more than I was aware, because suddenly I felt very tired. I ordered the crew to rest for an hour, and then I fell asleep in the sand.

I dreamed that I was carrying two big pieces of furniture in a religious procession. They were like the headstand of a bed, but relics of sort. They were heavy and my back hurt. Then a military officer, perhaps an army general, said, "I need you to also go to Guatemala." I didn't know if he expected me to carry the heavy headstand to Guatemala or not. Then I looked around and saw that everyone else in the religious procession was just carrying a photo of a relic, not a real one.

I awoke thinking of the dream, of what was "fair." I wanted to feel sorry for myself, for sacrifice, for lack of sleep, for being scared. I hoped my crew couldn't see it in my voice or actions. I continued to lie in the sun, looking at the sky. Five minutes more of peace, then "saddle up."

We boarded and searched fishing boats until evening then returned to base. I was tired. The night before we had been on ambush, quietly lying offshore. Just off a river mouth, looking through the starlight scope. Hoping the eerie green light of the scope would identify a boat running contraband. Silent. Just watching.

I thought of an article that I read about orphans in poor countries. Lying in cribs alone, they didn't develop very well. Sensual deprivation. I wondered what the opposite of sensual deprivation was called. "Sensual overload"?

DINNER CONVERSATION (CONTINUED)

Back from patrol 24 hours later, I sat at the same table with the same men. The conversation continued as if it had not been interrupted.

Elliott, always the scholar, was trying to get the other officers to listen to his theory that all fighting units throughout history have been dysfunctional. "Listen," he said, "Achilles hated Agamemnon at Troy. Even the Round Table, which we consider the flower of knightly virtues was chaotic. Sir Kay was a coward, Sir Gawain plagued by guilt, and Lancelot killed Sir Gareth. Lancelot was wounded by Arthur's knights, so when blood was found on the bed sheets of Guinevere, it was assumed that the queen had slept with her wounded lover . . ."

Some Swift skippers paused with the thought of blood on her sheets, but not Fox. Fox was explaining his latest business venture. He had found a seamstress in Ohio who would sew Viet Cong flags for him. She sent them 20 in a package. They were only eight inches by ten. Fox was selling the "souvenirs" for $30 each to new arrivals at the army base. "They only cost $5 to make and there's no postage for shipping here! $500 bucks profit. Net. For a few hours work." Fox went on to say that he was negotiating to buy a better motorcycle with his first week's profit. "And the best thing is that the quality can be shit. The flags look more authentic if my seamstress uses faded blue material and cheap red. The yellow star can be any goddamned shade . . ."

Trying to recapture attention, Elliott lectured with an arched eyebrow, "Not only did the "Once and Future King"—Arthur—have his problems, but the forces have always been against the warrior . . . look at Hercules. Jealous gods put two serpents in his cradle to kill him, but the infant was so strong that he strangled both snakes, one in each hand!"

Like the others, I found the Hercules story somewhat interesting, but I wanted to hear more of Fox and his commercial venture. But by then someone was telling a story with the grand introduction, "Now I won't shit in your Easter basket, this really happened, sport . . ."

> "A guy had a *lucky .50 caliber round!* He carried that big bullet in his left shirt pocket night and day. He said it was to protect him. The other guys teased him at first, and then let it drop. Well, anyway, the guy had been in-country about 11 months. He was getting short, and on this recon patrol, all of a sudden they got ambushed and out of the jungle a goddamned V.C. Bible came at him. The fucking Bible was going at the speed of sound and it hit him. Splat! Right in the heart. But that lucky .50 caliber bullet that was in his pocket absorbed the shock of the supersonic Bible. The .50 had a big dent in the brass casing, but it saved the bastard from getting wasted."

No one spoke. No one could top that story. It received the reverent silence it deserved. I was learning so much here in Cat Lo that I wondered if there was any reason to go to graduate school after the war.

PROFESSOR RUSSELL

Professor Russell was a legend. He taught an honors course at the Naval Academy, Philosophy of War. He was a sweet little old man, well beyond retirement age. His classroom consisted of a gigantic map, which covered most of the floor. Chairs were arranged around the perimeter. He would get down on his hands and knees and move the markers across terrain. The great battles of Alexander the Great and of Caesar came alive. He would dive into the smallest details; one day he spent an entire hour on one page of Caesar's *Commentaries*. He even stressed which kinds of oats were fed to war horses. He showed us how each sentence yielded clues to warfare, to success, and to life itself.

Russell was a teacher who surprised us: each lesson was taught differently. After digging into tiny facets of one campaign he would then go to sweeping generalities of the next. For example, the class on the Battle of Trafalger began not with a map, but with a slide showing a beautiful woman. We midshipmen stared at her with admiration. Then Russell explained, "This is Lady Hamilton. Nelson had a long affair with Emma under the nose of her husband, under the nose of the admiralty, and in full view of London society. Her husband was a very influential man in government. Had he wished, he could have destroyed Admiral Nelson's career. This, gentlemen, is *audacity*. If you understand audacity, you understand Nelson. If you understand audacity, you will be victorious. There is no need to discuss the Battle of Trafalger. You all know it by heart. Strategy and tactics will not bring you victory unless you couple them with an ability to do the unexpected. Class dismissed!"

We sat in shock. The lecture for the day had been just one word. We looked at the beautiful Lady Hamilton projected on the wall and stood up to go. Suddenly Caesar, Alexander, Patton, MacArthur, Nimitz, and all other great captains crystallized.

As I sat in the quonset of Cat Lo thinking of Rocky and of the war, I realized that literally every principle of warfare that had been taught to me at Annapolis had been forgotten by our senior officers. We Swifties didn't think of the clowns in the Pentagon or Saigon as our "superiors." They were anything but that. It was as if collectively our Army and Navy had forgotten all of the lessons of history. Of Alexander *growing* his Army as he made new allies, of the Duke of Wellington's guerilla warfare in Spain against Napoleon. Our Chief of Naval Warfare, Admiral Morer, and our Secretary of Defense, McNamara, were clueless.

A week after the Trafalger lecture, Professor Russell had asked, "Did you wonder why, when General Washington was starving nearby at Valley Forge, the British did not attack from their warm and comfortable base in New York?" Not a single midshipman could offer an explanation.

"The whores! The whores of New York!" He grinned. "The British generals could not muster their troops because they couldn't find them! The lobster-backs were scattered all over the town, living with their American whores! We should not have statues of generals in New York today; we should have a magnificent statue of a lady of the night in the middle of Central Park!" he screamed with a wicked smirk and a twinkling eye. I laughed with all the rest. Three years later I thought of the lessons that I had learned and how little they were put to use here in Cat Lo.

I hadn't seen Rocky, our C.O., in three days.

THE RED BULL DIVISION

One day we unscrewed the explosive head of an 81mm mortar shell from its propellant shaft. We used waterproof tape to seal a concussion grenade over the opening. In this manner, we constructed a gigantic explosive grenade that was much too large to be thrown, but would obediently explode in the allotted eight seconds after the pin was pulled.

We dropped it overboard. There was a huge explosion. A few seconds later some colorful fish floated to the surface. We scooped them up and fried them. They were small, but it was good to eat a fresh fish dinner.

I had constructed hybrid ordnance 14 years before. I was 11. In sixth grade, Bobby Mac had taught me more than I should have known, and later I passed the secrets on to my friend, Bill Bickley. Our Nebraska National Guard, the Red Bull Division, had declared one Saturday as "Muster Day." The public was invited to see the National Guard display its weapons. Bill and I enjoyed watching the display of smoke grenades. Yellow. Red. Blue. All were fired on a field behind the armory for the crowd's enjoyment. To our great interest, five of the shots were duds. I marked each in my mind. When the exhibition was over, the sergeant called everyone back inside the armory to observe another demonstration. As soon as the crowd had gone inside, Bill and I looked at each other and grinned. In an instant we were both in the vacant field of fire and within less than a minute we had collected all five dud smoke grenades. We put the unexploded ordnance under our shirts and strolled through the crowd and back to our bicycles. In delight, we peddled home with five live rounds under our shirts.

The next day was Sunday. We opened each grenade with a wrench and carefully tapped the powder into a pile in the middle of a round aluminum pan sled. Then we placed the olive green grenades in the middle of the powder and lit it.

The ball of fire was enormous. Far more than we had expected. Blue, yellow, green, black smoke billowed from the red-hot flames. A huge cloud of smoke drifted down the street engulfing houses. The entire south side of my own wooden house was covered in soot. The apricot-colored boards had been blistered and burned over a six-foot area. We were delighted. We were terrified that we would be caught. Finally, we were amazed at the damage we had done to my parents' house.

Four years later, when I was 15, a friend of mine asked if I wanted to go with the Red Bull Division to Fort Ripley, Minnesota, as an orderly. The job was truly a dream. I would spend the summer with the National Guard in the Minnesota woods. Far away from the mind-numbing ranch work in hayfields. Instead, I would spend the morning shining shoes and tidying up for the Army officers. Just running small errands. Butterbar lieutenants would pay me $5.00 per week, First Luies $10.00, the Captain $15.00 and so on. I would be making about $60.00 per week, living like a soldier, and I'd be finished with work by noon, leaving the entire afternoon and night free. I jumped at the chance to get away from being a summer ranch hand.

The job was even better than I anticipated. After finishing my work at noon, I was free to join the troopers on their field exercises. Soon I was packing ammo and carrying the unbelievably heavy machine gun known as a B.A.R. Ambushes. Squad tactics. Company movements. I was the most enthusiastic soldier in the field. I fit. I was a quick learner.

There was a surge of pride beyond anything I had ever known. I was learning how to be a real soldier. Not boyhood games. This was the real deal. The drill.

I had been elevated far beyond my peers. They were mowing someone's goddamned grass for their summer job. I was learning how to destroy a village with mortar fire. They were eating candy bars at the swimming pool. I was learning how to silently cut a man's throat from behind. Was it any wonder I felt that every other teen-aged boy was contemptuously inferior to me?

And this was only the National Guard. The real Army, with jumpschool and jungle warfare would be even better. I couldn't wait.

Eight years later, I was in the Navy, not the Army. The real thing, not practice. It all came together. As if every boyhood experience contributed to my skill. As if this career as a combat officer was inevitable.

I wanted excitement—even before I started school. I remember once when I was about four or five my mom and dad bought a little swing. They put it in the front yard of our house. I sat in the swing for about five minutes. It was boring beyond belief. As soon as they went inside, I climbed on top of the swing and tried to run from one end of the support bar to the other. I slipped off the top of the swing, fell to the ground, and shattered my left elbow. The pain was so intense that I curled into a little ball. During the car ride to the hospital, I vomited on the carpet floor by the back door.

An Army bone surgeon named Doctor Riddell set my arm. He did a magnificent job. My arm grew to look almost normal. It doesn't go straight; it is shaped quite differently than the right arm, but happily the Army doctors at Levinworth 13 years later didn't notice. I passed my service physical. It was 1961.

When I was in kindergarten my parents gave the swing away. I had never used it as a swing. My folks gave the swing to a poor Mexican family in Scottsbluff, Nebraska; a family that worked in the sugarbeet fields. Doctor Riddell put a massive cast on me. My left arm was across my chest with my left hand touching my right shoulder.

Doctor Riddell, Bobby Mac, the Red Bull Division, smoke grenades, they all led to a singular path. Perverted, odd, improper experiences all contributed to my becoming an officer. They all gave me skills needed in combat or to get fresh fish for dinner.

STARLIGHT (CONTINUED)

Back on the boat, 24 hours later. Another river patrol. The Mekong had been a Communist stronghold for decades. Some of the strongest cadres of Communism were in the southern-most provinces of the country. We didn't know that at the time. It was the type of information the Navy didn't bother to share.

As we pulled away from the dock, Thompsen told me that he had heard that one Swift officer had put himself in for a Purple Heart claiming that he was wounded while destroying a V.C. village. The enlisted men had heard that the officer placed a concussion grenade in a crock of rice and walked away. The grenade exploded sooner than the skipper expected and it blew a small piece of the crock into his butt. Thompsen heard the story at the enlisted men's club over a beer or two. The officer in question was an odd duck. I couldn't confirm what had happened, but it wasn't a surprise. Officers seemed to get more medals than the enlisted men. Some were undeserved. If life is unfair, war is even more so.

I looked down at the chart. One village was named Song Trang (4). Four goddamned vils with the same name. My thoughts began to drift back to the incident on the Jarvits when we shelled the wrong village, but before I could dwell for the thousandth time on that tragedy, Thompsen was telling me about a book that he had read by Kurt Vonnegut. *Slaughterhouse Five*. It was about Vonnegut's experience in the allied firebombing of Dresden, Germany, where he was a prisoner of war. February 1945, 135,000 people burned to death. The allied bombers conducted incendiary attacks that killed 84,000 in Tokyo. More, far more, than the 71,000 who perished in the atomic bomb blast at Hiroshima.

For a moment I wondered how many Americans had died in Vietnam. Someone back at Cat Lo would know. But it was all so abstract. It didn't really apply to us. Not the C.B.S. news. Not the newspapers. We were part of it and yet we were totally insulated.

I watched the dark green jungle go by, and thought of Hiroshima again. 71,000 were killed by the bomb, but how many others died later? Birth defects, cancer, the eventual fallout from the explosion would never be accurately tallied. Tonight we would again park off a river mouth waiting for a target. In another four hours, the starlight scope would get a workout.

The mangrove swamp moved slowly past the pilot house. At the time, we did not know of the "fallout" of Agent Orange or its eventual toll.

The roar of the engines. Wet, sweet, stink of the jungle. Bemused detachment.

THE LEARNING CURVE

I was learning how to fight a guerilla war, but it was overwhelming. Like taking a kid into the New York Public Library and telling him, "Read." Charlie poisoned the water supply at Cat Lo, then he attacked with rockets at night, then he tried to blow up the boats at the pier, then he planted a girl spy in our hooch, then he . . . there was simply no way to anticipate.

Back at the Naval Academy, Professor Russell taught each class differently. He would discuss politics as we studied Alexander the Great, then for an entire hour, he would focus on only one paragraph of Caesar's *Commentaries*, then he would dismiss Nelson by showing one slide of Emma and saying "Audacity!" It was impossible to know how to prepare for the class. But *that* was the lesson! The old professor taught that a great commander does *not* prepare for what he thinks the enemy will do. Good commanders do that. Great commanders prepare for all of the possibilities that the enemy *might* do. The Romans didn't think Hannibal would attack from the North, they expected him to come from the South. But Hannibal *could* cross the Alps, and he *did*, surprising Rome.

But the V.C. could do anything, any damned thing. I was trying to learn. Processing odd facts: eating peaches could bring bad luck, our interpreter might be a V.C., the starboard engine used oil. I was trying to learn the correct way to seal a body bag so it was airtight. Remember the locations of sand bars in the Cua River. Unending.

Once as a kid, I fell through the ice in a farm pond. It was an amazing experience. Each time I put my hands on the ice to pull myself out, the ice would break again. As I struggled, I thought about the physics of it all. As my wet body elevated, it put more pressure on the ice. Ice that by definition could not hold my full weight. So just as I came close to pulling myself up, the ice would break again. Pieces as big as a small desk. With each exertion, I became more exhausted. I could mentally compute that it was probable that I would reach the shore. Not certain, just probable.

The Swift bases were not visited by clergy. We would get our ass out of Vietnam alive if we had trust in our fellow boats, our crew, and our weapons. Move, shoot, and communicate. Communicate with other skippers, with air cover and with medevacs. Don't bother with God. The closest we got to religion was the occasional greeting, "Kill a Commie for Christ."

In the early days of musket warfare, armies faced each other in straight lines. They stood and fired. Finally, one army or the other could no longer stand its ground. The loser would retreat.

They "couldn't *stand* it."

But in guerilla warfare there is no space to hold. It was all fluid. What does it mean to be "able to stand it?" It was too overwhelming to truly understand, so we broke it into fatalistic but digestible pieces.

"Join the Navy, go interesting places, see different cultures, meet exotic people and kill them."

"Uncle Ho, he shall live in the hearts of his countrymen . . . as long as his countrymen live."

"Go home? Back to the Land of the Round eyes. Jump your old prom queen? Ha! Neva happen, G.I., neva happen."

IN COLD BLOOD

We were lying off the mouth of a river. Lights off, just looking at the radar screen. Quiet, hoping something would show up. With so little activity, it was not unusual to have three or even four people in the pilot house. Family time. Sometimes we just sat in the dark silence taking turns looking at the rhythmic green sweeps on the screen. The silence could last for hours. Just an occasional bump of a coffee cup on the aluminum. But sometimes a story would emerge. This night it was a story that would be profound if told in most company. Truly horrible. Sadly, in this environment it was only slightly unusual; everyone could tell of at least one aspect of their lives that wasn't like Ozzie and Harriet. Perhaps that was what made the whole situation even more bizarre—how "normal" the story seemed. In the dark, the voice of one crewmember of Inky Bite 97 began softly:

"My folks fought a lot; both drank too much. One night they came home late. They woke me up with their screaming. I was 13, so my sister was only 6. She was still asleep. Suddenly it was violent. I got out of bed and found my dad strangling my mom with his bare hands. I didn't even think, just sprang at him like a little wildcat. One hundred twenty pounds, I was about 40 less than my dad, but it didn't matter. I hit him so hard that he literally flew against the wall of the hall. He was stunned. Surprised at my power and too drunk to continue. I won. I saved my mom. I loved her. Three years later she ran off with a truck driver to a town 200 miles away. I had just gotten my driver's license, so to save her again, I loaded a deer rifle and drove there. I had two clips. Five rounds each. I chose 130-grain soft-nosed bullets for a nice flat trajectory. I parked one block away from where he worked. I waited for his truck to arrive. I had positioned myself so I had a clear shot when he left his vehicle and entered the office. Four hundred feet. The 30-06 rifle had a good scope and was zeroed in perfectly. It wasn't as if I was afraid of jail or the electric chair, or anything. Ice water flowed in my veins. I was that, well, that *indifferent* to it all. Just quiet and numb and focused. Oddly, I had only one concern: there was a slight wind with little gusts. I was almost sure that I should aim one inch to the left. But still the wind bothered me. Two inch drop at that distance. One to the left from wind, maybe two. I knew a headshot would be foolish. Play the odds, and put the first round in mid-chest. What was surprising was that I had absolutely no feeling at all. A lean, mean, killing machine. Not one worry, except for that slight gust of wind.

Well, apparently my mom's lover's schedule had been changed. I laid in ambush from the car for four hours and then gave up. I drove past his house. Nothing. Then I headed home. I drove back the 200 miles and I went to bed at about 3 a.m. I slept soundly, eight hours of goddamned driving and four of ambush for nothing.

Oddly, I never tried to kill him again. I guess that's good . . . at least for him.

*   *   *

Oh, one other thing: I knew that after I hit him with the first bullet I should pump another four or five rounds into the body on the ground. That seemed odd. You'd never do that to a deer. It would ruin too much meat. But one round in the chest of a truck driver might not be enough. You never know what some hotshot doctor might do; he could even save him. Better go with five or six shots to be sure."

The story was truly horrible, but none of us paid particular note. We all had a story of our own. The moral issue wasn't as significant as whether it was best to aim one inch to the left or two. A head shot or go for mid-chest?

*   *   *

We sat in silence thinking of the story and watching the radar screen. Lazy green sweeps. Each of us eager to see a little white dot. A white dot that indicated an enemy boat coming out of the river mouth. Collectively hoping to find a target. To grease a boatload of V.C. with the twin .50's. Just hoping for happy hunting. No such luck this night. Shit.

NIGHT AMBUSH

Quiet. Another covert insertion on a riverbank. Six of us volunteered. Dog tags taped so they would not rattle against each other. Nothing moving but eyeballs. Step off the boat, slink up the hill in single file. Three hundred meters. Hunker down in the grass by a rock beside the path. M-16's ready. Now wait for the prey, hope for good hunting. Radio silenced. Noises of bugs and nearby lapping water.

Hours pass. Slowly the moon begins to come up. Backs ache, knees hurt. Skin is sticky and my sweat stinks. The moon is full and bright. I'm afraid. In the dark it is easy to convince myself that because I can't see, neither can Chuck. That's fair. In a night firefight, you try to use grenades first so the enemy can't see your muzzle flashes. But the moon makes it all very different. The path that had been dark is now shining unbelievably brightly. Thompsen is to my right and I can see him *much* too well. I must be as obvious as he is. Goddamned moon. Charlie *can* see me. But I can't see him. Give me light or dark. This faint light is all to my disadvantage. I tell myself it is illogical to think so. Sure. I'm still scared shitless.

Thompsen leans over and whispers the first words I've heard for three hours, "Skipper, if I had some ham, I could make us ham sandwiches if I had some bread."

I grin. I love him. For the next two hours, I smile. It's the funniest joke I've ever heard. Think of ham sandwiches. No bread. No ham. No ham or bread. A Zen koan. I feel the oily comfort of my M-16. Four bulges against my breast. The friendly caring touch of two concussion grenades and two frags. My weapons make me safe.

Not like that cold, evil, goddamned full moon.

SAINT DOMINIC AND BUGS

In World War II, the Marines claimed that they could always tell the new guys because they were the ones who picked the bugs out of the oatmeal. The seasoned men ate the oatmeal, bugs and all. The Marines could also tell who should be rotated out, who had been there too long . . . . They were the ones who *added* more bugs to their oatmeal.

I had been in-country about two months. I was still picking some bugs out and eating others. We were supposed to be "winning the hearts and minds of the countrymen." That didn't square with what I heard. The weary guys would say, "Kill 'em all and let God sort it out." They didn't mean it. At least most of the time. Later I read that the phrase was actually very old. Saint Dominic said, "Put them all to the sword. God will know his own." A saint had said the same horrid thing! In the year 1209 Saint Dominic and the French army of Simon De Montfort put the entire city of Beziers to the sword. Men, women, and children. Dominic died in 1231; ten years later the Dominicans were put in charge of the inquisition . . . Jesus!

With this kind of thinking, it was clear that going from the Mekong to R & R, then back to the Mekong, and finally back to the land of the round eyes was going to be difficult. I began to suspect that the very skills that we needed in-country would become *big* liabilities some day. Plato asked, "Can virtue be taught?" Here, the question was, "Can it be forgotten?"

It was taking longer than I expected to learn how to lead. The guys with time in-country could *smell*. They could smell danger before it happened. Like a cop. They would avoid missions that looked okay to me and then they would volunteer for crazy stunts.

Amazingly, the easy ones often turned into a mess and those that appeared difficult to me often went off with ease.

The question of bravery was also more complex than a person would expect. Here is a story involving a patrol torpedo boat (PT), the predecessor of the Swift boat or patrol craft fast (PCF):

> In the Pacific in World War II, John F. Kennedy was skipper of PT 109. It was night; he had the engines at idle and out of gear. His boat was waiting in the dark to ambush any Japanese ships transiting the Pacific islands. Suddenly, the 109 boat was surprised to find a large ship, a Japanese destroyer, bearing down on it. Before Kennedy could get underway, his boat was T-boned. Sliced in half. Two men died. J.F.K. saved one other man by pulling the injured sailor to shore by a strap he held in his teeth as he swam. The Navy brass thought that Kennedy was guilty of being unprepared, unprofessional, and obviously lacking appropriate vigilance. They recommended a court-martial. J.F.K.'s father thought he should get the Medal of Honor. He got neither.

Earlier in my life, I thought heroism was simple. As a young boy, I read that two thousand years before, the Persian general told Leonidis that the massive Persian army would fire so many arrows at the tiny band of Greeks that the sky would turn black. Leonidis looked him in the eye and said, "Good. We can fight in the shade."

Our phrase was also laconic: "No guts, no Navy Cross."

But deep down I knew that it just wasn't that simple. Not for J.F.K., not for me, and it probably wasn't for Leonidis either.

TOENAILS

It was a perfect patrol. Dull. Dull is good. Kid tried to scrape the jungle rot from under his toenail with a knife. He was bleeding and shouting, "Fuck!" The blood came from his right big toe. The other nine toes also had the telltale hard green-black scab growths protruding from the edges. A week before I had recommended that Kid go to sickbay and have his toenails pulled off so the fungus could be treated properly.

Kid didn't do as I had instructed. That was okay. I didn't order him to go to sickbay; I just suggested it. Hell, I wouldn't go see Doc either. "Doc" wasn't really a doctor; he was just a 19-year-old medic with iodine and a pair of pliers.

I told Kid to keep his feet dry even though I knew it was impossible. Then I told him to put alcohol on his toes and wrap them. To my surprise, he did.

Thompsen and Kelley teased Kid that he had gotten the fungus at The Red Horse from the whore named C-4. I didn't know how a little 90-pound whore got nicknamed after our plastic explosive. I'm sure there was a good story behind her acquiring that name: "C-4."

The quartermaster and the engineman teased my radioman for another 20 minutes. Then they grew tired of the game or else they realized that being wet all the time, they, too, would get a bad case of jungle rot some day. And it might be in a more embarrassing place: their privates, or the crack in their ass.

Ah, well, that's life in the tropics.

PAPA TANGO

Phan Thiet isn't much of a town. Its initials are "P.T." or "Papa Tango" in the phonetic alphabet. We called it Papa Tango, but its real name is just as good.

From the distance, it appears to be a tiny village of dark houses clustered upon six or seven small hills overlooking the South China Sea. As the visitor approaches, however, he begins to realize that what appear to be houses are in fact miserable huts with tarpaper, wood, and metal scraps covering, or almost covering, the bamboo frames.

As the visitor continues to approach from the sea, the water becomes progressively covered with a dirty white foam, dead fish, and garbage. The unmistakable odor of human sewage becomes apparent and the eye detects that the black shoreline is in fact a jumble of hundreds of tiny fishing boats. A few boats cross the harbor carrying a handful of peasants hunched over the tiny seats. Each boat is painted black, no more than 20 feet long, and only 3 or 4 feet wide. The gunnels are within 18 or 20 inches of the water. In each boat, one fisherman is picking through the nets. The people all appear to be busy; on the other hand, they actually accomplish very little.

Ashore, things are much the same. The streets are crowded with people scurrying back and forth to avoid being run over by the Honda motorcycles. There are no cars; all houses look miserably the same. The visitor can take the main road that runs parallel to the beach and follow it around the gentle curve to the northeast, past the last pier and then inland. The houses continue; the same tiny size, the same thatched roof, the same naked kids looking out empty doorways. Walk on for another six or seven blocks—that's a distance, actually there aren't any real blocks in Phan Thiet—and the road will slowly merge with another. At the crossing there is a tiny white house of cinderblock. The visitor is slightly startled by its appearance. It is much cleaner than the other houses and painted too. A fence surrounds it and tied to the fence is a 200 cc Honda with a chain. This is probably the only house in the entire city of 55,000 that looks clean and dry and happy.

The door is bolted, and a small white buzzer protrudes from a box on which there is a little window for a piece of paper with the resident's name. There is no name in the little window. The house itself looks as if it is in two distinct parts: one is a living facility; the second is attached but is smaller as if it is used for storage. It sometimes is used for "storage." The house belongs to the Navel Intelligence Liaison Officer.

Mark was with me. We were going to get a one-on-one briefing with the spook. We rang the bell and when the door opened, Mark poked a finger into the belly of Peachy, "Umm, well you're not exactly losing weight ol' buddy. My crew threw three pounds of bacon and some bread in a sack for you. I also brought eggs, peanut butter, and a *Playboy*."

"Thanks. When your time's up, I'll give you a souvenir rifle to take back stateside when you're ready."

Mark shook his head, "As I understand it, they are searching everyone who returns home pretty carefully. I don't know about officers, but bringing a Chinese Communist automatic weapon probably isn't worth putting my ass on the line."

"Up to you!" Peachy shouted. He had returned with a long bundle from which he was unwrapping some rags. "This one is a real beaut. Brand new, and look at this." He pointed to some finely inscribed writing on the stock, "Know what it says?"

Mark squinted. "No, other than the guy's name was Nguyen."

"Well, look. See this says 'Nguyen Do Son.' Do Son is about six klicks from Haiphong. Right at the harbor mouth. In other words, the poor son-of-bitch walked the full Ho Chi Minh Trail with this AK-47! That's 600 air miles, so he must have carried this thing over a thousand miles through the goddamned jungle! I took this one apart and found this photo of a girl wrapped in plastic behind the butt plate in the gunstock. She's probably sitting up in Haiphong wondering when her boyfriend is coming back, not aware that her hero carried his AK-47 all the way to Papa Tango only to get shot."

"How did you get it?" I asked too quickly.

"Uh, my Viet counterpart was trying to get some stuff out of ol' Nguyen. He had been wounded; they gave him first aid and brought him in here."

From the tone, I could tell that ol' Nguyen had probably had a tough time of it. The intelligence officers were generally straight guys. Peachy had probably just stood in the corner as his "counterpart" in the South Vietnamese Army interrogated Nguyen. The wounded prisoner would have received medical help, but the speed and quality of his first aid depended on his condition and whether he was willing to spill the beans on other regular North Vietnamese Army troop dispositions.

Mark was a couple of steps ahead. "Well, where are the bad guys?"

"We don't know," Peachy replied. "He was in a group of five when he was shot six days ago. There could be up to a thousand near here. At least the RVN seemed to think so . . ." His voice trailed off and he looked thoughtful. "Yesterday the general called me and he mentioned 4,000, but that's not possible and so we're back in the dark."

"Look, Mark, I don't know where they are, but I'm not uptight about it. I think the RVN generals want to blow this up so Saigon will request more troops for Papa Tango to protect the general's farms and whorehouses and whatever else they own."

"It's a goofy business. The other day I got a message from another Naval Intelligence Officer up in I Corps. He told about a small base in his area where a little girl had been delivering something . . . like laundry every day for the last two years. One day she was really straining to carry her little package into the officers barracks so a lieutenant offered to help her. He picked up the package and noticed that it was about five times as heavy as laundry should be. He opened it and saw explosives. The little girl just went into hysterical crying. A couple of guys interrogated her and right away she told them what happened. The V.C. came into her village, took her mother and sister and said, 'Look, kid, you want to see these two alive again then take this package into the base . . . . '"

Just a typical patriotic story. But the "stories" are coming faster and faster. Closer. "Vietnamization of the War" means, "Losing the War."

*   *   *

That was how we interacted with naval intelligence. A giant of a man, "Peachy," was also an accomplished musician. I assume that he learned Vietnamese very well. Most musicians are skilled linguists. He was probably a good interrogator. We passed a little data back and forth in that hour. But data isn't actionable information.

All that I learned from this visit was that a young man named Nguyen was a North Vietnamese regular who had earlier been shot. The wounded man was interrogated by a South Vietnamese army officer. The AK-47 rifle that he had carried one thousand miles contained his ID and a photo of the girlfriend that he had left behind. The small photo was wrapped in plastic. She had big eyes and long hair and a puzzled smile. Perhaps that was the only time she had stood before a camera. Now her boyfriend or her husband was wounded or dead. But she didn't know that yet. She might not ever be certain. It would be easy to dismiss it all with "Xin Loi," but I couldn't. She was small and delicate and pretty. She didn't know that her love had struggled in the cleanest prettiest little house in Papa Tango.

Her photo was captivating. We fought "Communists" and killed "V.C." and we were ambushed by "little bastards." We were in firefights with "the enemy" and had operations against "N.V.A. regulars." Oddly, it was always a slight surprise to realize that those were all . . . well . . . they were actually *PEOPLE*.

HOW TO STRANGLE A CAT WITH A ROSARY

Oscelot had just come back from a check ride with a new kid. The kid's name was Tarzan. He arrived in Cat Lo two months after me. His dad was Governor of Montana. No kidding, the governor. We called the new kid "Tarzan." No one wanted to give him an insulting name; maybe his old man had clout. Maybe we would want a job in politics someday.

I had been on the fantail of the 97 boat looking at a problem with our aft .50 caliber. The debrief by Oscelot in the adjacent boat was so funny that I just sat on my ammo box with my back to his boat, which was moored alongside, and eavesdropped. Here is what I heard him say to Tarzan: "You've got a good crew. Solid. Nice job training them. Tell your radioman to spend some time with mine to learn the unofficial frequencies and call signs. You've got to know who is who, 'Mary Poppins,' 'Preparation H,' 'Kentucky Colonel.' You've got to know 'em all. How else can you talk to 'Baby Fats' or 'Toxic Organ'? Memorize the frequencies cold . . . . Without the 'freaks' you will not know where to meet us for picnics or water skiing. Don't borrow the skis until you've been on patrol for two or three weeks. Board and search fishing boats offshore until your crew gets comfortable. And for Christsake don't run over the water skier. Last week Hank's boat drifted back onto Barry and the engineman put it in gear with Barry floating almost under the stern. Now if the screw of the boat had cut off his wire, how would we explain that? How would you explain getting your cajones cut off by a propeller?"

Tarzan didn't seem to have an answer, so Oscelot continued: "So you girls just have a quiet time and keep your head down and

don't feed the dog. He's getting too fat. Now some guys believe
that eating peaches is bad luck and others don't, but if you trade
for lobsters give the goddamned peaches to the local fisherman
anyway. And another thing, girls, don't go up any rivers until you've
been with one of us vets once or you will never make it back out. If
you get stuck on a sandbar up a river, you are a sitting fucking
duck for a B-40. That happened in the Bo Di last month. We
know that you have hair on your chest so don't try to prove it. Oh,
and please don't call my Viet 'Zipper-head.' As you saw he took a
round in the scalp and the Viet doctor who sewed him up did a
lousy job, so now he has a big zipper scar on his head, but he's a
gutsy little guy. Tougher than a boiled owl. So I'll appreciate it if
you treat him well. You are a new kid, so there is so much to learn
that you'll feel like you are drinking water from a fire-hose. Well,
just wait a few weeks until you're an old vet. Then . . . you'll still
feel like you are drinking from a fire-hose."

Tarzan looked dazed, but Oscelot went on. "When we say
'punt,' drop three channels on the radio and you can speak in the
clear, like if you want to brag or cry or borrow Tabasco sauce or
something."

Sitting on my boat, I felt that I was hearing first hand the
Cheshire Cat lecturing Alice. Oscelot went on, "Next month, you
are all free to do whatever blows wind up your skirt. Later. Not
now."

"You are in the big game now. This is Zipper-head Memorial
Stadium and you are beginning to understand, just beginning to
understand, that the trophy is your ass. I don't mean to repeat
myself, but for a few weeks, I'd appreciate it if you don't do anything
to prove you're brave. Just enjoy life here in this shit-hole. I really
do not want to pull your young ass out of a jam right now. Now
I'm busy. Really. I'm making an 8mm movie and writing a novel
about this place. Do a good job and I'll put you in my book."

I turned around and saw Oscelot give the surfer's two finger
sign to Tarzan as he walked away. Tarzan stood alone. Stunned. I
caught his eye. Like Alice, he was in a strange and dangerous
environment and he did not understand the advice of a cynical

Cheshire Cat. Tarzan was a virgin. Alice in a little blue dress and innocent white schoolgirl stockings. Alice should have strangled that goddamned cat. With her belt or her bra or a rosary. But if she had done that, if she *had* garroted the Cheshire Cat, she wouldn't be Alice anymore, would she?

What poor Tarzan didn't know at the time was that logical instructions were probably not as appropriate as those that were insane. As for new kids, the old vets didn't give a rat's ass about them. Yet, they would give their lives to save them. The seasoned Swifties cared for the virgins and despised them at the same time.

Tarzan, you're not in Montana anymore. You are up shit creek and it's called Mekong.

MY LECTURE TO TARZAN ON MACROECONOMICS AND HOW AMERICA CAN BE A CAPITALIST BEACON FOR THE WORLD

I found Tarzan at supper later that evening and I sat beside him. "Oscelot is like Wild Bill Hickock who said, 'I mean everything I say when I'm drunk but don't do anything about it till the next morning.' Oscelot is from Hawaii, you know. He often talks more like a San Diego surfer than a naval officer, but believe me, he's a good skipper."

Tarzan grinned. "Is he really writing a book?"

"Yup. The tentative title of his war novel is *How to Strangle a Cat with a Rosary*. It's about misapplication of good intentions. I've never read any of it, but he does have a great ten-minute movie of a river raid; it shows a B-40 rocket coming straight at him. It missed, of course, but the crazy guy kept his camera going!"

Tarzan was quiet, so I went on, "Look, the tragedy of the war is that you can't convert people to capitalism by shooting them. This poor country would be better off with a hybrid of capitalism and communism. They need the education and the historical culture to make 100 percent capitalism work. Did you know that in the North of China the rivers are prone to flooding and in the South of China the rivers are more serene? So in the North everyone must work together. 'Gung Ho.' That means 'work together' or 'pull together.' If the guy upstream does not keep his portion of the levee in good shape and it floods, you are screwed if you live downstream. Down in the southern part of China everyone can go his own way. The river doesn't need constant attention and no one depends on the work of others. So, for centuries, the North has been cooperative-socialist and for centuries the South of China has been self-centered and aggressive. 'Viva Yo.' So the people up in Beijing believe they are cooperative and that the people in the South are selfish. The people in the South think they are free to do what is best, but folks in the North of the country are lazy and want others to do the work. Communist or capitalist? Hell, it's all a function of North/South geography and rivers. See? We attack them for being 'them.' Aesop said, 'Any excuse will serve a tyrant.' The French have an even better saying which is: 'If you want to drown your dog, accuse him of having rabies.'"

Tarzan said that he saw my point. He still looked puzzled, so I went on.

"Look, the best way for America to influence the world is to be perfect instead of running all around and accusing people of having rabies so we can justify killing them. We should focus on ourselves: America's poverty, its crime, and poor education. If we make our country attractive, the other 190 countries on the earth will want to imitate us. What nation wants to duplicate us if we riot in L.A. and run around shooting the hell out of people?"

"These folks in South Vietnam want to join with the North. They do not want to be ruled by a puppet of Washington's choice. President Ky is an out-of-touch Catholic. We're supporting a Catholic in a Buddhist country! Jesus."

"America's citizens are so goddamned dumb, they think the President and the Pentagon cause war. Hell, you know from high school civics that it is the Congress that funds the war and the Senate that conducts foreign policy. It's in the goddamned Constitution! So anytime the 435 congressmen and 100 senators want, they can shut this operation down. But the gutless sons-a-bitches let Johnson and McNamara and the military take the heat. They should stand up and admit they are in charge and not default it all!"

Up until then, I thought he had been following my logic and enjoying the lesson on political science, but I noticed that Tarzan was now looking at me with a blank stare. My ranting had made less sense to him than Oscelot's Cheshire Cat-like advice. Actually, my lecture was worse than that. Tarzan stared at me like I had been dropped on my head as a baby.

*   *   *

I realized that I should have skipped the macroeconomics lecture; instead I should have followed Oscelot's surrealistic advice with a sequel. I should have told Tarzan about a moose and a lesbian.

FISHERMEN

The days merged into one another. Sun. Blue water. Trade a can of C-rats for a fresh fish. Joke with the kids. The Viet fishermen prized eggs. Apparently they didn't get many, so we tried to save eggs to give to fishermen with kids. The little girls looked like dolls. Parents with feet as wide as they were long. Toes that spread out like a hand, the effect from standing on rocking decks since they too were children. Life was good. Poor honest people. They didn't even make a dollar a day in this country. Yet the kids were happy. They certainly got lots of time with their parents. They ate nuoc mam. The Viets make special fish oil from fish and salt. It takes days to ferment. It smells; "Enough to gag a maggot" said Kelley.

We would shout, "Dung lai" at the fishermen. They would stop and show us that they had nothing to hide. No gun running. No trouble. One night a boat that was skirting up the coast refused to stop. As we closed on it we could see them throwing things overboard. By the time we caught them, there was nothing left aboard. What evidence had they destroyed? What were their intentions? Hell, it really didn't matter. If they had been running guns or supplies, the goods were now gone. If they hadn't, no harm done. It wasn't worth the effort to arrest them. If we did, they would be free again by midday. So Kelley grabbed a teenage boy and shook him. Screaming as if he fully intended to kill the kid. The other two boatmen looked on in fear. The kid assumed his death was eminent. Suddenly, Kelley grew tired of it all. He muttered a profanity and climbed back aboard the Swift. The young gunrunner's expression changed from terror to wonderment at being free to live. By the time we left, he was again staring at us with a penetrating look of anger and fury.

Scare the bejeesus out of one. Give an egg to another. We were not winning the hearts and minds of the Viets, but we were definitely fucking up their heads and stomachs. Random events. Random action going both ways. Wanna lobster? Wanna bullet between the eyes? Cute girl, give her an egg. Do we have a Coke?

We had the power of gods. Gods that didn't give a shit.

That's the way the celestial clock ticks.

"Dung lai"—stop. "Di di"—go.

One day we came across a little boy who had a fishhook embedded deeply into his foot. His parents were very apprehensive when we told them that we would take the child to a medic and have him back at the same location later in the day. Reluctantly, they agreed. Within a few hours we had reunited the child. Big grin. Big white bandage on the little brown foot. One step forward.

We called the non-combatants names that fit them well. Administrators in Saigon were "R.E.M.F.'s"—"Rear Echilon Mother Fuckers." The people at the Pentagon "drove L.M.D.'s" (large mahogany desks). We respected the North Vietnamese soldiers. We respected the V.C. We had only contempt for our own military people who were not in-country. Our hatred of those Americans far eclipsed our feeling toward the enemy.

The news reported that a Marine officer, Major William Corson had learned Vietnamese so well that he had challenged a Viet Cong politician to a public debate in the village square. In Vietnamese! What would the war have been like if all Americans had been willing to work so hard? I was glad to see Major Corson's name again. He had taught Economics at the Naval Academy three years before. He gave me an "A."

What grade did the major deserve . . . as opposed to our cowardly Congress?

COBRA

The hooch at Cat Lo was simply a quonset hut. The first 20 feet were partitioned into a lounge; actually, it was a third rate bar. Predictably named, "The Cat House." Nondescript, irregular chairs, a table or two, and a refrigerator. Behind the partition, the sleeping quarters: simply a long bunkroom with cots on each side. That part remained dimly lit so officers could come and go 24 hours a day.

Tarzan was talking. He said, "It is incumbent on all of us to . . ." He was cut off by catcalls upon saying "incumbent." No one wanted to hear fancy words—they reminded us of politicians.

I suggested, "Use Navy words. Obscenities are fine; just *never* use the words of a politician again." He needed my advice.

The bar was always open. Toss a coin into the chipped ashtray and take a beer from the fridge. With luck, your Budweiser would be somewhat cool. At other times, you had to settle for warm beer. A San Miguel or a "33." The important thing was that there was always beer.

Metal quonset huts are hot. Hot in the day. Hot at night too. Not much breeze, so we left the front door open. One night a cobra came in. That's right. A cobra just came into the Cat House Bar. One half-drunk guy turned and pointed, "Hey look, a cobra!" Not too imaginative a statement, but certainly accurate.

So the Swifties just sat and watched the confused snake slowly moving through the open entrance to the quonset. Then something absolutely amazing happened. Rocky stood up and shouted, "I'll show you what you do with a cobra!" He staggered over to a red chemical fire extinguisher that was hanging on the wall. He took it down from its place and clumsily walked a few feet toward the snake. Then he turned the extinguisher on and blasted the cobra with the freezing snow-white chemicals.

The snake writhed, then moved slower, and finally straightened. Frozen stick-like in death or near death. Rocky picked up the frosted reptile by the tail and threw it out the door. Later the camp dogs ate it.

The amazing thing was not that the cobra came into the bar. What left us all in shock was the fact that Rocky had actually done something appropriate. It was the only intelligent thing I ever saw him do in-country.

PANDORA'S BOX

Naval intelligence said we would definitely catch "Charlie" at a food resupply dump in an abandoned village. It was pitch dark when we began a sweep of a vil with about 30 dilapidated hooches. My heart was pounding furiously as I opened the first door. A bat flew directly into my face. When I kicked open the second door, a mongrel dog raced past. Each hooch was a Pandora's Box of rats and other animals. I was very frightened; the entire sweep was simply unreal. When it was over (between ten minutes and an hour later—I have no idea which), my clothes were so wet it looked as if I had been for a swim. There had been no contact with the enemy. The night provided no danger, just white-knuckle stark terror.

Nobody gets medals for just being terrified; maybe they should.

BUDDHISTS

We saw a whale shark while on patrol. We parked the boat and dropped a concussion grenade on it. It probably killed the shark. The Viets believe the shark has special Buddhist qualities. Nguyen, the most popular name in the country, is a reflection of an ancient legend of a shark deity. In America, little boys often kill without hesitation when they see an insect or an animal. Without thinking. Young men in the U.S. Navy should know better.

I should have known better than to let Kelley shoot 81-millimeter rounds into a cemetery. I said nothing. I just watched until my eye caught the stern face of our Viet interpreter. He looked at me with a sad resigned expression. Only then did I order Kelley to stop blowing up the tombs. We had lapsed into vandalism. It was easy.

Perhaps at the time, we thought that we had a reason to hurt the shark. Maybe we even had an excuse for destroying tombs. Aesop said, "Any excuse will serve a tyrant."

Twenty years later, I lived in a Buddhist monastery in Thailand. It felt appropriate.

SHIT MAGNETS

Here is the problem. Chairman Mao's *Little Red Book* ordered the Communist troops to retreat if they were outnumbered. It told them to attack only if they had the advantage in firepower. Because they were indigenous, it was difficult to surprise them. Consequently, when our forces were strong enough to beat them, we did not find them. When they were superior, they found us.

Not good.

Curiously, W.C. Fields said much the same: "Never kick a man unless he's down."

So we devised a method to draw them out. Appearing weak, we would invite their attack. When they did fire at us, we would then call in air strikes on the newly identified position. Our job was to find them by having them shoot at us.

Shit magnets.

Another way to get your young ass shot at was to participate in what was called "Psy Ops." Psychological operations. The Navy mounted a loudspeaker on the radar antenna of our boats. It was connected to a tape recorder. We were given tapes in Vietnamese that said things like "Viet Cong, you are losing the war. Lay down your weapons and come out of the jungle. We will not hurt you!"

That idea was remarkably stupid. By making each Swift boat into a noisy, insulting, propaganda speaker, we insured that any enemy soldier worth his salt would come running to the river to fire at us. It was simply amazing how well it did work for drawing fire.

Within a week, every boat found that its tape recorder no longer worked or that the propaganda tape cassette was lost. A life-saving coincidence.

It was at about this time that we began going up rivers backward. Remember Chairman Mao's *Little Red Book*: If you got shot at, you were already outgunned. By definition. Thus it was more important to get out quickly than to duke it out like John Wayne. Cut and run. Call in an air strike. Turning around in the narrow channels took too long. Go up the river backward so you could get out fast.

I'm sure the old World War II vets would have a hard time understanding that approach. Well, Xin Loi. That's why we didn't join the V.F.W. upon our return stateside. We simply had little in common with vets of other wars.

On the other hand, perhaps some would understand. They didn't all have apple pie-and-motherhood memories of Roosevelt and Truman. The U.S. government was remarkably silent even after it knew of the atrocities in the concentration camps. Our government looked the other way when the occupied Dutch and French citizens turned Jews over to the Germans. Our borders were closed to many Jews seeking asylum. After World War II, the U.S. Army helped the Communist Russian government round up "White Russians"—those who had fought the Communists. We turned them over to Stalin to be sent to the gulag and executed. My dad was ordered to do just that; it bothered the hell out of him. Many were just kids.

To kill without remorse, it is best to dehumanize the enemy. Make him sub-human. Call him a gook or tell stories of his savagery. Say that it is he who holds life cheap. The problem with that is that you cannot do such things and simultaneously win the hearts and minds of the adversary. You lose both his heart and mind. Then you lose your own heart, your own mind.

*   *   *

Finally you make it into a joke:
"Get them by the balls and their hearts and minds will follow."

ARCLIGHT

At night the B-52 bombers would deliver their ordnance. Tons of bombs falling from the night sky. To the observer on the ground it was as if long strings of explosives on the face of the earth simply erupted in an "aweful" manner. We couldn't help feeling literally, full of awe. It was puzzling to us that the Air Force could know where the friendly forces were located. I doubt they did. Clearly our movements were along the river; friendly forces mixed, deliberately so, among the enemy. The Air Force did not know where we were, so how did they avoid bombing us? Probably it was simply dumb luck.

On one hand, we were pleased to see the power of the American military. On the other hand, the power did not appear to be delivered in an effective way. In fact, America dropped several times the ordnance needed to wipe out the entire Viet population. The U.S. military used that fact as evidence of how careful they had been. Perhaps. Or perhaps they were just inexcusably ineffective.

The primary measure of accuracy is "circular error probable." It is the circle around the target in which the bomb has a particular probability of landing. God only knows the accuracy of those B-52s. It is not just how well the bomb falls versus the location predicted by the bombsight, it is also the simple question of where the hell the bombardier was aiming in the jungle. Much of the territory in which we Swifties operated was a "free-fire zone." These were areas where by definition, "if it moves it is the enemy." That was the area where we moved too. Shooters, targets, people, aircraft, bombs, boats. It was a dangerous stew.

While all of the B-52 activity was going on, we also had the amazing experience of being surrounded by attacks by aircraft affectionately called "Puff the Magic Dragon." These were old C-47 prop aircraft armed with mini guns. The minis shot 6,000 rounds per minute. That computes to 100 bullets per second. A small percentage of those bullets were tracers that glowed a bright pink when fired. The result was a bright wavy stream of bullets coming from above. To us on the ground it appeared that an invisible giant was pissing on us from the dark sky.

The Air Force moved and shot, but seldom communicated with us. Unlike them, we river rats could see our target most of the time. Kelley, the engine man, made us move. Kid handled communication, and Jake, the shooting specialist, coordinated all of our weapons when things got hot.

A year earlier, on the J. Jarvits I had destroyed the wrong village. My shots were off by three kilometers. I questioned the effectiveness and damage done by the Arclights and Puffs. Their fire was often off by *much* more than three klicks.

Perhaps those questions, like many others, should not be asked at all.

INTEL BRIEFING

Evening was approaching; the Ops boss stopped at our breakfast table. We had awakened at about 1700 and were scheduled for night patrol. "Intel briefing," he said and moved on. We nodded and went back to eating cornflakes and powdered milk that would get us through the night. "Neanderthal" became quiet. We kept our distance. The genius was now at work.

Nervously we filed into the hooch. The squadron C.O. introduced the speaker as "Mr. Smith." We smiled politely at the joke. All Intel types were "Mr. Smith." We were eager to hear what he had to say, especially since this was a new briefer who did not know Neanderthal. He began: "At present we have no evidence of meaningful activity from any point in this area," he said as his hand swept over the center of the map in front of us. "Basically your operating area is, and should remain, quiet." A long pause followed. Then came the part that mattered. "There is, however, a regular N.V.A. sapper battalion at the coordinates Bravo November twenty-seven sixty-six." He said it slowly and very carefully. The map hung innocently in front. Mr. Smith's hands remained in his pockets. We knew. The map coordinates BN2766 were in Cambodia.

For the past year politicians in Washington had been careful to stress that America had no intention of expanding the war into another country. Daily, the President denied that any American troops were in Cambodia, or that the U.S. conducted any military operations there at all.

Note that we had not been ordered up that river. We were not even told to go into that country at all. He simply told us where the enemy was. Only later, did I learn the phrase for this: "plausible deniability."

Next came our measured and polite and very careful questions. "Will air support be up on all nets and will Dust-offs and Snakes be available at all locations?" one of my fellow Swifties asked.

"Yes," was the expected laconic reply.

That was all we needed to know. The spook had just told us both Navy and Air Force medevac helos and gunships would follow us, confirming that other operational units would be violating the "neutral" country. Now he was eager to get away from us; he started toward the door. Tension was high. We bit our lips to avoid showing emotion. We *knew* what was coming next.

Neanderthal raised his huge hairy arm. "One question," he said as politely as his booming voice would allow. "Do you think the high salt content of the Viet diet contributes to their aggressiveness?"

Neanderthal's questions were insane. His dark brow hid emotion as well as any poker player. Ridiculous, and yet . . . nothing was normal. And so, such marginal, crazy, odd questions caused us to pause. The spook was thunderstruck. He looked at the other eight of us. It was difficult, but we didn't compromise Neanderthal. Each of us had the innocent look of a student eager to hear what a brilliant professor had to say.

The new spook shifted. He looked at Neanderthal's face and learned nothing. Predictable, measured words came out, "To the best of my knowledge, no study has yet been done on that." Then he was out the door.

We all broke into grins. Humorous, innocent, pathetic retaliation of third grade school boys who had pulled one off on an unsuspecting principal.

The faceless Mister Smith had encouraged—or ordered—us into Cambodia and we in turn, had confused him. If we were lucky, he would pass the question back up the line. If we were lucky, perhaps some odd analyst would even wonder about it, or actually research it. If we were *truly* lucky, the mission to BN2766 would be a cakewalk.

Cat Lo River Rats

Swift boat

A Swift fantail after a firefight
(note spent mortar boxes)

Lt. (jg) Blinn

On patrol, breakfast

"Home"

L.S.T.
Hot Rivers

U.S.S. MADISON COUNTY (L.S.T. 1100)

My crew and I were just trying to get by without screwing up. After three months in-country all we knew was that we were still very, very naive virgins.

Upon return from patrol, I washed quickly and proceeded to the Cat Lo mess hall. It was oddly quiet. As I sat down with my tray, the buzz was about a W.I.A. on the T—Barry had been wounded for a second time while operating off the L.S.T. mother ship. He had been hit in the eye or the temple or the nose or a combination. He had taken something. Exactly what wasn't known; the speculation revolved around a piece of mortar shrapnel or a bullet or a piece of his own boat. That wasn't clear, but we did know that he was still conscious when they medevaced him off the landing ship tank called the Madison County.

I ate my boiled potato and beef gravy in silence and listened. Attentively.

"So you're next." It was the voice of Pat Lang from behind me.

"What?" was my reply.

"You'll go to the T to replace Barry. His crew will bring his boat back to Cat Lo without him."

It took a moment for it to sink in. My boat would go next. The Navy sent replacements wherever there was a gap in manpower. By definition, the newer crews went wherever there had been a loss. Stated another way, the system insured that those who had recently arrived went to the hottest spots.

It took Lang only a few minutes to sketch what we were to do. Early the next morning we would get under way and proceed down the coast of Vietnam. Past all six of the Cat Lo southern patrol zones, each of which was about 15 miles long. After we were 90 miles south, we would see on radar the L.S.T. Madison County, a large Navy ship stationed about four miles offshore. The mother ship was over a hundred nautical miles from Cat Lo. It would be our next home.

The Rung Sat Forest covered the southern tip of Vietnam. It had been called the "Forrest of Assassins" far back in Vietnamese history. The area was like the Everglades; consequently, it was impossible to build a proper base ashore. So the Navy stationed a ship offshore as a floating Swift base. The Cat Lo boats were assigned to the T.

I nodded with more confidence than I possessed and went to find my crew. We had to top off fuel tanks and deliver extra supplies as well.

The next morning the weather was perfect. Four hours at high speed brought us through all six Cat Lo patrol areas. We chatted briefly with each boat as we transited its assigned area.

I began to regret that I hadn't met Dad and my sister in Hawaii a few months before. Six years ago I had left my home in Nebraska. I didn't have a home anymore. I started to wonder if people simply become emotionally dull in-country. It was a self-preservation factor. A dulling that makes it difficult to feel or to love or to even care. Perhaps that was what was wrong with my relationship with the mother I no longer knew. Or Victoria. Or Diane, a wonderful girl that I had dated for three years while at the Naval Academy. I stared at the deep blue sea. Lost in thought. Not confused though, just dull. Like having had too many San Miguel beers in Olongapo.

At 1200 we had it on radar. Fifteen minutes later it appeared. A big, beautiful, gray Navy ship. My mind snapped back onto something real. Coming aboard, meeting those Cat Lo skippers I had not yet seen. Learning the procedure down here in Indian Country. As we pulled alongside, I grinned up at the people watching our arrival.

I stepped aboard the U.S.S. Madison County. The smooth gray hull reflecting the sun. My mother ship. Home.

MOTHER SHIP

The two best duty stations in the navy are the one you are coming from and the one you are going to.

Robert Adair Beed, Master Chief Petty Officer, U.S.N.

The U.S.S. Madison County nearly missed World War II. She was commissioned 1 May of 1945. Landing Ship Tanks or L.S.T.s are the big ships that you see in old war movies. The bow opens out like doors. They put their nose on the beach and open those doors and out come tanks and jeeps and troops. Heavy stuff for amphibious landings. They have no armor, no weapons to speak of. They are basically the equivalent of a huge seagoing truck. They pick up cargo in one place and deposit it in another. L.S.T.s displace 2,000 tons and can carry 4,000 tons in cargo.

L.S.T.s brought the first U.S. ground combatants to Vietnam. But the amphibious landing of our first Marines at Danang had been a very long time ago. Now the L.S.T. was used as an offshore base for Swifts down by Cambodia. At the southern tip of Vietnam where the notorious prisons with "tiger cages" housed men destined to die. Prisons with four solid walls and bars on the roof so guards could walk above the prisoners and look down on them. Down by Cambodia where it was always hot and sticky.

The Madison County was commanded by a wonderful officer. Five foot eight, olive skin, 40 years old. We called him "The Greek." We were on patrol 24 hours and then off for 24. An entire day to eat, enjoy the air conditioning, read, and watch a movie. Good food. Good company. Rest.

Working off "The T" was heaven. No Rocky to order us to do something dangerously stupid. We operated almost independently.

We covered each patrol area for a full 24 hours each day, but it was all flexible.

It was dangerous, but somehow the "pucker factor" wasn't as high when we had control of our own missions. One old timer, named Buster explained, "Everything here is relative . . . like the smell in an elevator . . . it is different to a midget." I liked these guys; Buster told me that his family's motto was "Frequently in error, never in doubt." He didn't make errors in chess or in poker. He was so smart; he had *seven* wisdom teeth. At least that's what he said.

Buster repeated the story of when Admiral Lord Nelson was ordered to withdraw from a battle. Nelson put his telescope to his blind eye and said, "I do not see the signal." On the T, we could do much the same to the signals from the brass in Saigon.

For a few weeks, I took a special interest in the fishing boats. Their movements, their cargo, and the technique of fishing from a sampan. Once again Thompsen and I took a basket-boat out to see what we could find. From a distance we appeared like local fishermen, but on a closer look, our stealth mission looked rather silly. Two Americans paddling in circles, clueless as to how to fish or even maneuver the keelless basket boat. As time went by, I became even more convinced that every "Water Born Logistic Craft" that the Jarvits had shot at, every "WIBLIC" that it had sunk the year before, was just a poor fisherman. The U.S. didn't know what it was doing. Like Perseus, every time we cut a snakehead off our Medusa, several more grew back. Every drop of blood of innocent people converted into another V.C. willing to risk it all for revenge. In short, Sea Dragon and much of the war effort down south simply created a bigger and more defiant enemy. Our strategy for the war was simply stupid.

I no longer had visions of flying to Honolulu to explain it all to the Commander in Chief of the Pacific Fleet. Instead, on the T, I just joined the others. We turned out the lights and watched an old John Wayne movie. "The Duke" said something profound in that movie. He said, "Life is tough; it's tougher if you're stupid."

YOU HAVE TO GO OUT

The Coast Guard has a great motto: "You have to go out; you don't have to come back." In W.W.II the P.T. boats "were expendable." Swift boats were part of that heritage.

After patrol, each boat came to the T alone. We changed crews and rearmed and then the next crew took the boat out for another 24 hours. About six crews would be on the T at a given time and six boats would be on patrol. Twelve crews, six boats. Badger and I were on the T at the same time. I shared my boat with another skipper.

On patrol we often tuned to a special radio frequency. By using unofficial call signs that we had given one another, we could talk in the clear. We would plan missions, get together for lunch, or just gossip. There was no way Saigon could tell who was breaking radio discipline. We were not on a Swift boat frequency and we were using fictitious names. My official call sign was the same as the boat that I commanded: "Inky Bite 97," my unofficial call sign was "Sweet Pea."

"Sweet Pea" wasn't very complementary, but most of the others were worse.

Earlier, back at Cat Lo, the procedure was different. We left in small groups together from the pier, and often returned in a pack. Before departing, we would check the communications systems. This consisted of one boat radioing, "This is Inky Bite 37, radio check." The next boat would respond.

"This is Inky Bite 45, read you loud and clear. How me?" And so it would go.

One day Badger skipped protocol. He just started singing "Come on, come on, touch me babe, don't you know that I am not afraid." I think it was a song by the Doors. Badger sang it surprisingly well, but he was unconvincing about the "I am not afraid" part.

The new approach to radio checks allowed us to be rebellious, expressive, and personal all at the same time. Soon new songs appeared. The most haunting was one another skipper sang: "It's a strange, strange world we live in, Master Jack. No hard feelings if I never come back . . . ." He sang it in a sad folk song voice. It was my favorite. It was a very appropriate way to start each patrol.

One guy tested his mike with "What a friend we have in Jesus Christ Almighty what a pal." He sang it all as one sentence. Enough irony to make us forget how scared we were, or to forget how that particular "pal" hadn't been helping us much lately.

Steel Wool would simply announce "The 6:17 is departing for Scarsdale on Track One."

One or two guys tried to sing, "Tell me over and over again my friend that you don't believe we're on the eve of destruction . . . ."

I stayed with my favorite by Leslie Gore: "It's my party and I'll cry if I want to, cry if I want to, you would cry too if it happened to you."

Still giggling, we would pull away from the L.S.T. Six boats with fresh crews. Rearmed, refueled and ready. Young men in touch with each other.

THE SOUTH CHINA SEA

Life on the T was heaven. Ice cream. Movies. After each patrol, a full 24 hours off duty. Buster was so good at the game of trivia that no one would play with him. He knew more facts than anyone I had ever known. Once after answering, "Who is on the front of a $1,000 bill?" we asked, "How do you know all this goddamned stuff?"

Buster could only answer, "I read it once." Later he confessed that he had been on T.V. The "G.E. College Bowl." Buster was on the team from Villanova University; they held the record for victories. Buster knew the name of Tonto's horse; more importantly, he knew every card that had been discarded. I played poker with him once. Just once. The goddamned horse was named Scout.

All in all, it was a bright group of guys. Three from Harvard, one or two from Yale, several from the Naval Academy, and one each from Michigan, Texas, Wisconsin, and the University of Oregon. Good, solid, and smart. Every one.

Some of the more senior guys had skin diseases. Big, white spots without pigmentation. Most had jungle rot too. Still, we were in remarkably good health.

The area was wild and beautiful. The spits of land had French names like Cap Ferrat and Cap St. Jacques. Later I learned that Cap Ferrat is actually a very exclusive residential area on the French Riviera near Monaco. Decades earlier, the French had named much of the coast of Indochina after landmarks that they knew from the Mediterranean.

We just did our job for 24 hours and then relaxed for 24. I started reading Plato, going deeper than I had ever gone in college. Once I missed supper; I had been so engrossed with a dialogue that I forgot to eat. After Plato came Nietzche. Nietzche fit so well with our position. Plato gave a glimpse of the ideal, Nietzche of reality. He said that the only appropriate prayer is "Thank you." Nietzche wrote that we have already been given all that we will get; to ask God for more is sacrilegious. People who pray for things or power or ability are in fact asking God for . . . magic. They will never get it. So, it is healthier to put it in the past; what you have now is all you will ever get. For those who pray for more—that is more magic—God is dead. I believed that. Philosophy was a great diversion.

Safety, sanity, honorable conduct, or war. No question was too big or too small that it was not addressed by those two philosophers.

My favorite quote was from Nietzche. He said, "The only serious philosophical question is whether or not to commit suicide."

SKIPPY'S BRAINS

Skippy took a round through the left eye. The shell removed the upper left front quarter of his head.

His crew carried him up the ladder of the L.S.T. mother ship and laid him on the dining table of the officers' wardroom mess. The corpsman called for us to hold the wounded down, three officers on each side. One half of the young sun-tanned boy was tranquil, the other side contorted violently. We six looked down at him and then back at each other in silence. Then the medic took a very big piece of gauze and smashed it directly into the gaping hole where the eyeball had been. A few pieces of skull fell on the table with the blood.

"I don't think you should just push a bandage onto raw brain. That might hurt him," I thought. My second reaction was "What in the name of God should you do?" The medic seemed to know what he was doing.

Then one officer looked at the body and spoke: "Jesus Christ, he's gone."

The medic fixed his fiery eyes on the speaker and snapped "Shut up. He might hear you. Now rub his hands and talk to him!" The medic definitely knew what he was doing.

So we all obediently began to rub Skippy and tell him he was going to be okay. I couldn't help noticing how half of the brain was gone and half of the body squirmed while the other half lay peaceful and still. His hand lay in mine trustingly. Guilt came over me because I was thinking like a doctor or someone detached from it all. No feeling. Just abstract. By now I had blood all over my hands and on my pants and I felt . . . nothing. Angry with myself for feeling nothing at all. Absolutely nothing.

*   *   *

Twenty-three years later in Washington, D.C., I placed a small white flower at section E-28 where Skippy's name is inscribed. Standing beside the Wall that rainy night, I cried, I trembled, and finally, I *felt*.

Later still, I read that psychologists discovered that the first reaction of men in combat to the wounding or death of another is . . . *joy*. We humans can't avoid the selfishness; "It wasn't me!"

SALT

We beached two boats and went into a village where the main industry was dehydrating saltwater to obtain salt. Travis was with two of his crew and I had Tex and Kelley with me. We left the rest of our crews on our two boats. Little children scrambled about covered with salt crystals. Their work in the salt flats left their skin dry and cracked. We hiked about ten minutes and soon stood in front of a large cement building covered with graffiti. It said "Die Americans!" and showed our aircraft being shot down, American soldiers laying wounded and dying, lots of blood and flames. It showed V.C. shooting westerners who held their arms above their heads. "SAT" was written across the building too.

The six of us stood looking at the artwork that forecast, or at least hoped, for our death. An old Viet lady sat in the shade of a nearby hooch. She seemed to be the only person in town. Travis asked the old girl if she knew who had painted the mural. The toothless hag indicated that she had never seen it before. Christ. She lived ten meters from the damned thing.

The war was so insane. V.C., friendlies, they were all alike. Only Tex was smart enough to realize that this town would be a very appropriate place for us to get shot. The other five of us just stood solemnly and stared at the painted war scene. The Viet Cong artist had been remarkably skilled. He had lots of detail. You could even tell that the aircraft was a U.S. Air Force Phantom II.

Briefly we talked about painting over it, but that would have involved getting brushes and paint and returning. It wasn't worth the work.

I was sorry I didn't have a camera. It would have made a good photo. All of us Swifties with our M-16s and grenades grinning in front of a "Die America" mural. "SAT" (Vietnamese for "kill") in big red letters before an American flag.

The artist showed dead American soldiers and U.S. aircraft falling out of the sky in flames. He showed victorious V.C. conquering the hated enemy.

He didn't paint a single sinking Swift boat. He didn't include us. That disappointed me.

SANCHO PANZA

The round that went through the kidneys of Sancho Panza's gunner looked like one from an AK-47. It was just a small, deformed piece of lead and steel. The point was flattened. After going through flesh, it hit the pilothouse and Sancho picked it up.

Later, when his boat docked alongside the L.S.T. mother ship, he carried the bullet that killed his man up the ladder with him. He was making funny sounds when he breathed. No tears, just little squeaky whispers as he rapidly breathed in and out. He sat down at the table where eight of us were off duty and waiting for lunch. Obviously, Sancho had not yet done the paperwork on this "incident." In his action report, he would have to explain how he lost his crewman. I felt sorry for Sancho. He was a good person. A teddy bear with a British-freckles complexion that didn't do well in the sun of the Mekong. Today he somehow looked *little*. He and his crew had been in-country only a month; my crew and I had been in-country 16 weeks. He was a "new kid"; I was becoming an old man in every sense of the word. When he talked about what had happened, he was also trying to create a story that was defensible. But I didn't concur with what he was saying.

I could tell from what he *wasn't* saying that, in my opinion, he had been aggressive. He had been close to a notoriously hot riverbank. One that was dangerous to patrol alone. Some would say Sancho was courageous, which is what a warrior should be. But I felt that if you lose a guy, then it isn't commendable. It is simply tragic.

Suddenly I began to realize I was now thinking *exactly* like the idiot Rocky, squadron C.O. in Cat Lo. Sancho might be right and I wrong. I was now what I had hated only months before. I was just trying to minimize loss—not win. Angry and cynical, not leading. Tired and beaten, just like Rocky. Just like the stupidest officer I had ever served under.

But that's not the point. What bothered me was that Sancho sat at the table with us on the mother ship and he kept picking up the round and dropping it. He'd pick it up about three inches and drop it on the table. He just kept picking it up and dropping the bullet on its flat point while he was breathing fast and shallow and his eyes were misty. No tears though. The rest of us were silent. We just watched as he would drop the round and then spin it around on the table. Then he would pick up that tiny piece of metal in his big fingers and drop it again. Over and over.

Some people told him to eat his sandwich and some told him to go lay down. I wasn't sure I could eat my meal with his goddamned playing around with that bullet with no point. I wanted to tell him to throw the thing in the garbage but that seemed sacrilegious. He should at least have put it in his pocket. Two ridiculous thoughts went through my mind. First that he should save the bullet as "evidence" and next that he should send it back stateside to the kid's parents or to his girlfriend. I have no idea what caused me to think such curious thoughts at the time. Maybe it was the goofy situation that caused some random electrons in my brain to fire off in an odd direction. Anyway, his dropping the piece of steel and lead—thunk, thunk, thunk— bothered me.

Another thing bothered me: Sancho's watchband. It was a brown shiny leather watchband. The main feature was that it had a cover that fit over the face of the watch with a black snap at each end. The glass was covered so it wouldn't reflect. So the moonlight would not bounce off the face and the illuminated hands would not shine. But every time he opened it, the snaps made a "click" sound. I wouldn't wear such a noisy watchband, not on a night ambush or anyplace. I wanted to tell him that, but I wasn't sure it was appropriate. He had enough on his mind at the time.

I also wanted to tell him that being "aggressive" wasn't good. Every time we lost an American KIA, it got on TV and in the papers and the people in that kid's hometown would ask themselves if the war was worth it. Jane Fonda and her type would hammer away at it, and America would become just a little more alienated from the war.

Our objective should be, like Mao's *Little Red Book* recommended, to attack only when we had the advantage. To retreat when we did not. To *never* trade an American trooper for a V.C. Giving a pawn for a pawn strengthened the relative position of the enemy and weakened ours. Hell, I wasn't sure it was worth trading 1 American for 100 V.C., but on this tour I'd been in-country for several months. Okay, trade one for ten.

The point is, by trading one for one, we lose. But it wasn't the appropriate time to discuss that either.

I never pointed out to Sancho my grand strategy of how to fight the war by Chairman Mao's own advice. I did not tell him his watchband was ugly and noisy and dangerous to wear. I remember him picking up that goddamned pointless bullet and dropping it a hundred times. What I do not remember is the name of the good-looking blonde boy who was pointlessly killed in action that sunny afternoon.

TRASHBERRIES

At about this time, there was a Lil' Abner comic strip that we adopted as a Swift mascot:

One cartoon character said, "Trashberries is poisonous out of season."

A second hillbilly replied, "Trashberries is poisonous in season."

To which the first responded, "Can't be too careful wif trashberries!"

For the next month or two, a large portion of our discussion, whether about V.C., mortars, river runs, or anything, would end with the phrase, "Can't be too careful wif' trashberries!"

OSCELOT 39

I was just back from patrol. Oscelot approached me and led me away from the wardroom. "I'm going out in an hour; I need your gunner."

"Goddamn it, find someone else."

"No, I need *your* gunner, Sweet Pea."

"Look, Oscelot, Jake is tired. There is no reason to take him. What's wrong with your gunner?"

"He needs a rest."

"He needs a rest. We *all* need a rest."

He stood silently. His eyes told me there was more to the story. But I wasn't giving in. When new Marine officers get their commission they are told five words: "Take care of your men." I regretted the Navy did not have the same tradition.

But he didn't move. He didn't speak. He just looked at me.

"Oscelot, what's really going on?"

In a voice almost too soft to hear, he said: "We lost Skippy. It was an accident. My gunner needs a day to rest, to think it through. If not, I'm afraid he will kill himself."

"Christ."

Oscelot answered with his eyes as much as his soft voice, "Don't ask."

And so, my gunner, Jake, went out as a replacement that day. Probably wondering why officers make such curious decisions. And Oscelot's gunner . . . well, he became the best goddamn enlisted guy in the division. A bit quiet, but *very, very* good.

And Oscelot, years later, rose *very* high in government. I couldn't think of a better man for the job.

GETTING INTO
INDIAN COUNTRY

One day after lunch and the movie, we six Swift skippers who were not on patrol just sat in the wardroom of the L.S.T talking. Ordinarily we would break into small groups and read, or chat, but most guys just went back to bed. Twenty-four hours on duty left a person weary once he was back in a safe haven like the T.

All six of us chatted about life and death and how we all got there. One guy said that in Europe, he fell off a big rock face. On the way down, plummeting through the air, he had just one thought: "Suzy Farber was a bum fuck." That was it. His last mortal thought. Then he miraculously landed in a fig tree at the bottom of the cliff. He was almost totally unscathed, but tore the hell out of the tree.

Fox roared in delight, "God almighty, your last thought as you were about to die was about your *worst* fuck! Oh man that is great. You should tell her!"

Needless to say, that advice probably went unheeded. Yet we could all appreciate the existentialist humor of the delicate incident. I was still reading Plato. Urged not to take the poison, Plato said in effect that he couldn't argue for life because he was ignorant of the reality of the alternative: death. That seemed logical. Miss Suzy Farber made dying funny. Plato made it a learning experience.

I commented that after the Battle of Austerlitz, Napolean allegedly said, "It amazes me what men will do for little pieces of ribbon." All of us were slowly acquiring medals and ribbons; we grinned at Napoleon's remark.

Hank told about how the Viet geese and ducks were good at sounding the alarm if an intruder came. Viet dogs barked, but the geese and ducks were better; they would give you away if you tried to approach a sleeping village. None of us could think of a way to put this novel fact into a moneymaking concept for the U.S., so we moved on.

Why did we volunteer? One guy said it was impossible not to do so. He had broken his right wrist, shattered his left elbow, broken off six teeth, busted his nose, broken two toes, and had a tooth hole in his hand from a fight. All before he was 16. How could he not go on looking for excitement?

In a crazy way, it made sense. The best volunteers were people who had accumulated experience of doing odd things. Exciting, wild, dumb things. War is exactly that. Give me people who are bored with routine, normal life.

We marveled at the losses of prior wars. Twenty million Russians in World War II. Our own Civil War chewed up half a million. That's right. The Civil War inflicted ten times the casualties and our country was only one-tenth the size in population. In other words, it was like *one hundred* Vietnams. Three or four major battles like Shiloh and Gettysburg and Antietam each accounted for almost as many men as America had lost in Vietnam. By those standards, we had it easy.

Buster said that to incapacitate medieval archers who were captured, the enemy cut off their bow fingers. So to show your enemy that you could fight, you held up your middle finger. That gesture of contempt continues today.

I told an old Japanese story about a man who was chased by a tiger. He climbed over a cliff and hung by a vine to avoid it. A few minutes later, a second tiger appeared at the bottom of the cliff. Just then, a mouse came out of a hole in the cliff and began chewing on the vine. With the mouse chewing away his handhold and a tiger above and a tiger below, the man trembled. But then he saw a strawberry nearby. He reached over and picked it. It was *the* most delicious berry he had ever eaten!

Badger said when he was ambushed a week earlier, he watched the bullets coming at him and said to himself, "You're dead." That was succinct.

I said that in the book *The Man in the Gray Flannel Suit,* the protagonist tells himself, as he is about to parachute over Germany, "This should be interesting." One of my own experiences had been similar. On an icy highway two years before, my car began spinning lazy circles as it sped toward a bridge embankment. My thought was a casual one: "Oh, so *this* is how I die."

The question was why we were in Vietnam. Not why America was here, but why we as men were here.

I thought of my strawberry story. How it paralleled my dad's asking the guy beside him as the boat approached Normandy, "Wanna cookie?"

And so we continued to beat the horse until it was no longer quick. Then Oscelot said laconically, "We are all somewhere between Calvin, Christ, and lizards."

*   *   *

It was at about this time that the V.C. got an improved version of the rocket-propelled grenade. The B-41. It had three times the range of the old one.

R & R

Rest and relaxation. We were each entitled to a week of R & R during our year-long tour. It was based on seniority, time in-country. So if you wanted to go early you had to go to an unpopular spot like Kuala Lempur or dull Singapore. If you were willing to wait and go after mid-tour, you could go to Hong Kong. The married guys met their wives in Honolulu at about the six-month mark. Sydney was considered the best. I hoped to go to Australia.

The stories coming back from down under were fantastic. One skipper was taken to a ranch house deep into the bush. The rancher had two beautiful daughters and . . . . The story was like the classic "Farmer's Daughter" joke. Another guy just walked into a bar and bought a girl a drink. When he asked if she wanted another, she said, "Why don't you just buy a bottle of wine and let's go to your room."

It was all hard to believe, but everyone coming back from Australia told a similar story. Compared to that country, America was still surprisingly puritan.

But to me there was a bigger question. I was fascinated by how few Americans tried to avoid coming back. It had to have crossed everyone's minds, yet each year half a million guys went to a safe haven and then a week later, half a million voluntarily came right back to Vietnam. They didn't try to run or hide, they just did it.

I understood their behavior, but just partially. It made me think about Highway 101 and wonder where Victoria was. She hadn't written.

TRANSMISSION PROBLEMS

We were on patrol off a hot coast. It was full of V.C. and consequently it was designated as a free-fire area. We stayed out of small arms range; there was nothing that we could see to attack.

Surprisingly quickly, an Army helo came from nowhere and hovered in front of our bow. The radio came alive, "Navy Boat this is Bull Rider; I am having transmission problems."

I could almost look in the pilot's eyes. I picked up our mike and responded, "That is negative, I hear you Lima Charlie." ("Lima" is the phonetic word for the letter "L" and "Charlie" corresponds to "C." I had told him that I could hear his radio transmission "L.C." e.g. loud and clear.) His angry voice came back with assorted obscenities. The helo began to make odd noises. It went down in front of us with a splash.

We looked at the bird as it settled into the water and watched the crew toss off helmets and open doors and windows. The rotor splashed the water and then stopped spinning. We crept forward and a couple of my men jumped into the water carrying life vests. When we got the crew of three aboard, the pilot continued cursing. I explained that there was no reason why I would have known that a goddamned helicopter had a transmission like in a car. Hell, prop and jet aircraft don't.

Finally he cooled down enough to thank us. If his crew had been forced to swim ashore, the V.C. would have greased them before they stood up on the beach. Later I realized the poor guy was just scared and confused. Men who are scared and confused often show the only emotion left: anger. If he had been cool about it, he could have just said, "Little Navy Boat, pick us up when we crash in front of you." That's a clear order. I didn't give a rat's ass what part of his goddamned Huey wasn't working; I couldn't fix it, for Chrissake.

Anyway, he cooled off and by the time we got him back to base he was very, very nice to us. Perhaps he realized that when he wrote his after action report he would have to mention the 97 boat. Once he did that, there was a chance I would be asked to describe how the Army had lost a million-dollar helicopter in a sister report. Maybe he realized that if he pissed us off, we would say the idiot was flying badly and just crashed, that from where we were, it looked like pilot error.

That is really too cynical, but the truth is that the after action reports are read by clowns in Saigon or Washington, D.C. They can't help you. An admiral at a desk can't pull your wet, frightened ass out of the water.

ANTIGONE

Athens

As the war dragged on, I became obsessed with Vietnam's parallel to a typical Greek tragedy. Those dramatists of twenty-four hundred years before often set the conclusion before the play ran its course. On the "T," I read the play *Antigone*. A beautiful young virgin's brother is killed on the battlefield. The victorious enemy king orders that, on punishment of death, all such bodies of his foes must remain unburied. Antigone has a heart-wrenching choice. She could properly bury the decaying body of her beloved brother so that he may go to meet the gods, or leave him to rot on the battlefield. She knew that she would be executed by the victorious king if she dug her brother's grave.

Once in-country, we were all like Antigone. The play would end as a tragedy. There was nothing we mortals could do. A chorus of protesters stood on our stages in America chanting. They told us of insight, of betrayal. They also warned of danger. But as in the Greek theater, none of the principal actors listened to the chorus. Few acknowledged their presence. The doom foretold comes on. Unabated. The gods had so willed it long ago.

Washington, D.C.

Another chorus: "We can't pull out of Vietnam. We've lost 20,000," it said.

"We can't pull out of Vietnam, we've lost 30,000," it said only a few months later.

"We can't pull out of Vietnam, we've lost 40,000," it repeated in 1969.

Years later, in graduate school, I learned that businessmen have a name for that concept. It is called "sunk cost." Today's decision should be based on how it will impact the future. That's what they teach in business schools. In short, the past does not matter; it is a sunk cost. Act on how you can best influence the future. Good decisions are made *only* on the basis of going forward.

In 1969, I didn't know about the concept of sunk costs, but our Secretary of Defense, Robert McNamara, had gone to Harvard Business School. He had been a "Whiz Kid" at Ford Motor Company. Really, that's what they called him. He should have heard the term. He ran the war effort; he advised President Johnson.

I wasn't a whiz kid; I was just a lieutenant junior grade. I was just a girl, Antigone, looking at corpses rotting in the sun.

O DARK THIRTY

My eyes open fast. Instant alert. Ready, but it is still pitch dark. It takes a while for my heart to slow down and for my body to relax. Feeling stupid. Afraid. Ashamed of being afraid. I focus on my watch: 0240. Not even 3 a.m. yet and I'm wide-awake and in my bunk on the T. In a real bed. The comfort of the engine's sounds in the officers' bunkroom. Too dark to tell who's in and who's out. Probably only two or three other Swift skippers in their racks. I'm awake. Not hungry, not hot, not thirsty. Don't have to pee, but the sweat around my olive drab T-shirt smells like urine. A night of sweating and it isn't even that hot. My skivvies are also wet with sweat. Cold too. My watchband stinks. We never take off our watch—it takes too long to put it back on if you have to scramble.

I stare at the pipes overhead in the cabin for a few minutes before I realize I'm swallowing blood. Not much. Just a little of the sickening sweet smell of blood in my mouth. The inside of my cheek is raw. I've been chewing it again. Lately, when I'm scared, I find myself chewing on the inside of my cheek. I don't *feel* emotions. I *detect* them from effects, like finding I've chewed into my cheeks from the inside. Both sides are raw now. This is the first time I've come awake with blood in my mouth. Jesus. I'm wearing down. I'm even scared just sleeping on the T.

Some days, I resign myself to the fact that I'm already dead. Then some days I forget and assume I'll make it back. That must be normal. No one *really* believes he's going to die—at least not for very long.

So anyway, I keep still in the bed and I'm embarrassed that I'm so goddamned scared and then I think, "So how are you going to get out of this?" And then it comes:

Get shot.

The answer is easy. I'll take a round.

But where? The guys who have been shot say it's like getting hit with a hot snowball.

So where do I want an AK-47 round to poke a hole in me?

I do a survey. Not a shot in the head. No way will I become an instant idiot. Not like that SEAL back at the Amphibious Base at Coronado. I don't want a sucking chest wound, not a hole through the lung. Frothy, bubbly blood out of the mouth, or out of the nose, or out of that hole in the chest.

Once as a kid I shot a deer in the rump with a 270 rifle; the bullet did not penetrate. It just exploded on impact. It blew a huge chunk of flesh out of the deer's hindquarter. Like a giant bear had bitten it. The deer bled to death. I don't want to get shot in the butt.

Gut shots aren't any better. Take one in the leg and be crippled? Lose an arm's motion? So I lay on my bed trying to think of just one place I'd be willing to be shot. I can't find a single goddamned spot.

High-speed bullets tumble inside flesh. They also ricochet; entry hole in the side and the bullet could stop anywhere. Turn left or right, up to the neck or down to the butt.

When you shoot a big animal or a person from a distance, the sound of the bullet hitting is like hearing someone kick a watermelon. I don't want to hear that sound from my body. So getting shot is not the answer.

Could I get out by asking for a mental? Sure. I can tell Lang I am about to crack. That I need some quiet time. He will give me a couple of days off. So what? I would just have to make up the missed patrols later. The downside is that everyone will know. A nut case? No way.

So getting shot and going goofy are not acceptable. Then I think that the only way out is to be a woman. I grin. That's it! You don't have to go back out on patrol if you are a woman. Hell, I wouldn't even be in-country. I'd be back in some college right now. I'd be a good-looking coed with a light course load. Brit Lit or something. I'd be reading books and listening to Joan Baez and I'd be concerned about some goddamned cause or something.

This is fun. I'm imagining being a woman. Lipstick and dresses. That would be interesting. But hell, I don't even know how to walk in high heels or act or talk or sit like a woman. No. That's not logical. If I were a woman I wouldn't know how to act like a man. Just once it would be amazing to know what sex is like from the other side.

If I were a woman, would I look like Joan Baez? That would be nice, but life on campus would be so, so insignificant. Reading Hardy would bore me to death. Sure it would be fun to feel . . . really *feel* what it's like to be a woman. But Christ, to have to read *Jude the Obscure*? It would drive me crazy.

Then I turn it around in my mind again. No, it wouldn't drive *me* crazy because if I'm a woman, I'm not me. I can't say if I were born a girl I'd be bored by Brit Lit and volunteer for a combat nurse job, because "I" wouldn't know what "I" was. It is incomprehensible. So there are three ways to get out: get shot and get medivaced, go soft in the head, or to have been born a girl 25 years ago.

I grin at the ceiling. I'm not afraid anymore. I'm relaxed. It's been fun playing a mind game that took me away. My watch shines 0325. For 45 minutes I was awake. For half of that I imagined being safe in a campus back in the land of the round eyes. One big breath. One big sigh and I roll over. Later, we patrol the "Rung Sat." The Vietnamese words mean "the forest of assassins." But that's still two hours away. I no longer taste blood. Lying on my stomach, I fall back asleep wondering what it would be like to lay on my own breasts. Even better, to sleep in a soft dry bed that smells good. A feather pillow would be nice.

RUNG SAT

The Rung Sat is a special part of the Delta. It is like the Everglades. Indian Country. Four hundred square miles of swamp with small rivers between the trees. Worthless and dangerous. As a result, the entire area was declared a "free-fire zone." In other words, *everything* in the Rung Sat was presumed hostile. No friendlies. We were supposed to fire at everything that moved.

It was a bright, sunny morning when my gunner manning the twin .50 calibers shouted down to me from the gun tub, "Skipper, we've got two bad guys in a sampan to starboard. Five hundred meters." I could see the small boat turn away from us and head up a thin tributary. We accelerated after them.

Again he shouted, "I got 'em skipper. They'll get away. In my sights. Permission to fire?"

"Hold."

By now our boat was closing. Roaring up the narrow river. No support. This was the classic "draw 'em into the ambush" technique and we were going right into it. A totally stupid move.

"Dung lai!" we shouted into the loud speakers. No response— the little sampan continued deeper upriver. Both figures hunched over.

Thompsen looked at me with the silent quizzical look enlisted men give officers who are doing something dangerously stupid. I was risking six young men in my crew following a boat into a trap and I did not have an explanation. The correct thing to do would be to say, "Fire at will." Blast the fleeing Viets apart and go no further. I didn't give that order. I knew that if we got ambushed in this situation, and if I lived, I'd be court-martialed.

By now we were next to the boat. They stopped. We stopped. I jumped onto the boat while Kid covered me with an M-16. I grabbed the Viet at the helm, and picked him up by the back of the pajamas with my left hand. The .38 in my right hand was aimed at his belly. Magically, he almost flew into the air. The combination of no weight plus my adrenaline rocketed the little body upward and around.

I found myself looking into two *huge* eyes and a tiny face. A girl of no more than 12 looked at me as if I were truly the devil. She expected me to kill her.

Partly out of shock, I dropped her back down into the sampan and turned to the other one. He was humped over hiding something. "So this is how I will die," flashed through my mind. Perhaps exactly the same words the little girl was thinking. I reached down for the second person. This time absolutely certain the V.C. would turn and shoot me. Oddly I didn't care. Numb curiosity.

The second body floated upward almost as fast as the first. Weightless. I jerked it around and as the yellow straw hat fell to the bottom of the boat, I stared into a face from hell.

No nose, just a hole. Teeth forming a hideous grin. Lipless. Earless. No fingers. He was a leper whose disease had progressed far beyond any I had ever seen. Most die of respiratory infection before the flesh death proceeds this far. A toeless gnarled foot extended from the pajamas and one hand, if a hand without fingers can be called a hand, fumbled to reach for the fallen hat.

My knees weakened, my hand recoiled. I climbed back into my boat. "Give the girl a few boxes of Cs, Kid, and anything else we have. Jesus Christ!"

I went into the cabin, and proceeded to scrub my hands with soap as thoroughly as possible. Thoughtfully, deliberately washing away the leper and asking *why?* Why didn't I give the order that would have killed that little girl and her leper father? No answer. Luck from the gods. Not judgment.

I had refused to give the "correct" order to fire.

*   *   *

Fifteen years later I was watching my own son at play. He had just gotten a new Mario Brothers Game Boy. The object of the handheld game was bizarre. The little firemen characters ran around below a burning building with a safety net. The player manipulated the firemen to catch the people as they jumped from the windows of the burning building. The building's inhabitants jumped one after another. Faster, faster. Until sooner or later the player made a mistake and a victim would miss the firemen's net and hit the ground.

As my little boy played intently, I realized that his game was closer to the world of combat than anything I had practiced at Annapolis. Decisions come upon a person faster and faster. Overload is inevitable. Sooner or later you blow it, and sadly that one bad decision eclipses all of the previous good decisions. Every person I knew in-country eventually made a stupid, tragic, mistake one day. Happily for a leper and a little girl, this was not that day. Sunny, strange, lucky morning.

PIEDMONT

In the movie of Somerset Maugham's novel, *The Razor's Edge*, there is a grizzled battle-weary sergeant named Piedmont. He drove an ambulance in WWI. Whenever a soldier died, Piedmont simply stated: "He will not be missed." At first, such a statement shocked the other soldiers; later they too brushed death off with the same curt statement.

Elizabeth Kubler-Ross wrote that, upon experiencing death, we go through six emotional stages: denial, bargaining, anger, depression, fear, and acceptance. In Piedmont's case, he was so hardened that each death was accepted. Numbness. Nothing in between. Or so it seemed. In truth, he was a caring and sensitive old man. There just wasn't time to process all of the emotion. The losses came cascading one after another. So it is in combat; a person is still trying to make sense of one death when the next comes along. Denial, bargaining, anger all get mixed together. Death of others, fear of dying yourself, and acceptance. It is all a big emotional stew. It would be overwhelming were it not for another factor: weariness. Lack of sleep over a period of weeks and months is very helpful. Like tossing bread into the spicy stew, it softened it all. It de-presses it all. It doesn't matter if you get hurt on a Monday or on a Saturday. Very little matters if you are tired enough. It is almost like a narcotic.

Later I read that in scientific studies, safety experts found that people who drive exhausting hours also cannot properly process danger. As their car goes off the road they look at it all abstractly, as if it isn't really personal danger to them. Not real, not imminent.

Today, my emotions still seem embarrassingly incorrect. When people die, including my close friends, I have little sympathy. I know that I should cry; that would be the proper thing to do.

Instead, I am embarrassed at being dry-eyed and feeling nothing. Yet I often cry while watching movies or while reading books. Odd.

There is a similarly curious theme in the novel *Lord Jim* by Conrad. In that case, the inappropriate behavior is bravery, not sympathy. In the book, Jim imagines that the ship's hull will burst apart and that the ship will sink; he then jumps in a life boat and abandons the passengers. The ship does not sink and for the next several years Jim believes—no, he now *knows*—that he is a coward. Later, in another situation, he is sentenced to be executed. He willingly volunteers to die even though he is not at fault. He is given the opportunity to escape and live, yet he walks of his own free will to his death. The odd thing is that Jim's earlier fear, through imagination, was profound. Yet his triumph over real and present danger was total.

Having inappropriate feelings is bothersome. Improper sympathy. Inappropriate bravery. Emotions, strong where they are undeserved, lacking in other situations where it would be correct. Perhaps all humans occasionally get out-of-sync on such things; perhaps war just causes men to be a little further off track.

Later in the movie, Piedmont is also killed. It does not matter. He will not be missed.

IF I DIE IN THE COMBAT ZONE

If I die in the combat zone, box me up and ship me home.

That was what the Greek chorus chanted repeatedly in August. We had a new kid KIA. They put him in a body bag and laid it on the deck of the T. Right at the entrance to the wardroom. To go in or out you had to step around him.

At first people would stop with reverence and step carefully around the body. Later they just stepped over it.

Normally the Navy puts cadavers in the meat locker with the food to keep them cool until they can be removed. We had called for a helo to get the kid out, but things were hot, so the helos were busy on shore with medevacs and firefights. Removing bodies is low on the priority. Apparently the L.S.T crew thought a Huey would arrive any minute, so they just left the zippered rubber bag on the deck. Chopper time is valuable.

So we stepped over the thing for about six hours. You could see in that short time the psychological change of the living. They went from shock and reverence to indifference and finally irritation. We didn't want reminders lying around. All in six hours. From a person, to a body, to a cadaver, to "it." Just six.

Later I had a squadron skipper who was a nice, caring guy. That was his trouble. The war was *really* hard on him. Being too human is a very dangerous weakness. His problem was that he went to Harvard and was not good at forgetting.

HE DOESN'T HAVE SENSE ENOUGH TO POUND SAND DOWN A RAT HOLE

When I was a teenager, I had a job unloading trucks. I worked with a man who was slightly crazy. Tom would tell me things like:

"General Grant liked apple pie, but Thomas Jefferson liked Budweiser even more."

"General Sherman's parents were so poor they had to give him away."

It was always a pleasant surprise to hear what Tom had to say. It was even nicer to learn that some of his facts were accurate. Later I read that little "Cump" Sherman was, in fact, given to the local banker to raise because his own folks were too poor to feed their kids. The local banker helped William Tecumseh Sherman get an appointment to West Point. "Cump" even married the banker's daughter. Jefferson didn't drink Budweiser, but he did brew his own beer. As for Grant, I assume he liked apple pie; if Tom said he did, who was I to disagree?

As I tried to think about preparing young men for combat, I occasionally wondered about the curriculum. Perhaps working with a crazy guy isn't such bad preparation after all.

Actually, it wasn't significantly different from my first tour. On the Jarvits we received $65.00 a month for combat pay. One day, Warrant Officer Bearton computed that we were being shot at an average of 13 times a month. Warrant Bearton was amused, that the pay computed to $5.00 for every time we got shot at. He asked rhetorically what the average person in America would insist on receiving if a rifleman were to ask them to stand across the street and allow him to shoot at them. Instead of rifles, how about heavy artillery? The consensus was that $5.00 seemed somewhat low. Of course, that was assuming that the willing target was mentally sane.

Occasionally Thompsen would curse, "He doesn't have sense enough to pound sand in a rat hole." I liked that phrase. For a split second, the person hearing it says to himself, "Gosh, *I've* never pounded sand in a rat hole; am I okay?"

Six months before, upon our arrival in-country, we were shocked to see body bags out in the sun at Ton San Nhut Airport. Our new crew had to walk through them. Five minutes in-country, and that was our introduction. At the time, I thought it was crazy. With further reflection, I realized that it might have been a *brilliant* welcome. It sure as hell reminded us to be careful.

We were doing so many night ambushes that I decided to quit smoking. A glowing cigarette can be seen almost a quarter of a mile in the dark, so smoking on ambush was not, repeat *not*, a good idea. As long as I was going 12 hours without a cigarette, this seemed to be an appropriate time to quit. Smoking shortened your life.

Of course, other things shorten your life too. In the rivers, once our mind/body had reached a certain level of adrenaline, it was uncomfortable to go higher, but equally uncomfortable to go lower. If things were too hot for too long, we would turn off our radios and just slack off. We would beach at a tiny offshore deserted island and have a picnic.

Conversely, if it were quiet for too long, we would literally go looking for trouble. Even senior officers did the same. Once on the Jarvits a year earlier, we had a very quiet week. To balance it, the captain brought the ship in very close to an area by Vinh where we usually received a meaningful amount of fire. Then he did something truly wild. He took our destroyer between the mainland and an island. We could have tossed a baseball ashore. The astonished North Vietnamese didn't fire a single shot at us. The crew was delighted, they grinned from ear to ear. It was necessary for us to keep the adrenaline balance.

So why did we enjoy taking unnecessary chances? Thompsen would say it was because we didn't have sense enough to pound sand down a rat hole.

LETTERS

Mom

A letter arrived from my mother, long divorced from my dad. I was eager to get some news. Good thoughts of Nebraska. Instead, the letter told me that she was ill. That she was struggling for money, that her life was difficult. Hell, I didn't want to read that kind of stuff. I had enough problems of my own. There was nothing that I could do to make her better. She had caused her own problems. Didn't she understand that I didn't have sympathy for her? I was getting shot at, for Chrissake. I was sick, tired, scared and weary. *Her* job was to cheer *me* up. Not the other way around.

So I told her not to write again.

She didn't.

Dad

When they were married during World War II, no matter how bad things were, Dad wrote to Mom "I never had it so good." I thought I should do the same. Dad's infrequent letters were upbeat and happy so I wrote back that everything was lovely. I told him that it was totally quiet in the Mekong River Delta.

He had a TV. He knew I was lying.

My Crew

Two members of my crew were married. The letters from the wife of one were not always good. There was nothing I could do. If the Navy wanted him to have a wife, they would have issued him one in his sea-bag. Tex subscribed to the *Congressional Record*. He read it with care. Our elected officials said some amazingly stupid things about the war. On the record. Literally.

Official

Meanwhile Armed Forces Radio and *The Stars and Stripes* newspaper told only light happy stories that hardly qualified as news. Childishly simple stories only.

In Short

I lied to my dad, a wife lied to one of my men, America's congress lied to all of us, and *The Stars and Stripes* avoided it all by saying nothing important—just baseball scores.

Only my mom told the truth.

ODE TO BOBBY MAC

We had fired so many rounds through the twin .50's that we had to replace both barrels. The inside bore had been worn away so badly that the rounds didn't fire with the velocity that they needed. The guns jammed too much. Gas was blowing by the bullet's sides instead of pushing each projectile from behind. It wasn't a big deal; I had experience in these things. I studied "blow-by" when I was in seventh grade.

Bobby Mac was my best friend when I was a kid growing up on the prairie. Like me, he lived on a ranch. He lived with his mom, Ann, who was a tall redhead, and his stepfather. Bobby Mac had a stepfather because his dad was killed over Germany flying a B-24. Everyone in America saw Bobby Mac's dad get killed.

A German fighter sawed the right wing off the American bomber. The photo of a plane in flames going down was in *Life* magazine. The plane was at the bottom of the photo and the detached wing was falling above it. Like a leaf. It was and still is, one of the most amazing war photos ever taken. I couldn't take my eyes off it, wondering what that last minute of freefall was like.

Perhaps because of his father, Ann treated Bobby Mac very well. He had more toys than I did. He was a genius too. When we were 12 he went into Peters Hardware in Valentine and asked to buy pistol powder. (It is stronger than gunpowder.) Mr. Peters wisely refused. But that didn't stop us. A week later Bobby Mac made an astonishing discovery: he found a 500-year-old Chinese recipe for gunpowder in some obscure book. We made a cannon by crimping shut one end of an aluminum tube and drilling a tiny bunghole one inch from the crimped end. We filled the silver tube with about two inches of our homemade powder and then rolled a big marble down the barrel. We touched a match to the bunghole and the cannon shot the marble into the side of the barn. We were delighted, but after a few firings, we concluded that the marble was slightly too small. It needed to fit more snugly to prevent blow-by.

So we coated the marble with a thin layer of paraffin. Performance of our cannon improved dramatically. But on the third shot using paraffin, the cannon exploded in a truly dramatic way. Pieces of aluminum went in every direction, some embedding themselves a full inch into surrounding buildings. We stood with our little mouths agape. All of the shrapnel had missed us. Neither of us was scratched. Neither of us could hear. We grinned at each other for a full minute. It was exhilaration that was indescribable. In that moment we were brothers. We were superior to every other boy in the world. A macho high. We were 12 years old and he and I could fire a marble (bigger than any existing military rifle bullet) through a barn, through a German Messerschmidt, or even deeply into a buffalo! It was totally our invention. Our secret made us powerful, confident, proud, and invincible.

Five years later Bobby Mac went to Harvard. Some time after graduation, he got in his car, closed the garage door, and killed himself.

I didn't mention that Bobby Mac had a huge purple birthmark that covered half of his face. It made no difference to me as a kid. I'm sure it made a big difference to my best friend.

The irony wasn't lost on me. He went to Harvard and he was dead. I had now spent a year and a half in Vietnam and all I had lost were two toenails to jungle rot.

Bobby Mac would have made a great Swift boat skipper. He had a lot of experience in ordnance. More importantly, he would also have thought of some different way to fight this war. He was a tough little cowboy and a good shot.

I still miss him.

LUCK

When asked to name the single qualification for generals he considered most important, Napoleon responded, "I chose generals who are lucky."

I had a series of missions that were reasonably uneventful. Luck did not seem to be distributed equitably. Hank took a B-40 through the hull. It exploded in the main cabin blowing all the windows out of the boat and making the aluminum hull more rounded in appearance. Hank and his crew were unharmed. They managed to put a wooden patch on the six-inch hole and return to the T where shipfitters sealed the hull.

Two days later, he was back on patrol. Hank was eager to share a quote that he had heard earlier that morning: "We the unwilling led by the unknowing do the necessary for the ungrateful." He thought it was a funny quote, and was fond of repeating it. I thought of the rocket hit and wasn't amused. Perhaps we were "doing the unnecessary for the ungrateful."

Oh well, we were lucky that there wasn't quite as much vegetation on the riverbanks as there had been before. Thank God for Agent Orange.

DESERTION

After my second tour of four weeks "on the T" it was time to again cycle back to our lovely home, the mud flat, Cat Lo. It was a 100-mile trip. We arrived at mid-afternoon. It was a beautiful day.

I walked to the quonset without seeing any Swifties I recognized. Just new kids. As I entered the Cat House Bar I was surprised to see how small it seemed. It was also cleaner than I had ever remembered it. Sunshine beamed through the window onto the red fire extinguisher that Rocky had used to kill the cobra.

Upon passing through the bulkhead to the bunkhouse end of the quonset, I had the happy feeling of being home. With a devil-may-care attitude I tossed my gear onto the "sniper bunk." It seemed the nicest; bright sunlight beamed through the window onto the empty bed.

From the back, Anderson entered. He had just come from the latrine. He gave me a big warm smile and welcomed me back asking about news from the south. He mentioned something about "slicks."

Half listening, I found my mind wandering. Words linked with one another and for some odd reason I was thinking of dancing, slow easy dancing, with a girl. How your right hand rests on her rump. How some girls wore slips that moved against their bodies and their dresses. How it was "slick."

After two-tracking the conversation for a couple of minutes, Anderson talked about Huey helicopters. The code for Hueys was "slicks" and I thought of firm butts of young women under smooth skirts: "slicks." I surprised myself by asking, literally out of nowhere, the question that amused me that night on the T, "Anderson what would your life have been like if you had been born a woman?"

He looked at me with big eyes and his mouth dropped open. Apparently the thought had never crossed his mind. "What?" he asked.

"Yeah, you know. Did you ever wonder about being born as a girl? Did you ever think, 'This macho shit is going to kill me?'"

Anderson grinned. It was starting to sink in. Then he grinned more. "Sweet Pea, you *are* crazy. Really crazy." His eyes went to the bunk I had selected upon my return. There was no reason for me to have picked the "sniper bunk," there were others vacant. I just did.

"Yeah," he said, "this macho shit is going to kill us." He slapped me on the back and walked away grinning. Halfway down the hall he turned back. "Oh, Lang wants to talk to you."

I went into Lang's office. As usual Rocky was gone. Pat Lang rose and gave me a warm handshake. After asking about life on the T, he dropped the bomb, "You and your crew are being sent to Cam Ranh."

I stared in disbelief. "Why?"

"Rocky wanted it."

"Pat, it doesn't make sense. I just finished two tours on the T. My crew has done a great job. I shouldn't be punished by being sent to Cam Ranh. What can I do? Can I talk to him or is he drunk?"

Pat looked at me sadly. The decision wasn't a logical one. It wasn't a good one, but it wouldn't have been a Rocky decision if it had.

I was sad, embarrassed, and angry. I was being ordered to leave the Black Cat Division. My home, my friends, and a territory I knew well. I was being transferred from COSDIV 13 to the next base north. Out of the Mekong to a base that was known to be safer, cleaner, better. With a real dining room and rumored to have real beds. I was mad as hell.

"Pat, how can you send a seasoned guy to a pansy-assed soft base? Send a new kid who doesn't know what he's doing. My crew can operate down here safely. We are in *much* less danger than a virgin crew." He shrugged. The decision had been made.

"How soon?" I asked.

"As soon as possible. Lifer is being ordered north too. Can you go tomorrow? They now want to cycle crews from base to base. Give everyone a chance to be in a hot area. Seasoned crews are supposed to get a rest in a less stressful base."

"It's a stupid policy. Once you know the Mekong you are like a street-smart cop. You are *much,* safer than when you first arrive. It's better to send new kids to a cushy slot."

"Probably. Gary, I'm sorry."

We shook hands; I walked out of the office and saw Kelley crossing the tiny dusty square. "Is it true?" he asked.

"It's true, we go tomorrow," I responded. Once again surprised that the enlisted intelligence network knew what was going on before I did. "Tell the rest of the crew," I said sadly.

I went back to the quonset and began unpacking my sea bag for the things I would need for one night only.

Anderson came in again. "So?"

"Yeah, the son of a bitch is sending us north. The guy hardly *knows* us."

"I know," Anderson said. He gave me a hug. "You know you are lucky to get out of this shithole."

"Damn it, Anderson, it isn't right," I said avoiding the obvious. "I want to stay with you guys. Cam Ranh is for pussies. This is where the 97 boat should stay."

Anderson wanted to end the conversation. He felt as badly as I did. He understood. Cat Lo was dirty, dangerous, and worthless. But in spite of that, we were still proud of ourselves. Actually, these factors *contributed* to our being proud. The Black Cats had a worthless C.O. so we ran the place by ourselves. Like kids with alcoholic parents, we were a level above our peers.

A tear ran down my cheek. I hoped Anderson wouldn't see it. I know he did. "Take care of yourself," I said. "Keep your head down."

He grinned. "No problem," he said. "Maybe you'll be back," and turned to walk away embarrassed at my sadness.

I sat down on "my" bunk. The sniper bunk. Twenty minutes

ago I was happy to be home. Now I was angry at being thrown out. Being part of Cat Lo's Division 13 was like being in absolute poverty with thoughtless and abusive parents. We brothers were all the more emotionally linked to one another. We cared for each other more than Oliver Twist and the Artful Dodger. It was the only life we knew in-country.

I resolved that I'd do everything I could to get out of cushy Cam Ranh and back to Cat Lo. They couldn't keep us up there for long. Cat Lo would have more casualties and we could come back as replacements. But until then, how could these guys get along without us? Without us, somebody here would get hurt.

I felt like a coward. I was betraying them all. It was desertion. No other word for it.

Desertion.

L.S.T.

PCF

After a minor recon mission
in a sampan

River Raider

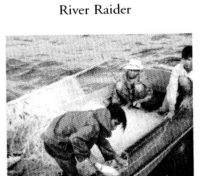

Fishermen

Medevac helo taking
wounded off the L.S.T.

Swift boat being repaired after
taking a B-40 rocket hit mid-ship

CAM RANH

*Though I could do a fair impersonation of a man who knew
his stuff, the act wouldn't hold up forever. One problem
was that I didn't quite believe in it myself. I was at a
distance, watching this outrageous fraud play . . . the
assassin . . . and in that widening distance between the
performance and the observation of the performance, there
grew, subtly at first, then intrusively, disbelief and
corrosive irony.*

*In time I lost whatever certitudes I'd had, but I didn't
replace them with new ones.*

In the Pharaoh's Army
Tobias Wolff

THE NEW KID
MEMORIAL LIBRARY

"What are they going to do to me, send me to Vietnam?"

The heart of the Cam Ranh Swift base was a bar. The door said:

New Kid Memorial Library
And Coffee Mess

Inside it was dark, no books, but certainly messy. Beer cans here and there, with a pool table with a torn green surface in the middle of the room surrounded by smaller card tables. A few broken chairs and a scuffed plywood bar. Like Cat Lo, the fridge had beer, and on occasion it was even cold. The bar functioned without a caretaker. One guy would drink a beer and actually pick up two empty cans. The next would drink three and put only one in the garbage. On occasion someone would restock the fridge or put the ashtray of money away. The floor was always sticky.

The barracks was a long two-story white frame building. Individual rooms. Real beds, not cots. Best of all: sheets.

A sweet little old lady named Ba Cuc kept the top floor and most of the lower floor tidy and spotless. Sensibly, she avoided the portion of the barracks that housed the "New Kid."

When I arrived, the only vacant room was directly above the New Kid bar. I expected that I would move to quieter quarters as soon as a better room was available. In fact, I stayed in the original room for the balance of my seven months left in-country. The reason was simple. When I returned from patrol I either joined the

247

party in the New Kid, or I was so tired I went straight to bed. In either case, the noise was not a bother.

The squadron skipper was good person. Competent, bright, and cheerful. He liked jokes and allowed his boat crews maximum flexibility. He understood. For example, on Christmas Day, no one really felt like patrolling. We tried to make holidays unimportant. To make them disappear. But 25 Dec was just too important. The boats went out, and then radioed back that the sea was dangerously rough and that they were coming back. The skipper looked out at the water and saw that it was not smooth, but certainly not so rough that operations needed to be curtailed. Nonetheless, he radioed, "I concur, sea state too rough to patrol *today*." We grinned and gathered at the New Kid. We sang Christmas songs for a while. Then someone began to add obscene lines to all of them; he was remarkably imaginative. Finally, we just drank Budweiser.

If you entered the bar, you would find no one at the damaged pool table; it was so uneven it was difficult to set a beer can down on it. As your eyes adjusted, you would begin to see individuals around the perimeter. Whale, a giant of a man with hair so blonde it was almost transparent, would be at a high stakes poker table. One night I saw him take a Coast Guard skipper for over $10,000. Nearby would be the squadron C.O. playing rummy or pitch with two or three of his Swift skippers. The stakes were much more modest: 25 cents per hand. Andre was usually at that table. A guy, who had made a daring run up a canal that was later named for him, would be selling something. Anything. Swedish pornography or Korean pistols or a Commando knife. We drank a lot; actually, of all the drugs for reducing anxiety, alcohol is still one of the best.

A newcomer would also notice the language. Much of it unique to barracks-room banter. "Dustoffs," "LZ's," "wahoos," "snakes," "slicks," "Hooligan Navy," phrases that were our shorthand. Whale would be talking about his desire to become an air traffic controller, while another skipper would be reminiscing about interesting women in Bangkok. It was noteworthy that no one said an American had been "killed"; instead we used the word "wasted." By using "wasted" we showed that we thought the war was a useless waste of young people. Not a noble battle, just a senseless foolish squandering of good men.

One person who didn't spend very much time with me was John Kerry. He spent his time across the street in the Ops hooch typing letters to Boston newspapers. He was obsessed with politics, had gone to Harvard, and was already campaigning. (Actually, it worked. He eventually did become a U.S. Senator for Massachusetts.)

The guys of Squadron 14 had distinguished themselves a few weeks before I arrived by intercepting a North Vietnamese trawler that was filled with weapons. They put a couple of white phosphorous rounds into the pilothouse, peppered the ship with .50 caliber rounds and eventually it beached. This event, later called the "Skunk Alpha Affair," marked the end of the North trying to resupply the South by means of coastal freighters. They gave up. They used the overland route exclusively. The Ho Chi Minh trail. So our attention turned from the coast to the rivers.

Jack Daniels had been on a sweep. The eight men came over a hill and approached a hidden V.C. whom they had wounded earlier. The V.C. shot at Jack Daniels hitting him where he was holding his rifle. Jack Daniels said his M-16 just magically flew up into the air in a big red mist. It took a second or two for him to realize that the red mist was his own blood. It took another second or two to notice that the V.C. bullet had blown off two fingers.

On occasion the dogs, Ralph and New Kid, would wander into the bar and beg for food or lap the spilled beer off the floor. Once their bellies were full, they went back outside. Too many Swifties smoked Marlboros; Ralph liked fresh air.

As we brothers talked, laughed, and drank, it occurred to me that this was as important as any military training. Within days I would be at home here. I would trust these guys with my life. They would feel the same toward me. Just as my crew was one unit, so too were the crews to one another. We knew each person's strengths and weaknesses. We worked together as cells in a muscle. We were indistinguishable, all something more than individuals.

A team. A bond developed that went well beyond friendship. It was brotherhood. Love. There was no hesitation between one person being in difficulty and the other coming to help. Not danger . . . action, but dangeraction. Automatically. As if the signal did not need to take the time to reach the brain. Instead, any cell, even a muscle cell, could commit us to act to help one another. This knee-jerk reaction was faster than thinking. A fraction of a second saved which could, in turn, save a life.

Three of my favorite people were not Swifties at all. One was a Seabee. He was a good-natured guy from Kansas. Bright and fun. He was also short; Ba Cuc called him "Ti Ti Trung Uy." "Small Lieutenant." Ba Cuc's nickname stuck.

The other two guys I enjoyed were "Red Dog" and "The Old Man." "Red Dog" was a carrot-headed junior officer who was an advisor to the Viet Navy. His close friend, "The Old Man," was a Navy Mustang. A man who had climbed the enlisted ranks and had become an officer. Both worked with the Yabouta Junk Forces. Their "Navy" consisted of long black Viet boats much like large fishing boats. They had pitch-black hulls with big white eyes printed on them. The Viet Navy patrolled the coasts and rivers and also conducted ambushes. "Red Dog" and "The Old Man" were responsible for missions much like Swifties. They just had less in terms of weapons, boats, communication, speed, and comfort. They ate like Viets most of the time. Nuoc mam. Fish oil on rice. That is why they enjoyed being with us. Drinking real Budweiser.

In short, Cam Ranh was as comfortable as I had expected. Good crews, good leaders. Even two good dogs. Thompsen began practicing on a typewriter; he said that he would need the skill in college. We began to look to a future. Life was good.

I never did understand who the original "new kid" was. At first I thought the bar might be named for the white mascot, but the guys said that particular dog had been around only a year or two. The "New Kid Memorial Library" was apparently named after a Swifty who had "bought the farm" long before. No one knew his name anymore, but he would certainly be proud of the scroungy saloon that was his namesake.

NOTHING ON BUT
THE RADIO

Marilyn Monroe was once asked, "What did you have on at the time?" Her response: "Nothing but the radio."

At Cat Lo we walked to and from the shower naked. Just a towel over our shoulder. It only took a day or two to get over being self-conscious walking past the Viet women. When I arrived in Cam Ranh, I did the same. I threw a towel around my neck, picked up a bar of soap and walked out the door toward the "rain locker." I had gone only 20 paces before I realized that the Viet women were holding their hands over their eyes. One or two shrieked. I froze. Staring about, I slowly realized that Cam Ranh was almost civilized. My conduct was considered barbaric. What a difference two hundred klicks make.

It wasn't a big thing to unwrap my towel and put it around my waist. It made me a bit sad though. I realized that I had enjoyed being a nudist for a few minutes each day in Cat Lo. Oh well, welcome to the modesty of Cam Ranh.

At supper I was teased by several guys. All in a light-hearted way. Actually, most thought that my sauntering down the street naked was somewhat macho. Back in Nebraska, the Lakota consider it a complement to say something like, "That ol' Bill, he don't give a damn about *nothing!*"

Only two days later I eclipsed my nudist stroll. The base C.O. decided to do an exercise in which it was assumed that the base was being attacked and overrun. We Swifties who were not on patrol ran to our boats and were ordered to lay off the base 500 meters and stand by to provide mortar and automatic weapons fire. Obviously we didn't actually shoot, but later my boat was ordered to provide illumination. So we began to fire 81-mm flares. They are very, very bright. They burst in the air and come down slowly by parachute. I put six or eight rounds above the mess hall.

Upon completion of the drill, we returned to base. To my surprise I saw that one round had malfunctioned. The parachute did not open and it had gone through the mess hall roof leaving a gaping hole.

My reputation was established. I was the barbarian nudist who put a hole in the roof of our own mess hall.

PRISONERS

The day after the mess hall incident, I was ordered to transport ten V.C. prisoners on my boat. I was unwilling to put them inside the cabin; the small arms and ammunition were stored there. So I left the prisoners out on the aft deck, above the hatches to the engines. The aluminum deck there was extremely hot; the prisoners had no shoes. I really should have cooled the deck by throwing water on it. That would have been the proper thing to do. Instead the V.C. squatted on the hot metal.

Earlier, I had been called "Ho Chi" Blinn. After the shower, the hole in the mess hall, and the prisoner incident, I found that more people were using my other unofficial call sign, "Sweet Pea."

Today, I'm sorry that the prisoners burned their feet. In 1969 I simply didn't care.

BROWN BETTY

A dangerous and very memorable incident happened when we were returning from a night patrol. The course took us close to an Air Force base by the coast. As routine, we radioed the machine gun perimeter defense (code name "Brown Betty") that we were transiting. This was a common occurrence, but that particular night, for reasons never explained, the Americans manning four sets of quad .50-caliber machine guns opened fire on us from point blank range. With tracers going absolutely everywhere, all we could do was scream on the radio a cry of "Cease fire!" as we departed as fast as our little craft could go.

This was not supposed to be. The general wisdom was that Cam Ranh was safe, Cat Lo dangerous. Yet this was one of the closest calls we had experienced.

"Can't be too careful wif trashberries."

RON

Ron went to Harvard. His dad was a physician. Upon graduation, Ron applied to Harvard med school; he didn't get in. Consequently, he joined the Navy, got a commission, and volunteered for Vietnam. He said Harvard was the only med school that he wanted. If he couldn't go there, he wouldn't be a doctor.

Ron was married. He had a five-foot poster photo of his wife. She was a lovely looking young woman, but the rest of us thought it was strange. Behind his back we joked about the poster. I don't remember why now. Perhaps she looked too human, or too big, or too vulnerable, or too caring.

Ron carried a lot of baggage.

HUGHES

The skipper of Cam Ranh was due to be relieved.

It isn't good to have to follow a fearless leader. The phrase "fearless leader" sounds fine in war stories, but the fact is that such men are goddamned dangerous. I'd much rather work with someone who had sense. Someone cautious like Chairman Mao who advised his guerillas to attack only when they had the advantage.

It reminded me of a classic quote of Calvin Coolidge: "Always buy stocks that go up. If they don't go up, don't buy them."

The departing base commander had told us earlier, "I don't know anything about my replacement except that his nickname is 'Nails.'" We worried that our new skipper would be a gung ho idiot. Instead, Hughes was smart and cautious. It was a good joke on us. We were glad "Nails" was only a joke.

THE MEASURE

It was the end of another 24 hour patrol. I was glad to be bringing my little boat back to base. Even if it was for only 12 hours of sleep before we went out again at 0400. Rearm, fuel, add water and food to the galley, and bolt down a C-rat. With luck I'd be back in my bunk by 5 p.m. Maybe even have the luxury of corpsman to look at the jungle rot on my toes.

One klick out, the radio came alive, "Inky Bite 97, upon docking proceed to H.Q. Out." Shit. What did the skipper want now? I was dog-tired, I hurt.

Hughes, Lt. Commander, greeted me. "Sweet Pea, I hate to say it, but you've got to take a check ride with a virgin crew. The new kids are ready now, take 'em out and tell me if they are safe to patrol on their own. It's boat 38."

It figured. Boat 38 was a pig. The new kids got the worst. A slow unreliable boat was bad. We didn't duke it out with the V.C. We went up the rivers until Charlie shot at us. Then we ran like hell while returning fire. Nothing John Wayne about it. But there was no choice. Hidden, the Victor Charlie sat in the nice tall elephant grass with B-40's and fired those rocket propelled grenades at us while we stood out like a sore thumb in the middle of the river. So you get shot at, you run away at 30 knots and you call in an air strike on the position. We were shit magnets, not warriors.

The skipper was still talking, "The new officer in charge is Don Futrell. I think he's a classmate of yours from Annapolis."

I flushed. Futrell. Dull. What the hell was he doing here? He should have been on an oiler in the Atlantic.

Within an hour I was out on PCF 38. Two hours later I made my report. "Commander, that is the worst crew I've ever seen. Dangerous to themselves. The quartermaster couldn't navigate the river, the guns were not ready, and the engineman is worthless. On the 38, you must have a good engineman. Send them back to the real world or give one of the people to each of six other boats. We can train them one at a time."

Hughes looked at me sadly. "They can't be that bad, Gary."

"Skipper, let me put it in my best Swiss boarding school English. They are a whore's wet dream. They *will* be hurt if they go out."

Hughes was silent. The next day another skipper took them out for a second check ride. Another failure. Badger, who had been transferred from Cat Lo to Cam Ranh three weeks after I moved, gave them a third "down." Called them a walking disaster. Finally, someone else gave them an okay.

A couple of weeks later, 38 was sent to An Thoi. I was pleased to have them out of sight. Don was hurt that I had evaluated him so poorly. I didn't care.

Sometime later Whale met me by the operations hooch, "Did you hear about Futrell? Yesterday the 38 boat came under heavy attack. Automatic weapons fire and B-40's. A rocket blew Don overboard. His crew tried to pull him aboard. The incoming fire was intense. To save his crew, he shouted from the river for them to go. To leave him wounded in the water and save themselves. I don't know how many times they were driven off, but eventually they got back to Don and fished him out. The boat is Swiss cheese. Unbelievable, but they're all alive."

My reaction was astonishment, but also envy and perhaps even anger. I felt like I did because Don had been tested at the limit and found to be very, very brave. Would I have had the guts to do the same as he? To order my crew to leave me. I don't know. Perhaps . . . or perhaps not. I'll never know. He *does* know.

For his heroism, Don Futrell earned the Navy Cross. Second only to the Medal of Honor.

None of us ever saw Don again. He has never come to any of our Swift boat reunions.

BA CUC

"How much time you got left in-country, Ba Cuc?" we asked of the weathered old lady we paid to clean our hooch. Ba Cuc was a sweet old girl. No more than four feet high in her black pajamas and rubber shower shoes. But she always smiled—especially when we gave her attention. Our gallows humor joke was beyond her limited English. While each of us had less than a year left to serve, Ba Cuc would be in Vietnam until she died. She would probably go no further than a few kilometers from her village.

Sometimes I wondered if we would fight the war differently if we knew that we would not go home until it was won or lost. Obviously the mindset of America's soldiers in World War II had been much different, knowing they would be in Europe or the Pacific until the war was over. "For the duration." We just served our time. Like prisoners. But there was the promise of the day the Freedom Bird would take us back to the land of the round eyes. Ba Cuc did not have that option. If the V.C. won, she would probably be mistreated for aiding the Americans.

She cleaned the hooch well, always pointing out mud with the phrase "Bad, numba ten bad," or smiling at photos of wives and girlfriends. One day I asked Ba Cuc if she had a husband. She looked at me for an instant and then tipped her head back with her mouth open and eyes half closed. She held the pose for several seconds.

I asked "Sat?" and she nodded. Dead. Then she smiled. No need to dwell on it.

Ba Cuc went back to cleaning. I looked at her long gray hair and weathered skin. She was someone's mother once. Someone's caring wife. There was nothing I could do for her but give her a few piasters of currency or some candy. Then she found one of my

259

khaki T-shirts and held it up. It was a good shirt, just a small hole in it, but she pointed to the tear and asked, "Survey?" "Survey" is a Navy phrase for destroying damaged goods.

I grinned and said "Yes, Ba Cuc. Survey." She put it in the oversized bag she used for both a purse and container of cleaning supplies. The shirt would go to one of her grandkids.

She and her family had a long time left to serve in-country.

CRISPY CRITTER

It was a beautiful day, warm, sunny, and over. We were exiting a river and on our way home. Midmorning, we were alert, happy and listening to Armed Forces radio.

From the port side, from a small sandy island-like area we began to receive small arms fire. Nothing big. Just rat-tat of small arms and automatic weapons. We responded with five or ten times the firepower. Still, it was a fair fight. They could see us.

The words sound strange, but it was good-natured boyish stuff. Each of us shooting ineffectually at one another. In such a case, the radioman comes up automatically and reports to "Big Brother." A factual timely report such as "Taking small arms fire from coordinates CO6354." No big deal.

But to our surprise, Big Brother came back with big news: "Two fast movers with jelly in your neighborhood. Do you want assistance?" Translation: two jets loaded with napalm were at my disposal. I repeated my coordinates and within seconds, I was speaking to one of the F-100 Super Saber pilots. They arrived in about two minutes.

They confirmed our position, saw our green marking smoke, rolled in on the target, and then it was just like the movies. Two V.C. stood up and started to run across the sand just as the jets swooped in.

The napalm was beautiful. Big. Close. White. Red. Black. Yellow. Right on top of those little guys. The heat and size and speed were something that would fill your senses. Full. Awe-full.

I hate to admit it, but this time the performance of the Air Force was flawless.

Those two little guys shouldn't have run. Maybe if they had hunkered down they would have lived. It wasn't a fair fight after all.

261

The pilots circled once. We thanked them. They sounded chippy. We grinned at one another on the boat and once more headed out to sea and to the rest and safety of the base. Kid reported the result on the radio. Five minutes later, Big Brother came back on the net, "Return to the site, find the bodies and search them for identity and papers."

It was an odd request, or at least it seemed odd to us. We bitched to one another but obediently turned around and proceeded back to the very spot where we had duked it out with the Victor Charlie. We cautiously nosed the boat onto shore and Kelley and I stepped ashore to find the toasted remains.

Nothing remained. We walked over the hot sand and burning vegetation. We stood in the middle of the napalm strike and we saw no trace of our enemy.

The jets had rolled in at low altitude, they dropped napalm directly onto the two running men, and then they disappeared. The jets disappeared. The two guys in black pajamas and AK-47s disappeared. Just flat-assed disappeared. Kelley tried to joke about the little Buddhists burning up just like on T.V., only faster. I thought of a Norman Greenbaum song, "Spirit in the sky, that's where I'm going when I die, take me up to the spirit in the sky." I couldn't believe it. Neither could Kelley. "Skipper, they were French kissed by a Mack truck and the little bastards just turned into vapor . . . like, well, Jesus!"

That time I did laugh. But not too loudly. I was scared. Standing there wondering. We looked around again and returned to the 97 boat. We backed off the beach and radioed Big Brother that we found nothing. Big Brother was slow to accept what we said. The big cheeses wanted to know something. We didn't know what, but they thought there was something special about our little friends who were now crispy critters. Maybe. Or maybe Charlie ran down a big rabbit hole like Alice in Wonderland.

After that I didn't speak so badly about the Air Force. Yes, they did almost sink our boat at Brown Betty and much of the time they seemed to just be converting jet fuel into noise, but today what they did was awesome.

Years later whenever I saw the black flag of POW/MIA in front of our local V.F.W., I thought of my little friends. Oddly, they were thoughts that were almost fond. Those two guys were shooting at us, sure, but it was a fair firefight. Oddly playful. And then the fast movers with jelly made them disappear. The Samurai had a word for the honorable code of fighting: Bushido. The early Japanese warriors used swords even after they possessed firearms. The F-100s violated that code of the Samuari. Two V.C. KIA, or two Victor Charlie dead, or "Chuck bought the farm." One phrase is military; the other makes them real people. People present "on the eve of destruction." These two got included in the Pentagon's body count that would be reported on T.V. the next day. I hope they lived somehow, but I know it is unlikely.

This is the stuff that separates me from the World War II vets in our town. They know how they feel about their war. I don't. They fly a black flag at the V.F.W. for soldiers missing in action; they think that we should be able to account for those people. I know better.

4-H

With the exception of Rocky, I had the honor to serve under some of the most truly impressive people in the world. Officers in Vietnam worked hard to mentor us. To train us, to baptize us in fire. They honed us to a sharp edge with meticulous care. With fatherly love.

When I was growing up in the prairie, most of us were in 4-H. "Health, hands, heart, and head." An organization built around rural youth. A major project was the annual livestock show. The young people would each select a calf from the family's herd. They would then give the animal special food and grooming and attention. After months of care and development, the day of the fair would arrive. Each 4-H boy or girl would then show his animal before the judges. The cattle were simply beautiful: young, fat, perfect. Coats glistened from brushing.

After the awarding of prizes, the animals were then sold in the sale barn. Usually the major restaurants would compete for the purple ribbon winners. But, blue ribbon show animals, red ribbon cattle, and all others eventually were resold to the packing house. Within a day these pampered pets were slaughtered and made into sirloin. It was often a difficult time for the young 4-Hers. To know the animal they had pampered for a year would be eaten. The older 4-H students handled the show better. They knew that the rancher's job was to husband the cattle for months and then give them up. The same March calf that was born in a snowstorm and fed by hand with a bottle inside the ranch house in the warm kitchen would be sold for meat a year later. Without remorse.

On occasion I marveled at the parallel. The same mid-level officers who we called "the old men" must send us to a fate no different than that of the yearling Black Angus. They prepared us with care. With love. Professional career military officers must face the anguish of seeing their own children hurt badly.

Civilians, especially politicians, couldn't understand, but I think ranchers would.

TYPHOON

All fighter pilots have hemorrhoids. They pull positive G's; the blood rushes down from their heads and bursts blood vessels in their butt. It's an occupational hazard. An occupational certainty.

Put a 50-foot boat in three-foot swells with four-foot waves and you get a scary ride. Crank the boat up to 20 knots and you get a bone-jarring experience. The shock on the spine and knees is as if you jumped off a picnic table. Only it happens every three seconds. For hours at a time. Twenty-four to be exact.

After a patrol in the monsoon season, which in the south is most of the summer months, the crews would climb off the boat as tenderly as if they were 80 years old. Soaking wet. Sprained backs, aching necks, headaches, and disks that screamed in pain. Swollen feet. The worst were knees. They felt as if they had endured a 24-hour football game.

No desire to eat. Just crawl into a dry bed. Eat aspirins by the fistful, washed down with a couple of beers.

The monsoon season lasted about three months. Superimposed on that period of incessant rain was another problem: typhoons. A typhoon is a pacific hurricane. Most guys experienced only two typhoons in their year's tour. At sea, that is two too many. Up north by the Cua Viet River a 30-foot wave picked a Swift up by the stern. The little bow dug into the trough of the wave and it simply did a forward summersault. PCF 77 sank within two minutes of being up-ended, drowning three. Heavy seas in a 50-foot boat are remarkably like a car wreck. The Swift crew must stand up. No seats. No seat belts. If you get washed overboard, you drown. Damned little chance that even the strongest swimmer can make it in a windy storm. The reason is that it is not water with air above. It is three layers: water, then frothy sea, and then air. The frothy sea is too soft to swim above and the wetness covers the person's head. Try to breathe the air/water mix coming out of a bathroom shower and you will get the point.

But that's not all. When the South China Sea comes aboard the boat, it does its first work on the electronics. Huge sparks fly from radars and radios and sonars. Electrocution is a real problem. Then the weapons and ammunition come loose, as well as food and freshwater. Mattresses, charts, and food. Tarps, spare parts, boathooks; it is all a jumble. Finally the engines give up. They simply cannot ingest so much water. Each time the boat's screws come out of a big wave they go from biting water to over-revving in the air. Finally the drivetrain breaks.

In the monsoon and typhoon season, it was not unusual to see Swift crews that looked as if they had been in a bar fight. Bruised, cut, and limping. One or two such patrols was manageable. Every other day for months at a time was like being required to run a 26-mile marathon every other day. A human body just cannot do it without permanent damage.

The monsoons made me miss the long hot summer days on the ranch. Haying season. So dry we would gulp down a half-gallon of ice tea with our lunch. Wide expanse of hayfields with sweet clover and timothy hay. Grasshoppers. Happy. It was all so golden dry.

Wonderfully dry.

SAPPER

To the living we owe our respect, but to the dead we owe only the truth.

Voltaire

We were out on patrol that night so I didn't see it. I didn't see them fish the little boy out of the water. They said he looked about 14. "Little swimming trunks" was what they said he wore. Actually it was probably just his underwear, but the lights on the pier weren't very bright.

For once Naval Intel got it right. They said we would be attacked by a sapper unit that would try to sink our boats at the pier. On any given night there were five or six boats tied up. Mostly boats that needed repair, the rest would be on patrol. Guarding the boats were four enlisted men doing two hour watches. Two slept on board boats while one stood on the pier and one walked from boat to boat. The rest of the off-duty crews would be asleep in Cam Ranh's wooden barracks.

A "sapper" is an engineering phrase used to describe small units that attempt to destroy the enemy's equipment and facilities. Naval sappers often use limpet mines. A limpet is a small explosive that magnetically attaches itself to metal and then is timed to explode later. They work very well on the hull of a boat. They stick on the hull just like a barnacle.

Because of the alert by intelligence, the squadron skipper doubled the guard and ordered that they throw occasional concussion grenades into the water to kill any underwater swimmers approaching.

That is exactly what happened. A sailor on guard duty threw a concussion grenade into the dark night water and a little body came up. They fished him out with a boathook and laid him on the pier. I imagine he looked cold and very wet. I also imagine that they saw blood coming out of the boy's nose and ears. Underwater concussions do that. They also blow water up your ass; that causes internal hemorrhaging.

When you hear an explosion in the air, it goes "boom." When the explosion is underneath the water you hear it as it truly is. Just a very, very sharp short "crack." It sounds like you hit the hull with a hammer. Almost a "click." Maybe the boy heard it. Probably not.

Anyway, he had his little swimming trunks and he had a limpet mine tied to his waist and only one other piece of equipment: he had two baby nipples stuck in his nostrils. That was his scuba gear. Two baby nipples in his nose. He probably wasn't even a very good swimmer; sticking something in your nose before diving is ineffective.

Still, with luck he could have sunk a boat or two. He was a gutsy little bastard. I'm sorry I didn't meet him.

Or at least see his body.

MALARIA

Jerry got malaria. He didn't look very bad. In fact, he looked almost normal. When he had attacks of chills and sweating, he stayed locked in his hooch. After the attack passed, he would emerge looking okay. The doctors worked on him for a few weeks while Jerry rested.

It was a reminder to all of us to take our anti-malaria pills. We were ordered to take them weekly. Even the radio would remind us each Sunday to do so. Yet it was difficult to remember. Taking a pill every week was too hard to do given our irregular schedule. We joked that given our forgetfulness, if we had been women we would all be pregnant. Oddly, Jerry was the only one to get malaria. Black malaria. Jerry said that, although that particular strain sounded serious, there were worse. Finally they sent Jerry back stateside to D.C.

All in all, there weren't as many mosquitoes in Vietnam as you would think. Not as many as in Minnesota where the mosquito is the state bird. We wondered aloud if Jerry was lucky getting bitten by a malaria-infected mosquito. We missed him.

Years later, I met Jerry in Washington. While in the hospital, he started reading law books. One thing led to another, and while recuperating he enrolled in law school. Now he was in the Judge Advocate General Corps. J.A.G. A Navy lawyer.

The war changed us all, each in a different way. In Jungle Warfare Survival School we were taught that if you are in a survival situation in the bush you do not need to fear big animals. It is the insects that are the most dangerous.

The little things certainly add up.

SMELL

Two years before, one of my first flight instructors was a giant of a Marine. A suntanned Greek god. He started every discussion with "Listen up! I'm gonna tell you two things. If you do them, you will live. If you don't, you will die."

He kept it simple. In the air he did the same. He would show me how to handle the aircraft properly. Then he would partially (or sometimes fully!) show me what not to do.

You just had to divide life into: 1) the important things that kill you, and 2) the rest of life—which is trivial.

Two years later, the advice of my flight instructor was still sound. During briefings in the Swift ready-room, I tried to keep the bipolar world in perspective. Some missions were dangerous; some were a piece of cake. The hard part was telling which was which. Often what appeared to be a routine mission proved dangerous. The trick was to volunteer for those that look dicey but were actually quite manageable.

Psychologists tell us that in combat 83 percent of men hesitate, about 3 percent totally freeze in fear, and only 14 percent immediately fight or flee. Most Swift skippers did not hesitate. We either attacked, or got the hell out and called in air strikes. The point is that you always wanted to know— *really* know—the guys on the other boats and what you could trust them to do.

With a covert wink in the briefing room, two seasoned Swift skippers would communicate with each other. Two hands would go up. Lock in a mission that smelled okay.

There was a second trick. Always volunteer enough that you stayed ahead of the game. That way, when a mission that smelled spooky came along, you could sit on your hands and have the other guy take the patrol that didn't feel right to you.

I imagine veteran cops acquire a similar sixth sense. Sensing/ feeling solutions for situations rather than thinking.

BB

Battleships are designated as BB's in the U.S. Navy. One was on patrol in Vietnam. The U.S.S. New Jersey.

Here is a quick thumbnail comparison of a BB and a Swift:

	New Jersey (BB62)	Inky Bite 97
Crew	2,748	6 plus 1 Viet
Displacement	59,000 tons	22 tons
Length	887 ft.	50 ft.
Guns	16 inch	.50 caliber = ½"

In short, a BB like the New Jersey displaced 2,700 times as much water as our boat and it had a crew composed of 2,741 more men than I had on board.

One day I was ordered to "protect" the New Jersey. Infuckingcredible.

We were told to find the ship and board it. Finding a battleship isn't particularly difficult. It was shooting at targets deep inland and so it had maneuvered parallel to a grassy shoreline with ten-foot high elephant grass. I brought my boat alongside the gigantic ship and went aboard. The captain told me that he was worried that the ship might draw fire from the enemy. He asked if it was likely that a force of V.C. could be ashore. I wanted to tell him that it wasn't "Mr. Rogers' Neighborhood." Instead I told him that we had been shot at enough to confirm that bad guys certainly lived here, but that it was highly unlikely that the enemy had anything strong enough to sink a battleship or even scar its paint. Recoilless rifle and B-40 rockets, which would sink my boat, would bounce off his hull harmlessly.

The old bird looked at me for a few seconds and then said, "I disagree. I want your boat between me and the shore." He was only a half-mile from the shore at the time, so he was asking me to put my boat literally under his massive guns. I stared at him in open-mouthed disbelief; then I gave the proverbial "snappy salute and a cheery aye-aye."

Within minutes we maneuvered 97 to the other side of the ship. We had barely arrived on station when the huge guns erupted, shooting shells heavier than an automobile at the enemy deep inland. Each shell flew at supersonic speeds just feet above our heads. The concussion of the shot was truly impossible to describe. It was like having the round explode in your skull. The second volley caused the windows of our cabin to blow out. The entire plastic window just popped from its rubber frame. Each volley left us with fewer windows. The radar screen broke. Pieces of our boat simply flew off from the concussion.

By the sixth or seventh volley we could no longer hear anything but a shrieking/ringing in our ears. I looked at Jake's wide eyes and half expected blood to be running from them.

Against orders, I engaged the engines and fled to the safety of the open sea. I radioed the New Jersey that we simply could not hold station without suffering serious loss to both the boat and men. The battleship recognized the damage that they had inflicted on us. After a few minutes, they radioed that we were excused.

Tex was furious. "Skipper, it will take us an entire day to replace all of the plastic windows in the pilothouse and main cabin. At least six are gone. Blown overboard! All the rest are so weak that they must be resealed." My bosun had every right to be angry. My gunner, quartermaster, engineman, and radioman also had damage to report. Our Viet interpreter just sat on the pilothouse roof with an astonished look on his face. He had now seen real American firepower. Up close and personal.

The New Jersey had 70 officers aboard; at least 60 of them outranked me. I knew that the original order was stupid, but I had no idea just how stupid until my boat started to disintegrate under my feet.

I would like to say that this was an unusual day. It was not. Each week we found ourselves doing foolish things. We learned from our mistakes of course, but the war presented so many new and odd situations that we were always in the middle of another goofy experiment. Each such incident cost America money or material or men. This screw-up was actually cheap.

Chuck had a huge advantage over us. He just had a little pair of shorts and an AK-47 and a little pouch of rice. Not much could go wrong, no technical problems for him. He didn't have a battleship. He had something better: common sense.

*   *   *

I'm 56 now. I have a strong ringing in my ears, probably from 97's .50 caliber machine guns. But perhaps New Jersey's massive guns contributed too. We vets could seek revenge by pissing on the graves of the clowns who mistreated us, but instead we will just pop open a cold beer and laugh. Laugh at the cosmic jokes of Mars, the god of War.

FORTUNE 500

We were eating toast with cheap Navy institutional grape jelly when Hughes stopped to tell us that sometime the next day a group of VIPS would tour. The Navy had promised them a demonstration ride on a Swift boat. They were spending an entire week in Vietnam, a few days with each branch of the service. As the details were fleshed out, the visit was both preposterous and predictable.

Apparently, the brass in the Pentagon decided that to get U.S. industry behind the war effort, they would invite the chief executives of major Fortune 500 companies to come to Vietnam for a week to see the war firsthand. Like Bob Hope, they would travel around and meet people and see demonstrations.

We had less than 24 hours to get six boats ready. All of the other boats would stay away out on patrol. The 97 was in good shape, so my crew and I were to be one of the six. "Lifer," a balding young skipper, was a full lieutenant and his boat was also chosen; he took charge of the exercise. After all of the boats were ready, we took them out to practice running in tight formation. Twenty-five knots and only ten feet apart. It was screwy, but we did it anyway. We had never run six abreast at that speed, or so close to one another. It beat going on patrol. It was insane, in a novel way.

Next we had to find a real uniform for each crewman. Blue for enlisted, khaki for officers. That was much harder than it sounded. Most of the time we were dressed in just an olive drab T-shirt and either swimming trunks or cutoff shorts. Even good shoes were hard to find. Normally we went barefoot on the boats, like Viet fishermen. Bare feet stick to the deck better than shoes. Shoes just stay wet and full of mildew.

The real wahoo part was that they decided to fill some 55-

gallon drums with gasoline and put them on a safe riverbank nearby. We were ordered to sail past at maximum speed and shoot at them. The entire exercise was becoming progressively sillier.

Finally, the time arrived. About 30 distinguished businessmen in their fifties and sixties arrived in a bus. Each had been issued nice green fatigues with his name on the pocket. I didn't know which person ran which big company. Some of the biggies were friendly, almost fatherly. A few were still pompous and filled with self-importance. Most were as puzzled as we were about this whirlwind tour.

Our portion of the exhibition was bizarre enough. I couldn't imagine going through two or three such demos per day for a week and then having to put up with briefings too.

Anyway, they were experiencing the dog and pony show to end all dog and pony shows.

The 30 men split among our six boats and off we went at full speed. My crew was dressed so well I couldn't believe they were mine. Kelley even wore his false teeth. My boat was clean and shipshape. The businessmen were hanging on for dear life as we bashed our way through the three-foot choppy waves at top speed.

Suddenly, Lifer gave the order to turn abruptly into the nearby safe river. Screaming into the channel, we opened fire on the target oil drums. Six boats in a perfect row, like ducks at a shooting gallery. Each firing mortars, .50 calibers, and M-79 grenades at the same target. Happily we hit the barrels and they started to burn with a lazy black-red fire. Not an explosion, but it looked only slightly less real than the Hollywood version.

Before the channel narrowed, Lifer ordered us to turn around and proceed back to port. I slowed down and two or three of my guests started to ask questions. "Where are you from, son?" type of questions. Like I said, most were nice guys. Some worked for defense companies, others worked for companies that simply did a little military work on the side. For example, Brunswick, the company that made bowling equipment also made weapons. So did Continental Can Company. I didn't know many of the firms they represented. With a little more time and in a quiet place, most of us skippers would have loved to talk to them. We all wanted to interview for a job; someplace nice to work when our tour was up. Our boats soon docked at the pier; the bus was waiting to take the executives off to their next Mickey Mouse exercise.

Before the last businessman disembarked from my boat, he called me aside. The gray-haired man's question was blunt: "This isn't real, is it?"

I hesitated only a second before telling him the truth. "No, sir, it isn't. This entire hour has been phony. I'm sorry we couldn't have shown you the truth."

At that moment, I knew that these businessmen weren't buying the Defense Department's stream of bullshit. The brass underestimated these men; they didn't get to be top dogs in Fortune 500 companies by being gullible.

The kindly gentleman put his hand on my shoulder, and squeezed it. With his intense blue eyes fixed on me, he softly said, "Keep your head down, son. Good luck."

A rush of admiration rolled over me. He was a World War II vet. I knew it.

RALPH, NEW KID, AND FAYE

I read that four dogs accompanied George Armstrong Custer and the seventh cavalry. They trotted all the way from Fort Lincoln to the Little Bighorn. I thought that it was ironic that one of Custer's dogs was named Swift.

Coastal Division 14 had two very special dogs: Ralph and New Kid.

Ralph was as majestic as a Viet dog could possibly be; he had beautiful golden brown fur. Well, okay, he did have a few mange spots and scars from dogfights. But he walked *so* regally. New Kid was his sidekick. Smaller, fat, white, and unbelievably stupid. With his dirty spots, and impetuous nature, New Kid could be relied upon to overestimate his ability and underestimate the adversary.

We loved both mascots equally. They reminded us of long gone childhood pets of the real world. And so we fed our dogs the best we had. The beef stew in our C-Rats, even the cherished pound cake. You could count the ribs on every dog in-country except Ralph and New Kid.

One night at the base, we hung a sheet between bamboo poles and had an outdoor movie, "The Thomas Crown Affair." Steve McQueen and Faye Dunaway. God, she was beautiful.

The black dog mascot of the Seabees foolishly wandered into the middle of our audience. New Kid sprang to the attack. The boat crews cheered their fat furry white mercenary. The black dog howled in pain as teeth closed in on his butt. After initiating the fight, New Kid left the serious fighting to Ralph. Perhaps he wasn't that stupid after all.

To the great embarrassment of the Seabees, their black dog beat a noisy retreat, yelping as he was pursued. Happily, our alert projectionist had shut off the movie so we could all enjoy the mercenary dogfight. Ralph received congratulatory pats on the back. New Kid was fed. Tails wagged. The Seabee dog had been disgraced; so had the Seabees themselves.

Sultry Faye Dunaway came back on the screen. Round eyes, long blonde hair, luscious lips and big breasts. To us, she was unreal.

And later we Americans left those little quadrupeds who had fought for us. We left them to an uncertain future. We abandoned our biped allies too.

Viets eat dog. Especially fat ones.

R.O.K.

There was a lovely little harbor near Nha Trang. Oil tankers unloaded their fuel along a tiny pier that jutted out from a mountain shaped like a pyramid. There were huge boulders all over the face of the mountain. We called it the "Rock Pile," but there were several mountains in-country that had that name. Sometimes we anchored for an hour in the harbor while we cooked lunch. Slowly the Rock Pile became inhabited by V.C. Then they struck. They sent some sappers down the hill. They placed a limpet mine on one of the tankers as it unloaded fuel. It sunk within an hour of the explosion. The tanker just settled on the bottom with its superstructure above the waterline. A big oil spill polluted what had been a beautiful little blue harbor. The pier was suddenly worthless, a home to a derelict.

So Saigon decided to sweep the V.C. off the hill. The terrain was like that of Iwo Jima. The corps commanders decided to give the job to the Korean Army. Republic of Korea: R.O.K. So the "Roks" swept the rock pile and reported that they had killed 115 V.C. They had neither captured nor wounded any. Every enemy they found, they killed. The Roks were tough little guys. They did not report their own losses. Ever.

Things were quiet for a couple of months, and then the V.C. reinfested the Rock Pile. So, the Koreans were called in again. The second sweep resulted in 53 KIA. And one WIA. The Koreans had actually brought one V.C. back alive—at least partially alive.

We joked that by not killing 100 percent, the Koreans were growing soft.

The Koreans, the White Horse Division, had a solid reputation. American bases would get mortared by V.C. hiding in nearby villages and farms. The Koreans were never fired on. The reason was simple:

they told the Viets, "If we get mortared we will kill every man, woman, child, cat, dog and water buffalo for a radius of eight klicks. Believe it." We as Americans couldn't do such things. The Koreans knew that such brutality was not brutal at all.

Alexander the Great was able to conquer two-thirds of the known world by the time he was 32. He did two very simple things whenever he approached a new city. He said, "Open your gates and no one will be hurt; if you do not do that, I will kill absolutely every living thing." The people opened the gates. Next Alexander said, "What is your biggest complaint? Taxes?" The people said, "Of course!" So Alexander called for the tax collectors and killed them. Then he instituted tax reform with new tax collectors—Greeks. In general, the conquered cities were delighted with the change. Alexander honored the customs of the lands he occupied. Those citizens became his allies, and as Alexander's army moved onward it *grew* as others joined its ranks.

Carefully used, brutality, tax reform, and respect for the culture were three interlocking keys to minimizing loss.

Probably not more than one person out of a hundred in the field or in the Pentagon had read Arian's *History of Alexander the Great.*

War is an art form.

THEY JUST DON'T HAVE
THE RIGHT PERSPECTIVE

Some big cheese was coming from Saigon to give us an important intelligence briefing. Everyone not on patrol was ordered to the operations hooch. The "ops shack" was tiny, hardly room for the ops boss and a radioman and a yeoman. Now there were a dozen Swift skippers packed in with nothing to do but tell dirty jokes and smell one another.

About ten minutes later, a bespectacled intelligence type arrived. He wore pressed and starched green fatigues and shiny jungle boots that had never seen the bush. He was an Army light colonel. He looked earnest. He looked "urgent" too.

He started waving a pointer all over the map telling us about pacification and secured villages and how the North was losing its will to fight. He told us how Sea Dragon was strangling the enemy because they could not get supplies in or down to the South. He went on and on, about air strikes, about everything.

The room got hotter, and that made us sweat even more. The spook didn't seem to notice that none of us gave a rat's ass about what he was saying. For an intelligence type, he wasn't very good at picking up clues.

Each week, men who had been in hot areas like Cat Lo and An Thoi were now getting rotated to Cam Ranh; they were very aware of how the war was progressing and unafraid to speak up.

One of the more thoughtful Swifties raised his hand. He said, "Sir, you say we are winning, but look at the map. Here in our operations area, things are getting worse, not better. We put a red pin on the map to mark spots from which we took fire. Six months ago, the map was a map. Now there are so many of those little round-headed red pins on it, the damned thing is just pink!"

Another Swift Officer-in-Charge raised his hand. "To follow up on that, there are islands where we used to beach the boats for a picnic lunch. Now we get our ass shot off if we get within a thousand yards!"

Six more hands went up. The light colonel looked as if he was losing control of the briefing. We were not being impolite to him. We just wanted him to know the facts. We were trying to give him valuable intelligence. Instead of listening, he was acting like a goddamned cheerleader trying to convince the team that it was not losing the big game.

In exasperation, he almost shouted, "Your problem is that you see only a tiny portion of the war! If you could get the *big picture perspective*, if you could see what we see in Saigon and Washington, you would know that we are winning!"

His white face was slowly turning pink. Sweat marks began to show on his pressed fatigues. We looked back at him with faces that were puzzled, angry, sarcastic, and sad. He decided to quit and said, "Dismissed" just a bit too loudly.

As we exited, we gave a sidelong glance to our squadron C.O. He didn't seem particularly irritated that we had forced the briefing to a close. He was probably both pleased that we had told the truth and saddened by the fact that some higher up might interpret our action as a sign of poor morale.

As we filed out, a few skippers wondered aloud if perhaps the war truly was going better in other sectors of the country. That perhaps, as the colonel said, our operating area was an exception.

Most of us just called him what he was: a goofy clown from Saigon trying to blow wind up our skirts . . . that was our "perspective" on it.

THE PHOTOGRAPHER

Show me a hero and I'll write you a tragedy.

F. Scott Fitzgerald

The rumors came first. They always do. A journalist or a photographer or both were coming for a ride. *TIME* magazine. The question was who would want them. Most of us told ourselves that we wanted them on someone else's boat. Photos of us in cutoff khakis and barefoot would not go well in Saigon. Whoever escorted these clowns would have to get their boat in shape, take down the flags of rats and pirate skulls and put up the Stars and Stripes. Perhaps even put the head back into working order since most of us had long since shut off the stool.

So anyone who got those guys would have to make a lot of changes. Starting with finding an unadulterated Navy uniform. Worse, the crew would have to wear the damned things.

Within a day or two the rumor was confirmed. One person was coming. A woman. Everything recalibrated. Now, every skipper was eager to host the journalist. Obviously it would not be a new kid. None of us wanted to admit it, but we were all yahoos. We didn't want Saigon to know what the hell was going on, but we would love to show off in front of an American woman.

Her visit got delayed, and delayed again. She arrived the day that I was departing for R & R. She was very small and looked surprisingly feminine in spite of the green fatigues she was wearing. She was young and pretty. Most of all, she looked innocent. Her fatigues were still starched and her boots were not broken in. Her eyes were big, but her countenance was business-like. She looked like a young woman that I had known, a woman I missed. I wished that I could have talked to her, but she already had more attention than she needed or wanted.

*   *   *

When I got back from R & R they told me what happened. She had gone out with an old timer on what was supposed to be a routine patrol. Instead the boat drew heavy fire from automatic weapons. With bullets peppering the Swift, the skipper pushed her down the stairs into the cabin and shouted for her to lie on the deck beside the small arms locker.

Amazingly no one was hurt. She hadn't taken a single photo of the firefight. That was good. I didn't believe that any photo was worth a 25-year-old girl getting shot. But she was a photojournalist, she would have disagreed.

Later, when she stepped on the pier as the boat docked, it was clear that she had wet her pants. The Swifties were courteous and pretended not to notice. She departed the base within a couple of hours.

I didn't really know the girl. I was not on the patrol. Yet, I was sorry she had that experience. It was all so unnecessary.

She didn't get a single combat photo. Not on film anyway.

To the best of my knowledge no one admitted to her that men also pee their pants in combat.

SYDNEY

Finally, after nine months, I was eligible to go on R & R to Australia.

A few weeks earlier, one of my friends had been hurt in an Army training exercise back stateside at Ft. Carson, Colorado. Jon Jones had burned his hand on an incendiary round. He had time to write letters from the infirmary. His penmanship was okay; I was glad to see that. Jon said I absolutely had to see "The Graduate." So that was the first thing I did upon arriving in Sydney for R & R. I found a nice hotel, washed up and went to the movies.

Benjamin, the movie's protagonist, did what he was told. Just like most of us. Sometimes you wondered if he would ever outgrow his confusion. He was almost paralyzed by it. The adult men were shallow, but his girlfriend seemed to know where she wanted to go. His girlfriend's mother, Mrs. Robinson, *definitely* knew what she wanted: sex. Ann Bancroft played the role perfectly. She was simply bored with life. It was a great sixties movie. Most of the characters were clueless, fortunate, bored, and confused. The only person not confused was Mrs. Robinson and she was busy doing the wrong things. Just like America. Just like war. Only funnier.

Sydney had a beautiful modern movie theater with thick carpets and nice food. Even alcohol. As a kid in Nebraska, I went to the movies at the "Rialto." Kids called it "The Rat Hole." We didn't know what "Rialto" even meant. I still don't. Anyway, the Australians had placed a full set of samurai armor in the middle of the movie lobby. Its purpose was to advertise the next movie coming after "The Graduate," a Kurasawa movie from Japan about samurai. I couldn't help just standing there looking at that beautiful armor. Shiny leather, bright black and red. Little horns coming out of a sinister helmet. The armor stood barely five-foot high, but indirect lights made it seem bigger than life.

I stared as if in a trance; it pulled me back out of R & R. What would it be like to face just one opponent? Armed only with swords. One on one. What happened to people who were badly cut? No surgeons, no antiseptic, no way to kill the pain. After nine months, I was getting proficient at fighting in the rivers, using guns, radios, jets, helicopters, and each of our tools of war. I realized that I would be totally naked trying to fight like a man. Like a samurai. I would also be completely at a loss how to fight a modern war in the desert, or in the snow, or in a mountain range, or any place except where I was now. The skills didn't seem to transfer.

More accurately, I didn't think I could be of any use any place else except Vietnam. Looking at the armor frightened me. Fighting as a samurai was foreign and strange. Vietnam was familiar. I knew that didn't seem quite right.

For two hours I had been laughing in a dark movie theater on "rest and relaxation." Now I was mentally pulled back again. I walked back to my hotel and crawled into bed.

I stayed there most of the next day.

VILLAGE SNIPER

A week after my R & R, we were lying off the dock at Nha Trang harbor waiting for a passenger when a sniper in one of the houses in the town proceeded to shoot at us—methodically: one round every five or ten seconds. With the engine in idle, my quartermaster and I simply stood on the side of the boat and stared through binoculars to see who was shooting at us. Actually, it mattered very little since we certainly couldn't have returned fire into a "friendly" village. I was extremely curious to determine where the fire was originating. After a period of time of hearing bullets whiz by our heads, Thompsen finally asked, "Wouldn't it be a good idea to depart?" As if I were awakened from a dream, I responded that his idea did have merit. We cruised away after being willing targets for a sniper who probably shot 15 rounds at us as we casually stood full view. To this day, I do not know why I acted as if I were invincible. Probably just stupidity.

ONE OF OURS

Nha Trang. The coast was stunningly beautiful. Limestone climbed from the sea in majestic towers. We skimmed across a China Sea that was as flat as glass. Perfect blue glass. The roar of two V-12 engines gave a sound like a tiger. Kelley in the gun tub, sharp eyes watching beyond the occasional flying fish.

The smell of Navy coffee from the galley. Primitive warm liquid awakening our viscera. The Navy. Our Navy. An institution of love. A Spartan mother who shouts to her departing son "Come back with your shield, or on it."

Kelley grew up in the poverty of West Virginia. Jake was getting a great suntan. Thompsen just wanted to save money for a car and college; earning money by getting shot at was better than bussing dishes for Mrs. Rich Bitch's daughter in some sorority house. Tex was staring into space with the look of an enlightened Buddhist dog. Kid was on the radio checking codes. I was 25 years old. I was the Old Man. The Navy might be an odd home, but at least it was an exciting one, full of vigor and violence. All of us had come from difficult families. We had no complaints. It was pure and true. In short, we loved each other. But men do not use that word.

A helicopter was suddenly on top of us. I was embarrassed that I had been daydreaming. The radio cackled with a strange voice, "Swift boat this is Iron Maiden."

"Roger, we copy" responded Kid.

"Request you come left 30 degrees and proceed one klick."

"Roger" we responded and turned to obey the Huey Cobra above us. A "snake." Gunships that always came to our aid when we needed them.

"Three hundred meters ahead and to your left," called the pilot. "Do you see it? A floating body?"

"Roger, we see it."

"We relay. Please retrieve the floater and take it to Nha Trang harbor pier."

"Roger, out." We replied as we stopped alongside the cadaver. Kelley came down from the gun tub, muttering like an old man.

"That goddamned thing will stink up the whole boat, Skipper. Please! Let's just tie onto it and tow it to the pier."

He had a point. The floater was bloated to the size of a Sumo wrestler. Bleached white. Soft stinking flesh. Kid tried to pull it aboard with a boathook. A big piece of flesh fell off the rib cage. It reminded me of Annapolis. Each holiday, Jake Cohen received a Jewish care package from his mom. Among the goodies was a gefilte fish. Yip, I thought. This guy is like a big hunk of gefilte fish! I found myself muttering obscenities right along with Kelley. Eventually, we got the mass aboard.

"Look, he's got no hands or head left," said Thompsen. "Just fishing line all tangled up around him. 'Coc a dou,'" he said using the Viet phrase for "cut your throat."

We waved at the helo above and it banked off. Within 15 minutes we were at the pier with our cargo. Kelley rolled the stinking hulk onto the cement pier. "Can we go now, skipper?" he asked. Although I had only revulsion for the carcass, it didn't seem appropriate just to leave it there. So we stayed awhile.

I looked at the white rot, drank my coffee and sat on the top of the pilothouse. Beyond the pier, I could see the little village come to life in the morning sun. It was amazing to watch the local Viets who worked at the pier. They averted their eyes and walked around that ivory garbage as if it were a crate of goods. Not one Oriental even gave the body a second glance.

"God," I thought, "these people are now so callused, so truly numb to the horrors inflicted on them, even kids don't give a cadaver a second look, and this is a dilly of a cadaver!"

Then a jeep arrived. A Green Beret colonel from Fifth Special Forces and a civilian with cold, fishy eyes. I climbed down from the gun tub and introduced myself.

"Thank you," said the colonel. Polite. Curt. Then his eyes went to the civilian. "Is that one of ours?'

"Yes. It is," said the guy in the checkered shirt. His strong French accent gave him away. A C.I.A. spook.

I knew that there was nothing more that they would say in my presence. I asked permission to depart, climbed aboard and we left. As we resumed the trip down the coast, I sat cross-legged on the top of the pilothouse. Below me I could hear my crew discussing the incident. I did not volunteer to them that even though our passenger's head and hands had been removed to prevent identification, those two men knew it was one of their "assets." The spy had been tied in fishing line and weighted down. Somehow 007 had floated free. This work was not as glamorous as Ian Fleming had made it out to be.

A year later I was in a barber chair in Arlington, Virginia. The big white cloth fell around me. I looked like a fat white maggot or a Sumo wrestler. I was reading *TIME* magazine. It reported that a colonel, formerly of the Fifth Special Forces in Nha Trang was being investigated for murdering a double agent. Actually, the Green Berets had not said to "murder" him. They used the words "terminate with extreme prejudice." A nice turn of phrase. *TIME* went on to say that the court-martial did not proceed due to lack of evidence. Lack of evidence. Uh huh. From what I had seen the year before there was definitely evidence that a double agent had been at work. He had changed one of our spies into a floater. The problem was that the evidence had turned into gefilte fish.

Just like Jake Cohen's Mom lovingly mailed to him.

ELEPHANT DUNG

I was sent on a mission to resupply a Navy advisor and his Viets. We loaded ammunition and food and proceeded up a particularly foul-smelling river. Flat, stinking mud. No real water. The screws of the boat churned through sludge the consistency of potato soup.

We arrived at what was to be the rendezvous point but I saw no village, no boats, no people. We stopped while Kelley checked the cooling pumps which had ingested so much mud that the engine was overheating. I looked at the chart a second time, certain that we had been given the wrong coordinates.

Suddenly, a man was walking toward us. Knee deep in mud. No shoes, no shirt, just khaki shorts and a .45 in his shoulder holster. As the wretched soul approached I realized that it was an old friend of mine. Mike Dodge was sunburned and sickly. Hollow dark eyes. An enormous grin covered his face, like a kid who had finally seen Santa Claus with presents.

Mike climbed aboard. I tried to look cheerful, but the poor bastard resembled a holocaust survivor. I couldn't imagine what his life was like. Being an advisor in this godforsaken place was like being dropped off naked in the poorest slum of Calcutta. Mike was smiling, but he wasn't shy or modest about begging. We literally gave him everything on the boat. Food, flashlights, ammo, candy from home. Everything. Even the stuff in the first aid box.

Slowly a few of his Viet fighting men crawled aboard. Each loaded a pack or sack or simply filled his hands with what he could carry back across the mud flat. Mike explained that the river had "moved a bit" so his village was no longer a Navy base. It was simply an outpost. Past the mud, we could see a poor hooch or two under exhausted banana trees.

Mike and I talked for a while about the old times. Three years before we had been in the same company at Annapolis. Mike was from Guam. From a Navy family. He was a bookish little guy, not a football player physique. As a child, he studied the World War II Pacific campaign to such an extent that he was an encyclopedia of knowledge on war in the Pacific and in China, Burma, and India as well. One day in speech class he explained the technique of how to climb and harvest a 30-foot coconut tree and how to unhusk the coconuts with a nail.

Mike also told me a great story when we were students. He said that in the '40's in Burma the resistance had only very limited resources. It was impossible to have men monitor the large land mines that the Brits placed under the road. With an observer, you can detonate a mine manually thus destroying only enemy vehicles while allowing friendlies to pass. By chance the British Special Forces under Colonel Slim noticed that the friendly natives avoided the piles of elephant dung on the road. Not the invading Japanese forces. They seemed to enjoy the novelty of driving over elephant dung and splattering it. The solution was elegantly simple: put the mines under the dung. Allegedly it worked perfectly. The Japanese truck drivers swerved out of their way to run over the mines!

If anyone could make it out there, Mike Dodge could. I knew that. Yet when I shook his hand to say goodbye, tears started streaming down my cheeks.

Christ. There he was standing ass-deep in mud waving goodbye with a grin. The only American in eight, maybe ten, miles. The Navy had basically forgotten him. Malnourished, with guts full of parasites, and no supplies. Nothing.

I was convinced that it was the last time I would see him. I knew that sooner or later his pathetic outpost would be overrun.

Sadly and predictably the Navy never gave such men the promotions or recognition that they so richly deserved. The guys who can live on nothing, the men who can make weapons out of elephant dung, scare the corresponding shit out of the

Navy brass. By definition such guerillas are not easy to control. By definition those men do not fit the conventional mold for a sailor or naval officer. Perhaps the Admirals know, like Kipling, that the Gunga Dins of the world are better men than they are.

ENTERING PETITE PASS

To enter Cam Ranh Bay, a boat can take one of two routes. One is a broad open seaway. The other is through a narrow channel through a giant crack in the rock face. It is treacherous. The sea waves crash against the sides as they compress into a slit only a few feet wider than a Swift.

The proper route involved a long soft curve. The more dangerous Petite Pass shortcut saved only eight or ten minutes. We almost always took Petite Pass. At the time no one questioned the gravity that pulled us to the more dangerous route.

Perhaps there is no reason. Wrecking a boat would certainly have led to a court-martial. We wouldn't have considered that a deterrent. So why did we do it? I realize now that perhaps it was simply boredom. Swifts were the most decorated of all the Navy boats operating in Vietnam, yet most of our patrols were uneventful. Most coastal patrols involved no contact with the enemy. We had driven the enemy away—or at least under cover. The river patrols were certainly more dangerous, yet even in the rivers our contact was sporadic and brief.

In earlier wars, less than half of the people who died perished as a result of enemy action. Most died of disease or accidents or other causes. Like the 750,000 Germans who died at Stalingrad primarily from freezing to death.

An even more awesome statistic is that the U.S. lost almost as many men in three Civil War battles as we lost in our entire Vietnam War. Almost fifty thousand died in Gettysburg in three days. Imagine all Vietnam casualties compressed into 72 hours; now imagine how long the American public would have stomached the carnage.

Chronos the Greek god ate his children.

Another fact that causes us to pause is that something like 80 percent of the men and women sent to Vietnam never saw combat. In other words, only 20 percent of the people got shot at 100 percent of the time. At the time, the military had a measure called "the Teeth to Tail Ratio" which measured the fighting force versus the support staff. It would have depressed us all to know how many people were driving desks instead of helicopters.

The Marines in I Corps, the Special Forces guys in the highlands, the Americal Division and a few others saw much more combat than their fair share. All while other people filled Coke machines and shuffled paper.

So what does this have to do with Petite Pass? In truth, I'm not sure. Perhaps it was just that our level of adrenaline was often high and unused. Many days were simply boring, so we took occasional foolish risks for our own health—to get our internal chemicals back in balance.

In the *Odyssey*, Ulysses looks into the "wine dark sea." But he doesn't just look. He *sees*. War brings every sense into the moment. "Be here now!" the Buddhists instruct. Most people go through life unable to focus on the moment. Remember what it was like to bite a strawberry when you were a child? You tasted each bite; you felt it explode in your mouth, filling your nose with the sweet smell. Juice on your lips as you felt each seed crack between your teeth. It is difficult for an adult to eat a single piece of fruit with the attention of a three-year-old.

In combat though, life is lived that way. Buddhism is not a religion. It is a way of living. For those of us in combat, Vietnam was a Buddhist experience. Every Catholic, every Protestant, and every one of the agnostics was actually a devoted Buddhist.

We saw stunningly beautiful sunsets. My theory was that the dust from the bombings contributed to the beautiful colors as the sun's rays cut through those microscopic prisms. The adjective "stunning" is accurate. Even the crudest man would freeze for a moment as they looked at the brilliant pink sky.

Our most primitive sense, that of smell, was often overwhelmed. By nuoc mam's sickeningly strong fish odor. By diesel fuel and the hot exhaust that blew across the deck. By the salt of the sea, a smell that captures Homo Sapiens as quickly as the sight of fire captured cavemen.

No smell was as strong as the urine-sweat smell of our unwashed flack jackets. Days and weeks of fear-induced body fluid soaked deeply into the kevlar. The hot sun made this material give off odors from Swift crews that had been in-country years before ours.

Our eyes and noses were filled with conflicting, even overwhelming senses. Ears would be alert for every crack of the radio, every "slap/bump" of the hull against the water and every splash of the wake. We heard, primarily through our feet, the diesel engines on which our lives depended.

The entire hull vibrated from 24 cylinders humming up and down. Each one going up and down 20 times a second. Bare feet, sun on naked arms and backs, eye muscles forced into a squint for hours at a time as the sun reflected into our sun-burnt faces. We would absentmindedly pick at a scab of jungle rot, or wince as our knees screamed in pain from the boat falling through another sea swell and landing with a hard "splash/thump."

The taste of the sea was always in our mouths. All but the new kids knew every taste of the C-rats. There were over 24 boxes in the case; each became familiar all too quickly. Only last night's beer tasted differently, each time the "33" was belched back up.

And so we became sensing animals. Sensually aware, sensually alive. Perhaps more accurately, it was our senses that kept us alive. That's not surprising. War is primitive, animals are primitive, ergo to survive in war we became more animalistic.

It was no accident that we called ourselves "River Rats." That is a complement to the rat. Twelve animals came to Buddha's funeral. The observant, vigilant rat was the first to arrive.

PETITE PASS: THE EXIT

So did the previous chapter explain why, with hair blowing in the wind, we grinned as we sliced through the narrow crack in the earth called Petite Pass? We could reach out and touch the shadow cool stone rushing by at 30 knots. It must have been from sheer joy at being back. Being safe. Being "home."

If that explanation doesn't convince, let's try another:

When the great racing driver Jackie Stuart was asked how he was able to drive Formula One cars at 200 miles per hour, he responded, "It's simple: total lack of imagination."

Perhaps foolhardiness is related to bravery. Perhaps bravery stems not from something that we *have*, but from something that we *lack*.

THE INSPECTOR GENERAL

Some things are too good to miss. Unfortunately, I wasn't there when Ralph sent the Inspector General packing.

The stories vary, but they go something like this: Saigon was to send an Inspector out to Cam Ranh to assess us. Now how a staff type can assess the fighting capability of a unit is an obvious question, but that was what he was allegedly going to do. Perhaps he was to count paperclips and typewriters. I didn't know.

Anyway, I saw him briefly at breakfast but didn't speak to him. I rushed off to my boat for a 24-hour patrol. The Operations boss at Cam Ranh was Lifer. He was losing his hair but not his sense of humor. He was the primary caretaker of our squadron's two dogs, Ralph and New Kid. Both accompanied him and his crew when they patrolled. When he had about four months to go on his tour he was taken off patrol to become the Ops boss of Cam Ranh. It was the same job Pat Lang had back in Cat Lo.

He took good care of both dogs. Once I saw him feed them pizza. I don't know where he got the pizza, but both dogs enjoyed it. I wanted pizza too; both animals were growing fat and lazy. Both slept at the entrance to the command hooch. To enter H.Q., a person was forced to step over both dogs sleeping in the sand. We washed the dogs every month or so by throwing them overboard a hundred meters from the shore. They emerged from the unwelcome swim, sullen and wet, but all was forgiven when we offered an open can of beef stew.

But back to the story. As I understand it, upon finishing breakfast, the Inspector went to the command hooch. He asked a few questions of our C.O. and of Lifer and then stated that he wanted to go to the pier to see the boats. The boats were about one klick away on a single lane asphalt road.

He climbed into a jeep and insisted that he go without any of the regular officers. Those who met him said that he had a highway patrol/IRS agent "gotcha!" attitude. As he sat down behind the wheel of the jeep, Ralph jumped on the right side seat and sat at the ready. Startled, the I.G. looked and then in a condescending voice said, "Isn't that cute?" After being told that the dog could ride to the pier, he gave a curt nod to the Ops boss and our C.O. and then put the jeep in gear and started down the road.

What the I.G. did not know was that halfway to the pier, on the left-hand side, was the Seabee base. (The Seabees of the Navy were responsible for construction of facilities. The Construction Battalion—"C.B."—people literally built Navy bases in Vietnam from nothing.) As luck would have it, Ralph's archenemy, the Seabee mascot dog, was sleeping on the porch of his outfit's H.Q. near the road and in full view of the passing jeep. (This was the same black dog that Ralph had evicted from our movie two weeks before.)

Upon seeing his black nemesis, Ralph went ballistic. Barking furiously, Ralph did what any good Swifty would do, he attacked with fury. In order to do so, he had to jump over, or through, the I.G. Smashing between the steering wheel and face of the Inspector, Ralph rocketed from the right side of the jeep and out the left, tearing hands off the steering wheel.

Although the jeep was going only 15 miles per hour or so, it swerved to the left and overturned.

We Swifties assumed that again Ralph had gotten the best of the Seabee mascot. He would have attacked with full vigor. No question. We also saw that after the fight his rich red full coat remained unblemished.

As for the Inspector, needless to say he was less battle-ready than our dog. When the jeep overturned he broke his arm.

Within an hour the Inspector General was out of Cam Ranh, on his way to get medical attention and never to return. I don't know what he wrote in his report—perhaps with a broken arm he couldn't write anything. For causing the accident, Ralph was fed a triumphant feast by the Swifties and patted affectionately by all.

When I got back from patrol the next morning, Ralph was still the main topic of conversation. The jeep was turned upright; it suffered only a cracked windshield.

One wit even wrote a mock citation for bravery:

> "On 10 Feb 1968, on or about 1000 hours, mercenary Ralph attacked the enemy. Without regard to his personal safety and without support, he charged from a moving vehicle and inflicted serious damage upon the unsuspecting enemy force. His heroic single-handed action resulted in a clean sweep of the intruder from the base area of operation."

Lifer said that when the I.G. drove off at midmorning, he fully anticipated that the Seabee dog would be outside. He knew Ralph would get excited, but he had no idea our golden dog would be so magnificent.

Exactly what happened is obviously uncertain. The injured I.G. did not talk. Ralph simply smirked.

The Inspector came to judge us, to judge if we Swifties were battle-ready. Battle ready? Shit, even our *dogs* were battle ready. So convincingly so, that the son-of-bitches from I.G. never came back again.

ANDRE

Andre was a genius. He looked like an average guy, but at the Naval Academy he had truly distinguished himself academically. He was married, and I believe that he had a child too.

Being both smart and married, it was surprising that he volunteered for Swifts. He had been in Cam Ranh for his entire tour. I had spent the first half of my year in Cat Lo, a base much less safe and comfortable than Cam Ranh. At Cam Ranh, I learned that some of the married officers would often go to the main base where they spent time with the nurses. It was the married guys who chased nurses, not the bachelors.

Lifer asked if anyone wanted to go back down south to Cat Lo. Months earlier I had sworn that I would do everything possible to get back to the Black Cat Division and my friends. My bosun, Tex, had already gone south. Yet this time when they asked for volunteers I did nothing. I do not know why. Perhaps I was getting soft or I was lacking bravery. I did ask my five crewmen if they wanted to go back: two did, two didn't. Red, who had taken Tex's place on Inky Bite 97, did not vote.

The fair way to select would be to send people to Cat Lo who hadn't been there before. Instead the squadron C.O. decided to draw names. He drew Andre's.

So in the end, it was a married guy who went south with his crew. Down to a hotter area. Within a week Andre's boat was hit. It beached and burned to the ground. Andre took a rocket hit. Shrapnel hit his leg and chest. Part of his crew was saved. Only part.

When I heard what had happened, I felt like a coward. I should have volunteered. If I had taken 97 on the Duong Keo it would have been different. I told myself that my crew would have made it. We should have gone instead of him.

I didn't feel a loss for Andre as a person. Perhaps because he was smarter than I, or perhaps because he was not as close to me as other skippers. Or maybe because I had served my time in Cat Lo already . . . . Or could it be that just because he was married, I improperly imagined that he too had spent nights in the little silver trailer house of the nurses and I hadn't?

It really didn't matter. They would need more boats to go south during the next month, so we would all head to Cat Lo or An Thoi sooner or later anyway.

Steel Wool's boat was with Andre's at the time of the ambush. Steel Wool wrote a touching eulogy. It concluded with a description of how, while Andre was laying on the deck bleeding to death, the Swift just turned lazy casual circles in the water. The boat was out of control, no one was at the helm and it was taking heavy fire. So the craft just motored around and around in casual circles, as it burned and sank. Steel Wool, who wrote well, described with haunting serenity the final minutes of the man and the loss of his boat.

The Cam Ranh squadron C.O., had often played cards with Andre, his favorite of the dozen skippers who were under his command. He took the loss of his friend very badly. It weighed on him. After all, he had picked the name out of the hat. He had sent his friend to his death. In retrospect, the C.O. should have called me into his office two weeks earlier; with a one-on-one plea, my pride would have forced me to volunteer to go.

Andre went. I didn't. Andre died. I didn't. A mistake.

DIVE

A few weeks later, I thought about the cadaver that we had pulled from the water near Nha Trang and I decided to return to see if there were other bodies in the area. Perhaps that spot was an underwater cemetery. We might find a surprise.

It was curious that the men from Fifth Special Forces had not thought of looking for other people or things there. They didn't even ask about the location of our find.

A few days later, we took 97 back to the same place. Standing on the boat looking into the water, we thought that we could see other shapes on the bottom. Dark shapes. Perhaps bodies. Perhaps just seaweed. It was hard to tell. The water was 20 feet deep or more. In the bright sunlight I resolved to return the next day with fins and a scuba mask. I would borrow them from the SEALS. I could free dive down 15 or 20 feet and take a look. I imagined finding several more bodies of people assassinated by the V.C.

Upon return to Cam Ranh, I was ordered to the Ops hooch. There, the Ops boss told me that my orders had arrived. As volunteers for Swifts, we had been promised plumb assignments after our tour. I shot for the moon: I asked for Headquarters, Naval Forces Europe. London. Lifer told me I had gotten exactly what I wanted! In two months I would be on my way to England. An apartment in a lovely section of London, a "flat" in Kensington. Three wonderful years in Europe. This was what the Navy was all about. *The* perfect post!

In the excitement, I forgot about going back to look for more bodies. Further exploration might result in more intelligence, but I didn't care about the outcome of the war enough to volunteer to do extra work. It didn't matter; I was going to London.

THE WARRIOR

"What do you want to do? Live all your life?"

CPL. Robert F. Blinn, U.S. Army

Psychologists say the warrior type of person is typified by having energy. By definition, warriors must limit imagination. They develop silence, action, awareness and bravery; all are keys to hunting animals—quadrupeds or bipeds. Believing in invulnerability helps; thus good warriors should be young. No reason to be dramatic. No reason to take things as personal. Detachment helps.

Psychologists also say that warriors are often unsure of their own worth. Unsure of what they want. They hate the weak, because they fear becoming weak. They fear the coward that lurks within every human. We were, in fact, like that. The men in Vietnam understood one another, but not America. Not the politicians, not Jane Fonda, and not the scum who fled to Canada.

The unpopularity of the war has even prompted some later observers to state that, because of the unique situation, Viet Vets may someday be remembered in history as the most patriotic of any soldiers in America's history. That would be nice. It would also be inappropriate. None of us gave a damn about apple pie or motherhood, or the stars and stripes. We only cared about each other. To that extent we were less like patriots than mercenaries. Poorly paid ones at that.

We were, for the most part, children of dysfunctional families. We fled those flesh and blood families to join the blue and gold family of the U.S. Navy. We fled one dysfunctional family only to join another.

KIT CARSON SCOUTS

The Viet Cong who defected to our side were rewarded; they were trained thoroughly, paid well, and offered a job as mercenaries. They were called "Kit Carson Scouts." Switching sides was encouraged through a program called "Chu Hoi." The quality of the fighting men that we got through the program was difficult to assess. Most were tough little bastards. The trouble was that their loyalty was in question. They switched once; they could switch back again. Or perhaps they had just pretended to change allegiance; some definitely were agents infiltrating our forces. Normally, the Kit Carson Scouts were commanded by a spook, a C.I.A. type. Often a Frenchman.

Now let me take a moment to tell you about the depth gauge on a Swift boat. Like sonar, it told the depth of the water. Our boat drew two and a half feet of water; the keel lay only 30 inches below the surface. The screws protruded below another foot. In theory, if the water was over about 45 inches, we were fine. The depth gauge had two settings: shallow and deep. We *always* used it on shallow. If the sea floor was on the second ring of the sonar's face we were okay. Each ring was two feet at the "shallow" setting.

The more seasoned skippers were normally chosen to do insertions and extractions of SEALS and Kit Carson Scouts. I was told that I would insert a team of ten scouts as soon as the moon settled. At about 0300 we were to drop them off for an ambush on a rocky island. Not a tough assignment. Later at sunrise, Steel Wool, who had come back from Cat Lo, and I would extract them.

As we approached the rocky shoreline, I throttled the boat back. When the depth gauge read four feet, I brought 97 to a full stop. Dead in the water. We were still about ten feet from shore. The Frenchman who was the C.I.A. advisor to the team expressed concern. He thought that I should be able to put the boat's nose onto the rocks and that his men could jump ashore. I pointed out to him that the depth gauge was showing two rings: four feet. Even a foot or two closer would put our screws into the rocks below. We would be trapped. He was unhappy, but he understood. He ordered his men overboard.

Something near panic spread among the mercenaries. Men with the eyes of cold-blooded killers were transformed into sissies. Each afraid to get into the water. Slowly it occurred to me that many of the former V.C. did not know how to swim. Most of my work had been with Navy SEALS, men who were among the best swimmers in the world. I simply had not imagined mercenaries would fear the water.

The Frenchman whispered an order, and the first man went overboard. He sunk to his neck and began a swim/walk to shore, holding his rifle high. One by one the others followed, but only after protesting, banging weapons around, and violating silence in a hundred other ways.

Admittedly, the water was high, and these guys were barely five-foot tall and weighed down with gear, but the level of noise they made on insertion was truly ridiculous. SEALS are perfectly silent. Perfectly.

After the insertion, we backed the boat away. About an hour later, as he was tidying up the pilothouse, Thompsen called me to his side. He pointed to the depth gauge: the goddamned switch was on the "deep" selection. Somehow, it had been bumped. I should have known. I should have tested it. I could have put those men *much* closer to the beach. Four or five feet closer. I was an old-timer and I had made a mistake typical of a new kid. I was embarrassed and angry with myself, but it was okay. Just a "brain fart," no harm done.

*   *   *

Two hours later, I learned that mission had gone badly. One Kit Carson Scout had been shot through a lung. A sucking chest wound. With each labored breath, bloody foam went in and out of the hole in his chest. We took the little trooper's shirt off, and laid him in the cabin. We knew that this wounded trooper had to come back by sea; medevac helos couldn't be spared for a Viet. In other words it would be two hours before he could get medical attention, not 30 minutes by air.

They said the Frenchman was concerned that only two shots were fired on that pitch-black night. It was inconclusive if the team had even been in contact with the enemy. The French C.I.A. commander worried that perhaps another Kit Carson Scout had shot the wounded man. If it were an accident, well, okay . . . but if this wounded guy had been shot by a V.C. who was operating from the inside, one who hadn't changed allegiance after all, then all future operations could also be compromised.

We were amazed that none of the other nine scouts who came aboard gave their wounded comrade a second glance. On the contrary, they all began to eat breakfast. We couldn't believe that they were casually talking and eating C's within a few feet of a dying fellow soldier. They showed no human compassion. Zero.

While the story unfolded, I was concerned about my gigantic screw-up. If the enemy caused the wound, it was certainly my fault. I had not checked the setting on the depth gauge. I had dropped them off too far from shore. Yes, they made noise, but it was because of my *totally* inexcusable mistake. That noise would have been enough to alert the bad guys.

If our mercenaries walked into a trap, I contributed to their defeat. I should have known better.

CONSOLATION

Later I tried to rationalize it away. Perhaps the wounded soldier was a V.C.; perhaps our friendlies greased him. Two shots. Very odd. That isn't the way it happens when a force of ten men goes into an ambush. There could easily be several hundred shots. Never two.

Blood from the lung is frothy and bright pinkish red; quite different from a gut shot, which is much darker and thicker.

It is hard to put a measure on how much I contributed to the sad result. Misreading the depth gage sure as hell affected the mission.

Lawyers have a phrase, "contributory negligence."

*　　*　　*

Mark was thoughtful and compassionate. Because he went to Yale, he often used odd references. He didn't know why I was depressed; Thompsen and I kept the depth gauge screw-up a secret. Still, Mark knew that I needed cheering up. He stressed that we all contributed to this odd stew. That everyone had several examples of things that we had done that we kept as deep secrets.

Oddly, we quickly forgot the things that we did that were good. Mark reminded me of our removing the fishhook that was deeply imbedded in a boy's foot a few weeks earlier. Of not killing the leper and the girl. The good outnumbered the bad ten to one, but in memories, it is the other way around.

Don Quixote said, "Such are the fortunes of war which more than any other are subject to change." He and Sancho Panza stumbled along. Actually the author, Miguel Cervantes, had survived one of the biggest naval battles of Spanish history. At the Battle of

Lepanto, his ship was sunk and he was taken prisoner. He knew what he was talking about, yet he made it into a comedy.

I was reminded again of the poem:

> As flies to wanton boys,
> We are to the gods.
> They kill us for their sport.

My cousin Linda was a newly-minted elementary teacher at a Catholic school. She said that each morning she asked the kids what was on their mind, what they wanted to pray for. Often they would mention a relative who was ill or in trouble. But the most frequent request in her kindergarten was to pray for animals. Especially road-kill. When she told me that I laughed. Later I remembered that as a little kid, I had a recurring dream in which I was a dog on a busy highway. Each time I tried to go left or right, another car would hit me. The cars didn't stop for me or swerve; they came too fast to avoid them.

In the *Odyssey*, when Odysseus went to Hades, he met only naked souls. He reflected in ways not possible elsewhere. Dark and isolated. In such an environment, he explored who he truly was.

A dead scout, road kill, a nutty Spaniard jousting at windmills. Naked souls in hell. All pieces of a mosaic of myth and reality.

But that's not consolation.

So did the mercenary live or die? I don't know. We didn't keep track of things like that in 1969. Today, it is different; now I care. Against all odds, I hope the little guy made it.

Cam Ranh

Ba Cuc

Ralph resting by sand bags at Operations hooch

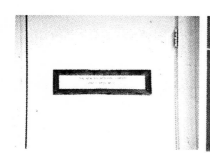

Door of "The New Kid Memorial Library and Coffee Mess"

Night fight—.50 caliber tracers

New Kid, the dog, ashore at Barracks #50

Inside the New Kid Library

SHORT TIMER

*I feel myself driven toward an end that I do not know. As soon as
I shall have reached it, as soon as I shall become unnecessary,
an atom will suffice to shatter me. Till then, not all the forces
of mankind can do anything against me.*

Napoleon

ICE CREAM

The C.O. came to my table with a smile. He sat beside me and leaned over with a conspiratorial wink. "We've got a virgin DD coming today, do you want it?"

"Sure, Commander. Thanks." We Swift skippers were basically divided into three types. New kids, seasoned, and finally, short timers. I had been in-country ten months. Although rank among us meant little, seniority now allowed my crew first pick of assignments. That is why the skipper offered us the opportunity to be forward gun spotters for the destroyer that would be off our coast.

The job was simple. Go up the river to the target and then direct the destroyer's big guns on to it. In theory we were supposed to be close enough to see the shells landing. That was the theory. In fact, you'd have to be out of your mind to get that close. Not one of us in the "Brown Water Navy" trusted the "Squid Navy" enough to let them shoot within 500 meters of our boat. The deep-water guys in a new ship with a new gunnery officer had to earn our trust first. Until they had been with us a week or more, they were considered wahoos who would make mistakes. Mistakes like landing shells on us rather than the enemy. So for the first or second day, we played it very safe.

But that was not the point at all. The issue was *ice cream*. The first boat to go out to the destroyer was always the lucky one. And so, on a sunny afternoon we cruised alongside the new destroyer, our chance to show off. We approached it at 30 knots. Each of us wore only a ragged olive drab T-shirt and a khaki swimming suit.

The crew of the destroyer looked down at our boat with a mixture of awe and pity. We wore no hats, no shoes, no insignia. What the destroyer men did see was a very fast little black-gray

GARY R. BLINN

boat with badly patched bullet holes here and there. Each member of the ship's crew looked first at his own specialty on our boat. That is, the men who manned the destroyer's guns noticed that our .50 calibers were spotless. The destroyer's quartermasters would look into a pilothouse that had charts and radars in perfect condition. The snipes on the man-of-war could tell from the sound that our engines were tuned like a Ferrari at Le Mans.

Red brought our boat to the ship's ladder. By now 100 men were along the rails. Thompsen, Kelley, and I climbed into the quarterdeck. The ship's officers in their starched uniforms were at a loss to even guess who was in charge. We were sunburned warriors; they were not. "Request permission to come aboard," I said. "I'm Lieutenant Blinn. May we meet your weapons officer and your gunner?" The officer of the deck shook my hand and stared at my impoverished dress. Soon we were in the wardroom, being served coffee and freshly baked cookies, of which Kelley ate a dozen before he sat down.

The ship's C.O. entered. He was an odd duck. He looked like Calvin Coolidge, and Calvin was upset that we were impressing his crew with our Clint Eastwood act. In due course, we covered the details of their intended target and explained precisely where we would be when they started shooting. Finally, we could get to the real business at hand: begging.

"Captain, do you have any extra ice cream?" I asked. Calvin Coolidge squirmed for a moment and then said the most ridiculous thing in the world, "No, we can't spare any!"

I couldn't believe my ears. This anal-retentive, coward was the type of officer who endangers the Navy. Not a brother. Not worthy of the imaginary bullet I wished to put between his eyes. Most C.O.s gave us five gallons and even an extra treat like a pizza or salami.

We beggars were fearless. What could he do to me, send me to Vietnam? So I asked again: "We do not need much. Just a gallon or two and some cookies for the rest of our crew."

"We can't spare it," he said. His crew of 300 versus mine of 6. It was a joke, but apparently he had to keep face. I gave him a devilish grin, which puzzled that poor unsuspecting bastard. I smiled at the weapons officer; Kelley ate four more cookies, and we waved good-bye.

Two hours later the gunshoot began. The destroyer fired upon the target and came remarkably close. Kelley reported that the round was lost. He asked them to fire ten rounds of white phosphorus. Again, we reported to the ship four miles away that they had hit nothing even though the target was now destroyed. And so it went for most of an hour. The ship continued firing and we continued reporting their failure. Finally the ship called off the gunshoot.

Word got to the other boats. The destroyer left two days later. It had fired most of its ordnance and had hit *nothing*, or so we said. I was careful to report their "failure" to Saigon. So much for Captain Coolidge.

Later, I was posted to the Pentagon. Systems Analysis. We analyzed data from Vietnam. Such data included targets destroyed, ordnance expended, and the effectiveness of Naval bombardment.

I had a healthy suspicion of the data that crossed my desk. For what it's worth, the ice cream in the mess on the fourth floor D ring of the Pentagon isn't bad at all.

BODYSNATCH

A bodysnatch is a kidnapping. It isn't easy to kill an enemy without getting hurt yourself. It is substantially harder to capture someone alive, especially a V.C. general who is protected by soldiers. No one would be crazy enough to do that. Except Navy SEALS.

We worked with both SEAL Team One and Team Two. Usually our work involved transporting them to sites where they would establish an ambush. Insertions and extractions. One evening at supper I sat beside Tim Wettack, the C.O. of Team One. He was studying a tiny Navy chart of a pear-shaped island. On the chart, the island was only the size of a thumbnail. It had no name, but it lay off the entrance of Nha Trang, a major Viet fishing village. Lt. Wettack said that a team was going on a night mission there and asked if my boat had been assigned. I told him that Oscelot would do the insertion, and that I would be going out at 2000 to a patrol area further north.

I finished eating turkey and biscuits and left him studying the tiny map. The mission appeared to me to be ridiculous; that island was only the size of two city blocks. My boat had passed the steep, rocky little lump many times. A pathetic place which looked devoid of life to me.

Four hours later my boat was scrambled. From our northern area, we were told to rush south. The SEALS on the mission had encountered resistance. The bodysnatch had gone badly and the leader of SEAL Team Two, Bob Kerrey, had been wounded. The V.C. that they had hoped to capture could not be found. Word came down to us that perhaps some of the bad guys had attempted to swim ashore to escape.

So while Oscelot's boat extracted the SEAL Team, I was given orders to search the water between the island and the shore, with instructions to look for a swimming V.C. general. It was pitch dark when we arrived about 80 minutes after the firefight. The likelihood of our success seemed small. I was sorry that Kerrey had been wounded; at the time I didn't know how seriously. Unlike Wettack, a Kansas athlete who drank beer with us, Kerrey was both quiet and introverted. Consequently, I didn't know him as well as the other team leader.

*   *   *

On a typical mission, it was usually very, very quiet. As the six-man team prepared for an insertion, there was *total* silence. Dull black tape covered grenades, dog tags, radios, everything. Clothing tucked in, not a visible piece of silver or brass to reflect even a moonbeam. Not a single thing that would make a noise if touched. The team members do not talk to each other. They communicate in silence. Painting one another's faces with flat black and olive grease paint. Checking the weapons, especially the M-79 grenade launcher. It was an odd little thing that looked like a very short single-shot shotgun. The M-79 fired a golf ball-sized round that was made of tightly wrapped, thin stainless steel wire. When it exploded, the wires flew out in ever-expanding circles. Victims looked as if they had been in a violent knife fight.

After the insertion one team member remained on board the Swift to operate the radio. He did not talk to the men on the ground. Instead he would simply key the "transmit" button, which changed the radio's sound from static to a different sound of silence. By clicking the transmit button, SEALS sent coded messages without words.

Just before the insertion, SEALS paired up, faced each other, and gave a final check to weapons, radios, and overall readiness. Unconsciously, our Swift crew stood in silence watching what the V.C. called "devils with painted faces."

Hairy-chested stuff. Our Swift boats just made the insertions and extractions. We were taxicabs. Glad that we were not getting

off at hellholes where intelligence had promised that it would be
unusually dangerous. We worked closely with the SEALS, but when
it came to thrills, they were out of our league. Way out.

*   *   *

But the night of the bodysnatch, things hadn't gone well. Inky
Bite 97 motored in a search pattern looking for a swimmer, a black
head of hair bobbing in the warm South China Sea. Six square
miles to cover with a searchlight that covered ten square feet of
black water. Ninety million square feet of water and at any moment
we could look at ten. A one in nine million chance that our light
would be on the fugitive.

Slowly more information trickled in. Bob Kerrey had had his
right foot blown off. Later he was awarded the Medal of Honor for
that mission. I don't remember many other details of that night; it
was not particularly memorable compared to others. My boat played
only a minor part in this particular drama. A routine mission, yet
no day or night was truly routine. The amazing thing about war is
that it floods a person with a variety of experiences that are beyond
belief. Beyond life. Beyond the imagination of a sane person.

I'm sure the V.C. who escaped that night would agree.

*   *   *

Bob Kerrey returned to his home state of Nebraska and became
governor. That career seemed odd to me; he had been so quiet in-
country.

Twenty-six years later, when John Kerry, the Swifty, was a
Senator from Massachusetts, and Bob Kerrey, the SEAL, was also a
U.S. Senator, I ate a fish dinner with my wife and son at the site of
the insertion. After the meal, six old Viet fishermen dressed in
tattered clothes joined us for tea. They were proud of the fact that
they had many children and wondered why I had only one. I
couldn't explain that having many children was not as common in
our culture. Between sips of hot tea, I glanced up the steep hill

and thought how green and peaceful it now looked in the bright warm afternoon sunlight.

My son Rob had just turned 19. He could tell how much I enjoyed being with such men, how much I respected them. Missing teeth, wide flat fishermen's feet. Big smiles. Perhaps some of these very fishermen had been soldiers on that island in 1969. My son was much too polite to ask.

THE COURT-MARTIAL

I was ordered to be a judge at a summary court-martial. I had taken a course at the Naval Academy on military justice, so it took only an hour or two to reread the book, *The Uniform Code of Military Justice*.

It was a hot, bright day when we took our place at the big green felt table. All of us were officers; the defendant was an enlisted man. An engineman on a Swift boat.

The facts were simple: three days before (well, three and a half), he was drunk and driving a jeep at 0200 on the one-mile road from Cam Ranh to the pier. At the same time another Swifty was drunk and walking in the middle of the road going the same direction, wearing camouflage fatigues.

The result was predictable: the jeep emerged unscathed. The driver was okay too. The pedestrian was flown to a hospital in Japan; his condition was between "sort of okay" and "not too good."

As I looked at the defendant, all I saw was a good-looking young guy with a rock solid body and sad eyes.

In the end, we judges reduced the engineman in rank and fined him. His naval career was now over, but he would be back in combat the next day.

The pedestrian would not be coming back. Maybe the collision saved him from getting killed by a bullet. Maybe he would get disability pay from the Navy for the rest of his life.

Before the trial I thought that justice sorted out the good and the bad. During and after the trial, I realized that the only question was: Why did this sorry event have to happen? There was now no way to make it right. Before the court-martial, I was not involved; during and after the trial, I became part of it. It sounds strong, but

I became partly "dirty" because of it. Like the war, the legal system mixed both good and bad into an indigestible stew.

As for careers, I realized that I would make a very poor lawyer or judge back in the states. Law school was off my list. Hell, I wouldn't even make a very good police desk sergeant in Olongapo, Philippines.

TRAVIS

Travis went to Yale. He was a serious looking guy. Heavy eyebrows, dark eyes, a soft and thoughtful voice.

Travis was the resident philosopher. He was interested in two big questions. What made us volunteer for this? He was constantly asking why we went out of our way to get here. The Navy had hundreds of thousands of easier jobs. Why did we feel we had to volunteer for this?

The other question that bothered Travis was the definition of bravery. It wasn't as simple as it appeared. I told him how the one torture at SERE that haunted me was to have my eyelids cut off. Just the thought of having my eyeballs dry out made me tremble. Travis understood. Everyone has a different perception of danger. Look at a photo of people on a roller coaster. Some are laughing; others are hanging on with white-knuckle fear. Some hang out the side, others close their eyes. It's the same experience, but vastly different levels of emotion.

I told Travis that I had parachuted out of aircraft and had photographed sharks underwater, but I didn't have the courage to live in a wheelchair. He understood completely.

Travis said a writer named Alvarez had studied mountain climbers. He found that certain guys just keep trying progressively more dangerous climbs until finally they were attempting mountains that had a high probability of killing them. At what point does it become suicide? It is okay to climb Mount Fuji. Mount McKinley is much more of a challenge. K2 or Nanga Parbat or Everest can kill you. The Eiger is notorious. So at what point should we stop? Even if the chance is one percent, do you dare repeat it ten times? Twenty?

Travis was the only Swift skipper to become fluent in Vietnamese. He would chat with each Viet he encountered asking "How's the wife and kids?" or "How's fishing?"

He was strange, but in a good way. Years later he married a lovely, bright and shy young woman. She was blind.

THINGS THAT GO BUMP
IN THE NIGHT

Our patrol of area 4B ended at 0400. Four a.m. and we were on our way back from Hon Heo to base for dinner and a good day's sleep. We began transiting area 4C, a restricted zone. An area where it was prohibited for all Viet boats. In theory it should all be open water.

The night was pitch black. Thompsen gunned the engines to full speed and within a minute, Inky Bite 97 was high in the water, skimming across the still and flat South China Sea. Roaring home in the dark.

Midway through 4C, there was a huge "thump." A sound like we had run over a log, which is almost true. A fishing sampan is a log-sized piece of wood.

My guts sank. In my mind's eye I could imagine that we had T-boned a fishing boat. Two men cut into pieces by our boat's screws. Those propellers would chew up the boat, the fishing gear and the people. They were turning at 1800 rpm, 30 times per second.

We made a slow 180-degree turn to port and retraced our path at a crawl. Ahead I could hear humans in the water moaning. Soon our searchlight illuminated a piece of wood. Then more. Finally an area the size of the lawn of a house. Just pieces of black water-soaked wood. The little Viets' heads were hard to see in the water. Their black hair blended with wood and sea. Finally Kid saw one. We pulled the wide-eyed fisherman aboard. To my astonishment he had all four limbs! Not a scratch. He turned back to the dark sea and pointed. The moans grew. We found another man. Again, he was unscathed. I could hear a child cry. A minute later, he too came out of the water like a wet fish. Whimpering.

Loudly. A little boy of six. Unhurt. Finally another child, a girl about eight. Miraculously all were unharmed.

As the shock wore off, the two adults started protesting that they had lost everything. We were sympathetic, but, hell, they shouldn't have been there in area 4C. The offshore restricted areas were often designated in an area where the V.C. had been smuggling arms ashore. If these guys were not red commies, they were certainly bright pink. Still, they had a point. Their livelihood was destroyed. A fisherman without a boat is in deep guacamole.

After half an hour, my Viet interpreter was able to calm them down. We told them to find the local province chief and ask if he could help get a replacement boat. We told them that we would drop them off at the next fishing vil.

I wasn't happy. It was still 30 nautical miles to base, and Inky Bite 97 was not running well. A big vibration indicated that we had bent a shaft and a screw when they bit into the wooden hull. I didn't want to take the time to encrypt a message to base that our boat was no longer battle-ready. Encryption would take half an hour and we could be back in two. So we dropped the four lucky souls at a pier and limped home.

It was 0700 when we arrived. Hughes was already on the pier. He was furious. Those little Viets had gotten to their province chief at sunrise. The chief, in turn, called the Naval Liaison and he had called my squadron skipper. Hughes wanted to know why I hadn't notified him of the collision at 0430. I didn't have an answer except that our encryption system was ridiculously slow and this wasn't info I could send in the clear. Hughes, the squadron skipper was also angry that I had bent a screw. Inky Bite 97 would have to come out of the water. A big job for the shore facility. I was sorry to have damaged my boat, but also pleased that I had avoided decapitating a kid. I also wondered how illiterate fishermen in a boat the size of a log were supposed to know where a prohibited zone would be. They had no radar, no navigational charts. All they knew was where the fish were schooling. So I stood on the pier looking appropriately apologetic. Hughes vented his spleen on me and eventually grew tired of shouting. I then shuffled off to get soup and a sandwich. Red, my bosun, went to the repair facility to schedule the dry dock.

For the next week or two we would have to borrow another boat. One that didn't fit. It was like borrowing someone else's shoes. If they were not Jake's guns on 97, I couldn't trust them. If they were not Kelley's two engines, we couldn't be sure. Kid's radios on our boat worked perfectly, how could we be confident of others? This was not an issue of "preference"; it was an issue of added risk to our lives. 97 was a trusted warrior; she had proven it time and again. She was a tough and honest little bitch.

Maybe those commie fishermen felt the same about their boat, the one that was now just flotsam. Two days later, the U.S. province advisor authorized buying them a replacement at America's expense. Eight days after that, my crew and I were back on 97. We loved her. No other word for it: Love.

THE CHURCH

One night I had a great dream. Memorable. It summarized much of the reading that I had done earlier. It also convinced me that I would finish my tour of duty unscathed. In my dreams, a priest was droning on about the hereafter. I was less convinced than I thought I should be. As I tried to hide my lack of belief in what the Padre was saying, I felt warm breath, like sticky sweet blood, behind my right ear. I turned to look into the yellow eyes of a beautiful silver-gray wolf. The wolf spoke, "Don't bother to listen. You already know."

"What? What do I know?"

In my dream, the wolf talked without moving his mouth. He talked with his eyes. "You know the same as I. All you can depend upon is yourself. You can enjoy the sun and sea. You can enjoy the earth, the stars, your body, and your mind. You can appreciate freedom, the excitement of the hunt, and a full belly. You can know, enjoy, and appreciate life. What you cannot get is magic to overcome life's insane difficulties. So let's go. Get up!"

"Who are you?"

"A dog. An answer. A wolf. You. What does it matter? There is no way to *understand*. If I as a wolf run down a rabbit, is it a 'tragedy' or a 'warm meal?' It's all in the perspective. The *true* story cannot be told. Impossible. So let's go outside and enjoy the fresh air and go for a brisk trot in the country. Listening to this clergy fool babble is a waste of time. For two million years man has tried to understand life and death. He must have either more brainpower or God must give him more clues."

I got up and the wolf and I trotted out of the church. As I looked back I saw myself in a coffin.

I had just walked out of my own funeral.

I awoke with a grin. Happy. Confident.

DENTISTS

The dentists wanted to participate in the "Win the Hearts and Minds" program. They decided that they would like to do some free dental work in a Viet vil. It seemed like a good idea, so we selected the tiny island of Binh Ba. The people on the isle were primarily fishermen and their families. The Viet Navy also had a small detachment of Marines and their dependents on Binh Ba as well. Good little guys, they had two American advisors living among them. "Red Dog" and "The Old Man." A young Lt. (jg) and a 25-year veteran mustang. "The Old Man" had started as a seaman, worked all the way up to chief, and then gained a commission. They were both good men. It was nice to do a favor for their village.

The island was three klicks across Cam Ranh Bay from the Swift base. The junk base was on a tiny beach nestled below a rusted French six-inch gun emplacement. Originally, it had also been a base for the French Foreign Legion. Dependent children scurried over cement bunkers and through the tunnels.

So on the prescribed day, the 97 boat carried three dentists to Binh Ba. We dropped them off on the pier and they set up shop in front of the one room schoolhouse. My crew and I were invited to join the fishermen. We ate squid and rice cakes. Drank a beer or two with the two advisors and watched the kids play on the beach. The beer was local: "33" or "Ba Muy Ba" in Vietnamese. The nicest thing I can say about "33" is that it came in big bottles. The kids were truly happy. So were we.

As the sun began to set, the dentists returned to the pier. I asked the quiet one how their day had gone. He said simply, "When I opened the mouth of the first patient, a teenage girl, I said to myself, 'there is a month of work with just this one child and we've got a hundred here!'"

I'm sure he overstated the case. But clearly the dentists had overestimated their ability and underestimated the task at hand. I thought to myself that there was no need for him to be discouraged about it; all of us had done the same. America. The U.S. Navy. All of us. Even the dog, New Kid; we had all overestimated our ability and underestimated the task at hand.

LUCKY LITTLE GUYS

Once there was an old lady in Nebraska who told her daughter that it was time for her to die. The daughter said, "Oh, Mom. How do you know?"

The old lady answered, "I know, because I am no longer curious." We were all growing tired. Too tired to even care how the story would end.

*   *   *

We came upon a very suspicious boat one night. The small craft made a run for the beach. We gave chase. With a spotlight we could see three little guys jump from their sampan and run ashore. They ran to a place where six fishing boats were overturned with their hulls up. Nets lay across the boats to dry. The sides of the boats were held by logs about a foot above the sandy beach.

It was pitch black. Our Swift's spotlight was on the boats. The fugitives were hiding under one of them. Kelley said from what he saw, he was certain they were armed. Red agreed. I wasn't so sure. Perhaps it was just kids who were scared. Still, why had they been out so late and in an area where there was only poor fishing?

So that was the situation. My Swift was 50 meters offshore. Six fishing boats laying on the beach, and three little guys hiding under one of them. Behind the boats was a tiny village. My choices were limited. We could fire at the boats with the twin .50's. Chances were good that we could kill or wound the guys in black. But it was also certain that some bullets would go into the hooches, bamboo and grass huts that probably contained sleeping women and kids. Furthermore, there was a chance that once we began to shoot, the men would run into the village. Kelley was a good shot, but it was expecting too much to be confident that he would kill the suspects without hurting the innocent folks too.

And "suspect" was the correct word. Armed men? Unarmed kids? V.C.? No way to tell. The spotlight remained fixed on the black hulls. "Let me have 'em, Skipper!" Kelley said in a hoarse whisper from the gun tub.

I had one alternative. We could beach Inky Bite and put three men ashore. They could circle between the vil and the fishing boats. We could flush them out that way. But that plan involved danger to us. First, a beached Swift at a questionable vil would be a perfect target for a B-40 rocket. Second, the searchlight would light up our shore party with their backs to the vil. Easy targets for a shooter from the hooches which were only a few meters inland from the six overturned boats. Finally, the boats were resting on big logs. The bad guys were under one of the six. They could fire at my shore party before we knew exactly where they were hiding.

The searchlight continued to bathe the immediate area in light, but beyond it was just black jungle and a dark vil. As usual, Kelley was on an emotional high, ready to shoot. I called to Thompsen beside me. We explored options, but there was simply no solution without risk. Risk killing innocent villagers or risk the lives of my shore party? Choose.

We had been grappling with the problem for almost ten minutes. I'm sure to the people under the boat it seemed like eternity. Our Viet called to them on the loudspeaker to come out with their hands up. They stuck tight. Smart move.

Finally, I made the decision. "They are unarmed kids, we are pulling back." Kelley cursed.

We were within a few weeks of ending our tour. I wanted to get my crew home alive. All of them. It wasn't worth risking them to kill one V.C. or even three.

There would still be lots of V.C. to kill later. Our replacements could figure out how to do it. I was growing too weary to care.

*   *   *

Upon my return to Can Ranh the next morning, I was told that my orders to London had been cancelled. Instead, I was to be sent to the goddamned Pentagon. A section that did systems analysis and war gaming. Solving problems. I would work with the McNamara "whiz kids" making war a game. Oh God, oh God.

A COSMIC JOKE

Imagine being a poor fisherman with rags for clothes.

Imagine living your entire life in a little jungle village on the other side of the world. Imagine in 18 hours, you get transported to a city in the U.S.A. Imagine you are given a gun and told to go out and shoot the American Republicans but not the Democrats. Or the agnostics but not the regular churchgoers. Shoot Baptists not Episcopalians. Imagine that the people in the U.S. are all told to shoot back at you as you try to sort them out.

If you do that exercise, you begin to get an idea of the frustration of an American in a country fighting guerillas. Outsiders can't help in a civil war. Thomas Payne said, "Belief in a cruel god makes a cruel man." Who in the hell could believe that God was benevolent with this going on? Our world was like a fishbowl where all the fish are on the attack. No place for a guppy to hide from the sharks or piranhas. No fish owner looking through the glass. No General Sherman to end it mercifully by showing no mercy.

One armored personnel carrier had paint on the side that said, "Fighting for peace is like fucking for virginity."

My quartermaster, Thompsen, had a solution that was as good as any. He proposed that we put all the Viets on a big boat and take it out to sea. Then we burn the country with napalm from one end to the other wiping out *everything* . . . then we sink the boat.

We sang two songs over and over: "If I die in the combat zone, box me up and ship me home."

And "It's my party and I'll cry if I wanna, cry if I wanna, you would cry too if it happened to you."

Curiously, we stopped singing "We gotta get out of this place, if it's the last thing we ever do." The two other songs were more fitting. Some were starting to seriously doubt that we would get out. God's competition recommended abandoning hope if you entered. Not bad advice.

Clearly having a functioning brain is not an advantage. Having imagination is worse. Being tired is good; it numbs you so you do not take the cosmic joke personally. It isn't as if God cared for you or heard your pleas specifically. He simply didn't give a shit.

I know no one, no one, in Swifts who went to religious services. Nietsche said the only proper prayer is "Thank You." We didn't pray. We knew no one was going to get our ass out alive for us. We were on our own.

The most common religious reference I saw was "Yea, though I walk through the Valley of Death, I fear not . . . because I'm the toughest mother in the valley."

Months before, just for fun, we shot up a beautiful Buddhist shrine near the beach. Later we felt an odd sense of shame for our destruction.

We too were omnipotent gods with no sense of mercy. But a little remorse came to us later.

I hope someday God regrets what he did to us. By us, I mean both Viets and Americans. I hope someday He is sorry he allowed that cosmic joke to continue for years and years and years. It wasn't funny.

PHILOSOPHY OF WAR

26 April. They said that as the boat came out of the Cua Giang River, the aft gunner on the 79 boat fell down. He just "fell down." The sniper's round entered the American's side just an inch below his flack jacket. It came out the other side. The exit hole is bigger. He was dead before he hit the deck.

When I heard the news, my first thought was that it seemed like a nice way to go. I wondered how the message got back to families. Moms and dads and brothers. Would they say, "He just fell down," when they broke the news to his kid sister? Especially his sister. My little sister was just finishing high school. It was late April. Buying a prom dress. No, not really. It was 1600 in Cam Ranh, no one buys a prom dress at 0400. Twelve hours difference in time zones with Nebraska. Even a different day. Who buys a prom dress at 4 a.m.? Pink or yellow?

An hour before, a young Swifty had died. Because of that, my mind went through five or six abstract steps and ended up on a yellow prom dress. A man died and my brain went into fucking gaga land. I stared at the bulkhead and asked, "Am I going nuts or is this the way to keep from going nuts?" Jesus. I didn't even ask the kid's name.

Wasted.

"No guts, no Navy Cross," we said to each other. But an American kid with 12 years of education at, say $3,000 per year . . . so the education in his brain alone is worth $36,000. His earnings, if he had lived, could be $15,000 per year for, say, 30 more years or $450,000. A $450,000 man versus a little Viet who will earn $100 per year for 40 years . . . so economically, a V.C. is worth only $4,000 or $1/100^{th}$ of an American. Tell the Viet's mom and dad that. Mr. and Mrs. Nguyen wouldn't buy into such a goofy analysis. But maybe McNamara would. Tell the Pentagon that we will trade only one American for one hundred V.C . . . . any other loss ratio is unacceptable. There I go again. Navy Cross, to value of a brain, to a speech, to the Secretary of Defense.

If this double-loop thinking sounds insane, it may be. But that is the way we talked. "The real advantage of suicide is that it creates total freedom," said someone at supper. Can't argue that. It is like a mental jigsaw puzzle. None of the pieces fit anyway, so put them together however you wish. It makes no difference. Such were our thoughts. Conversation too.

In theory, with four years of college, my brain was worth $100,000. It could be put out of order by a bullet worth 2 cents. (Lead is only 16 cents per pound.) Now 2 cents doesn't sound like much, but in China when they execute someone, they send a bill to the family for the bullet. See, $100 annual income per person is 30 cents per day, so a bullet is worth almost an hour of work or $6.00 converted into American money for an American. Maybe we in America should send the condemned American prisoner's family a bill for $6.00 of electricity used by the chair.

Alexander the Great conquered two-thirds of the known world by the time he was 32. He changed tax systems, governments, political and economic systems, alphabets, architecture, language and everything else. In contrast, Hannibal just went from battle to battle. Hannibal won often, but the moment he vacated the battlefield, it all returned as before. America was like Hannibal; we left no political or economic reforms. A few mopeds, a few whores, but no real improvements.

We were all nuts. That's why Heller's "Catch 22" was so popular. It is better to think of your kid sister's prom dress than a gut shot boy just two years older than she.

Later I realized that, again, Kipling had written the same thing before I had thought of it; he wrote:

> "Two thousand pounds of education drops to a ten rupee
> Jeznil . . . shot like a rabbit . . ."

(Kipling, *Arithmetic on the Frontier*)

*   *   *

Later still, I read that in 1812 at Waterloo, after the battle, the men were eager to care for the horses . . . they could release emotions with the animals which they could not give to other combatants. We didn't have horses, but Ralph and New Kid served the same purpose.

JESUS, WHAT A FRIEND

Each morning for radio checks, someone sang the sarcastic theme song, "What a friend we have in Jesus Christ Almighty what a pal." I heard it every other day. For a year. It reminded me of the assurance I had gotten earlier when someone quoted Kafka: "The Second Coming of Christ *will* happen . . . the day after the world ends."

The song repeated every day. Every day. Some poets repeat lines again and again. They say that we do not really hear things the first time. The same phrase takes new meaning each time it is repeated.

Buddhism is based on three pillars: great faith, great doubt, and great perseverance. I like that. To them it is natural that doubt should be equal to faith.

Spiritually, we river rats had that down cold. We had doubts up the wazoo. We doubted the war, Washington, ourselves. We doubted heaven, our wives, our girlfriends, our leaders, and our sanity. We doubted humanity and our mortality. Faith was non-existent except for each other, our weapons, and our trusty little boats.

As for perseverance, we had it too: "How much longer you got to go in-country?"

"Sixty-six days and wake up. I'm so short I can parachute off a dime. I'm so short, you have to dig a hole to kick me in the ass. I'm so short . . ."

* * *

If a man loves God, he can become holy in twenty years.
But if he hates God, he can do the same work in two years.

Author unknown

MY KID SISTER'S BIRTHDAY

10 May 1969 began on a happy note. I thought of my sister, now 18. I wondered what she had planned for her birthday. Pretty, blonde, smart, and young. An entire exciting life ahead.

The sun was just coming up as we left the pier. My boat and Badger's. We were scheduled to patrol adjacent areas just south of the base. At 20 knots, the sea air felt great, Badger's boat was on my port side. We ran parallel, each crew making signals and grinning at the other.

Suddenly Kid came up to my side. I could tell from his face that the news wasn't good. He motioned me down into the cabin. On the radio was a frantic "May Day," the international signal for "I am in danger." The voice was familiar. It was The Old Man. He and Red Dog and 30 Viet Marines were pinned down on the beach. I could hear heavy automatic weapons fire in the background as he spoke on the radio. They were unable to advance. Unable to retreat. Laying on their bellies in the shallow sand dunes of the narrow beach. V.C. bullets whizzing above them. They were dying.

I picked up the mike and said, "This is Inky Bite 97. I will be on site in 20 minutes. Hold on. We will extract you. Inky Bite 36 is with me. Do you copy?" The response was emotional. The Old Man said he had heard the message loud and clear. He asked us to hurry. Badger joined the conversation saying that he had heard it all. Our base operations officer also reported that he had heard the radio traffic and asked us to keep him posted.

From that moment on, everything happened automatically. Literally. Everything just happened without input. Kid kept upbeat radio messages going crisply, giving confidence to the two American advisors.

Inky Bite 97 turned in a giant sweeping turn to starboard

342 GARY R. BLINN

hugging the coast. We didn't turn the boat. Inky Bite 97 turned her own little bow straight into the direction of the firefight. Almost two hundred years before, John Paul Jones had said, "Give me a fast ship; I intend to sail in harm's way." Our little boat raced to the coordinates at 25 knots. We didn't guide the boat; she went as instinctively as a terrier chases a rat. I simply stood in the pilothouse door sensing. I could tell from the metallic "clack" that Jake had the twin .50s loaded and ready. Extra ammo boxes by his side. The GM diesels screamed as the hull rose above the water. Kelley already had 81-millimeter mortar rounds out of the cardboard tubes, their fuses set. Kid had automatic rifles loaded and distributed while Thompsen bounced in the pilothouse with a steady hand on the wheel. His eyes were trained ahead looking for the tiny bursts of light ahead that would indicate the muzzle flashes of the V.C. shooting at our friendlies. Kelley was singing, "Over the river and through the woods, to grandmother's house we go." Over and over the same phrase. It was oddly comforting, funny, and appropriate. Detached amusement.

Sixteen minutes later we were in the hot spot. Bullets whizzed around us as we nudged the nose of the boat onto the shore in the center of the fight. Our twin .50s were laying down a barrage of bullets, firing over the heads of the men pinned down a few yards in front of us. Badger was to our port side, his boat's nose also on the beach. We didn't communicate, not with the radio. It was mind to mind. The Swifts shot at the enemy behind the dune. The V.C. shot at the Swifts. Red Dog and The Old Man were pinned down with their Viet Marines between us. They had the tough job. Lying on their belly in the sand while hundreds of bullets whizzed a few feet above them in both directions.

I didn't do anything.

It sounds ridiculous, but the firefight was proceeding as if it were all choreographed in advance. As if my crew had been on H.M.S. Victory. The boat was taking a few hits, splashes were everywhere around us, but mostly the fire was from us to the bad guys. Kelley was perfectly on target. Jake's fire was murderous. Kid and Red were emptying clips one after the other. It was beautiful. Like a perfectly functioning machine. Like a beast that had been trained to do a complex trick. Each muscle, tooth and sinew in harmony.

Slowly the friendly Viet Marines gathered the courage to run toward us. Just a few at first, then more and more. They had been under fire for almost 20 minutes. Unbelievable. We pulled them aboard like fish. Finally The Old Man and Red Dog came running; both carried wounded. Wild eyes. Fear. Grins. Curses. And bullets. Even more. Whizzing about. Harmless splashes in the water. An occasional "thunk" as a bullet hit the aluminum of our little boat.

Badger had retrieved about as many friendlies as we had. Red Dog shouted that he was confident that they had left only dead ashore. To me, it was all proceeding like a slow motion ballet. The noise was there, but I didn't hear it. To me it was actually quite peaceful. A perfect extraction of a very screwed up operation. Most of the men should have been killed. Instead, the majority were now safely aboard our two boats.

Inky Bite 97 backed off the beach at the same time as Badger's 36 boat. I was simply and quietly giving commands. No thought. No fear. Not really aware of any danger so to speak. This was the way it should be done. So it was. All in slow motion, so it was unhurried and simple. Peaceful. Directing suppressing fire, medevacs, and mortar fire kept me simply *busy*. Not brave, just *busy*.

Detached. Floating above it all. Lucky to be with Badger. I knew we would be successful and that my crew would be safe. The incoming bullets didn't matter. We had it mastered. Ecstasy.

The Navy awarded me a Bronze Star with a combat "V" for heroism that day. Badger got one too. It was a mistake of course. I wasn't brave. It was all done by someone else who just floated into my body.

Christ, I should know. If I had been there on 10 May 1969, I would have been scared shitless.

SLACKER

When Red Dog and the Old Man clamored aboard my boat after the big ambush, they were carrying their Viet Marine commanding officer, a colonel. He looked okay to me, but he had his eyes partially closed and was moaning. Not much, just a little.

The Viet pointed to his forehead. A little bit of blood trickled from a groove between his eyebrow and his hairline. So we laid him down in the main cabin and the three of us huddled. Red Dog said he really didn't know what was wrong. "The guy wouldn't retreat from the beach, so we carried him. He looks okay to me. Is he faking it?"

"Probably."

"So what do we do?"

The Old Man shook his head, looked at the wounded, and said, "He isn't a bad officer exactly . . . he just isn't very good."

That didn't help, so I asked again, "Is he a coward?" After getting the same response, we huddled over this "wounded" soldier. Light pulse. Pupils looked okay, or at least not particularly strange to me. No cold sweat, no clammy skin. "He's got to be faking it. He's not in shock."

So we went topside and took care of counting who was on our boat and compared that with the headcount on Badger's boat to get an idea of our losses. Then we ate a snack.

A Viet sergeant came up to us and said, "C.O. bad. Get helo."

So we went back down. The guy looked a little worse. We decided to call for a medevac.

The "Dust Off" came up on the radio. The medevac pilot asked if the wounded was an American. We said no, so he asked us to come further out to sea where it was safer.

So we did. It took about 20 minutes, and soon the big helo was right over our boat. I expected him to lower a stretcher but all he had was a jungle penetrator. They look like an inverted mushroom.

So we dragged the Viet colonel out on the fantail, sat him down on it, and shouted at him, "Hang on!" He put his hands around it and the helo wrenched him aboard and flew off. That night we learned that the colonel died en route to the hospital. We couldn't believe it. We felt somewhat embarrassed by it all. That wound didn't look bad at all. It looked as if someone had taken a fingernail and deeply scraped two inches of skin from his forehead. Nothing more. Head wounds. The Viet died in less than two hours of a head wound that looked insignificant.

It didn't make sense. Skippy had lost a big chunk of his skull. He had a gauze bandage holding in his brains. He didn't die until he got to Japan.

THE PIER

Hughes was on the pier waiting for us. Our squadron C.O. had followed the entire firefight, monitoring the radio channels as Badger and I extracted the two advisors and the 30 Viet Marines. He heard us call for air support, for medevacs, and knew of the casualties.

He was relieved to see both of his boats back safely with their crews. He shook hands with Red Dog and The Old Man. He had ordered the two ambulances that were also waiting on the pier. The medics whisked the seriously wounded Viets away. The Viet C.O. who had been taken by helo from our boat 45 minutes earlier had died en route to the hospital. Those remaining casualties who had suffered only light wounds were not lucky; they would be back on patrol again within a day or two.

Hughes looked relieved as he patted Badger and me on the back. He looked tired, like a parent who had been worrying about his children. When I looked into his eyes, I saw all of my mentors. My dad. Captain Tarr. Professor Russell. Major Love. Each one was a father to me. Each taught me a skill that I had used this day.

As I debriefed Hughes, my crew was busy rearming the boat. We had fired every .50 caliber round on board, over 1,000 rounds. Most of the mortar shells were gone too; over 70 had been shot. We inspected the hull. It had taken surprisingly few hits. My crew was still on a howling testosterone high.

Within minutes Inky Bite 97 was rearmed, refueled, and ready to go out again. Deep down I knew there was no urgency. We could go back to the ambush site, but it was unlikely that the V.C. would still be there. They would have removed their own KIA's by now. Nothing but a few blood spots in the grass and sand would remain. Red Dog would collect his own KIA's tomorrow.

I was sorry the fight was over, yet pleased at the result. It could have been much worse. Badger and I were confident that we had done a pretty good job. We had extracted two American advisors to the Yabuta Junk Force. A redheaded Lt. (jg) and a grizzled Mustang. We had gone in to save two Americans, two guys who played poker with us. In the process, Badger and I also saved 30 Vietnamese Marines.

We saved the Americans because they drank beer with us. We saved the Viets because they jumped on our boats first. The two Americans bravely waited to get all of the surviving Viet Marines on board safely before they themselves left the beach.

I hadn't been to church for three years. God and I had not been on speaking terms. But that particular firefight on my kid sister's birthday was truly a perfect white-light spiritual experience.

The magnitude of what Badger and I had done did not register with me until I spotted The Old Man. It had been ten minutes since we dropped him off. He had not left the pier. He was just standing alone with a numb and vacant look, a look of disbelief that he was alive. Near him, also at the point where the pier touched the beach was Red Dog. His back was turned to us, but I could tell from his shaking shoulders that he was still crying. Uncontrollably.

HONG KONG
HILTON REVISITED

I returned to my bunk and began to read. Within minutes I was in a deep sleep. Two hours later I was awakened by Badger. He was excited, but that was not unusual. He blurted out, "We're going on R & R! Our tour is over!"

I couldn't understand him. "Our tour is over. What do you mean?"

"Skipper says we can squeeze in a second R & R! We can go now. By the time we get back, we will have only two days left in-country. Just time to pack and wrap up."

The news was enough to bring me wide-awake. "Why does he want to do that? He's short-handed. We could go on at least three more patrols."

Badger became serious. His mustache twitched as he said, "I think the skipper just wants to make sure we both get home safely. This way he is assured that it will happen. I think he is haunted by the losses of some of his men. This is his way of insuring that the two of us finish safe and sound. Dammit, let's go, before he changes his mind."

Within an hour, I was packed and we were bouncing along in a jeep to the airport. At the R & R check-in desk, the Air Force sergeant said, "Everything is full except Hong Kong. Without advance orders, you will have to go standby. How much time you got in-country?"

Badger and I grinned. Standby was based on seniority in-country. Only someone who had extended his tour could bump us. "Three hundred fifty-five days," we said.

The sergeant didn't even look up. "Gate two in one hour."

We checked into the Hong Kong Hilton. I had wanted to stay there. Familiar. After a year of wild surprises one after another, I just wanted routine. But even the Hilton had changed. It wasn't as exotic anymore. It was just a good comfortable hotel now, far different from my wide-eyed first visit two years before. The lounge looked tiny. Smoky and dark. No longer magic like the night Neeley danced his soft-shoe routine on top of the bar.

Back in my room I stared at the crisp white sheets. I bent down like a wolf to smell their fresh scent of dry sunlight. I stripped off my uniform and turned the shower up as hot as it would go. I stood with the steaming water massaging the back of my neck and shoulders. I stood there for an hour letting my confusion drain away.

I put on a clean uniform and walked through the lobby, enjoying the attentive looks of the hotel staff. Outside the tropical sun was shining brightly. I stood on the stairs and looked at the bright green park across the street. Little old Brit ladies, all dressed in white were playing at lawn bowling. The Union Jack flew from a nearby flagpole, its lanyards clanking rhythmically. The white ball bounced across the grass. "The Colony" was still a magic place. I grinned and waited for the pedestrian light to change so that I could cross the street and sit in the park. I wanted to just watch the people playing lawn bowling; I wanted to learn how that leisurely game was played.

As I stepped off the curb, I realized that a young woman with long brown hair was beside me. I smiled at her. When we reached the park, I stopped and asked her if she knew the game. "Certainly," she responded in a clipped British accent. "Sit down and I'll explain."

Five minutes out the door of the hotel and I had already met a round-eye girl. Hong Kong was still a magic place.

Ann was from South Africa. She was to meet her boyfriend in Hong Kong. He had a job on an offshore oilrig and hadn't arrived yet. That was disturbing to her. It was just fine with me. We talked for an hour, enjoying the sun. She explained the rules of lawn bowling and then I invited her to dinner at the Hilton.

We found Badger and went to the formal dining room on the top floor. We had a leisurely, luxurious dinner: escargot, Chablis, fillet mignon. A Margeaux. Best of all, the dinner didn't end. Not just chocolate mousse for dessert but also a crepe. Badger ordered cognac and cigars. As a kid from Nebraska, I had never had cognac. Hennessy V.S.O.P. Badger knew what he was doing. A Chinese girl with incredibly long black hair brought a big box of cigars. I had only smoked a few cowboy cheroots in high school. Again, Badger, the guy from Chicago, led the way. He picked out a cigar for himself and a different brand for me. Ann had a second cognac. I wondered if she cared whether or not her boyfriend ever showed up.

I winked at Badger. He raised his eyebrows conspiratorially.

I loved Badger. I loved all of my brother river rats. I wanted to explain that to Ann, but Badger was talking to her.

No three people ever had such a wonderful meal at the Hong Kong Hilton. Not ever. We sank into the deep red chairs. Ann took off her shoes and tucked her feet under her. Tiny feminine toes wiggled beneath her nylon stockings.

Badger was touchingly emotional. He needed time to unwind. He needed to talk. Having a quiet soft woman join us made the chemistry perfect.

Lieutenant Ken Badger repeated over and over how he couldn't believe that our year in Vietnam was over. That we were alive, safe, and going home. To say he was relieved isn't strong enough; he was far beyond that. He was giving a prayer of thanksgiving. Not to God, but to our little trinity.

He asked Ann for advice about what presents to buy in Hong Kong for his mom and dad. I imagined both of them in their house in Chicago welcoming their son home. In just days. Incomprehensible. He asked Ann about his next post, Indonesia. She wasn't much help, she hadn't been there, but Badger enjoyed her attention. I watched in a detached way. I decided that Badger really did need to fall in love. He was ready for it. Ann appeared to enjoy my company slightly more than his, but to her credit, she also understood that tonight Badger needed to talk. He really, really needed her to listen. And she did.

He talked about booby traps and about his mother's lasagna. He talked about his high school girlfriend and a firefight in which he said to himself, "You're dead," as bullets whizzed by his face. (I wasn't on that mission, but I remembered when it happened; there were dozens of new holes in the hull of his 36 boat all around the pilothouse door.) He talked about his dad's bad heart and then he ordered more cognac. He decided to sample the Courvoisier brand. When the waitress brought it, I studied the little picture of Napoleon on the label. It was getting dark. The harbor was beautiful with the lights of boats bobbing in the darkness.

As he talked, I realized that perhaps Badger may have been more frightened than I. For a whole goddamned year. It seemed as if he was confessing it all to Ann. Confessing that he had expected to die and now he couldn't believe his good fortune.

I didn't have the heart to tell him that his next assignment in Indonesia would be a screaming bitch. That the dictator Suharto was facing riots and that Badger's job at the embassy would be to work with the creepy intelligence spooks trying to prop up or undermine the tyrants. Just like Vietnam in the early stages. I didn't want to upset Badger. He was just getting his feet back in the real world.

I thought briefly of a girl I had left in Maryland. Diane was married now; she had a future. I had been long forgotten. Rightfully so. As confused as Badger was, at least he had plans. Plans for the future. Not only didn't I have a goal, I didn't really want the future to come at all. The best of all worlds would be to freeze time. For this very night. To stay with my best and most loyal friend. To have a lovely young woman with her bare feet tucked under her. A catalyst for coming alive. To look at Hong Kong, "Fragrant Harbor." Lights of skyscrapers and old colonial buildings. The Star Ferry and lawn bowling. Cognac and cigars. For that one night, the three of us were on a gravy train with biscuit wheels. We were in heaven. No, really. I mean it; we *were* in heaven.

I thought of the Greek myth of Prometheus. He stole fire from the gods and gave it to man. He did the improper thing. He upset the gods. Would our god, or the gods of yore, be upset that we were coming home alive? That we did not fulfill a destiny? We broke the link with deity. The contract remained unfulfilled. We were not expendable after all. Instead, as the Nebraska cowboys would say, I was "fine as frog hair." I thought how perhaps God did not cast Adam and Eve out of paradise. They probably walked out of their own accord. Why stay in a boring place like heaven when you can become an expatriate? Cast yourself out, leave paradise and go to Vietnam or Antarctica or Indonesia. Who wants "fair winds and smooth seas"?

I realized that my thoughts were getting both confused and morbidly philosophical. The cigar was gone, so was the brandy. Ann was looking tired. Badger was still talking, but his speech was slurred. If he talked much longer he might break down. Perhaps he was talking only because if he stopped, he would begin to cry.

I smiled at the raven-haired Chinese girl in a short red dress and asked her for the check.

LAST ITEM ON
THE CHECKLIST

On my last day in-country, I did one check ride.

A new crew had arrived skippered by Matt Friend. I took Matt's crew out for an inspection check ride. Apparently the training back in Coronado was getting much better, because these guys were almost flawless.

When we tied up, I handed Matt his checklist and shook his hand. He grinned. Before he put his report in his pocket, he skimmed it proudly. Then said, "Oh, we forgot to cover first aid."

"No sweat," I said. "Assuming all of your guys read the manual, I'll just signoff. No need to test. I trust you."

"Thanks. They know it, Gary."

I initialed the only remaining blank box and Matt started to walk away. He'd only gone a few paces when I found myself calling out, "There is one point I forgot."

He turned to face me.

"Head wounds," I said. "They are hard to judge. They can be tricky."

"Oh, yeah. Sure . . . ," he responded blandly. He was eager to get going.

OUR LITTLE BOATS

It had come full circle. On my last working day in Vietnam, I was ordered to talk to a naval architect about how the Swift boat could be improved. My bags were packed when I was told that the engineer from BUSHIPS had arrived on base. When the war flared up, the Navy had no small costal boats. There wasn't time to design a specific boat from the keel up for the mission. So the Navy looked to see if there were any boats in existence that could do the job. They found a little company called Stewart Seacraft of New Orleans that was producing 50-foot boats used to service offshore oilrigs in the Gulf of Mexico. The Navy made a few modifications, such as adding a .50-caliber gun tub, a mortar, and an ammo box, but basically the design was unchanged. Stewart made 118 of the hulls.

The engineer from the Bureau of Ships in Washington came to interview only the most senior Swift skippers to see how the boats could be further modified to make them better. He asked if I would have liked to have had armor. I told him that it was futile to get into a duel with shore batteries, that as shit magnets we needed to run more than to fight. Armor would be nice, but armor is heavy and that would slow us down. If we were up to our ass in alligators, we needed every knot of speed we had.

The engineer asked if, during the year, I had wished for more weapons. I told him that we already had more than we could shoot. As for the aluminum hull, I asked him not to strengthen it; often a B-40 rocket would go in one side and out the other without exploding. Oddly, the aluminum hull was better because it was so thin. I stressed that if naval architects tinkered with our boats, it would do more harm than good.

The best thing Washington could do for us was to leave us alone.

MEDALS

Within an hour after the engineer departed, I was told that in addition to the Bronze Stars from America, the Vietnamese government had awarded both Badger and me the Vietnamese Cross of Gallantry with Palm Leaves. For their country, the Cross of Gallantry was a fairly high medal, equivalent of our Silver Star or Navy Cross. Instead of being honored by the award, I felt slightly ashamed. My Swift went in to extract two Americans. I went in primarily to save two advisors who liked to drink beer. The fact was that the South Vietnamese honored me for saving over 30 of their Marines. Those lives were collateral to saving Red Dog and The Old Man. Those two advisors waited to be extracted last; they waited for their men. That was why I saved 32 instead of 2. Or so I thought. Maybe I was lying to myself again. Maybe I would have done it all the same, even if the force pinned down did not have American advisors.

Probably. And yet, I never felt right about that green and bronze medal with palm leaves.

The 10 May 1969 ambush by the V.C. had been executed perfectly. Absolutely perfectly. In fact it was too lucky. There was no doubt in my mind that the Yabuta Junk Force was infiltrated by V.C. Someone inside that Marine group had given the V.C. advanced notice. Red Dog and The Old Man had led their men into a trap; the V.C. knew when and where they were coming.

So I got a medal for heroism and for saving 30 Viets who had been in a savage firefight because some traitor in their own organization had tipped off the V.C. who were then able to lay a perfect ambush.

Firefights, bravery, traitors, medals. It was all so unpredictable. I did not know how I was supposed to feel. Proud and happy, or sadly ashamed?

KELLEY'S LAST DAY

I stopped my Q.M. "Thompsen, what's wrong with Kelley? He has an all time hangdog look. Did someone clean him out at poker?"

Thompsen paused. It was clear his answer wasn't going to be funny. He didn't want to tell me, but I knew if I just waited, the enlisted code of silence would be trumped by authority. "Dunno, Skipper. He got some news. He'll get his head straightened out. I'll watch it."

That phrase, as encrypted as it was, was all I had a right to know. Or so I thought. It was 18 May. We were scheduled to go out on the Freedom Bird on the 20th.

The night of 18 May, for reasons that I never got clear, Kelley demolished the enlisted men's head (bathroom). He was a giant of a man. He was drunk. He tore washbasins out of the wall with his bare hands. Like an animal in a rage.

When I saw him the following afternoon of 19 May, he was scheduled to go before a captain's mast. A mast is just one step under a court-martial. The rest of my crew and I were scheduled to fly home in 24 hours. Kelley would have to stay two days for the disciplinary proceedings.

I saw him in the late afternoon, in front of the barracks. I asked if I could help. He shook his head sadly and said, "No, Skipper." Then I walked away. The next morning I flew back to the U.S.

In the U.S. Army, a calvary soldier could not eat until his horse was fed. As a Naval officer, I should not have left Vietnam until all of my men were out. Not most of my men, but *all* of them. Yes, what Kelley did was foolish, but plumbing can be repaired. Other men had made mistakes that couldn't be corrected.

Mistakes that killed people. By comparison, this was a minor event. I should have skipped my flight back to San Francisco. I should have testified on Kelley's behalf even if it meant staying in Vietnam an extra week.

He had a spotless record for 363 days. He had a wife and kid. He was my engineman. He shouldn't lose a stripe or be fined. We could have fixed the goddamned plumbing. I could have paid for it.

At the time, I thought that I was eager to get home. My orders to the states were cut, the date set. I followed orders. That was stupid. Nothing was more important than loyalty. There was nothing important in the U.S.A., not anything as important as helping my engineman. Instead, on 20 May I boarded the aircraft and flew home.

Short Timer

Children with Blinn

Nha Trang Harbor in 1994

Fishing junk
(note eyes to help the boat find its way to fish and safety)

THE REAL
WORLD

The only war is the war you fought in.
Every veteran knows that.

Allan Keller

FREEDOM BIRD

So I had a roundtrip ticket after all!

The flight home did not proceed as smoothly as I expected. The base from which we were to depart was attacked the night before. Runways were damaged, so we waited half a day. Finally, they were ready. We were told that everyone would be inspected carefully upon arrival at Travis Air Force Base in California. Zero tolerance for drugs, weapons, or anything else. Before boarding the aircraft, every man walked through a little hallway with curtains at each end. In the middle of the hall was a big black box. We were to toss everything into the box.

I didn't have anything illegal. I barely had one uniform that was fit to wear. Most of my clothes were full of holes. Rotted T-shirts, skivvy underwear that had been washed by mamasans in the river and pounded on rocks. Old camouflaged cutoffs. Almost everything had been given away to Viets. Even though the clothes were several sizes too big for them, they would still get more years of use.

Some people rejoiced when we boarded the aircraft. They shouted "di di nha"—go to U.S.A. Most were just too damned tired.

There was a massive shout from the passengers as the aircraft's wheels left the runway. Then the troops started singing old songs like, "We gotta get out of this place, if it's the last thing we ever do." The pilot announced that we had crossed the coast and were out of Vietnam airspace. Another shout came from the 250 men, "Feet wet!"

I thought about the transition, of words describing the geography below. We were flying from "in-country/the war zone/ Indian country," to the Mekong, to the Tonkin Gulf. From the

Tonkin Gulf to the South China Sea. South China Sea, a softer name, a safer place. And finally to the Pacific. A word that means peace.

I took a window seat and laid my head against the plexiglas. When we had arrived exactly one year earlier, helicopters were shooting up the city of Saigon. The war was a year older. Grinding along, too big to stop or change directions.

I felt very tired and unsure of myself, like I wasn't supposed to be on the flight. In school I ran track. After every race, I felt regret because I still had a tiny portion of energy. Somehow that was evidence that I hadn't given it my all. If I hadn't given every ounce of energy, I had, by definition, held something back. So I hadn't done my job.

I was still alive, so therefore I had failed.

I felt depressed, numb, and guilty all at the same time. Embarrassed to be leaving my friends. I dreaded the reality that I was to face, and wondered how I would face Dad, Mom, and my kid sister. There was a weary sense that I should probably be crying, or celebrating, but not just staring out the plexigalss window at the vast nothingness of the wide, blue Pacific.

NIGHT FLIGHT, CATNAPS, INSANITY

It was night. The aircraft was midway between Vietnam and California, over the Pacific with cabin lights turned down. The Viet Vets fell silent. I closed my eyes. I dreamed, I imagined, I slept.

The Pearly Gates

When I die, I meet Saint Peter. He looks me in the eye. "So you missed a gunshot target by three klicks? That's close enough for government work."

I shuddered. "Well, Sir, it was government work," I responded truthfully. Relieved.

"I know. I know. 'XIN LOI' as we say up here. Welcome aboard Lieutenant." As I step off the big green parade field from mortality to Heaven, the band plays "Anchors Aweigh."

"A Prayer for Non-Believers Passes" through my mind. It is a song St. Mary sang with Peter and Paul in the 60's.

Buddha

I die but go nowhere, not up, not down. As the last oxygen molecule is burned in my brain, the tissue flashes pure white as it dies. I see Buddha holding one small white flower. He smiles. It is the most eloquent sermon he taught. I heard it. I was there.

Silence *is* the voice of God. You make your own Hell. Make your own Heaven.

The Philosophy Student, Providence, Rhode Island

"Deal with it," Rob says, crystallizing Zen.

The Bushdo code of the Samurai can be partially distilled with those three words: "Deal with it." The Samurai warriors attended their own funeral. Having already "died," they then had nothing more to fear. Every day of life beyond the funeral was a pleasant surprise.

Intelligence Officer, Pentagon

"Look, it is simple. We are all ants on a log. Just ants on a big log that is rushing down a river." Glen went on, "Each ant is hanging on so he does not drown. Every single ant believes that he alone is in charge."

It's funny, but years later upon the assassination attempt on the President, those were the very words used by General Hague: "I'm in charge! I'm in charge!" He was a very hyperactive ant.

Diane

"You look tired and full of tension," she says. "Roll over on the floor and I'll give you a backrub." The tension disappears as my neck and shoulder muscles ease into a relaxed state. This is Heaven. The touch of Love.

Hera

"Ha! Your problem is that you believe that delusional fool. That mortal. That Moses!" She sneers as she tosses her long raven hair back behind her. Stunningly beautiful in her pure white dress, she looks at me as if I were a child.

"We Greek gods use you mortals as playthings. As gods, we bicker. We fight. We love and deceive each other. Why do you think Zeus and I, or any of the other deity, should treat you mortals differently?"

I have suspected as much all along. The bickering gods of three thousand years ago are more logical to me than a single inconsistent one.

Hera touches me on the shoulder, "Look what I did to the sailor Jason and his Argonauts. Did your boat expect better? Look what we did to Ulysses and Achilles. Reread the *Iliad*. Homer told the truth! The other gods wish to kill you as they did Hector and drag your body through the dirt. Perhaps I can intervene. Perhaps not. It depends on how I feel at the time."

"Thank you, goddess," I respond. "It is not good news that you give, but it certainly helps me understand."

"Good!" she says. "You think you alone are responsible for killing?" We gods caused Medea to kill her own children. Egotist! Show some respect to those of us who have changed and will continue to change your life simply by raising a finger.

*   *   *

Daydreams. Dreams. My mind was bouncing from one bizarre thought to another. I was on my way back to the world. A place that was normal. The thought of reentry was terrifying.

BACK HOME

In late May of 1969, after landing at Travis Air Force Base, I went straight to my dad's house.

I arrived in Nebraska in the afternoon. We talked late into the night and then I picked a few things from by sea bag: a Bronze Star, the Vietnamese Cross of Gallantry, and some shrapnel that had come within an inch of killing me. I laid it all out on the stark white kitchen table. I expected Dad to be proud of my accomplishments.

He wasn't. He just looked at me sadly and walked away. I should have known. I swept the stuff off the table; eventually it found its way into a dark shoebox-sized safe deposit box.

QUIET

After only three days in Nebraska with Dad, I drove to my next duty station—the Pentagon. Some people say that silence is the voice of God. Perhaps, but it can also be frightening.

In Arlington, Virginia, I found that I could not sleep in my new apartment. I spent the final five minutes of each evening adjusting the television sound so that it would be just loud enough to keep me company as I fell asleep. Total silence reminded me of night ambushes. I was afraid of the full moon and the "whap, whap" of helicopter rotors. A person who lived nearby owned the Klink Insurance Agency. He had a vanity license plate: "KIA." Every time I saw it I shuddered; the idiot was clueless of his poor taste.

Back in Valentine, some ranchers hunted coyotes with wolfhounds. When the wolfhound attacks, it does so in total silence. It runs down the coyote and then bites it in the throat, crushing windpipe and arteries alike. The coyote fights and dies in total silence.

As a kid I had spent much of my free time hunting. After the war I gave away the guns that I had owned since childhood. Shotguns, .22's, deer rifles, pistols. Even those that had belonged to my dad and grandfather. I didn't want any of them. Some nights I just sat alone in my dark living room. Vigilant. Out of place.

Over time, I began scuba diving again, hang gliding, rock climbing, driving a "Ninja" motorcycle. Those activities seemed to give an adrenalin boost.

Some people overcome fear by confronting it. Teddy Roosevelt was a sickly child who deliberately did the very things that frightened him. Similarly, Mick Jagger of the Rolling Stones had once been afraid of death; he obtained a part-time job as a gravedigger.

But what do you do if you are afraid of silence? I was also afraid of noise. On the Fourth of July, I closed all the windows and turned up the volume on the T.V. Some guys say, "I died in Vietnam." I didn't have post-traumatic stress, but I was very much aware of many of the symptoms:

- Decreased ability to trust.
- Shrinking horizons.
- Using survival skills in daily life.
- Having minor events trigger thoughts. e.g. a goddamned "KIA" license plate. Killed in Action.
- Thoughts of suicide; it equals freedom.

I felt detached from others, but, don't we all? Slowly, I began to be able to eat rice again. And look at the moon. Road-kill didn't make me freeze. I became a Buddhist. There was a sad regrettable awareness that I had knowledge of things that I shouldn't have learned. Adam ate from a tree of knowledge. Then he couldn't go back home again. Let me give an example of the kind of things I wish I didn't know:

Do you want to learn how to kill someone with a knife in total silence? You do, even if you do not want to admit it . . . okay, here goes:

Approach the enemy from behind. Get close! Your chest should touch his back. Hold the knife with the point turned down in your right hand; put your left against the mouth as you bring your right hand over the right shoulder of the victim. Thrust the knifepoint down deeply into the hollow below the Adam's apple. Just above the sternum. The knife will sever the windpipe. Keep it buried to the hilt and push it right to left and back. That cuts the major arteries above the heart. Lungs, brain, and heart are now no longer connected to the circulatory system. It is perfectly silent except for a gurgle or two. Fast. You will never again look at the hollow of a person's neck without imagining a target. It is only the size of a quarter. Coyote, wolfhound, human. It is all the same. The best knife for the job is sharp on both sides. A K-Bar or a royal commando knife are the weapons of choice. Buy one today. Keep it in the drawer by your bedside. Keep it very sharp. You will sleep better. I do.

Do you see what I'm talking about? Why do we clutter our mind with such memories? We should be listening to kids on a playground. Good sounds; not scary silence. The memories keep grinding on.

At age 25 I was turning to the "Obituary" section of the alumni magazine first. The moment it arrived from Annapolis.

By definition, war is insanity. To deal with it, humans become partially, just partially, insane themselves. Then the insanity seems normal. And all is well . . . until you return to the real world.

The Navy SEALS have an appropriate motto: "The only easy day was yesterday."

PENELOPE

The battle at Troy lasted over ten years. When it was over, Odysseus and his men attempted to return home. The voyage was filled with obstacles. Huge obstacles. That Odyssey took seven years, almost as long as the war. It was also as dangerous as the war. Odysseus just wanted to get home to his wife.

His dog was named Argo. After 19 years of loyal waiting, Argo licked the hand of Odysseus when he finally returned. Then Argo wagged his tail one last time, and laid down to die. But Argo was the only one to recognize Odysseus; when Penelope saw him, she didn't believe it was her husband. He had changed that much.

Diane was teaching in a ghetto school in Baltimore. I called her from the Pentagon. Within hours she made the short train trip down to Washington. She was wearing a dress that had always been my favorite. We stood by the train tracks and looked at each other in disbelief.

At that moment, I knew that I wanted to marry her. What I didn't realize at the time was that she was willing to get a divorce and marry me.

PUZZLE PALACE

Stick close to your desk and never go to sea and you will be
ruler of the Queen's navy.

Gilbert and Sullivan

In-country, I had gone from 165 pounds to 145 pounds. Just gut worms and jungle rot, nothing serious.

The Pentagon was worse than I had expected. I was greeted by an admiral, a Georgia cracker who was a bully. A simpleton. He told me that if I worked very hard in my assignment, I could also take on a second job as his Aide-de-Camp. I stared at him in astonishment. He had clearly gotten his position and his stars through political pull, not merit. His chest was nearly bare of medals and those he did have were called "gedunk medals," awards given for basically just showing up.

Slowly, I said, "Admiral, after my last year in-country, if I just sleep this year, the Navy and I will be even."

He turned red and exploded. Slobbering, he screamed at me, "One more such statement and you will be court-martialed!" He continued to rant. I became very, very quiet. I don't remember what else he said because I was sitting in the chair facing him with my eyes slightly lowered. To him, I probably looked properly admonished.

Actually, I was looking at his pen and pencil desk set and thinking to myself. You can hold a writing instrument with the blunt end at the center of your palm. Make a fist with the pen or pencil protruding from between the second and third finger. Such a fist is actually an amazing weapon. The pen acts as an ice pick with its point aimed directly out. You can slam it very, very hard into a body because your elbow, wrist, palm, and the point are a straight line that will not yield. If you aim slightly to the left of the sternum you can drive the pen into a lung and, with luck, also hit the heart. Do not leave the pen in the wound! If the pen penetrates the heart and stays in, it will wiggle up and down from the heartbeats, but it will be sealing the wound. Pull it out and stab again. That way the blood flows out of the lung and heart wounds. Later you can drive the six-inch pen through the eye socket to finish off the job. You also have enough strength to smash the pen or metal or plastic pencil (not a wooden pencil) through the temple.

As I was thinking of how to kill the worthless piece of shit, I realized that the admiral was asking me if I "understood." He repeated the phrase several times as I mentally reentered the discussion. I stared into his eyes for 20 seconds. His rage turned to fear. He knew from my face that at that moment I was truly evil. He fumbled. I stared. Ice water in my veins, I just stood up, turned, and walked away. At the back of his carpeted office, he had a small desk for his personal secretary, a young woman named Sandy. She looked at me with very, very big eyes.

I returned to my desk in a room nearby. I began moving things around on my desk, unsure whether to be angry with myself or with the worthless piece of meat whom I had regrettably left alive. It was like a circular firing squad, everyone aware of the enemy yet shooting each other. I heard others say that we fought the war "with one hand tied behind us." With this admiral, the fighting was with one brain hemisphere tied behind him.

A few minutes later Sandy came into my office. She brought coffee and a little cookie. She looked at me with a look that clearly said, "I've never witnessed such behavior." She was a convert to the side of the good guys.

I was only focused on using the tools at hand to properly do the work. It wasn't as if his life were of any value; he wasn't a warrior. All he knew how to do was park his fat ass behind a desk.

I looked at the cookie from Sandy and knew that I was thinking like the guy who had told the story of laying in ambush to shoot his mother's lover. Worried about allowing for wind. One inch to the left, or two?

Simply concentrating on flawless execution . . . of the execution. Jesus! I needed to get back in-country. Fast.

PCF 97

I had turned my boat over to two new kids on 20 May.

On 25 June 1969 PCF 97 was ambushed and sunk by recoilless rifle fire off the mouth of the Gang Hao River.

Five weeks after I left her. Only five weeks.

GEORGE WASHINGTON UNIVERSITY

At the time, my sister was a freshman at George Washington University. Just a few blocks from the White House and Capitol Hill. She protested against the war. Once she marched to the Pentagon.

Meanwhile, I worked in the Pentagon. Systems Analysis. A group of one hundred of the brightest officers in the Navy working on problems. Sadly, the biggest "problem" was how to get more of the Defense Department budget for the Navy. Almost no time was spent on the biggest issue of the decade—how to win the war.

I deeply regretted that I couldn't "terminate with extreme prejudice" the pathetic admiral who was my boss.

Perhaps my sister and I were on the same side after all.

PENTAGON

An officer in a swivel chair in the Pentagon actually knows
nothing. All they do is collect paper facts.

Gen. G.S. Patton

After I was in the Pentagon a few weeks, I resumed reading books at voracious pace. I didn't want to go out at night. I didn't want to go to dinner or entertainment. I had not yet figured out how I felt about people. Oscelot had gone to Spain after his tour. He and Elliott were each trying to write a book. Neither man could bring himself to the required level of concentration. I understood. Even reading was difficult.

One piece that I read was Davy Crockett's account of the Creek Indian War in 1813. It was odd that America considered itself unprepared for guerilla warfare. We had a wealth of stories from our own Revolutionary War, Indian Wars, and other events. It was equally odd that we didn't read T.E. Lawrence and his desert tactics in Arabia. The American military hadn't even taken the time to read Chairman Mao's *Little Red Book* or other works by Mao or Che Guevarra. A few Navy SEALS did, or the guys in the Army Special Forces. Sadly, no one that I met in my year in the "Puzzle Palace" had a clue. Not a goddamned clue. Our generals and admirals in D.C. were ignorant, lazy, and worthless.

Back in-country, Charlie knew about guerilla warfare; he had been living it for 30 years of history. As an adversary, we respected him.

Eighty years before, Kipling had written of similar respect:

"Here's to you, Fuzzy Wuzzy, and your home in the Sudan.
You're a regular little heathen, but a first class fighting man."

REMF'S

Doubt is not a very agreeable state,
but certainty is a ridiculous one.

Voltaire

If I have been vague about what we did in the Pentagon, that is because I really didn't know what the hell we were doing. My department was one of the most highly classified sections of that monstrous building. We had the standard "classified," "secret," "top secret," stuff, but only there did I learn that there are many classifications even higher. The names of these classifications *themselves* were classified.

We were basically a think tank. The project to which I was assigned was to work on background material for the Strategic Arms Limitations Talks (S.A.L.T.), which were being held in Helsinki. The department had about 40 such projects at the time. Part of my job was to collect data. From the C.I.A., D.I.A., Navy Intel, and so forth. During the day in Helsinki, the negotiators would propose trade-offs. The Russians would say, "We will destroy 30 SS9 missiles aimed at your country, in return we want you to scrap two nuclear subs off our coast with their Polaris missiles aimed at us!" So my job was to help determine if such a trade-off was fair.

Hell, I was perhaps one of the least qualified people to know. I had just spent my time in one of the most low-tech jobs in the entire Navy. Separately, the Navy also had a group of systems analysts looking into the effectiveness of the Navy in Vietnam. I still had jungle rot growing under my toenails but I was never asked to join that group or work with them. Few men, if any, on that project had spent time in-country. You figure it out, but how do you get the right—perspective—with such insane staffing?

Almost everyone in our department was a bureaucrat. With one or two exceptions they were all REMF's or "rear echelon mother fuckers" as we called them in combat. The officers at the Pentagon were required to wear civilian clothes four of the five days a week. I was told that it was so the military did not appear to have such a big presence in D.C. I did not believe it. I believe the reason was that one look at their chest when in uniform and you could see they had never done a damned thing. McNamara talked about the "teeth to tail ratio," the ratio of our fighting men to the non-fighters. It is actually a good indicator, but no one in the Pentagon seemed to be advocating abolishing desk jobs and sending themselves to Indian Country.

I did.

I called my detailer at Bureau of Naval Personnel to ask to return to Swifts or anything back in-country. He said that the Army had problems with guys who spent three years straight in-country. As a result, men with two years of duty now had to wait out one year before going back. He was telling me that after three consecutive years of combat, men "go native"; they fit in Vietnam *too* well. They no longer even give a shit about the U.S. At least that was my take on it. Adding bugs to oatmeal.

Truly I had more respect for Chuck than anyone I worked with at the Pentagon. Oh, the secretaries were lovely and professional, but the men were clueless. The V.C. were gutsy little bastards and you only saw them on occasion. These Americans were packed elbow to elbow in the old gray cement building. At least in-country, I could turn my radio off; here some officer was shouting every damned minute. In the river, I was top dog. The Alpha Wolf. Here I was a full Navy Lieutenant and still at the bottom of the pecking order.

Adding to the urgency was the fact that many of the people in our group were submariners. They were bright, but wound too tight. They knew all about nuclear physics but they were basically scholars, not warriors. They didn't know that an American body would be booby trapped so you should not go near it. They didn't know that an old Viet lady could sit under a "Kill America" mural and tell you she had never seen it before. They didn't even know how to fire an AK-47. It was beyond pathetic.

I also was assigned a project to prove that carrier-based aircraft are superior to land-based aircraft. Several of us were working on the study; it was a major piece of work. As the junior person, I was the bagman. I had to run here and there to get more input data. Running around with a briefcase handcuffed to my wrist and an armed bodyguard made me feel important. Off to get statistics on the effectiveness of Air Force, Marine, and Army aircraft, C.I.A., D.I.A., and a dozen more. Then one day I hit pay dirt: my counterpart in the Air Force! A guy who was doing *exactly* the same study, only his was to prove how land-based aircraft are superior to sea-based planes. Un-fucking-believable! I had worked on the goddamned study for four months. Honestly believing that our work would help America defend itself more effectively. Instead it was just the Navy collecting evidence why it should get a bigger share of the Defense budget! The other services were wasting money the same way. Interservice bickering with the American public paying taxes for the foolishness.

At about the same time, I heard about the capture, torture, and execution of a good friend. We played rugby together at Navy. What the V.C. did to him is simply something I can't write.

In Vietnam, the intelligence briefer said, "You only see a portion of the war; if you were in Washington and could see the big picture, you would know that we are winning."

More than once in the Pentagon I heard people complain, "If we were in-country we would get a better idea of what is happening." It would have been funny if the stakes were not so high; irony is lost on the dead.

There was one Naval aviator who worked at a desk near mine. He had been on one tour as an attack pilot and wanted to go back again. He was friendly to me. We got along well. Then one day we talked about Tet. I told him Mao had written that only when guerilla war has succeeded could the insurgents move on to the next phase of more conventional attacks. Thus Tet showed that the Communists were convinced the war was nearly won. Conversely the American public learned that the V.C./N.V.A. could strike anywhere, anytime, and with shocking destructive power. Just the opposite of what the Pentagon had said. Yes, we lost fewer casualties than the attackers, but Tet showed that the American people had been told a gigantic lie.

I told the Naval aviator that the war was lost. Tet proved it and now everyone in America, except the White House and the Pentagon, knew it. He became angry. We didn't speak again.

Later that night I watched the T.V. news. Protestors threw their medals over the fence at the White House. One person who spoke on camera was a woman. She threw a Bronze Star onto the White House lawn. It was Andre's widow.

*   *   *

I hope that someone picked those medals from the White House lawn and put them in an appropriate place. I wish I knew the fate of those small pieces of ribbon and metal. Fate.

We Americans forget that, to Greeks, the fates were beautiful goddesses. They were the daughters of a god. The god named Chaos.

NAVAL CAREER

Riverboats were not considered a "career enhancing" assignment. The Navy promoted officers who avoided combat—who simply bored holes in the Atlantic—faster than the warriors.

I heard that Mike Dodge had gotten back; he lived through his lonely year as an advisor on a mudflat. He was posted to some god-awful place. Willy took heavy automatic weapons rounds through both legs; it was doubtful that he would walk again. Badger was sent to Indonesia; they were having a revolution at the time.

Professor Russell would have explained it well: In Rome, the army was composed of many, many foreigners. Rough, effective men. The best were the Praetorian Guards. Mercenaries. They were the elite. They took over the army. Then the mercenaries took over the government. Then all of Rome. Ever since, governments have been afraid of soldiers who are truly effective. Democratic governments cannot trust the elite forces.

U.S. NAVAL ACADEMY

Every five years I go back to "Navy," as the U.S. Naval Academy at Annapolis, Maryland, is called by its graduates. Each reunion brings smiles and camaraderie within the class of '66. There are really two distinct groups: those who did a tour in Vietnam and those who did not. A man who got no higher than first lieutenant in the Marine Corps but served in Nam has far more respect than the man who made it to admiral without being in the war.

As I look at the academic buildings, I feel angry. Angry with a curriculum and faculty that did remarkably little to prepare us. Playing rugby, studying physics, marching to meals. Christ, that was during a war! They did nothing to bring the war into the classroom. Not once did we study Marx. Nothing on Che Guevarra or other guerillas. Nothing on jungle warfare. The faculty and the officers of the Navy didn't respond to the reality of the war about them.

We midshipmen were like medical students who had only read books but hadn't yet seen a cadaver or a patient. No one had read the *Communist Manifesto*, but we had all memorized silly trivia of the past. We learned to respond to questions such as "How long have you been in the Navy?" with the answer: "All me bloomin life. Me mother was a mermaid, me father was King Neptune, and I was rocked in the cradle of the deep . . . ." Truly, that is what we learned at taxpayer expense. Because I was an honor student, I was allowed to take extra courses. Among others, I took Professor Russell's "Philosophy of War." It was the *only* course that I took at the academy that had been of use to me in the Mekong River. Probably less than 3 percent of the brigade was fortunate enough to have taken that course. Professor Russell translated everything into the real world. If we were studying Roman catapults, he would insist that we actually make and shoot one! (That particular project was more difficult than expected because two thousand years ago the Roman Army discovered that the twisting force of the power spring could be improved by using the hair of women instead of horsetails. We couldn't obtain enough human hair to get proper range.) Only one other instructor took time to tell real war stories— they interrupted class. (That person was Colonel Corson, the officer who went on to debate a V.C. in Vietnamese in the village square.) In fact, the war stories should have *been* class.

Our joke as midshipmen in 1966 was, "This is the only place in the world where you can get a $100,000 education . . . shoved up your ass a nickel at a time."

My ass was on the line in the Mekong. There I came to the conclusion that at Navy we learned character, leadership, and theory. What we didn't learn was how to kill and how to stay alive.

Annapolis should be a trade school, not just one more damned college.

BUPERS ONE YEAR LATER

"Gary, I couldn't do that to you. I gave you your second choice."

I focused on the fatherly face of Captain Donald Tarr, the man in charge of Junior Officer detailing at the Navy's Bureau of Naval Personnel. Earlier he had been the captain of the J. Jarvits. Shortly after he had been transferred to this job in Washington, the Jarvits was hit by shore batteries off North Vietnam. While the ship was limping back to Pearl Harbor, I decided that it would be boring to spend six months in Hawaii while it was being repaired; so I too asked to be transferred. I posted my Officer Preference Card asking for Nasty Boats.

Nasties were my first choice. I was impressed with their Napier Deltic engines, paper-thin wooden hulls, and speed so fast it was classified. I had wanted to run the rivers of North Vietnam. Almost every mission was secret.

My second choice was Swift Boats, which ran rivers of the South.

Fourteen months before, Captain Tarr, my former skipper, had seen my request when it arrived at the Bureau of Naval Personnel. Now he looked me in the eye and said, "Not one of the Nasty Boats survived."

"Thanks, Captain," I replied awkwardly.

What else can you say to a person who saved your life with a fountain pen?

IMPERMANENCE

Life is what happens to you while
you are making other plans.

I don't know why this was important, but it was.

When I was 12, a rattlesnake bit me while I was deer hunting. It was just a small prairie rattlesnake; he shouldn't have been out so late in the fall. I cut the bite open with a knife. My grandfather drove me to the hospital in the town of Valentine, Nebraska. For some reason, the doctor did not stitch my cut shut, so I was left with a two-inch long quarter-inch wide scar. The sun of the Mekong turned my body mahogany brown, but the scar tissue stayed silvery white. I noticed that everyone else's scars seemed to glow as well. Kelley had several on his back. Kid had two on his face. Old scars just seemed to become very, very visible. As memorable as those on a past lover. Why that aspect of the war was so significant to me, I really don't know.

After my tour was over and I was home, Betty, the wife of a childhood friend, said that I touched everything. I touched people and things just to confirm them, like a three-year-old.

*   *   *

On 5 March 1971, my former mother ship, the L.S.T. 1100 U.S.S. Madison County, was transferred to the Greek Navy.

*   *   *

On the J. Jarvits two years before, the Padre had told me how lepers die. He had served in the leper colony on Molokai, Hawaii.

The disease numbs the extremities, so they do not feel pain when the fingers and toes and ears get injured or infected. They eventually die and fall off. The disease also destroys the soft tissues of the nasal passage and throat, and so eventually the leper loses his nose and mouth too. With only a gaping hole, they breathe dust and dirt, inhaling things that eventually give them respiratory infection. That's how they die, of respiratory infection. We take air for granted today. Not long ago, they didn't. There was good air and there was bad air. Buenos Aires. Malaria.

The little girl who we had not killed had probably lost her father by now. I hoped that she was okay. How does a young girl survive in the Rung Sat, the Forrest of Assassins, after losing her father? A fishing family poor beyond our understanding.

On the sampan, she was in constant touch with the man. Using the same equipment. Sharing food. I hoped she didn't become a leper too.

DANGER, BRAVERY, AND RECOGNITION

GI Joe

Here is the way it happened in the comic books: the first frame would generally show GI Joe and his buddies in easy conversation. By the second frame, an emergency had arisen. The danger was always clear and present. Joe rushed into action (often alone). At this point, the magic of the comic book artwork allowed the reader to see Joe in single-handed action, while also noting that others were close enough to observe his heroism, but were simultaneously far enough away to be unable to come to his aid.

The final frame would show Joe being decorated by his C.O., sometimes in a formal ceremony, but often on the battlefield while he was still covered with blood and mud.

That's the sequence in the comic books, and that is the way I expected combat to be when I was in grade school. Curiously, after graduation from the Naval Academy, I still expected there to be a simple linkage: Danger, Bravery, and Recognition. In Vietnam, I learned there is often no linkage at all.

In my experience, I faced danger in The Brown Betty Incident in which the Air Force nearly sunk my boat. The village sniper had fired several rounds at us without our being brave; on the contrary, we were simply stupid to have been willing targets. Bravery was called upon to walk through a Pandora's Box village of bats while expecting an ambush, but there are no medals given for simply being terrified. Recognition and medals are awarded for doing things, like saving Red Dog and The Old Man . . . even if no bravery was involved. It was all very confusing.

The Real World

The idea that danger, bravery, and recognition are often unrelated came to me 20 years later as I was walking through the Lincoln campus of the University of Nebraska. A motorcyclist raced dangerously down a quiet street on one of the new 120+ mph "Ninja" motorcycles. A few blocks away, the state legislature was debating whether such foolhardy fellows should be required to wear helmets to protect their physical safety. A few paces later, I passed a young man in a motorized wheelchair who was almost totally paralyzed. He was clearly enjoying cool spring air and was maneuvering his chair so that he could face the sun. Between his teeth he held a plastic stick with which he was typing one letter at a time on a word processor mounted at the level of his throat.

I felt a humble awe for that young scholar. The time during which I have been truly brave is certainly measured in minutes; his is measured by a lifetime.

Reflecting on this, I really do not know how or where to teach these things to my son or any junior officer. I can only say that bravery can be found in thousands of places beyond the battlefield, and even there it isn't like it is in the comic books.

ONE FISH THREE FISH

Hemingway said there are only three sports: bullfighting, mountain climbing, and war. The others are just little games.

I like that.

When I see guys playing a ball game, I think of it as a damned poor substitute for the real thing. It is all watered down. Indirect. Like dancing with a woman. Somewhat silly as a substitute for making love.

Anyway, American men do not usually feel. That's why they whoop and shout at ball games; it is one of the few places they have where they can express raw emotions. Feelings. Most have never played the *big game*. I imagine men who have been in combat take less interest in sports. I know I do. But maybe it's just me.

After combat, the mind breaks humanity into two: "brothers," those you trust with your life, and "people"—the others. Your son, your wife, special friends—very special friends—fit into the former category. But almost everyone else—except other Viet vets—are just "people." There is no middle. No continuum of friendships. Either intense or not at all.

A racing instructor at the Road America track at Elkhart Lake, Wisconsin, gave a quote that I liked. He was asked how long you should keep your foot on the accelerator going into a curve. How late can you wait before backing off and hitting the brakes? His answer: "Keep your foot down. Don't let up until you see God."

Perhaps that is theology. I've never heard a Bible-thumper say anything meaningful, but when a person is in real danger it is quite possible to see God.

I read that when an underwater explosion occurs, it usually ruptures the air sack of the fish. For every fish that floats to the top, three others sink to the bottom. Fishing with explosives is not very efficient. Only a few float to the surface and show their underbelly. Only a few become fried fish dinner. The rest sink into the dark, dark bottom of the sea.

Perhaps the violence of killing does the same to people. After the war, for every casualty we can see, there are three others out of sight, sinking. Drifting downward. A lonely odyssey into Homer's "wine dark sea."

NATURAL HISTORY

One summer day, I went to the Natural History Museum by New York's Central Park.

They have a prehistoric skeleton that was found buried and covered with antlers. It is a young boy. In mourning, our relatives of 20,000 years ago covered him in red powder to give a more lifelike appearance to his small body. They stacked antlers to arch over him like angels. It looked so peaceful.

A body bag is primitive by comparison.

BADGER IN CHICAGO

In 1972, Diane and I were newly married. We had just moved to a small, but very tasteful, apartment near Lincoln Park. I invited Badger for dinner. I don't know what I expected to come of it; I was anxious for Diane to meet my brothers. Badger was the first. It had been three years since our cigars in the Hong Kong Hilton.

He was still animated and distracted. Almost as skinny and funny as he was in the Mekong. I asked what he thought of being sent to Indonesia after Vietnam. He said the riots against the dictator Sukarno were "okay." I knew he was a military advisor. I knew his job was dangerous. Thus I didn't understand his odd answer, but I pretended that I did. Diane looked at me with eyes that seemed to ask me to explain it all to her later.

At this point we could have discussed Sukarno in Indonesia, Marcos in the Philippines, Batista in Cuba, Samosa in Nicaragua, or any of the other dozen dictators our State Department supported. Diem in Vietnam fit right in. Earlier an American President had said, "He might be a son-of-a-bitch but at least he's *our* son-of-a-bitch."

Is it any wonder that we felt ambivalent about the Stars and Stripes? Is it any wonder that we had contempt for the Congress, the Senate, State, the CIA, the President, and the whole Hill of son-of-a-bitches that were *not* our son-of-a-bitches?

Badger enjoyed Diane's *coq au vin*. We drank far more Beaujolais than appropriate, which was good, because that led to more stories both appropriate and inappropriate. Soon he was doing his John Wayne impersonation. As he had teased in-country so many times, he would look us in the eye and growl, "Badges, we don't need no stinking badges!"

Badger actually had both a mom and dad; loving blue collar parents who were proud that their son had gone to college at University of Wisconsin, Madison. We both missed the Navy. Lang, fond memories of the Black Cats, and our little boats. We hated Rocky but we still missed him. Almost everyone who served under Rocky left the Navy. We didn't hate the V.C.; on the contrary, our respect for Chuck had grown.

The conversation changed from flippant to deadly serious and back to joking. Around and around, like a windmill. Funny stories like Rocky and the cobra would lead to serious thoughts of Badger's bad ambush and then, to lighten it up, we would joke about the 5:47 to Lake Forrest, only to remember the day I needed fast movers with jelly. And so it went.

I even called him Ken once or twice that night, perhaps because he was wearing a suit. Diane was gracious, quietly allowing two old vets to remember truths, tell lies, and to hide other truths from one another. I asked if Vietnam bothered him. Badger simply said, "Just the smells."

She didn't seem surprised that Badger was nervous and jumped from one subject to another. She knew when called upon he could be very, very brave. She knew that without his bravery, she would not be married to me.

Later she met other river rat brothers who had saved my life. Once on an airplane, I introduced Pat Lang that way. I said, "Diane, this is Pat Lang. He saved my life. More than once."

Pat said a soft dismissive, "Oh" and looked at his shoes for a second, then grinned and changed the subject. He was embarrassed at being a hero, yet I wasn't embarrassed about being saved. That seemed odd to me.

Badger worked in a big office on Wacker Drive. A huge insurance company, it reminded me of the Pentagon. I couldn't have worked there. He also seemed to enjoy his clothes. He liked wearing a suit. He took his tie off. Our stories were like the movie "Rashoman," all slightly different interpretations of the same events. Perhaps as time went by, those interpretations had become both more similar and more different. Looking at Badger made me realize how fearful

I was of growing old. My thoughts were jumping from subject to subject, reflecting Badger's coiled-spring personality.

Faster than I expected, we ran out of things to say. We sat in silence, and then forced a sentence or two. Instead of flowing, the conversation wound down to the point where continuing it was work. I was reminded of my trip four years before to the hospital in Hawaii. Now Badger and I were the raccoons.

In the end, we concluded that our special relationship with one another was truly unique, something of a fluke.

We vowed to get together again soon, and he departed. The following day, when I opened the vestibule closet, I saw the tie Badger had removed the night before. Freudians say people unconsciously leave something behind in places that they want to return. I felt pleased looking at the purple tie.

HOOD

Years later I saw a childhood friend of mine who had also served in the Delta in the Army. When we were 14, he taught me to ride an Indian motorcycle.

After his tour in Vietnam he had several very serious physical problems. He had pain in various parts of his body, was deathly weak, and some of his internal organs began to fail, especially in the gastro-intestinal tract.

He was in and out of V.A. hospitals; none could diagnose his problem. Some doctors thought it might be partly, or even mostly, psychological.

Finally, after ten years of unsuccessful treatment, they found the culprit: the Mekong River Fluke, a parasite that literally bores holes through the host's viscera.

Invisible holes in the guts. A fluke.

LIFE IS A FOOTNOTE

Eighteen percent of the population of Poland died in World War II—120 times American losses in Vietnam, in a country one-third our size.

After World War II the U.S. Army conducted a psychological study of Hitler's Waffen SS. The only difference that the psychologists could find between other soldiers and the feared Death's Head Storm Troopers was that the Storm Troopers were slightly more . . . *meek*.

Some of the statistics of man's inhumanity to man are equally sobering. Truly frightening. For example, *The Economist* reported that deaths from war during the twentieth century totaled 37 million. That was 30 million who died in international fighting and 7 million who died in civil wars. (Thus our casualties on the Vietnam Wall account for only 1/7 of 1 percent of the combat deaths of the twentieth century!) Although the loss of 37 million people is a tragedy, the loss in war is actually small compared to the killings governments conduct on their own citizens.

- The Soviets killed 62 million Russians in this century.
- The Chinese killed 35 million in the Communist Purge.
- The Germans killed 21 million from 1933-1945.
- The Chinese killed another 10 million in the Kuomintang Purge 1928-1949.
- The Japanese eliminated 6 million Chinese from 1936-1945.

In short, deaths caused by governments totaled 170 million or almost five times as many as killed in war!

Wes Nisker, a childhood friend of mine and a thoughtful author, wrote, "When an earthquake or flood occurs, we talk of a 'natural disaster.' But we don't consider our wars or economic upheavals as natural disasters. As if nature had nothing whatsoever to do with the way we behave."

It amazed me that we humans behave so differently from the way one would expect. For example, one day I was in the National Archives in Washington, D.C., where I saw a study of World War II vets who had won the Silver Star. They felt that they had been *less* brave and were *less* proud or confident of their achievements and ability than men who had not been decorated for valor.

Some people might find that curious; I could understand it very well.

Oddly, only a tiny proportion of men in-country actually were shot at. The odds of getting killed in Vietnam for the average person were remarkably low. But that masked the fact that the elite units took disproportionate losses. Swifts were the most decorated unit in the Navy, gaining more medals than any other group, but that was far less than several special units of the Army or Marine Corps.

Later statistics indicated that about one-quarter of the men thought it was impossible that they would die, but twice that number thought death an actuality. The other quarter was somewhere in the middle. Ninety-one percent of those who served said they "were glad they served their country."

*   *   *

In 1992 I died while on an operating table. It was like being slowly submerged in a numbing warm bath. Very, very pleasant. So pleasant that I remember wishing the doctors and nurses would stop trying to revive me. I just wanted them to leave me alone. The sensation was comfort, not curiosity.

When I was young, I went to see my grandmother. She said, "Gary, I'm just *so* tired." I knew that she was telling me that she was ready to die; it was a beautiful way to break the news.

In-country, people were not "killed"; we used the word "wasted" instead. "Wasted" was a commentary on the futility of the war itself. In any event, I hope all 58,000 of the guys who died felt that "numbing warm bath." I hope in that final second, they, too, just felt "tired."

I hope as they died they didn't feel wasted.

SEABEE

My son was born in 1976. When he was three, Seabee came to the apartment with a Christmas present. Seabee was five foot eight inches, the same height as most Viets. They called him "Ti Ti Trung Uy" (small lieutant). He gave our son Rob a plastic Thompson Sub Machine gun. It was battery powered and made a horrid noise in our little apartment. The Thompson was designed early in the 1900's. It was still in use in World War II and in Vietnam. Because of its shape it was called the "grease gun." Rob ran up and down the hall greasing everything in sight. The T.V. The fridge. Even the closet. He reminded me of Anderson when Anderson shot up his own locker inside the Cat Lo quonset with a Thompson. The only difference was that Rob did less damage.

When the batteries ran down or we hid the gun, Rob would be so disappointed with the loss of his favorite toy that Diane and I would eventually give in. Slowly, Rob learned to ration his batteries. Within a week, my wife and I had learned to live with a three-foot tall, in-house, gun-toting, maniac.

I didn't tell you that, at the time, Seabee was a bachelor. You probably guessed that. But I'll bet you didn't guess that it was Seabee's black dog that Ralph bit in the butt during "The Thomas Crown Affair." Perhaps my friend was looking for humorous revenge on behalf of his long departed mascot.

LINCOLN PARK

One day I was in Chicago with a close friend, Bob Probasco. He had been in artillery in Vietnam and he worked in the same bank as I did. He told me about a cannonball of granite in Lincoln Park, near Lake Michigan. Of all things, some people in the past had inscribed Lincoln's Gettysburg Address on that sphere. A speech inscribed on a cannonball is remarkably hard to read. Just phrases are visible.

... the last full measure of devotion ...

I can't read that without feeling guilty. I'm alive. Thus I didn't give it my all.

Later he said, " ... the brave men, *living* and dead, who ... " So Lincoln honored those who lived too. And yet ...

The subject of bravery continues to haunt me. We Swifties did not suffer even a fraction of the horror that the Marines saw. As a boy, I had a friend whose body was ravaged by polio. Yet Roger Shaffer was always upbeat, pleasant, and courteous. He was truly the bravest boy, and later bravest man, in our town. He taught political science at the local college; predictably he taught it with devotion and love for his students.

Bobby Mac, with his huge birthmark, was my best friend. Yet only a few years later, I was embarrassed to ask a pretty young girl for a date because she had a birth defect that caused her to have no left hand.

Sometimes I go to the Mayo Clinic. To visit my doctor, I must use the same elevator as pediatric patients. Kids with no hair from chemo and radiation give me a big smile. Kids in wheelchairs politely move to make room for me. Sad-eyed mothers of those children look at me with melancholy eyes; their exhaustion is *so* very visible.

I know that I am braver than some. I can look with pure contempt at cowards like Bill Clinton. But compared to a child with cancer, or with their mothers, I'm nothing.

So I looked at that cannonball in Lincoln Park, and I thought of my friends, both river rats and children, and I decided that bravery is more than a word. More than I can understand.

I know the men who fought at Gettysburg would say the same.

IN-COUNTRY 25 YEARS LATER

In June of 1994, I returned to Vietnam; I had been away for 25 years. The reason I went back was much the same as why I had volunteered to go there the first time: simple curiosity. At age 50, I found myself asking if the sunsets were really as spectacular as I remembered. Were the women truly that pretty? Were the insects that big, or was I embellishing things? My wife and son were also curious to see the country about which they had heard so much.

Before going, I had expected the trip to be reasonably heavy emotionally. In fact, for me, it was just the opposite—it was upbeat, refreshing, and renewed my confidence in mankind. The strongest impression I had was that Vietnam is a nation of *youth*. Fifty percent of the workforce was under 25 years old; almost 70 percent of the population was born after the war with the U.S. We traveled in-country from Hanoi to Vung Tau and did not meet a single person who was unfriendly. On the contrary, most young people were delighted to practice English with an American. In the late 80's the Vietnamese school system stopped teaching Russian and made English mandatory. (They called Russians "Americans without money.")

Economically, the country had barely progressed in the past 25 years, but there was an unmistakable eagerness on the part of the people to get on with life and catch up economically. The young were eager to talk about starting businesses, buying Hondas, and getting a better education. Having worked in Beijing in the late 70's, I expected to be bombarded with patriotic banners, Communist slogans, and so forth. The only such banners I saw were those reminding people to cross the street with care and to prevent AIDS. On a similar note, I was attempting to be politically correct calling our destination "Ho Chi Minh City" when my guide interrupted with, "Oh, hell, call it Saigon; everyone else does."

Hanoi's parks were well preserved and there was little evidence of past wars. After our prisoners were released, the "Hanoi Hilton" was used briefly as a metropolitan jail, but was vacant and scheduled for demolition to make way for, ironically, a new hotel. China Beach was still stunningly beautiful, but in need of an international resort or two to develop it properly. Saigon was noisy and crowded compared to the sophistication of Hanoi, but it teemed with as much entrepreneurial spirit as Hong Kong. The U.S. Embassy still stood vacant. When I asked why it wasn't being used, my guide responded, "We expect that sooner or later your government will want it again."

The ease with which special side trips could be arranged surprised me. Having lived in China and traveled in Russia, I was amazed how flexible and cordial the Viets were. A quick stop at the Vietnamese Naval Academy was no problem, and I even got back to Cat Lo. Cat Lo was still a naval base, so my guide strode inside to ask the base C.O. for permission to bring in "an important American visitor." Sadly, the C.O. was preoccupied at the time, so I was unable to go aboard the base, but my guide said that most of the time visitors were, in fact, allowed in.

Vietnam is 1,000 miles from north to south and the variety from the mountains of Dalat to the highlands of Hue to the swamp of the Mekong was amazing to those of us who saw only a small portion of its geography. With 70 million people, it was the fourteenth most populous country in the world. Foreign businesses were capitalizing on the opportunities there. U.S. companies were only beginning to enter. I believe it was good that we lifted the embargo. I hoped we could restore diplomatic relations reasonably soon. Five years after World War II, Germany joined NATO; it had now been much longer since we left Vietnam, long enough for many wounds to heal.

Perhaps I also went back to look face-to-face into the eyes of the people. If that was so, it was anticlimactic. The Viets just went about their business, too busy to give me much attention.

REUNION

We few, we happy few, we band of brothers . . .

Henry V

We found a boat. Almost 30 years after Vietnam, we found a Swift boat. It was one that had been used in our training. It was now in Panama. At the same time, the Internet also allowed us to find each other. After Vietnam we had scattered to the winds. Now we were back together.

We succeeded in getting the Swift boat up the East Coast and then up the Potomac River. At the Navy Museum in Washington, D.C., we dedicated PCF 3 to those men who had died. One skipper was now Deputy Assistant Secretary of the Navy. John Kerry, now a U.S. Senator, gave a speech that was quite good; the families of Swifties understood when he said, "We loved our little boats . . ."

Lifer was an admiral. He was instrumental in getting PCF 3 refurbished in its best fighting paint and on display. The others were there: one worked in the Pentagon and was married to a Marine colonel, a member of my crew brought his wife and kids, another skipper had recently retired from the Navy, and two great guys were both soon to retire from the F.B.I. Three hundred sat in Navy-issue gray collapsible chairs.

To the casual observer, we looked like normal fifty-something men. Yet deep down, each of us was a "Steppenwolf" as Herman Hesse called them. A wolf of the Steppes. A man/wolf who doesn't really fit back into society. Always alone. We loved each other as a band of brothers, as truly as the men who fought with Henry V at Agincourt. Each of us had a sense of values different from other

Americans, a deeper appreciation for life, a haunting understanding of the fragility of the world about us.

Our Cam Rahn C.O. didn't show. Futrell, who had won the Navy Cross, didn't come either. I had begged Badger to come, but he went fishing instead. That disappointed me more than anything, but I understood.

At the reunion, my cynicism bubbled up on several occasions. First, when the band played the National Anthem of the United States. "Oh, say can you see . . . ?" We are the only country in the world whose national anthem consists of two asinine questions about an obscure battle. A battle in a war America lost. We got our butt kicked. In 1812 the Brits burned down Washington. While England was in a life-and-death struggle with Napoleon and was chasing the French fleet, we were kicking England in the shins. So they burned our capital and sank a few of our ships, and after that tanning behind the woodshed, America left them alone. Our damned national anthem covers three octaves; no one can sing it. Oh well, no one studies history, so it doesn't matter. The words are as goofy as the notes. Still, I wish we had a normal inspirational national anthem like "Oh, Canada."

Tarzan was now a politician. He was singing right along. Enjoying himself. Maybe getting our ass kicked in 1812 wasn't so bad. By 1970 people were saying that Vietnam was the only war America had lost. If it took 160 years to forget the War of 1812, then by the year 2130 people will have forgotten we lost Vietnam. Maybe in 2130 our new national anthem will celebrate some battle in Vietnam, like Ia Drang where we got our butt kicked. While we are at it, the new national anthem may cover *four* octaves; that way only Italian opera singers will be able to hit all the notes.

By the time my mind got to the opera singers, the anthem was over and I was feeling guilty for being so cynical. Still, my image of Washington, D.C., in flames had been partially inspirational. I'll admit that.

Someone said depression is anger turned inside. I liked that quote, even if I didn't understand it. So do we feel guilty or depressed for losing the war? Some numb-nut U.S. general told General Giap years after the war, "*We* won almost all of the battles!"

The North Vietnamese general patiently replied, "That is totally irrelevant. We won the war." But losing isn't all bad. Pickett lost. Custer lost. The 300 Spartans at Thermopylae lost. In Vietnam, we lost big time. For many years it was like a cut that didn't quite heal; each time it is bumped, it bleeds again. The blood stains your shirt or your soul.

"No calamity is greater than underestimating opponents."

Lao Tzu

Some people said that America had fought the war with one hand strapped behind its back. We had seen enough dead V.C. to know how stupid that quote was. We were the ones with fast movers with jelly; we had cold Coke and medevacs. Chuck had a pair of shorts and an AK-47 and a little bag of rice. We had scuba gear and he had baby nipples stuck up his nose. Chuck was a gutsy little bastard and we Swifties were not ones to belittle his courage.

I realized that I was thinking exactly like my dad. He had huge admiration for the Germans who faced Patton's tank force; Dad felt more respect for the men he fought against than for the French Allies. The French nation had folded before the Germans; the Polish Jews of the Warsaw Ghetto actually held out longer against the Nazis than the French! Yet, my dad was patriotic. Somehow the word "patriotic" implies not so much that a person cares for America as much as that he has confidence in the American government. By that measure, most of my generation is more cautious than the men who fought World War II.

"It's not a great war, but it is the only war we have," we joked in the '60's, taunting the protesters. Quickly we learned that such a statement rang hollow. The things like body counts, that could be measured by McNamara and the presidents from Kennedy to Johnson to Nixon, simply did not matter. The things that could not be measured in such a civil war, like support for Saigon vs. Hanoi or the willingness to fight, mattered a great deal. Truly in this case, it "wasn't the size of the dog in the fight, it was the size of the fight in the dog." But that was just my perspective.

Later some analysts wrote that, given the lack of support, the men who fought in Vietnam were among America's most patriotic. Looking around the dedication ceremony, I could believe that. To a man, these guys had given it their best shot. One attendee said, "I try not to think of it anymore than I have to . . . but how much do I have to?"

As the speeches continued, my eyes drifted through the group, searching for a tall, quiet man; I wondered if he had become an air traffic controller. Did one skipper buy a boat and start a Caribbean freight company? I wondered if any others had become Buddhists like I had. Perhaps all the others also had deep regrets for their mistakes. Mistakes like shelling the wrong target or killing a basking shark. Perhaps they felt that the good things they did, like not killing the old leper and a little girl in a fishing boat, made up for it. Perhaps. It was impolite of me to ask.

Once I met a woman who spoke about going to psychological counseling. She said the biggest benefit to her was that the counselor helped her answer one vital question: "How can I tell when I'm lying to myself?"

Wow. Knowing that would help a lot. I rave and howl, but do I understand it or even mean it? Hell, I didn't really wish Washington to burn. Today I was having a good time in the city. Sitting all around me were good, solid men. No different than any others. No different from men who did not serve in Vietnam. They were all able to get on with it, I told myself. I must be the odd duck. I couldn't tell when I was lying to myself.

The speeches were ending. I heard less than half of what had been said. I put my arm around my son and squeezed my wife's hand.

I looked at the men around me, my brothers standing straight and tall. I thought of the myth of King Cadmus, the King of Thebes, who sowed dragon teeth in the Greek soil and warriors emerged. Standing firm and strong in perfect rows.

THE WALL

My son said that in feudal Japan, each new Samurai was initiated by attending his own funeral. Symbolically, having already died, the Samurai had nothing to fear.

The Vietnam Memorial in Washington, D.C., consists of a deep cut into the earth. Visitors to The Wall descend along the black wall to its midpoint and then begin the climb back up to the surface. Most visitors start at the west end, so as they emerge, they see the Washington Monument, a giant white monument pointing straight to the heaven. Walking along The Wall is like going into the grave with 58,000 souls and then emerging. The impact of The Wall is high, partly because it reminds us subconsciously of dying, dying along with those whose names are inscribed on the granite.

To me it is as if there are also other men down in that cut in the earth. Pieces of gray tissue. Bits of brain and drops of blood on the walkway, in the grass, on your hands, and on your trousers. Just small pieces of those who went in-country but didn't die. Each of them left a piece of themselves behind.

*   *   *

After the dedication of PCF 3, we went to The Wall to pay our respects. Some guys knew the location of every name, of each dead Swifty. By panel and by line. I don't. I would rather forget. Each time I go back to The Wall, I again go to the directory to look up the men I knew. To me that is better than having those panel locations permanently in my memory.

In 1990, I had a heart transplant. Once again I cheated my destiny. I cheated on the powers above, the singular God of the

Jews and Christians or the more colorful gods of the Greeks. Midway along The Wall, at the bottom, I usually stop. Reluctant to come back up. It seems improper, because I should be dead twice. It is all the more difficult to emerge when the sun shines on the Washington Monument. For that reason, and others, I usually go at night.

At the Naval Academy, we once had an officer of the British Commandos give us a lecture on the necessity of having a conflict now and then. He said that an occasional fight kept an army keen. Specifically, he said, "An army is like a dog; you must give it a bone in order to keep its teeth sharp." He really said that. Looking at The Wall, I am saddened that at the time I heard him, I believed what he was saying. I was 19.

Each name on The Wall stands out. Each is crisp and visible. Someone once told me that in hell each soul is naked; no one can hide. That is a good thing about our monument. No one can hide from it; no one can avoid its impact. Like the "whunk" of a round that lands nearby, it shakes your guts.

ROB

My son is 23 now. He works on Wall Street and lives near Central Park. Some days I think of him taking the commute hanging on a subway car's strap. I hope that he is imagining that the strap is actually the static line on a C141 and that he is looking the jumpmaster in the eye. He is about to go airborne with the 101st Screaming Eagles. I imagine that he thinks of quitting Salomon Brothers investment bank so that he can fall to earth with a beautiful white parachute canopy about him. I expect that he wants to quit business so that he can join an elite outfit like the Rangers or Tenth Mountain or Delta Force. Then I realize that it is *my* dream, not his. I'm the one who didn't get West Point.

I am not afraid to jump out of airplanes. I enjoy it. I am afraid of growing old. I don't want to be 55. I don't want to get older and weaker each day. As I go out my front door on my way to work, a jump school song comes to mind and I sing in my best Walter Mitty voice, "I wanna be an airborne ranger, I wanna live a life of danger."

BODY COUNT

And where is the source of understanding?
No man knows the way to it.

Job 28

Earlier, Steel Wool was intrigued with a four-box matrix he was constructing. He expected people to be "for the war/against protestors" or "against the war/for protestors." But some were "for the war/for the protestors" and even more "against the war/against the protestors." We all lost.

I told him that near the wall by the Lincoln Monument, a guy was selling patches. One said, "I'll forgive Jane Fonda when the Jews forgive Hitler." A year later I went back to buy one, but it was too late. Maybe Viet vets forgave Jane, so demand dried up. I'd rather believe Jane and Ted Turner threatened the patch maker.

Our squadron C.O. left the Navy mid-career. Sad and disgusted. He doesn't want any contact with any of us now. Rocky died; exactly how was a mystery. As far as I know, he wasn't garroted in his sleep by any of us.

MAGGIE

25 Years Later

I worked in a big Chicago bank, a new loan officer in the international section. Vietnam and business school were behind me. I was 29. I often worked late. I loved my new job.

At a desk nearby was a quiet, thoughtful, dark-haired girl just out of college. I'm seven years older than my kid sister; the soft young girl, named Maggie, was the same age as my sister. She brought out the "big brother" protecting side of me.

If we were both working late, she would occasionally ask a question about Vietnam. Not often, just a timid question sprinkled here and there.

We had worked together for over a year, and then one evening Margaret Lukins asked a particularly penetrating question. She asked if I had ever worked with "LURPS." Long Range Recon Patrols were a very special group of guys. They worked deep in enemy territory. Few civilians in America knew about them. I fumbled, and then asked her point-blank how she knew about that facet of the war.

Her eyes were dry. She looked straight at me and softly said, "My brother was killed there."

God! For almost a year I'd been answering her questions flippantly, curtly, carelessly, inaccurately, or insensitively. Not at all as I would have, had I *known*. But then again . . .

Maybe that's why Maggie Lukins had asked me. Perhaps my candor was why she had so trusted me.

Oh, hell. I did the math. She would have been only 10 or 12 when her brother died. Parents unable to explain, or perhaps too wounded to speak, about their lost son. Erroneously believing such a young girl wouldn't understand.

One of the Best

After Sancho Panza's gunner was killed, Sancho got Jim Luke as a replacement. Bosun Mate Luke. Blonde. A surfer type. Big confidant smile. Very quiet, most gunner's mates are. Professional. One of the best. He was quiet, serious, and smart. In December of '68, when they asked for volunteers for a particularly messy mission in Cambodia, Luke volunteered. He took a round.

The Wall

When I go to The Wall, I don't go during the day when the Washington tour buses are there. I go late at night. In the daytime, it's a monument. At night, in the mist and rain, The Wall becomes holy. I am among the gods in Valhalla. I take a few tokens to leave at the sight of each dead brother river rat. Usually I take small white flowers—they look good against the black stone. Sometimes I bring a few beer bottle caps, and once I left a piece of pound cake.

The names on The Wall are listed in the order of when each person was killed in action. To find a name, you first must go to a directory. It's like a telephone book, the names are listed alphabetically and then the location on The Wall is shown. Luke is in panel 37 West. As I read it, my eye froze on the next name: *Lukins*. Only one person named Luke died in-country, only one Lukins was listed. Together in the directory. Maggie's desk beside mine.

Since then, when I go to The Wall, I always bring one extra flower. First I visit each of the river rats I knew. Finally I stop at the sacred spot of a LURP. And when I put a white blossom by Lukin's name, I whisper:

"Your kid sister loves you."

It's been 33 years since I saw Maggie. Frozen forever in my mind as a beautiful 22-year-old girl. Her brother is, I'm sure, frozen in time for her as well, a big older brother. Age 18.

THE SUN ALSO RISES

So how are things today?

Every now and then as an ant crosses the picnic table, I reach out and eat it. When people catch me, I explain that I'm just surveying what kind of bugs live with me. Some live inside my head. Some ants taste sweet, some have little taste, and some are bitter like vinegar. On occasion, the other person will try one. I always hope they will get a good vinegar ant.

Add them to your oatmeal.

So things are okay. Or, as Jake would say to Lady Brett in Paris: "Isn't it pretty to think so."

The Real World

A gunrunner sampan
(note the false bottom)

Chicom weapons
B-40 on top and AK-47 below

Cat Lo Base in 1994 now in use by
Viet Navy

Map of Communist villages
faithful since 1936 clustered
along the Mekong and in the
deep south in the Rung Sat

Political poster displaying a bayonet in a U.S. Army helmet

P.C.F. dedication during 1995 reunion in Washington, D.C.

EPILOGUE

The fact that after war, all of the remainder of life is
but a footnote is not new.
Aeschylus, the greatest of all Greek dramatists won the
Athens playwright competition 21 times. When he died in
456 BC, he insisted that his tombstone say only:
"I fought the Persians at Marathon."

There is a wall ten miles high and fifty miles thick between those
of us who went and those who didn't, and that wall
is never gong to come down.

Milt Copulos

EIGHT EPILOGUES

I

After combat, all of life is a footnote. Admiral John Paul Jones was the father of America's Revolutionary War Navy. When asked if he surrendered, the young captain said, "I have not yet begun to fight!" He died in poverty in Paris. Emma, Lady Hamilton, lived long after the death of Admiral Lord Nelson. She too died in France in obscurity.

II

Who am I? The war is not a memory. It *is* me.

The Hong Kong Hilton was demolished in the '80's. Yet some nights I can again see Lt. Commander Neeley do his soft shoe on that bar. Whenever I drink cognac, I'm with Badger.

III

You may not like the writing style of this memoir. It isn't mine. It is the dictation of ghosts. Of river rats. Kelley, Skippy, Tex, and dozens of others. Ghosts.

IV

In nature, the animals with the tools for killing are also given a high level of self-control. Look at the wolf, an excellent killing machine. But wolves seldom hurt one another. They show their teeth, they growl, they nip, but rarely do they bite; a bite to the opponent's leg would cripple him. Which would, in turn, kill him.

Contrast the wolf with the chicken, which can inflict only limited damage on other chickens. Nature gives the chicken very little social self-control. They peck one another aggressively, but the pecks inflict only limited damage.

Men are like the chicken. Early man could inflict only limited damage with his teeth or bare hands. But modern man now has sophisticated weapons, which change it all . . . . A man with a gun has the self-control of a chicken and the killing ability of a wolf.

V

Psychologists say that those who fear often display arrogance. Bullies speak loudly. Confident people are noted for how quiet they are.

As men get older, their feminine side becomes more open. At least that is what Carl Gustav Jung said. The average man says 2,000 words per day; the average woman 7,000. Does this explain why I'm scribbling all of this down in spite of the well-known aphorism that applies? Especially to war:

> "Those who know do not speak.
> Those who speak do not know."

Hell, I don't know the answer. So bear with me, I need to put these things down on paper. They are like cockroaches that crawl out of the rug. If I put the ideas on paper, I can close the cover and trap the roach inside by closing the covers of this book.

A grand old Navy saying goes:

> "When in danger or in doubt,
> Run in circles, scream and shout!
> If the lights show red and green,
> Close your eyes and steer between."

A sailor can see both red and green running lights only if the other ship is directly approaching. This advice assures a head-on collision.

I wanted to write a book that tells what it is like to *feel* war. Not to describe battle actions, but to feel it. I failed. I'm just running in circles, screaming and shouting.

VI

Colonel Corson, my instructor at Navy, was retiring from the service. He wrote a book titled *The Betrayal*, which took issue with the strategy and policies of the Johnson administration. Colonel Corson had worked closely with the Vietnamese; he predicted that the policy of the government would not produce a win in Vietnam. On the contrary, he stated that it was truly a betrayal. Our government considered bringing him back on active duty so he could be court-martialed, but later dropped the idea.

VII

It is often said that military service is just hours of boredom interrupted by moments of stark terror. So perhaps some of the details that I have written are boring. Perhaps that is as it should be.

In *The Sun Also Rises*, Hemingway writes a story that stumbles along. Jake Barnes, Lady Brett, Cohen, and the others simply live. The novel really has no conclusion. It ends with the characters still in Spain, doing the same things they did at the beginning. Eat. Drink. Fight. Travel. Love. I came to Vietnam in May of '68. A year later the war was just stumbling along. No further ahead. No progress. By May of '69 we as people had all changed. All of the characters together. Badger, Jake, Fox, Cohen, Sweet Pea, Lady Brett. All in a big circle of life. Each impacting the other. Subtly. Permanently.

It seems that "karma" energy is just another name for centripetal force. The force that pulls us all toward the center. It balances the massive centrifugal force which attempts to fling all of us characters off the stage and away in all directions.

VIII

A well-known Buddhist story is about a monk who was traveling on a path. He reached a gate that was rusted shut. He picked up a big rock and smashed the gate open. After going through, he threw the rock away.

The story can also involve crossing a stream. Once the monk crosses the stream, he throws the raft away; no need to carry it further along the path.

A classic drawing covers the same thing. It shows a grizzled old monk, the sixth patriarch and founder of Zen, who is dressed in tattered robes. He has not shaved or bathed for months, perhaps years. He is tearing up his well-worn book on the teachings of Buddhism. As he tears up the book, he wears a wild grin on his face. The story is the same: once a person is enlightened, he can throw the book away.

I too am old and grizzled. Now this book is done.

Tear it up.

RATS IN A TRAP

Sancho Panza planned the thing. Three boats gathered a mile out to sea just south of a major river in Cau Mau. Sancho explained the plan, "We go up the river about a klick. You will see on the right side a lagoon-like thing that runs into the forest. The passage is narrow, and there is a sandbar, but once inside, we will be in a little isolated pond. On the shore is a V.C. village. If we do it fast, we will catch Charlie sitting on his ass."

We asked if Sancho had ever done the trick. Sancho responded, "No, but I'm sure that we can make it over the sand bar."

Five minutes later, three boats darted up the river, turned right, and entered the shallow little passage into the dirty pond.

There was some movement in the village, the first boat opened up with .50-caliber fire immediately. Cau Mau was all "free-fire zone." Everyone down there was assumed to be hostile.

No shots were returned. The three Swifts motored along the perimeter of the pond, past the abandoned vil. There were signs that people had been there recently, but now, there was nothing.

After half an hour, the lead boat turned to exit the channel. To our shock, there was now a log chain across the entrance. Charlie had drawn it tight, trapping the three boats. Sancho and the first boat began to shoot at the chain. The rounds were ineffective; the chain held.

Then the radio blared, "Cease fire." Luke jumped from his boat with bolt cutters. The water was chest high; he waded to the chain and after a full minute, he was able to cut it. We expected the enemy to shoot Luke. They didn't.

Three boats, three sitting ducks. Immobile in a hostile pond and yet not a single shot was fired at them. It made no sense.

Whoever tightened the chain should have fired volleys of B-40s. They did nothing.

Luke was pulled aboard the 95 boat and all three Swifts screamed out. The boats got out scot-free. Feeling stupid and vulnerable. And very, very lucky.

If the trap and been sprung correctly, it would have been "hair teeth and eyeballs."

BLIND MICE:
A GHOST STORY

So three river rats got mousetrapped. Three blind mice. I remember the details, but I wasn't on that mission. I must have been told about it.

Yet years later, as I was writing this story, I found an old yellow sheet of paper. It indicated that I *was* on the screwed up run. Perhaps I was there and memory wants to forget; perhaps I wasn't and memory wants to remember.

At about the same time I was puzzling over this, I read an account of a SEAL, Dick Couch, who said that he remembered his first firefight with diamond-like clarity; he then went on to say that *all* subsequent shootouts just merged into a blur. How can such profound events get lost in the muddy waters of the mind? Perhaps if they were all remembered precisely, the person would be insane.

Only a day later, I read in those same yellow notes that I had written in 1976 the account of the little girl in the Rung Sat who we did not kill. She was with a *blind* old man; his eyes were totally milky white. She wasn't with a leper after all. He was somewhere else. A different day. A different sampan. A different story altogether. Somehow I merged them in my memory, replacing a blind man with a leper on the girl's sampan. I reread the chapter that I had written earlier. It was obviously inaccurate, yet I chose not to change it. It reflects history as I remember it, not history as it was.

*   *   *

When I was working at the Pentagon, I took Diane to a Swift party. She was amazed hearing some of the stories other skippers told about me. On the way home from the party, she began to ask questions about some of the events. I didn't have the courage to confess to her that at least half of those stories about me were news to me too.

By the 80's, the ex-hippies were saying, "If you remember the 60's, you weren't there." Funny. I wish it were true; those of us in-country at the time remember much of it too well . . . but then again . . .

I wanted this book to be a memoir; I know now that parts are fiction. I tried to get it all straight. Thirty years later, I tried hard to make it accurate, to make sense out of it. I never will.

Perhaps it doesn't make any goddamned difference. I do know for certain that the doll-like 12-year-old girl lived. The blind man lived. Even the leper lived a little longer. That is true. Three boats went into the trap and three got out. I know that. I don't know if I was one of the three. Does it make any difference?

Sometimes we got medals when we didn't deserve them. That was okay. No one felt guilty, because much more frequently we didn't get recognized for the many brave things that we did that went unnoticed. Imprecise, but in the end it balanced.

I hope this book is like that too.

VETERANS DAY 2000

I sat at the hotel table looking at strips of beef and mushrooms. The Swift Boat Sailors Association reunion in San Diego had dedicated a second boat that morning. The 104 boat, a boat on which we had all trained. It had been discovered as a derelict in Seattle. With contributions of $10,000 it had been transported to the Navy Amphibious Base in San Diego. Back to her original home. Back to Coronado where we had undergone our preparation for Vietnam. Now we had a boat in D.C. and also one in California.

The speakers at the banquet told dozens of stories. I'll share just one:

> In 1999, a leg bone was found inside the hull of a Swift that had been sunk 30 years before. Six weeks before our convention, a DNA test on the femur had proven the identity of the sailor. His family had been notified, and so now we too could be told that the Swifty was no longer "missing in action"; he was now, in November of 2000, officially KIA.

I sat beside Fox. Fox, who, as legend had it, had been known to sunbathe stark naked, often boarded and searched Viet fishing boats wearing just a .38 pistol. (That colorful story was untrue.) Fox, who on a quiet day once beached his boat and hiked inland to stop to check papers of riders on a bus. (True!) Tonight he looked somewhat tired. Four bypass heart operations. It was Fox who once told Rocky, "The only way you can hurt me with a fitness report is if you wad it up into a little tiny ball and stick it in my eye!" He still looked impishly defiant. Fox whispered to me, "You know, Rocky thought that I had 'a difficult learning curve,' but if we had

followed orders, we would all be dead." He grinned and reached
for the soft touch of his loving wife's hand.

Two men were talking across the table about the entrapment
incident, an amazing coincidence. I listened intently. No, I wasn't
on that run after all. No rats, no trap. It wasn't me. Oscelot was
singing a song that went:

> "Last night, I had the strangest dream,
> I never dreamed before.
> I dreamed that all the world agreed
> To put an end to war."

Three hundred and fifty Swifties wiped tears from their eyes,
hugged each other, and looked at their drinks.

A guy sitting at a table adjacent to mine looked frail and much
older than the rest of us, with deep sad eyes and trembling hands.
Earlier I had been told that he was a skipper of a Swift boat that
had been sunk near Danang. He lost his entire crew. Every one. I
thought of the burden he must feel; like a mother who escapes
from a house fire only to learn that all five of her children perished.

What can you take home from a reunion? Understanding. That
is what we wanted, and that is exactly what we got. The officer in
charge of the boat is a father. The skipper *is* the old man. I felt
badly that 97 had been sunk, but other's lost boats as well. The
Navy still uses an archaic expression: "The boat went down with
five *souls* aboard." The melancholy skipper had lost his men. To
look at his trembling hands, it was clear to me that a sixth soul had
been lost as well.

The psychologist Erik Erikson wrote about the stages of a
person's life. Normally, at age sixty or so, we think of our mortality.
But this is particularly awkward for veterans, given that they
prematurely examined that issue more than 30 years before.

I went to bed. I had gotten all of my men back home alive.
Kelley, Kid, Thompsen, Tex, and Jake. Red, Tex's replacement,
also came back unscathed.

*   *   *

I awoke at 2 a.m. thinking of rats in a trap. At the banquet, I learned that I wasn't there after all, so why was I remembering it? Then the answer came, and it was so obvious that I was embarrassed that I hadn't seen it before.

Thirty years earlier, when I heard of an incident such as the one in which boats were trapped by a chain, my mind would begin to play it through. "I would not have made *that* mistake. I would be vigilant going into the slit looking for barriers; I would be careful to keep the exit open; I would never make the mistake of dallying; I would . . . ." Or so I told myself. I had perfected the practice of playing the events over and over, looking for ways to improve, trying to anticipate each potential for danger. News of such incidents drifts in through boat squadrons over a period of weeks. Retelling of the story by another person adds another fact or two. To me, the skipper's job is to avoid surprises. So each time I heard the "Rats in the Trap" story, I replayed how I would have reacted—how I would have avoided trouble. Over and over. Until, in the end, I would have actively imagined such an event a hundred times or more.

It was exactly what Admiral Lord Nelson would have done. Scenario planning. Mentally rehearsing. Over and over. Learning from mistakes. Adapting and adjusting.

But because of that practice, it became doubly difficult to get the facts right after the war. Real events and scenario events were irrevocably mixed.

The very skills that are vital in time of danger often become unhelpful later. What *really* happened was lost in the deluge of versions of what *might* have happened. That was sad, but it was also a very small price to pay for having the ability to learn to adjust, to adapt, and to anticipate.

No rats. No trap.

NEVER-ENDING POSTSCRIPTS

I

I haven't fired a single round since my kid sister's birthday in 1969. I still dislike the full moon. I leave lights on at night, like a little kid.

II

Sometimes I wonder about the odd things that I have learned. When I mention things like "in the end, lepers die from respiratory disease," people look at me with an odd expression. Only then do I realize that I said something inappropriate. Like the Padre.

III

A nurse wrote that after combat she could no longer work in medicine. She had no feeling. The trauma in-country forced her to be numb. After watching such young men die so violently, she could only look at people with small health problems as whiners.

IV

I built a house with big windows so I could get lots of light. It makes up for night ambushes. I built it far away from the city hospital so I wouldn't have to hear medevac helos.

V

The class of '66 of the U.S. Navy Academy formed a foundation to provide scholarships to the sons and daughters of classmates killed in action. It was very successful, providing funds to students who went on to some of the best colleges in America.

VI

So far the Swift sailors have found two boats. One is on display at the base where we trained in Coronado, California. The other is at the navy museum in Washington, D.C. We are still looking for another survivor. Hopefully it will go to Boston where "Old Ironsides," the U.S.S. Constitution, is berthed.

VII

I visited Dresden, Germany, in 1994. The people there plan to rebuild the cathedral. I asked if they were religious and if the cathedral would be used. They said no.

VIII

Levi Highhawk was actually quite sensitive. He cried and hugged my Aunt Vic. A short time later, he died in a car accident. His organs were donated.

IX

I was a guest at a Lakota ceremony for warriors. Basil Braveheart conducted it. I was painted in war paint; later a young woman ceremoniously washed the paint off. She performed with care and with respect. Then Basil fanned me with an eagle wing. The fresh breeze cleansed me. After I had returned to "the people" from my warrior role, the attendees formed a circle around me and each said "thank you." They thanked me for having fought. I was *very* touched. It was 1999. It was the first time that anyone had ever said "thank you" to me for being a veteran.

X

On 16 June 1968, PCF 19 was attacked and sunk. Of the four KIA, two bodies were not recovered. In late 1999 a few remains were retrieved and identified as those of Tony Chandler, Bosun Mate Second Class. The family chose to have a burial service on the thirty-third anniversary of the firefight. On 16 June 2001, services were held in Centerville, GA. Several Swift boat veterans attended.

XI

Several nurses wrote that when men died, they often called for their mothers. That gave me pause. I won't know until the time comes, but I suspect if I'm on my deathbed and truly scared, I'll call . . . BADGER!

A BOOK REVIEW

"So let me get this straight. If you had been on the 97 boat five weeks after you left Vietnam, she wouldn't have sunk. You feel guilty because if you had been on Andre's mission, you would have been safe and he wouldn't have died. As a matter of fact, if you had been on *every* mission where someone else was wounded or KIA, you believe that you could have pulled it off without loss."

Carol paused before she spoke again. "I don't know what to say . . . ." She let the silence fall again. I had hoped for insight. With her photographer's eye, she saw into nature. She saw into souls. To my disappointment, only stillness followed.

Finally, she whispered softly, "But . . . if Buddha were here . . . he would say that you have a *very* big ego."

Involuntarily, I exhaled the deepest sigh of my life. A single tear ran down my right cheek. Like Persephone, Carol lives among us mortals only half the time; the balance is spent in a land of myth. I would like to think that the tear I shed was the last drop of Mekong river water still in my head.

Printed in the United States
60075LVS00004B/2